10649396

The Devil to Pay

MARK DANIEL

The Devil to Pay

LITTLE, BROWN AND COMPANY
BOSTON   TORONTO   LONDON

First U.S. Edition

The characters and events in this book are fictitious.
Any similarity to real persons, living or dead,
is coincidental and not intended by the author.

Library of Congress Cataloging-in-Publication Data

Daniel, Mark, 1954–
    The devil to pay/Mark Daniel. — 1st U.S. ed.
        p.   cm.
    ISBN 0-316-17265-0
    I. Title.
PR6054.A469D4   1992
823'.914 — dc20   92-11547

10 9 8 7 6 5 4 3 2 1

RRD-VA

Printed in the United States of America

Book One

"NEVER LOOK BACK." It was one of the first things my father told me when I started riding races. "Never, ever look back. More races have been lost by overconfident bloody fools looking over their shoulders in the straight than anything else. It unbalances you, and the sods will come at you out of nowhere, out of your blind spot when you least expect it. Ride 'em out all the way to the post."

It's good advice, that. Euridice would have profited by it. Mrs. Lot should have trained as a jockey.

Sure. And you just try abiding by that good advice when all the devils in hell come hollering and howling at you from your blind spot.

You'll look back all right, and it'll unbalance you. You'll look back, as much for love of those devils as for fear.

It's love that'll do you. Every time.

"All right, all right." Joe Wade, the local potato merchant, held up a cigar-case hand. The clinking of ice and glasses and the seepage of Barry Manilow continued, but the people around us hushed. "A pint of best says you can't do us the Twelve Just Men."

It was closing time in the Rawcliffe Arms. The Rawcliffe Arms showed no sign of closing.

"Angry, that'll be," Hugh the landlord corrected. He had a high brow and dark hair, slick as a seal. His fist burrowed in a pint mug.

"'Sright." Joe nodded his sandy pink head. He gulped. "All right. Twelve Angry Men. All twelve. Pint on it."

"Ah, come on." A woman named Valerie laid her hand on my bare forearm. She was somewhere about forty. She had a good trick: she looked more and more like Jeanne Moreau with every minute, every drink.

About ten minutes back, I'd gone to the outside loo. She'd been waiting for me when I came out. She'd pulled my head down, breathed "Nick" into my mouth and followed the word with a fisherman's tale of a tongue. It started as a wriggling minnow and grew to a thrashing three-pound trout.

Like a sculptor with a deadline, she had urgently worked the convexities at my crotch, so I had politely done a bit of the same for her concavities. She had looked a lot like Jeanne Moreau by then, so I had kissed her throat and the bibs of her breasts. Then suddenly she had pulled away from me, all *farouche* and feral. She had sucked deep on her lower lip. She had hit me in the chest. She had snapped. "No! You think I'm just like the rest of them, don't you? Well, I'm not. No, no, no!"

I'd remember not to accept her dinner invitations in future. Get done for trespass halfway through the soup.

Now, of course, she was behaving as though she had somehow acquired proprietary rights over me. Her husband, a fat garage owner in an old-school tie, sat by the fireplace. He guarded his vodka and tonic with fierce jealousy.

"No, hang on. Easy." I rocked a little, heel to toe. I supped my pint. I laid it on the bar. "Ready? Okay. Four Just Men, incidentally, were Hugh Sinclair, Griffith Jones, Frank Lawton, and Francis L. Sullivan. Walter Forde directed —"

"Wrong!" Joe triumphantly struck the bar.

I swept on. "But the Twelve Angry Men — right. Count. Henry Fonda, obviously —"

"Lee J. Cobb," murmured someone at my right. Someone else said "Shh!"

"That's right. Henry Fonda, Lee J. Cobb, Jack Klugman, Jack Warden, Ed Begley —"

"Hold on. Hold on."

"Ed Begley, E. G. Marshall, of course, Robert Webber . . . George Voskovec . . . Edward Binns . . . er, Ed Begley —"

"You've 'ad 'im."

"Shit. Okay. Oh, Martin Balsam. How many's that?"

"Eleven."

"Oh, bugger. One I always forget."

"Aha!" Joe crowed. "Come on!"

"Hold on, mate." I frowned, though I had it already. "Voskovec, Binns, Balsam . . . Sweeney! Joseph Sweeney. Thank you." I held out a hand to Joe Wade. "Pint, please."

There was some cheering. "Boy's a bloody marvel!" Joe slapped his thigh. "Bloody marvel, eh?" he appealed to his friends. "Not as I'd like to wander around with all that useless lumber rattling around in t' bloody attic."

"Bit like a deformity, if you ask me." Hector, our ancient head lad, worked on his dentures with his gums. "Find a rabbit like that, you'd shoot the poor bugger."

"Sidney Lumet, nineteen fifty-seven," I finished lamely from habit.

"Here." Hugh handed me the sweating pint. "Eh, should you be drinkin' this, then, Nick?"

Dudley Knox, our local hero, a blond, stocky, experienced jockey, touched my arm. "Should go easy I were you, lad."

"'Sright." Hugh nodded. "Got our 'orse to ride tomorrow."

"Ah, I'll be all right." I raised the glass to him. "No problems with weight. . . ."

"Ah, well, remind you of that tomorrow." Dudley shrugged. "I'll be away any road. Night, all." He waved and strolled off.

"'Course he'll be all right," Valerie soothed. "Young chap like him."

"Ah, but it's not weight we're worried about, is it?" Joe bellowed. "Sharpness of reactions. Finding your way around. Finishing speed. Hands and heels, eh? All that. That's what matters.

Got to be sharp. Our horse, that. Cost us a packet. Lot invested in our Pip."

"I know, I know." I grinned. "Don't worry about it. I'll be okay."

"You'd better be." Joe stood and swayed toward me. I saw him in hand-held 16mm. "You'd better be, lad."

"Don't be fucking stupid," Valerie suddenly spat out. Her hand squeezed my thigh like a claw. "Nick'll be fine, won't you, Nick?"

"Easy, love," I crooned. "Yeah. No problems. Not exactly the greatest challenge of my life, you know, couple of times round Market Rasen. So. Shut up, Joe. Sit down. Have a drink. Pipistrelle and I will fly round that track tomorrow. You just wait and see."

I grabbed a high stool with something like urgency. Valerie lurched against me. The burbling bar spun like a fairground.

"'Ere, Nick. Word in your ear."

"Mmm?" I turned. Billy Stephens, village hothead, mother's boy, proud owner of a blind collie bitch and a Velocette that sounded like Tina Turner, shrugged his narrow shoulders and cocked his head against his upstanding leather collar. "Hi, Billy. What's up?" I asked.

"Sorry, um . . ." He raised his eyebrows and again jerked his head like a fighter dodging jabs.

"Excuse me, love." I extricated myself from Valerie's grasp. I slid off the stool. "Just a moment."

Billy's hand rested on my shoulder as he led me purposefully through the crowd. Finally he stopped and glanced quickly over both shoulders. There were bright spots of pink in his cheeks. "Now, come on," he said.

"What?"

"I mean, come on, Nick. No aggro or anything, but . . ."

"Billy." I shook my head. "I haven't a clue what you're talking about."

"Ah, come on. I mean, Jeez, I mean, he's sitting right there. I'm not stuffy or anything, but really, man."

"I'm still not with you, Billy."

"Shit, I mean, she's *married*, Nick."

"Yes. And?"

"Well, I mean, Jesus, come on. You know what I mean."

"You mean that she's married. I knew that, thanks. Any other information?"

The shoulders jumped again. Billy pushed out his tongue. His lower lip now jutted. His eyes narrowed. "You ought to watch yourself, you know. We don't want your dirty ways round these parts. You could find yourself in trouble, big trouble, you could. You hear me?"

"I hear you, Billy." I sighed wearily. "I wish I didn't, but I hear you loud and clear. Now, if you'd let me return to my friends . . ."

I waved back into the moth's-wing light. I called, "Night, then," and the door-frame jumped out and hit my shoulder. A male voice — Joe's, I think — called after me, "Night." Another, "Night, lad." A girl, "See you, Nick." The normal boiling bubble of chat resumed. The door swung shut.

I lurched down a step that some joker had built since I'd entered. I converted the stumble into what I thought to be a jaunty but graceful little leap, and landed in a tin-foil puddle. I looked quickly from side to side.

I smiled, just in case anyone was looking and might think that the manner of my exit had been less than scrupulously planned. A cat on the low wall at my left proved my only spectator. It made a noise like tearing canvas, arched its back, and raised its tail in an astonished question mark above a shocking-pink full stop. It undulated away. "Arsehole to you, too," I murmured.

The breeze was cold. It smelled of rain. I set my face against it. I grinned as I set off up the lane. I seem to do a lot of grinning. Nerves, I suppose, or congenital idiocy. Opinions vary.

I strode quickly through the village's soft puffs of light and out into the country. At my left, the crags, outcrops, and tumuli of Spaunton Moor were smoothed into homogeneity by the darkness. At my right, spruces shuffled and sighed, gowned aristos awaiting the chop.

I was a little surprised, if unconcerned, to find myself lurching from the grassy verge on one side of the lane to the ditch on the other. Rocking roads had become familiar hazards of late, and there were two sobering miles yet to go to High Rigg Grange. I whistled something that might once have been "Moondance," even put in a couple of quick skips just to make straight my path and raise my spirits. I crested the hill. And the horror hit me like a wall of glass. I stopped. A sort of keening seeped from me. I pushed the flopping hair back off my brow; I scanned the great black basin of moorland beneath me; I blinked up at the mantilla of cloud that shifted about the wan face of the widowed moon. Anything to keep the pain at bay. It got in under my guard nonetheless and punched me hard and low. I doubled up, eyes screwed tight. "Bastard," I heard my angry squeal, "How can you? How can you? How can you?"

My voice rose with each question until the last was roared and took frantic, fluttering wing across the valley. It ended on a sudden squeak as though swooped on from above. Then I was walking again, my right fist slapping into my left palm, echoing the call of an insomniac stonechat in the heather. And as I walked, bobbing from the waist, I growled and whimpered in time with my stride. "Bastard! Bastard! Bastard! Filthy, treacherous, cowardly *bastard!*"

The dart had struck on Cheltenham Gold Cup day in March. Now it was the first day of June, yet still the poison was active in my system, still I did not understand.

Only this afternoon, I had seen him on television in his bulging brocade waistcoat and his pigeon-gray suit. His silver hair was swept back in hermetic wings beneath the cocked trilby.

He stood in the Newbury winners' enclosure with that wife of his, Deirdre. Her movements and general responsiveness recalled nothing so much as an Easter Island statue.

He was talking to Peter and Dido Malpeters, an amiable, elegant, and prodigiously rich young couple who owned flat-race horses in a serious way and kept a couple of 'chasers just in case they should get bored in winter.

8

Your man's eyebrows archly arched. His thin mouth was tugged to one side in a lurid parody of a Gable smile. I could well imagine his account of the conversation: "Probably saw me on that bloody box. You know Peter and Dido, of course? Oh, Peter's a splendid chap. Splendid. Owns half of Nottingham, you know. Literally. Just bought himself a new Ferrari. He says he used to have Porsches, but they've become common now. And that Dido — you may think butter wouldn't melt in her mouth, but that's a naughty little number, I can tell you. Giving me the old come-hither and no mistake. She was telling me about how John Dorset" — oh, how he loved a duke's Christian name, even if it was the wrong one — "about how John Dorset got absolutely sozzled and turned his new powerboat over down at Antibes last week . . ." or some such nonsense, all delivered with much sticky crackling of his tongue and childish glee at his supposed intimacy with such luminaries and their mores.

"It's simple, Nick," Benet Kilcannon, one of my godfathers, had consoled me. "The poor old chap's jealous of you, that's all."

Oh, sure, the jealousy had been evident enough in "the poor old chap's" strutting and seething and slandering since he'd dropped the bombshell, but that could not be all of it. There had to be more to it than that.

"You're young and talented. You have the future. He's a drunken old loser. He only has the past. Pity him." This from Maria, my friend when others had failed.

Her perspective gave me, perhaps, some short-lived consolation, but whereas for her he was a figure only, an exemplar of this or that, for me he was, he must be, flesh and blood; his smiles, even tears, generous deeds and follies, silly songs, angry outbursts, jokes and heroes and laughable illusions all were as familiar to me as my own. And hate the man as now I must, I was nonetheless condemned somehow to love him, whatever that ridiculous, compendious term might mean as applied alike to mistresses, mentors, nations, lovers, babies, tortoises . . .

And fathers.

I had been so happy, so bloody pleased with myself that Cheltenham, only my second since turning pro. I had become stable jockey, somewhat surprisingly, at the beginning of December, after my predecessor, Stan Doyle, did a double-backflip-with-twist at an open ditch at Towcaster. That had merely crushed a couple of vertebrae, but a straggler's hooves had splintered his ribs, which in turn had punctured a lot of important internal bits. Stan, at thirty-eight, had decided to hang up his boots.

I had already had forty-eight winners that season and one at this Cheltenham festival. People were starting to sit up and take notice. Okay, so there were the old cracklings of resentment. The lads in the changing room made much of the silver spoon that they said I had had for a teether — only son of top trainer, all that. But even the most grudging of the cavilers had begun to acknowledge that the gilding of that spoon had been my work, and mine alone.

I had shrugged off the reprimand delivered by my father the previous evening. He reckoned that a moment's carelessness had cost us a place in the Champion Hurdle frame. Maybe he was right. But today was Gold Cup day, and I woke happy and apprehensive and fully alive.

The girl in my arms was warm and soft and limber, and her blond hair smelled faintly of cinnamon. It had seemed the night before that my mind could nestle into hers like a gun in its case, snug and secure from its noisier, more random and ramshackle functions. The tumbled bed was warm, too, and the sheets, once rough, were now waxed slick by our bodies. Had it been a Sunday, it would have been good to stay in there, to extend the shelter and luxury of the night, but the birds were clinking and shrilling and the gunmetal blue in the window was case-hardening.

And I was young, and impatient.

Her skin stuck to mine, releasing it only with a little *click*. Her thigh across my genitals was deadweight. I peeled it off me and rolled from the bed. Naked, I stood and stretched.

I reached for the light switch by the door. The trees jumped back and pretended they hadn't been peeking.

Light splashed cruel as cold water over the Heals mahogany bed with its New England patchwork counterpane; over the blue and red kilims on the yacht-varnished boards; over the remnants of last night's meal on the table beneath the window: scraps of smoked salmon, an empty bottle of Sancerre.

The girl moaned. She bunched her fists in her eye sockets. She said "God" on six notes, like in Handel.

I flicked on the Brixton briefcase. The latest Stock-Aitken-Waterman Saint Vitus' disco hip pop pap bounced from the speakers and rattled the windows.

"Oh, bloody hell!" She blinked pale lashes and screwed up her face. "What time is it?"

"Mmm? Half-six." I grinned with what I hoped was distasteful cheeriness. "Time to be up and doing."

God, I could be hateful.

"For you, perhaps," she croaked. "Come on, Nick, I'm not due in the office till half past nine. Jesus! Go away, will you!"

She flapped a hand at me, rolled over, and pulled the counterpane over her head.

"Uh-uh." I stepped into boxer shorts. I snapped the elastic at my waist. "Know what day it is? Come on. Up with you." I bent and tugged the bedclothes back.

She shrieked. She kicked long naked legs. She arose as though attached to the sheets. She covered her breasts with crossed forearms. "No, Nick," she pleaded. "Please. Christ!"

"Come on, love." I kissed her crown and rubbed the kiss away. "I've only got the one set of keys. Anyhow, do you good, see what a morning looks like."

She placed praying hands between her thighs and flung herself back on the skinned ticking mattress. She curled herself into a fetal comma. "Fucking *sadist,*" she mumbled into the pillow, then, "God, it is *freezing!*"

She jumped up and dressed quickly then, in clothes that she drew from a Harvey Nicholls carrier bag. She gathered together the other clothes — the powder-blue cashmere sweater, the gray box-pleated skirt, the black-spotted knickers — that lay by or beneath the bed. She folded them neatly before replacing them in the bag.

Her name was Jasmine. She was a natural ash-blonde of twenty-two. Her body was firm and fine, her face sharp and conventionally pretty. She would look pinched in middle age, pretty again at sixty. She worked for a Newbury auctioneer. Daddy was a brigadier and a Bembridge yachtsman. She spoke of him a lot. Of Mummy she spoke only occasionally as of a harmless idiot. I had known her vaguely since the days when we played pass-the-parcel and squabbled over jellies at children's parties.

"Jesus!" she shuddered. She pulled a toothbrush from her bag and clicked toward the bathroom. "It's meant to be March, for Christ's sake!"

"Yup." I ran a comb through my hair. It behaved for a moment as I peered in the looking glass. As soon as I stopped looking, it jumped up and started to play. "Been the coldest month some years past now. All our preconceptions about weather, you know? I mean, snow on Christmas cards. When'd it last snow at Christmas, Lord's sake? Hang on. News."

I sat and cocked my head. The only news that interested me was the weather.

The man on the wireless announced the news in the compulsively jolly tones of a children's entertainer. Another youth, he said, had immolated himself and four others at a Buckinghamshire self-service petrol station. Police had identified him as Anthony Adamson, seventeen and unemployed.

And unoriginal. This was the vogue among loonies that season.

And guess what, kids? Yes, the latest AIDS figures had been published, and they indicated that the number of HIV cases in the heterosexual population would triple within the year.

Jasmine walked back in with her toothbrush held erect like a sentry's saber. She said, "God, we ought to be more careful, Nick."

I shrugged and leaned closer to the wireless. The weather forecast was oracular as ever. Cloudy, with some sunny spells and the possibility of scattered showers.

"Right." I pulled one leg off the other. I slapped my thighs and stood. "You ready?"

"No, Nick," she sang, "I am not ready. I mean, for God's

sake, give us a chance, will you! I've got to brush my hair, get made up."

"Gawd!" I slumped back into the chair and slung one booted leg across the other. "So how long'll that take?"

"As long as it takes," she hummed. "I'll be as quick as I can. And if you'd let me have the one chair in front of the mirror, I'd be a damned sight quicker."

I spent the next few minutes pacing from one window to the other, peering out at the disappearing darkness and sighing deeply. I also drummed my fingers on such surfaces as came to hand. I switched off the wireless only to sigh and switch it on again. "Come on, woman." I sat on the bed for a few seconds. I looked at my watch. I sighed a bit more.

"The more . . . you . . . do . . . that, the longer I shall be." Jasmine coaxed mascara onto her long lashes. "I've told you that, Nick. I'm doing my best. Why don't you . . . why don't you do something useful for a change, like making a cup of tea, for example?" She snapped a tub of something shut.

"There's no bloody time." I resumed my pacing. Did the woman not realize what lay ahead of me today? "Got some schooling to do. And I want to see what that girl said about us in the *Mail*."

All of which was true, of course. I was itching to see the first-ever feature on me in a national daily, but my principal concern just then was to get Jasmine out of the way.

I would return after morning work, straighten out the bed, pick up earrings, stockings, or whatever accusing vestige of herself she would inevitably have left, and throw the plates into the sink for Mrs. Cox's attention.

I liked Jasmine. I even fancied sometimes that I loved her, despite the fact that she moaned "Oh, God!" with the conviction and regularity of a squeezed teddy bear, making her sound like a revivalist robot during sex. But those moments of amorousness were always when we were both evaporating into dewy breath, or late at night, when the lads had gone home and I was alone.

So now at last she closed her handbag, snatched up the carrier, and slung her Miyake coat over her arm. She bustled like a secretary to the cottage's front door with only a brief taunting moue at the hall mirror. Once outside in the washhouse-gray light, she made straight for her white VW Polo.

I turned from locking the door. I saw the car rock beneath her weight. Oh, bloody hell. I could not let her leave like that. Not today; I wanted to be carefree today.

I ran across the track. I called "Hey!" and bent with a smile.

She turned the ignition key. The corners of her lips were tucked into her cheeks.

"Hey, sorry," I crooned. "It's just — today *is* special. You know that, don't you? If I stay with you for a second, I'll want to stay for hours. You have this unfortunate effect, you know. Forgive me?"

"Maybe." She deigned to flash me a cool glance.

"Please?"

"God, Nick, you can be irritating!" She hit the wheel with the heel of her hand.

I considered for a second, then quietly sighed. I cobbled together a makeshift smile. "Look, since it's so early, why don't you come up on the gallops, watch us work for a bit?"

"Nah," she said without conviction.

"Ah, come on. Be fun."

She looked up at me without raising her head. Her eyes met mine and crinkled just a little. "Pig," she said.

I placed my hands on her tiny shoulders and I softly, slowly kissed her. "That's better," I breathed in her ear. I slowly backed away. "It'll be better soon. Promise. Just think, Provence in June. Be good, eh?"

But there would be no summer holiday. The day's events would see to that. June would find me swinging back and forth, drunk on a Yorkshire moorland road, and Jasmine would be long estranged and hundreds of miles away.

But now her clear gray eyes gazed cool as moonstones into mine and her pale pink lips formed, "Might at least be warm," and then, "Okay. Yes. Why not?"

"What?"

14

"Yes, I'd like to come up, see you at work, so-called. At least for a minute or two."

"Oh. Okay. Great. You follow me, okay?"

"Fine," she beamed. She revved up the engine.

I swung the door shut. I waved, turned away, and muttered "Damn" before clambering up into the jeep.

The hell with it. At least the day had begun.

I whistled as I let out the brake and swung the wheel. The jeep bucked and took off like an old quarter horse that could not kick the habit.

I hadn't far to go. The cottage, a fat oblong of gray stone and mossy slate, lay at the end of a narrow track. The jeep lurched into puddles, staggered around tractor ruts, and emerged on the road directly opposite the gates of Waylands, my father's house. Waylands, my home.

The flint gateposts were topped by twin stone pineapples. A squiggly sun beamed at the center of each wrought iron gate. Beyond, an avenue of limes shot straight as a dragster's trail to the house.

Waylands is light and lovely. It is built of flint and limestone. It has a big white lantern and twin colonnaded crescent wings. Behind the wing at the left, I knew, there would already be a quiet bustle — the froufrou of straw, the thud and rattle of buckets, the scratching of brushes on cobbles and concrete, the scraping and clattering of hooves.

In the old days I used to enjoy grooming and mucking out — private, rhythmical, satisfying activities — but such tasks were not now considered fitting for Waylands's son and heir, still less for its stable jockey. I swung to the left, therefore, and sped into the little village of Uffington.

I braked hard at the village shop. I jumped out to buy the *Daily Mail,* the *Life,* and a packet of Wrigley's spearmint. Mrs. Bruce became the first person of many to wish me luck that day.

I waved the folded *Mail* at Jasmine where she sat waiting. I climbed back into the jeep and drove fast up into the flesh-colored, fleshy downs.

15

I longed to open the newspaper, but you have to play these things cool. At my left as I climbed, the great white horse carved into the chalk loped across the hillside. Up to my right, Uffington Castle, a magnificent Iron Age fort, made a smooth stadium for the larks of the larks.

I shifted down. I sat back. The jeep plunged steeply into the mud track. I wanted to turn right. The car dissented.

I glanced back over my shoulder. The Polo's wheels were spinning, but Jasmine was still on my tail. My teeth rattled. The jeep jumped rather than ran down the old road. On either side the downs furled beneath me. The scrub was ruffled like breeze-blown fire.

A mile or so along, I braked so sharply that the jeep rocked. I got out, slid down, and clambered onto a raised oblong of turf surrounded by tall beeches. At the middle of the oblong, I sat on my favorite rock and looked up at the rooks in the trees above me. Jasmine climbed carefully toward me. "Jesus!" she squeaked. "I'll be lucky if I have a sump after that. Isn't there a road, for God's sake?"

"And what do you call that?" I plucked grass and flicked it impatiently away. "That, madam, is the Ridgeway, the first and the greatest of roads."

"Oh." She smoothed her skirt before sinking down beside me. "Big deal."

"You bet it is."

"And what's this place, then? Prehistoric petrol station or something? It's weird."

"Not far off, actually." I grinned. "In fact, it's a tomb. Megalithic chamber tomb built about five thousand years back. But — sense of perspective — I mean, the Iron Age seems a long way back to you and me, right? Well, this was over three thousand years old when Christ was born. So the Saxons looked at it and they hadn't a clue what it was. Must have been built by giants, though, and they've got a giant to fit the bill. Guy named Wayland — well, Weland, actually — great elfin swordsmith. So this is his smithy. Wayland's Smithy. Called that for a thousand years or more. So then — I don't know — the name gets known, and soon you have this tradition. Your horse loses a shoe on this

16

road, you leave the horse here with a coin, come back, your horse has been shod. So yes, in a sense. Ancient garage. You look around, you'll still find coins. Magic place. Often come up here before work, pay my respects."

"Is that it?" She peered over my shoulder at the paper. "Let's see. What's it say?"

It said a load of gushing guff. I loved every word.

It said that I was a rising star that somehow contrived at the same time to be meteoric. "Dashing," enthused the journalist, who was called Sally and had been sweet, and even "good-looking."

This, I knew, would draw derision from Dad. Despite his years, he firmly believed himself to be the undisputed Don Juan of the turf. I also, I have to say, stretched the truth a trifle. I don't mind looking at myself, and there's been many a woman and child of nervous disposition who has gazed upon my countenance without shrieking, but Gary Cooper I ain't. As you could see from the accompanying photograph, I am drawn in brushstrokes a little too bold. My eyebrows swoop in Slavic parabolas, my mouth is too wide, and my hands are too big for my five-foot-nine frame. "Acceptable," maybe, "amiable" at best. But like I said, this Sally was sweet.

She went on about how I was "storming" my way to the top in this most challenging and dangerous of sports, how I myself never placed a bet ("a mug's game," I said — I really did!), how I wore Turnbull and Asser shirts, liked girls with a sense of humor ("you need that in this game"), and had, so far, suffered nothing worse than a broken collarbone (three times) and femur (once) and a few sprains and dislocations. She mentioned that I would one day inherit Waylands, my father's "magnificent training establishment in the rolling Oxfordshire Downs," and that today I would be lining up for the Cheltenham Gold Cup on Ibn Saud, "heavily fancied for the greatest prize in the steeplechasing calendar." She said I was "excited" at the prospect.

Herein, for once, our Sally was miserly with the truth. I was elated, apprehensive, thrilled, terrified, overjoyed. See the appropriate section of *Roget*: "Huzza! Aha! Hail! Tolderoll! Tra-la-la! . . ." It will not go halfway to expressing the emotions that

17

at that moment made me feel as though an intricate electric train set with a whole lot of rolling stock had been installed in my stomach.

"Golly," said Jasmine. "I don't know this chap Storr."

"Nor do I." I grinned, but the piece was flattering and I susceptible. I handed her the paper with modest disdain. "Space-filling stuff." I stood and stretched. "Look," I said suddenly. "Here they come."

Here it came, rather, a meandering millipede, resolutely crawling up through the wispy mist. Then individual figures became clear: the skullcapped lads slouching in their saddles, the horses plodding somberly to work or tossing their heads and prancing, dancing in their shuddering blue and maroon blankets.

"God, you're lucky," Jasmine murmured at my side.

"Mmm?"

"To have all this. To have the horses, the downs, the way of life, all mapped out for you."

I glanced at her quickly. It sounded dangerously like a proposal. But she stared innocently ahead, shading her eyes with her hand, engrossed, awestruck even. And she was right. I was lucky. Incredibly so. "It's a wonderful life." I nodded. "Not all easy, though. And anyhow, maybe Dad'll leave the lot to a cats' home or something. Never know."

"Is that him up front?"

"Nah. That's Don. Headman. Dad's right at the back on the gray hack. See?"

I heard rather than saw her nod. My gaze rested now on the brown animal five from the front of the string. My baby. Later on today, in a very different place and watched by millions of people, his muscle and mine, his will and mine, his destiny and mine would be united.

"Come on," I said briskly. I led Jasmine down from the Smithy and over to a long low barrow two hundred yards away.

And still I watched that horse.

Ibn Saud was big, burly, bold, and beautiful, and he was mine, all mine.

Well, not exactly. He belonged, in the strict, nit-picking legal sense, to the man whose gleaming, desert-gold Range Rover followed the string up the hill.

Rashid al Iqbal's family was oil-rich, but Rashid was a poor relation in the relative way of these things. He had dedicated the first fifty years of his life to public service. He had irrigated the odd ten thousand acres, represented his country at the United Nations, that sort of thing. Only then had he decided that it was time for a bit of crack.

He may have been a latecomer on the scene, but he shared his fellow Arabs' predilection for horseflesh. Unlike some of them, for all his wealth, he did not wish to be seen as profligate.

Oh, he played the tables big, but he won. His predecessors might spend billions in pursuit of Derby winners; Rashid knew that there were cheaper and better tests of the animal that his countrymen had given to the world. He set out to win the Grand National and the Gold Cup. On such relatively modest aims, he was prepared to spend as much as anyone in steeple-chasing history.

Breeding a champion steeplechaser, however, is not so straightforward as breeding, say, a champion miler on the flat. Ninety-nine percent of male 'chasers are gelded because of the naturally discouraging effect of dragging dangling wedding tackle through the top of birch fences. Furthermore, there have been good — and bad — jumpers bred in the purple, and good — and bad — jumpers whose pedigrees augured little more illustrious than a career in a milkcart's shafts.

A flat-race champion needs speed and will to win. A jumper needs cleverness, guts, stamina, bone, brawn, speed, and will to win. Of these, speed is perhaps the least important.

I once read a description of a horse in an Irish folktale. He had, so it said, "twelve qualities combined: three of a bull — a full eye, a thick neck, and a bold forehead; three of a woman — full hips, a slender waist, and a mind for a burden; three of a hare — a swift run against a hill, a sharp turn about, and a high leap; three of a fox — a light, treacherous, and proud gait, to take in the two sides of the road by dint of study and acuteness, and to look only ahead."

That was Ibn Saud for you.

Frank Moran, Rashid's racing manager, had bought him for Rashid as a three-year-old. He had known at once that this big baby would not "come into himself" until his fourth or fifth year under heaven. There was too much bone to upholster, too much rangy waist to fill, but Frank had recognized the bold eye, the lop ears, the incipient second thigh, the lazy length of the animal's stride. "Reckoned as he'd have a pop in him," he explained.

Ibn Saud was lucky. He went to prep school, as it were, at the place where he was to complete his further education. I was twenty-one when he arrived, a gangling, overgrown baby no less than he.

We had taken to one another from the outset. In breaks from my accountancy course, I had lunged him and long-reined him. Later I had overseen his loose schools and ridden him on the schooling ground. I had soothed him back to confidence after his first falls. I had watched in trepidation as he was outpaced in a flat contest at Newbury at four. I had cheered him home in a two-mile hurdle there at five. Since then I had ridden him in his every race. He was eight now. We had grown up together.

An experienced pro would have given his full set of dentures for the ride on Ibn Saud. I had had him for my schoolmaster.

And now they were all about us, bays, browns, chestnuts, and grays, and their riders saluting me. The very senior mumbled "Morning, Master Nick," those who had been with us a few years just "Nick," and the more junior still, "Morning, Mr. Storr." The second group nodded with conspiratorial leers toward Jasmine.

"Morning, old boy." Dad's face was strangely expressionless as he nudged Florin, his hack, through the milling string. He was an exceptionally good-looking man. His fine bones made his grayish flesh seem a loose-fitting hand-me-down. His smile to Jasmine, however, was infectious. "And who's this, then?"

I took Jasmine's elbow and eased her forward. "You remember Jasmine? Jasmine Winterton?"

He reached down to take Jasmine's hand. It looked very frail and white in his. "Jasmine," he said, and he gazed wetly, lasciviously, into her eyes. "Now, let me see. Winterton. Not Toby Winterton's girl?"

"No." With her free hand, Jasmine plucked the white strands of hair from her eyes. "Toby's my uncle. My father's John."

"John!" Dad smiled indulgently. Still he held her hand. "Oh, of course. Infantryman, right? Did quite well for himself, I seem to remember. Didn't he get a brigade? Thought so. No, Toby, I remember old Toby. Splendid chap. How he could ride. Whatever happened to him?"

"Soggy brain." Jasmine was brisk. "A few Scotches too many, poor old dear. Serious illusions of grandeur. Struts around the clinic writing IOUs for millions of pounds and ordering people's executions. Thinks he's a maharaja or something."

Dad released her hand. He sat upright and gazed around the valley. "Ah, well," he sighed, "there but for a brace of cod, eh? Poor old chap. Still. What are you doing with this useless streak of piss so early in the morning, hey?"

"Oh." Jasmine shrugged and leaned back against me. "He just suggested I'd like to come up and see you all at work. Hope that's okay."

"'Course! 'Course! Delighted. You must come back for some —" He paused. For a second his bristling gray eyebrows meshed. "Well, not today. Things are a bit frantic. But another day, any time you feel like it, just give me a call and come along. Like to have the chance to talk to you. Properly, you know?"

I had been gesturing and hissing to attract his attention as he spoke. Ten yards behind him, Rashid and Frank Moran had climbed from the car and now stood waiting. Rashid, ever a mild-mannered man, looked merely disconsolate. Moran, once a hurler for Wexford, looked frankly furious.

"Dad," I said urgently.

Still he did not turn, just kept on wittering affably and lecherously to Jasmine. Moran looked at the gold watch on his profusely freckled wrist.

"Dad, for God's sake."

I forced my hands into my jerkin pockets and stretched my face into a suitably welcoming smile. I strolled over to where the two men stood. Moran now leaned back against the car in a blatant parody of drowsiness. The breeze made his cropped, pale orange hair stand on end, revealing mottled scalp. His baggy tweed trousers shook about his legs with a sound like a distant helicopter.

As for Rashid, he stood studiously upright in his dark suit, his thick fingers entwined before his crotch. He was a wiry little man with grizzled hair and a grizzled mustache. He had weary, slow, dark-brown eyes that were surrounded by cobwebs of deep lines. His left cheek was heavily pocked, the remainder of his face hairless and shiny as burn tissue. He somehow contrived to make a Huntsman's suit look like something from Jerry Lewis's neighborhood thrift shop. He moved with blinking caution, like a bee that had been too long on a window and had lost his faith in the air.

"Mr. al Iqbal," I greeted him.

He took my hand in his, which was dry and soft. His eyes scanned my face very carefully. He said, "Nick. How are you?"

"Excited." My grin was for Moran, too. "And terrified. Looks great, doesn't he?"

Rashid licked his lips. He looked concerned. Moran said, "Er, surely . . ."

"Nick! Come on! This isn't a bloody cocktail party!" My father's voice made me spin round.

"Sorry." I turned back to Rashid. "To work."

Orders were given. Today was a cantering day. Colts, then geldings, then fillies were to canter four furlongs on the collar, both to loosen them up and so that Dad, from his vantage point on the barrow one furlong out, could observe their action. The jumpers would go on to do more work, and there was to be a trial for two of the three-year-old flat horses, but that initial canter was to be the lot for Ibn Saud. A pipe-opener, no more.

Belfast, the lad who did the horse, dismounted with a rueful smile. "Bustin' out of 'is skin, he is. Swear as he knows it's the big day."

He gave me a leg up. And he was right.

Ibn Saud was not short of exercise — he did not need a deal of work at the best of times — but he was gassy as a four-year-

22

old on the first day of spring. He was up on his toes and looking about him as though wondering where the crowds and the grandstand had gone. "Now?" he seemed to ask. "Is it now?" And it was for me to draw in the reins and run a hand down his shivering neck and tell him, "Not now. Not quite yet, lad. Don't want to leave this one on the gallops, do we?"

Lord knows what it consisted in, this sense of almost bursting potentiality. He made no noise, yet it was like having a giant motorcycle revved up and ready to spurt off in a wheelie. He made no movement save impatiently to bob from foot to foot, irritably to rub his eye on his right foreleg before tossing up his head to sniff at the dry wind that swooped and scurried about the downs, yet he was as evidently charged with power as an unexploded bomb.

Older hands had described this to me, this conviction that an animal was absolutely right and ready. I had always thought that they were romancing.

I knew better now.

If Ibn Saud did not win this afternoon, it could only be because I fell off or because there was a still greater champion in the field. Ibn Saud for one did not believe that such a creature could exist. The form-book agreed.

So, with certainty now, did I.

Tolderoll.

I should have been immune, I suppose, but I never was. Perhaps it was all those childhood years spent with my mother in a scruffy cottage. Whatever it was, to pull up outside Waylands, to run up the steps beneath the portico, and to saunter into the high hall with its serpentine staircase and its towering cupola still gave me an almighty kick every time.

The books and the magazines and the visitors concentrated on the irrelevances. They oohed and ahed about the silver and the mahogany and the paintings in the dining room. I doubt that I ever ate there more than once a month. They drooled over the Chinese Chippendale and the yellow silk hangings in the morning room. I'm pretty certain that I never sat on the pierced-back chairs or set anything on the console tables. There were Sohos and Aubussons in the hall. I'd have missed them were they gone, but I passed them daily without a glance.

What mattered to me about Waylands was the underground kitchens with their huge ranges, the gun room with its three-seater loo, the flower room, the old nursery, Dad's study overlooking the walled garden, the trees, and, of course, the yard.

Dad had inherited the house from an old woman who doted on him. I was two at the time, and my father had almost immediately fled the coop. I had stayed there for perhaps one week every year until I returned to take up a job at seventeen. All in all, I had not spent much time there, but it was home because I knew no other. My mother's house, after all, belonged to my stepfather. For all his goodwill, I felt like a guest there. From the day of my return, Dad had greeted me and treated me like the prodigal.

I loved the place.

The smell of coffee from the conservatory drew me now through all that mahogany and silver in the dining room. There were male voices down there. I frowned, curious. I had not expected anyone but my stepmother to be there.

On the threshold, I stopped and gaped a bit.

Chris Wildman, the blond paunchy man with a baby face who sat at the left, was a rare visitor these days. Although his gaming and leisure business had its headquarters in London, he had lately preferred to oversee things from the warmth of South Africa.

As for Len Egan, I had expected to see his kippered face and long lank hair in the weighing room this afternoon. He was a well-known, hard rider, but he did not ride for us.

My stepmother, Deirdre, who sat facing me, might have been designed by a marketing committee. She was neither sweet nor sour, fat nor thin, fair nor brown, attractive nor ugly. The committee would no doubt have concluded, as with some powdered pudding, that thus she could offend no one. As with powdered puddings of such exemplary blandness, they would have been wrong. She reminded me of a potato print. Her face was oblong; her eyes were two inexpressive black dots; her mouth was a thin straight line.

Okay, so once, I understand, she had her attractions. When first my father met her and she was a dealer at one of Chris and Richard Heron's clubs, she was fluffy and sweet enough to pussy-whip a good man, but as far as I was concerned, all that had been lost with the acquisition of a husband and wealth and some tenuous position. She was tight now, and terrifiedly refined.

Each greeted me characteristically. Chris, my godfather and a generous friend, leaned forward. An oval of old gold engraved with his cipher glinted on his striped cuff. His jowls arose like stage curtains to show a corps de ballet of teeth. "Nick," he drawled. "Good to see you."

Len tipped his chair back. His cavalry twill trousers shot up to reveal a patch of hairy white leg above green socks. "Wotcher, Nick, mate." His voice was clogged.

Deirdre said, "I hope your boots are clean, Nick."

I dealt with them in reverse order. To Deirdre I deigned to cast a glance intended to be withering, but stone flowers take more than a breath of frost.

To Len I afforded a matey grin and a nod. "Hello, Len, what are you doing here?" I asked.

I shook Chris's pudgy pink hand and said, "And as for you . . . no one told me you were back, Chris."

Chris was a contemporary of Dad's, but his baby face and his flat, yellowish hair made him look a lot younger. He was built like a fighter, with broad shoulders and big hands, but the years had softened his contours. He was a craggy landscape turned into a golf course. Somehow fleshiness only served to increase his daunting, ponderous presence. His was the bulk of the chieftain. There were heavy wrinkled sacs beneath his eyes.

He said, "Back for good, Nick. Well, I think so." His voice was a smooth rumble. "Political situation's getting out of hand. See that bugger Mandela? Anyhow, it was getting too damned easy. I missed the rough-and-tumble, the cut and thrust, you know? Missed the birds, too. Oh, there are some tasty little

25

numbers in Jo'burg, all right, but half of them are smelly-socks brigade these days, and the other half doesn't exactly give you a wide enough field. And how about you, my old mate? Quite the young buck these days, aren't you? Gather you've been doin' pretty well for yourself with the gee-gees. Good on you! Never understood the bloody animals myself. Still. Nice for old Perry. Chip off the block, all that. My bloody boy's no damned good. My ex tells me he's got God and is into ethnic music, God save us, and my girl's a crazy mixed-up neurotic mess."

I poured myself some orange juice. Deirdre reached across and dabbed at the tablecloth with her napkin, thus staining two pieces of damask rather than one but making her point. Having made it, she sounded her habitual triumphal fanfare: she tutted.

Chris was my father's oldest friend and his one-time partner in gambling and philandering. Despite myself, I liked the guy. If, as the city pages always claimed, he was ruthless, he gave no indication of it in his playful, mock-roguish manner.

"As for me, Nick" — Len showed a crazy zigzag of brown teeth — "you know me. Just bein' chummy. Saw that guff about you in the paper. Gor. Which side of the bed was that written on, then?"

Deirdre sniffed. She bit a tiny corner off a triangle of marmalade-covered toast. "Your father invited Len," she said. "They have things to discuss. We can still do some things without consulting you, I suppose?"

"Oh, sure, sure." I shrugged. "Just curious. Well, I reckon I'll be on my way. Lot to do today. You be at the sports today, Chris?"

"Yes, mate. Yes. I thought I'd drop in, have a bit of a punt." He sipped coffee noisily and mopped his shiny lower lip. "Good to see you, Nick." He leaned backward to look up at me. He clasped my wrist and squeezed. "Good luck. See you later."

"Sure. See you." I hit his barathea shoulder. The lèse-majesté that established us as fellow bucks. No threat.

It never struck me at the time that the folded *Daily Mail* at Deirdre's left remained resolutely virginal, that no one else at the table had wished me luck on this, the most important day

26

of my life, and that Chris Wildman's tone and gesture had a decidedly valedictory tone and air.

Chris's eyes were full of pity as he wished me well. He always did take his godfatherly duties seriously.

I strolled back onto the steps beneath the portico. The lighting director up in the gods caught sight of me and turned a spot on me. The sudden warmth spread through my muscles like post-orgasmic glow, so I did all the usual things. Stretched. Inhaled deeply. Swallowed the moment to make it mine.

". . . minutes, okay?" I heard Dad's voice down at my right. He backed out from under the archway. He raised his hand in a half salute. "Fine. See you there, Mr. al Iqbal. Splendid, splendid!"

He swung round and walked toward me like a man with debts. He looked down at his feet. There was a thin diaphanous patch in the iron-gray streaks of his hair. His feet chomped on the gravel.

He looked up as he neared the steps. His frown dispersed like grime in ads. "Oh, hello. You away then, old boy?"

"Yup. Pop back to the cottage, then off to the sports. Want to be there early. Know what the traffic's like."

"Lord, don't I?" He climbed up and stood beside me. He too looked out over the landscaped paddocks, the greening limes, the distant downs. "God, like an impacted colon come lunchtime. Be there myself round midday."

"You had your jab, then?"

"First thing. Don't fuss. I'm not going to forget. Lived before you turned up."

Dad was a bad diabetic. A bad diabetic is not one who suffers diabetes worse than another, merely one who insists on the good bad things and so has to take compensatory insulin. Oh, he avoided chocolates and *crème brûlée,* but he could never resist the celebratory champagne, the glass of lager at lunchtime, or whisky after dinner. He said life was too short.

When first I arrived at Waylands, I quickly became expert at giving him the twice-daily jabs of Actrapid and Monotard. It became an affectionate sort of ritual, discontinued only when I moved out to the cottage.

"You didn't tell us Chris was here," I said lightly.

"Didn't I?"

A thing about Dad: his every sentence was preceded by a crackle of tongue and palate in saliva. It was as though each thought must be taken from its cellophane wrapping before use.

"Oh, yes, yes," he said. "Came over a week or two ago, but typically vague about when he'd actually turn up, you know? Just rolled up last night. Same old Chris. Says he's back for good this time. I'd not leave South Africa. God's country."

"Yes, Dad." I sighed wearily. This was one of his silliest affectations. On bad days he liked to walk into grocer's shops loudly declaring that he would only buy South African.

"No. God, I mean it."

"And what's Len Egan doing here, then?" I threw in a laugh.

"Oh, just a bit of business, you know. Ideas to discuss. Is that a redwing?" He leaned forward with narrowed eyes. "No. Pigeon. Oh, well. Glorious day, isn't it?"

"It'll do." I glanced at him, a little surprised. Apprehension about the race must be getting to him, too.

He took a deep breath. "Ah." He shook his head. "Nowhere like it, is there? Bloody marvelous. Think that every day. Nowhere in the world. Just to have this . . ."

"It's lovely," I agreed.

"Sometimes, you know, thinking of all the hard times . . . Well, we really are bloody lucky, eh?" Two more pensive crackles, then he was suddenly cheerful. He turned. "Well, good. Yes. So. See you later, then, Nick, old chap." His arm just whispered against mine as he passed.

I called, "Yeah, bye, Dad," but the ringing of his footfalls on the tiles told me that he was already too far away to hear.

The hypersensitivity of the meat eater, who would sooner pretend that a chicken is born oven-ready than wring a fowl's neck, condemns a million birds to live in concentration camps. Nothing, I mean to say, nothing is so cruel as squeamishness.

I am sure that it was such cowardice, disguised as clemency, that made my dad delay the striking of the blow until the very last minute. He always hated the sight and sound of pain.

So much that was hurtful and regrettable could have been avoided. My mates would have enjoyed a morning undisturbed by my unconvincingly cavalier calls. Innocent passersby on the road to Cheltenham would have been spared the cocky young ass in an open-topped jeep, grinning and waving and inflicting Jusse Bjorling and Charlie Parker on them. The gateman at Prestbury Park would have had one bruise less on his shoulder because I would not have punched him and bellowed "Morning!" as I lugged in my kit.

All this could have been avoided, and the humiliation and the horror would have been less public, had my father only had the guts to strike firmly and with the ruthlessness of mercy.

Instead, a nightmare now began.

When I was a child and pigs were pigs, not breathing sausages, I used to see the weaners being walked to the slaughterhouse, and I'd wonder, had these most intelligent of animals an inkling that this was something more than a country stroll? Did they pick up telepathic warnings or vibes of pity from onlookers, porcine or human, who knew the score?

I, a weaner on his way to slaughter, slowly, slowly got the message and began to drag my feet as I neared the inevitable, the already known, the unjust, unexpected, inexplicable. Blitheness gave way to curiosity, curiosity to anxiety, anxiety to panic.

The sky was pale and sulfurous, the breeze cold enough to graze whatever it touched. Normally at this hour on a racecourse you would expect to see only the pros — jockeys, lads, caterers, officials — but this was the annual fetid scrum that is Cheltenham, and already men with marbled complexions and bulbous noses were wandering about munching on sandwiches or taking snorts from their hip flasks; already pippin-cheeked girls in parkas were chortling and yapping while their burly escorts studied their race cards or their hands; already Irish priests in their black suits and dog collars were strolling about the place in twos and threes, frowning seriously as though speculating on the likelihood of the second coming this afternoon.

No chance. Arkle is dead.

Pete Straker's was the first familiar face that I encountered on the course. Pete, a stocky, dark fellow with thick eyebrows and a broad, ready smile, had been champion jockey seven times. Now he trained successfully near Swindon. He stood chatting with his wife, Gloria, and his headman.

I just said, "Pete," as one does, and I passed.

Pete looked up, that smile already creeping across his chops. It froze. Expressions flickered across his face like suits in a riffled deck of cards — concern, compassion, bemusement, even fear. At last he found a smile to replace the original and hung it in its place. This one was a fake. He vaguely said, "Nick," and turned back to his conversation.

I shrugged and strolled on over the concrete concourse. Curious, I glanced back. Gloria Straker watched me. Her eyebrows rose at the center. Her lips were parted to reveal a small lozenge of white. As soon as she saw me looking at her, she huddled with the two men again.

"Mornin', Nick." Pat Farmer, a foulmouthed, wizened, workaday jockey, swaggered by. "What's this I 'ear from your Joey, then, eh? Jocked off, and by your old man!" he hooted. "Fucking magic!"

"Oh, ha, bloody ha," I called after him, though a large weight had for some reason just shifted downward in my stomach.

A joke. That was all. It was a weighing-room joke.

I walked on. Two scruffy children scudded up to me and tangled around my legs like breeze-blown litter. Someone shouted below the stands. A kestrel flapped and glided above the course.

"Nick! Nick!"

Joey Beale, our traveling head lad for as long as I could remember, hobbled toward me from the weighing room as fast as he could manage. One of his legs was useless. He had to carry it like an artificial limb, which gave him a lurching, hobby-horse gait.

Joey had been with us back in the Wiltshire days. He was a teddy boy back then. He had taught me to ride, spent hours trotting alongside my Welsh Mountain pony while I bounced on its back like a pea on a drum.

Now all that remained of the Carl Perkins quiff of those days was a morning mist of white hair. The frock coats and drainpipe trousers slumbered in a trunk, awaiting the hour of England's greatest need or the last trump, whichever came sooner, to be replaced by more suitable — if less fitting — tweeds and twills.

A crazed bitch of a filly had all but shattered Joey's left leg, so the sunken cheeks and the trim, quick frame had filled out, but the pale eyes that met and held mine were youthfully clear.

He reached out a hand that felt like a bunch of grapes. "Nick," he panted. His voice was very high-pitched. "Nick, listen, I just wanted to tell you. I don't . . . I mean . . ." He drew a hand angrily across his brow. "I don't know what this is all about, but I think it's wrong, bloody wrong. There. That's it. And I've told anyone as wants to know and I'll tell the guv'nor, too, straight out, I can tell you. I have to obey orders, but I darn near refused to do the job. Unfair, that's what it is. Bloody unfair. So."

All sorts of small creatures were scuttling down my shoulder blades as he spoke. I shuddered. "Look, hold up, Joey." I shook my head and grinned. "What are you on about? This is a joke, right? I mean, what's supposed to have happened? You've got this all wrong. Must be some rumor got out of hand, something. Someone's having me on, Joey. . . ."

But as I watched him slowly and sadly shake his head, I knew that whatever this was, it was no joke. Joey was a serious, devout, even dour man now that his jiving days were done.

A mistake, then. It had to be.

"What are they saying, Joey?" I laughed. "Am I in disgrace or something? Who's been saying what?" My voice quavered. I had to swallow.

Joey continued with his head-shaking.

"Come on, Joey," I barked. I shifted impatiently from foot to foot. "For Christ's sake, what's all this about?"

"I'm sorry," he mumbled, "I thought as you knew. Shouldn't have said nothing. Can't believe he hasn't told you —"

"Told me *what?*" I yelped.

"I dunno. I'll not say nothing." He shuffled backward. "I'm not putting my foot in it again. Sorry, mate."

"Goddamn it!" I muttered. I turned away and took the last few strides toward the weighing room. Two people who should have greeted me on the steps turned to look at the hills as I passed inside. I picked up a race card and flicked through it. There it was: *Ibn Saud . . . N. Storr.* It had been in the *Life.* It was in print. It had to be so.

This bare room, furnished only with a single chair, a table, and the two sets of scales, was the racecourse's heart. Later in the day it would see chaos. Jockeys would rush this way and that to change between races, hop on the trial scales, adjust the lead weights in their saddlecloths, weigh out and weigh in, somehow contriving to fit in gossip, post mortems, and politics, while inside and outside on the steps, trainers, officials, and press babbled of prospects and odds, distances and sex. The whole place would rumble and rattle and ring.

For now, however, just a few people lounged about, none of them a suitable or reliable source of the information I needed. I barged through into the changing room. Four jockeys had made it before me and sat, still in mufti, on the benches, chewing the fat.

I ignored them. I needed the services of the oracle.

The oracle stood at my right. It was meticulously laying folded breeches on the benches. Its name was Alan. It was a jockey's valet.

The valets travel from course to course with our kits. They are our managers, counselors, and confidants. They know which horses we are to ride and which colors we are to wear. Theirs is largely an inherited job, and Alan was the son and brother of valets. He looked like an Italian waiter with his deft brown fingers, his sharp face, and his black hair slick and shiny as rubber, but he claimed Romany descent.

I slowed my pace so as to appear unconcerned. I tapped his shoulder. I said, "'Lo, Alan."

Alan looked up. He said, "Nick," only he spoke so adenoidally that it came out as "Ngeenk." He sounded like a music-

32

hall queen. "Hello. Good to see you, but . . . well, truth to tell, I wasn't expecting you. Still, always lovely . . ." He smiled kindly. His teeth were stained mahogany.

"Come on, Alan," I snapped. "What the fuck are you talking about? I'm riding in — what is it? T-Two? Th-three contests today? Leave it out, would you!" I cursed the stammer that always came back when the pressure got bad.

"Not what I've got down, Nick." Alan moved on to the next place on the bench. "So, what you been doing to your dad, then? Look fit enough. Thought you must be ill."

"Alan . . ." I wanted to pick the man up and slam him against the wall. I wanted to shriek. Instead I gave it another try. I jabbed the race card with my finger. "Look, what's the joke, m-mate? I'm on Ibn Saud in the Gold Cup. Come on."

"Not what we've got down," Alan droned again. "Len Egan's got the ride. Joey left specific instructions from your dad. And the rest of 'em. Looks like you've done something to offend the boss. Sorry, Nick. Probably a misunderstanding, but orders is orders."

"There's been a mistake," I announced in a voice that made the jocks at the other end of the room look up. "This is bloody ridiculous. Gerry," I called to one of the boys, "who rides Ibn Saud this afternoon?"

"The Pope?" offered Gerry helpfully.

"No, listen," I spoke with increasing urgency, "these guys are saying as L-Len's g-got the ride. Jesus. Has every bugger gone m-m-mad?"

"What's up, then, Nick? Screwing your stepmum, is it? No, okay, far as I'm concerned, you and that wog horse are a number. Still, your dad's pretty unpredictable. No knowing with a guy like that."

"You hear him?" I was shouting now. A panicking bird was looking for a way out of my rib cage. "You hear him, Alan? I ride that horse. Jesus. I was riding him this morning. This whole thing's fucking ridiculous!"

"Sure it is," Alan soothed. "Now don't bawl us out, Nick. Nothing to do with us. Just you sort it out with Daddy, right? I just do as I'm told. I'm told Len Egan rides. Look." He thrust the checklist at me. I did not look at it. "Seems crazy, but don't hassle me. I've got enough on my plate. 'Scuse us." And he consulted his list and brushed past me.

Later I would be grateful for Alan's bustling, housewifely calm. For now, it irritated the hell out of me. The world, his businesslike manner asserted, impertinently went on, regardless of my distress. I might not ride, but others would. I did not find this consoling.

The jockeys at the far end of the room had resumed their casual chat about Cheltenhams past and future. Many had won great races here. I had not. I was horribly alone.

Just to remind everyone that I was there, I growled "What the fuck's going on?" before swinging round and stalking off through the door.

I walked out onto the steps outside. A gray sky had slammed down like a dustbin lid on the lot of us. The crowd was already thickening. There was not much time left. Where should I go, then, to sort this fiasco out? I glanced at my watch. My father might still be at home. The telephone, then.

I stepped down into the winners' enclosure, and a short man with crimson dewlaps detached himself from a group by the weighing-room wall. He pursued me. "Nick," he called plaintively. "Just a second, Nick . . ."

I kept walking. Frank Trenchard of the *Echo* had to put in two scurrying steps for my every one. He was fat, but he had dainty, gleaming little feet. Twinkletoes. "What is it?" I demanded over my shoulder.

"Can you tell us why you're not riding Ibn Saud this afternoon?"

"I am. I will be. Far as I'm concerned, there's just been some sort of cock-up." I set my jaw and walked on.

"Your father," Trenchard panted. "I talked to your father . . ." He flicked over the top pages of his notebook. "He said, he said, 'Nicholas has done very well on one level, but we're talking about a whole different league here: Lenny Egan has the experience and above all the courage needed for a race like this.' Have you any comment on that, Nick?"

Something pushed down hard on my eyes like a murderer's pillow. Every word he spoke jabbed me. "I — I don't know what this is all about," I almost squeaked. "It must be — I don't know — there must be a joke of some sort. I ride Ibn Saud this afternoon. I ride all the Storr horses this afternoon. I am the stable jockey. That's it."

"Have you got a contract?"

"With my own father?" I snapped. "Don't be ridiculous."

"He can jock you off whenever he feels like it. After all, technically any trainer can jock off his jockey up to forty-five minutes before the off."

"Technically, maybe. But in practice they don't, in case you hadn't noticed. Ibn Saud is my horse, my ride. I don't believe my father said that. If he did, he's just joking, or he was pissed or something. I don't know. Whole thing's crazy."

"And what about the implication that you're — um — timorous . . . ?" I had reached the telephone box. I stopped now and glared at him. Alarm was evident in his bluebottle eyes. He gulped back his words. ". . . That you haven't got the nerve," he finished weakly.

I pulled open the door of the kiosk. I took a deep breath. "Listen, Trenchard. You write that, you'll find yourself a laughingstock and damned probably at the wrong end of a libel suit. I ride Ibn Saud, okay? And now I'm going to make a telephone call. If you're not fifty yards away by the time I get through, I'll give you a crime story instead of a sporting one. How does 'Hack Castrated by Jockey' grab you for a front-page splash?"

I stepped into the kiosk and let the door swing shut behind me. Trenchard smirked at me and walked away slowly, but at least he walked away. I shook as I dialed the familiar number. The receiver smelled of scrapbooks. It became a bristling pincushion of sound, then stabbed at my eardrum. Busy.

"Shit!" I slammed the receiver down, picked it up again, shifted rapidly from foot to foot. I wiped furious tears from my right eye with my upper arm. I dialed again, muttered, "Come on, come on . . ." There was a click. The telephones at Waylands, in the morning room, in the kitchen, in the master bedroom, in my father's study, jangled and shrilled in chorus.

"Come on!" I hit the telephone with my fist. "Come on, damn your eyes, come on. . . ."

A click. A rattle. Deirdre's distant voice: ". . . Yes, if you can just put it over there. No, that's fine . . . no, I'll see you later. Greet . . ." then, "Hello?"

"Hello, Deirdre?" No. Too urgent, too obviously distressed. Pause, then, breathe deep. Play it cool. "Hi, it's Nick. How are things?"

"Everything's fine, thank you, Nick." She sounded surprised. "Is there some reason why it shouldn't be?"

"No! 'Course not. Just . . . look, is Dad still there?"

"Hardly. Your father left at least half an hour ago."

"Was he coming straight here, do you know?"

"I'd have to know where 'here' is to answer that, wouldn't I?"

I exhaled through gritted teeth but managed to make my tone equable. "Cheltenham. The racecourse."

"Well, he's going at some point, obviously. I don't know precisely when. Why?"

My eyes were closed. My forefinger and thumb clutched tight to the bridge of my nose. Burglars had broken into my skull. The alarms clamored. "Oh, nothing," I managed with a little laugh. "Just — there seems to have been some sort of blunder, that's all."

"Oh? And what sort of blunder is that?" I could tell by her tone that she was doodling as she spoke.

"Oh, just something silly. Someone's . . . They've got the idea . . . It's nothing. Just confusion about jockeys. Someone's putting it about that Len Egan's to ride Ibn Saud."

"Yes," she said, as if to say, "And?"

"What?"

"Well, he is." She was cool. She was enjoying this. "Surely you didn't expect . . . ?"

"Expect what?" I barked. "I've ridden . . . What the hell's going on?"

"Don't shout at me, Nick. Thank you. I don't know why it should surprise you. Your father's been less than satisfied with

36

your performances for some time now. Ibn Saud needs strong professional handling. You can't really expect that you would ride him in the Gold Cup."

"Less than satisfied?" My voice cracked. I blinked away the oily tears. "What do you mean, 'less than satisfied'? He hasn't said anything about it to me. What's going on here?"

"Oh, do calm down, Nick, and stop being ridiculous. There's nothing special about you, you know. You're just a jockey like any other jockey, believe it or not, and your father is at liberty to employ you or not, as he wishes. The world doesn't owe you a living, you know."

"But no one fucking told me. No one told me anything!"

"I believe it was a sudden decision, and please don't swear at me. I've got to go now, Nick, or I'll miss the first race."

"What . . . ? Wait . . . look, what about the other horses, the other rides? How come . . . ?"

"Nick." She cut through my burbling. "You'll have to talk to your father about that. I've got to go. Goodbye."

"No!" I shouted at the bit of plastic in my hand. "You fucking come back here, bitch!"

But the bit of plastic purred at me as though satisfied.

I lay in wait for two hours. The crowds poured in through the gates like some thick lumpy fluid.

They laughed. They greeted one another with handshakes, slaps, and kisses. They mumbled secrets and speculations, bellowed jokes and salutations. Men doffed trilbies. Women clung to their crowns although the breeze was light.

And I stood somberly at the owners' and trainers' entrance, trying to be unobtrusive while waiting for my father, waiting for understanding.

They say that those who lose loved ones at sea grieve worse and for longer than those who can bury their dead. They say that burial is a sort of full stop, a cold fact to end the agonies of speculation. In much the same way, I now needed knowledge, no matter how terrible that knowledge might be, simply in order to end the devil's dance in my head. One fact I could face, but not these countless dreads.

No sooner did I think that I had subdued one demon than another leapt out and fired a blast of flame to sear an unprotected part of my brain. When I thought of Ibn Saud, now in the racecourse stables, grief and yearning threatened to choke me. When I thought of Deirdre's complacent malice, my fingers flexed in search of a yielding throat. I was by turns indignant, incredulous, scared, and self-pitying, but overlaying all these was a new and worse emotion for which I could find no name.

I harbored, or so I thought, no illusions about my father. He was a rank outsider in anyone's canonization stakes. He was often absurd, venal, cowardly, and treacherous. But I knew those vices in him as I knew them in myself, and I regarded them with the critical forbearance bred of long intimacy. Perhaps because he had played so large a part in the creation of my standards, I had preferred to admire the corollaries of those vices in him: he was funny, generous to a fault, zestful, and transparently eager to love and be loved. The very understanding of his weaknesses constituted some sort of love on my part, and the admiration of his strengths some sort of hero-worship. It was on his account that I had cultivated disdain for niceness, moderation, thrift, and middle-class propriety, on his account that I had placed generosity, courage, and greed for life at the top of my list of desirable traits.

If I had thought myself at twenty-six to be immune to hurt from him, I now discovered that I had been wrong. Very wrong. Suddenly I knew the meaning of that old phrase "sick at heart." It was as though some part of me had turned against me, and I could not fight it without fighting myself, or hate it without hating myself.

That he thought he had good reason I did not doubt, but as I stood looking out over the car park in search of his tall figure, I racked my brains to think of any motive sufficient to justify the brutal and public betrayal of his son. I could not think of one.

Money, sex, power — the usual human motives — would not suffice. It was unthinkable that the ties of blood and the intimacy of a lifetime could be bartered for cash. He was my father. He knew me. At what price could I set my own worth if he had traded me for something — *anything* — else?

I saw him.

He stood behind the open boot of his BMW, perhaps three hundred yards away. His back was toward me. He reached back over his shoulder to adjust the strap on his binoculars. A saucer-glass of champagne stood on the car's roof. Now he leaned forward into the boot. He pulled out his trilby and wedged it onto his head. He straightened, picked up his glass, and drained it.

A woman emerged in sections from the front passenger seat. Deirdre. So the cow had lied to me. Dad had been there even as I had talked to her on the telephone.

She wore a tube of herringbone tweed and a black hat with a broad, upturned saucer brim. Her mouth was a short, precise gash of pink gloss. She smoothed down the coat and inspected the soles of her low-heeled shoes. She looked angry and disapproving, probably because my father was drinking. She briskly said something, picked up her handbag, and started to walk toward me, leaving my father to lock up in a hurry, pull on his fawn overcoat, and set off in pursuit.

I had already started to stride toward them, but now I stopped. I sidestepped and crouched beside a red Rover. I wanted to confront my father alone, to challenge his memories and our common bonds without Deirdre's cold sarcasm. I had never liked her, nor she me. She might even be responsible for this.

She bustled and rustled past on the other side of the Rover. I gave her half a minute, then I stood. I damn near gave my father — and myself — a heart attack. He was no more than three yards away.

He recovered first. "Hello, old boy," he said with exaggerated casualness. He gave me a thin smile. He walked on.

"Hold on." I rowed myself along the bonnet of the car between us. "Don't you reckon you've got something to explain to me?"

"Mmm?" He raised his eyebrows. "No, not really."

"Ibn Saud. The rides today. How come you didn't tell me? You let me come here —"

"Oh, come on. Don't be childish. It's a perfectly normal situation. I simply decided we needed someone more experienced. I *am* the trainer, you know."

"You're also my father."

"So? Nepotism can only go so far, old boy."

I was three paces ahead of him now. I took the opportunity to squeeze between the bumpers of two Rolls Royces so that now I stood in front of him in the same aisle. I extended a hand to stop him.

"Please get out of my way, Nicholas." He was two inches taller than I. He did not meet my eyes.

"Okay, sure," I panted, "but first explain to me, why have you done this? What the fuck have I done wrong?"

"Nothing. I told you. I just thought we needed someone more experienced and with his mind more on the job. I mean, look at you. Drink, messing around with these tarts — no wonder you made such a complete cock-up in the hurdle yesterday. Sorry. I just can't trust you, old boy, and there's an end on it."

"You never told me, never warned me."

"No, well, I shouldn't have to."

"But . . . this is ridiculous! Okay, so you reckon I went the wrong way round yesterday. Okay, so I'm sorry. So I've learned a lesson, but . . . And how come I'm experienced enough for the Hennessy, experienced enough for the King George, but there's such a big difference in the Gold Cup? Come on."

"No, *you* come on, Nick." His right eyebrow rose. He smiled. "I really don't want to discuss this any further. You're just not professional enough. Let's let it rest at that, shall we?"

He made to walk past me, but I sidestepped into his path. "Look, look . . ." I shook my head fast. "I just don't understand, Dad! You've always told me Len was a crook, and since that blunder at Fontwell — okay, there was yesterday, but besides that — there hasn't been a race that I could have won but haven't. You know that. So why?"

"I really don't have to explain, Nick," he sang. "There are all sorts of pressures in this business that you know nothing about. . . ."

"So tell me."

". . . And as for my implying that Lenny was a crook — ridiculous. Perfectly good jockey."

"You did. You said he was a crook."

"I'd be careful if I were you, old man. You could get yourself into trouble talking like that."

A sudden gust of wind pushed me forward. My father's bloodshot eyes fastened on mine. He was alert, even apprehensive. He thought I might attack him.

"Look," I gulped. I waved and smiled. "Tell me the truth, Dad. What's this about? I can stand it if you tell me the truth. I can't cope with not knowing why you . . . why you want to jock me off, and why you've waited until the last bloody moment, made me a laughingstock . . ." my voice trailed off.

"I'm sorry, old boy." Still the same mocking tone. "I didn't want —"

"It's you who are making yourself a laughingstock, Nick." Deirdre's voice was sharp and hard behind me. "Behaving like a spoiled infant when his toy's taken away. Grow up and let your father pass."

I gave her one heavy glance. "You keep out of this, Deirdre," I snapped. "This is between me and my father. I need to know why this has happened, what I've done wrong. . . ."

"Oh, for God's sake." She sighed. "Your father's been bloody good to you. He's given you a hell of a leg up in this business, and now you're being asked to sink or swim on your own and all you can do is whine that it's unfair. Just grow up, Nick. You're not even very good as it is."

"That's a lie," I growled. "Tell her it's a lie, Dad. I'm bloody good. Okay, I've got a lot to learn —"

"Oh, come on, Perry." Deirdre reached past me. She took his hand. "There's no point in talking to a spoiled brat."

The rustle of her breasts on my back, the scent of Penhaligons' Bluebell, and the unjustified arrogance of her tone made

41

my temper snap. "Fuck off out of here, you bloody woman" —
I pushed her back — "and leave us alone. Who the hell do you
think you are?"

"That's not necessary, Nick." My father was stern. "Just
accept the fact that you have been dismissed, and I mean dismissed, like any other jockey, okay? And to answer your question, no, actually, you are not very good, and Waylands has to
have the best. In my day you'd have been regarded as a rather
cack-handed wimp, as a matter of fact. So. The decision is made.
That's it. You may not like it, but there we are. Now, if you'll
let me pass . . ."

He was raising his voice, but he had not lost his temper. I
knew him well enough to guess that he was performing for an
audience. As I stepped aside and leaned back against a car to let
him go, I saw the audience.

It was a large if unprepossessing one. Frank Trenchard stood
two aisles away, scribbling in his notebook. On his face was the
smug look of the journalist who has found his copy before the
day has so much as started.

I skulked like a thief in the vast, pulsating crowd. I spent a lot
of time in the loos, a lot of time down in Tattersalls', where, I
trusted, the journalists and the other jockeys would not deign
to come. When I saw a familiar face approaching, I covered my
head and dived into the cover of a clump of drunkards.

I would have liked to leave, to drive off to a quiet riverbank
somewhere where I could howl and hit the turf and try to bring
some strategic order to the crazy crossfire of ideas in my head,
but I had to stay. I had to subject myself to the familiar twang
of the course commentator, the bellowing of the crowds, the
ringing of the stands, the jubilant self-congratulations of winning punters and the sight of the lads riding out into the great
basin of the course, cantering up to the start, and enjoying the
borrowed might of their mounts' strides, the flying sensation as
they leapt, the hot joys of battle as they vied with one another
in the straight.

I had to suffer all this because I had to see Ibn Saud, my
horse, confronting the greatest challenge of his life.

I could not bring myself to go to the paddock before the big race. To see my father flicking Lenny up into the saddle and Lenny smirking down at me as he rode out would have been too much. I stood alone, therefore, on the stone steps of the stands as the other racegoers eyed up the horses and placed their bets.

"Hello, Nick, lad." A dark girl came up the steps.

I said "Hi" and pulled my race card from my pocket. I studied it very seriously. I knew her, of course.

Maria Thornton, the daughter of a fairly distinguished but deceased Middleham trainer, Colonel Sylvester Thornton, had worked at Waylands ten or eleven years ago. She had left suddenly and soon afterward had married Michael Wyatt, a piss-potical little trainer somewhere up in the wilds of Yorkshire. He had been killed in a car crash on his way back from Sedgefield one winter night. Maria had taken on his license. She was not often to be seen down south.

"So what's this everyone's saying?" she demanded. "You should be riding out there, shouldn't you?"

"Yup." I shrugged. I did not trust my voice to sustain more than monosyllables. "Still."

"You must be bloody furious. Know I would be. I'd not have that Len Egan up if you paid us. You're good, Nick. Surprised me. Bit bloody reckless, perhaps, but you're good."

Kindness was cruel. I swallowed down a large lump of something and blinked up at the gray sky. "Not what my — not what he says."

"What the fuck's he know? Perry Storr is mad. Always has been. I'd not worry about him. Right bastard. Sorry, but it's true. So, what's behind it? You done anything to offend him?"

"No." It came out as a sort of howl. "No bloody indication till — till I got here. Dismissed from the stable. Oh, God. Crazy." I tried to smile.

"Jesus Christ. So you're out of a job?" She lurched forward as a fat man squeezed in roughly behind her. Instinctively I reached out and grabbed her arm. I gave the fat man a hard glare. He appeared unmoved.

"Thanks. God, it's more comfortable on a rush-hour tube."

43

Maria dusted herself down. "So, tell you what. Come and work for me. I could do with a helping hand. God, couldn't I just. But I reckon that's not your style, eh?"

"Ha ha. Thanks, Maria, but no thanks."

"Just a thought." She refused to be offended. "I've got the best novice in the country, I reckon. You just wait and see."

"What's his name?"

"Pipistrelle. You wait. He'll win here next year."

I had heard of him. For the moment I could not remember just what it was that I had heard, but I knew it was good. I dismissed her rash dreams with a "Hm" and returned to my study of the race card. All I saw were those names: *Ibn Saud (Capt. P. Storr, Uffington), Mr. Rashid al Iqbal,* and, as mocking as a place setting on the *Titanic,* my name, *N. Storr.*

"Well, if you ever change your mind, let me know — you'd like the North York moors," Maria was saying. "Oh, look, here they come."

My head jerked up. Beneath us, the eight horses and jockeys paraded. I knew them all: Appalachian, the wonderful old gray who had won this race two years before; Kilgore Trout, the washy bay who had taken the Mackeson; Ballykealy, the orange bay Irish mare; Grimaldi, the young rising star who had beaten Ibn Saud once in the Leopardstown, and been beaten by him twice; Eyewitness, the outsider and Grimaldi's stablemate; then Grand Seigneur, the brown ex–Champion Hurdler; Prague Spring, another brown who had twice been in the Grand National frame: and Ibn Saud, my boy.

I ached with yearning as I saw him high-stepping, his checked quarters gleaming like conkers in the watery light. He looked about him, sniffing the air, taking in the big burbling crowd. He knew that it was there for him.

Was he confused, I wondered, to find another rider on his back? He looked content and alert enough, but soon he would know the difference. Len was good when he chose to be, but he was tough. He mastered his mounts. He drove them hard where I preferred to coax, to urge, to persuade.

Maria stood on tiptoe and craned to see him. "God, he looks bloody marvelous, doesn't he?"

44

"Don't," I groaned.

"Poor Nick." She laid a hand on my forearm. I looked quickly down at her. She was perhaps ten years my senior. Her hair was thick, dark, and curly, her eyes wide and dark as coffee, her face just slightly plump and quick to show pleasure or concern. She had a scruffy urchin's smile.

I turned away. "I'll be okay," I said. I pulled my binoculars from their case and followed Ibn Saud as he cantered up to the start. Beneath me, bookies hawked last-minute bets. Ibi Sword, I gathered, stood at 9 to 12, third favorite to Appalachian and Grimaldi. More people squeezed onto the stands. They jammed Maria and me tight together against the waist-high wall.

"God, I remember you when you were in short trousers — well, almost. You were a nice kid. Pompous ass, but bright. Good manners."

I smiled. "I had the hots for you. You know that?"

"Nick," she chided, "how could I possibly have known?" She grinned. "No. 'Course I knew. Didn't fancy 'em — what? — eight, nine years younger? Not then, any road. Still. Like father, like son, eh?"

"Don't say that." The hard rap of my voice surprised me. "You mean he tried it on?"

"Of course! Didn't you know? Why I left. Thought he was irresistible, silly sod. I resisted him, so he made my life hell. Bastard. I may have been only a lowly stable girl, but he made sure I swept the fucking yard three times a day, gave me two of the worst nags in the yard to look after. He drove me out."

"Come on. That's just sour grapes, Maria. You thought you were above such menial tasks, told yourself it must be because he wanted to get in your knickers. I mean, he never actually made a pass at you, did he?"

"Depends on what you mean by a pass," she hummed. "Is grabbing your tits and pressing himself up against you and breathing 'You know you want it' an advance or an assault? Moot."

"You must have —" I started, then said, "Come on. I don't believe it." But I recalled his leering smile at Jasmine this morning, and I believed it.

45

She lowered the glasses, and that impudent urchin smile flashed up at me. "I must have led him on? That it? Oh, Nicholas Storr, you're your father's son, poor sod. It wasn't just me. All those secretaries used to come and go, you remember? Just like me. Most wonderful girl in the world for a month or two, then when he didn't get his way, she was a common bitch, and he'd find an excuse to get rid of her. Katie — you remember Katie? There when I was. She got booted out 'cause she was engaged and wouldn't play. The next one — what was her name? Christina, wasn't it? — she came across. He'd be pawing her in front of all of us soon as old Deirdre's back was turned. Sort of 'Look at me, big man, I've got a girl.' Jesus, like a schoolboy."

"You've got it all wrong." I forced a laugh. "He's a flirt, that's all. Likes a pretty girl. So? He's a man."

"Which words are, as usual, offered as explanation for a hog's behavior," she said crisply. "Open your eyes, Nick. You're too old for fairy tales."

"Don't be so bloody patronizing," I murmured. But something had withered inside me as I listened to her story.

I thought of the many secretaries, who came and went with increasing rapidity these days. "We have to work closely on a day-to-day basis," he told them. "It's an intimate relationship, and obviously it can only work if we really get on and are totally at ease with one another." And Maria was right. He would gloat and sing the praises of each new incumbent: "Wonderful girl, broad-minded, charming, father's in the Blues and Royals, you know. Owns half of Manchester. . . ." But within weeks, this paragon would have become a "common, po-faced little bitch. Apparently she has a 'boyfriend' up in Worcestershire, some spotty young farmer. . . . Girl talks about 'toilets,' for God's sake." Within a month, the unfortunate girl would be gone and a new advertisement would appear in the sporting press.

Dad was getting old.

"And they're away," barked the tinny loudspeaker, and again tears sprang unasked to my eyes. I suppose that some irrational part of me had hoped right up to the last minute that the whole business would prove after all to be a dream or a joke, but now

I saw Ibn Saud springing off from the gate, saw Lenny crouched like a monkey, tucking him in at the back of the pack on the rails.

Even as they set off, soft rain swept across the course in successive veils. I knew what it would feel like out there, how exhilarating the cool touch of that rain would be on a face already hot with effort, as the saddles creaked and the horses snorted impatiently and the hooves pounded their mama-dada drumfire and now, yes, three-two and hup! Good. Ibn Saud was away from the fence like a deer. Lenny took in a reef, steadied him again.

I was mildly surprised to find myself rooting for Ibn Saud. Before the race I had fantasized that Lenny might make a complete cock-up and that I would have the satisfaction of gloating, but my love for the horse and my share in the years that had led up to this moment proved too strong. I wanted Lenny to die in agony, sure, but first I wanted Ibn Saud to come home in triumph.

They were going at a fair lick as they came down to the fence before the stands, Arkle's fence. Eyewitness, eight lengths in front, took it hesitantly. He was already coming back. Then in a tightly bunched group came Appalachian and Grimaldi, who jumped upsides, Ballykealy a length back, Grand Seigneur, who pecked badly on landing, Ibn Saud, who flew it, Prague Spring, and finally, struggling, Kilgore Trout.

"Going well," Maria mused.

"Yes," I said miserably. "Going like a bloody dream."

To the casual observer it would have appeared in the next few minutes that I had contracted some obscure neurological complaint. My shoulders were tense and heaving. With each jump, I twitched and sighed. I was riding my horse from the stands, willing him to take his fences cleanly. When he hit the last open ditch up the hill, my stomach contracted like some giant mollusc. When Prague Spring, too much on the forehand, too keen, hit the next and sprawled, flinging Terry Davis over his head, my whole trunk jerked forward as I steered Ibn Saud round the milling limbs.

And now as they came down the hill, the race resolved itself.

Its true nature became clear. It was a three-horse race. Ballykealy was too slow. Prague Spring and Kilgore Trout were fallers. Eyewitness had pulled up and Grand Seigneur had hit a plain fence in the back straight. Although he was struggling on, he had lost too much wind and too much ground to pose a threat in this last stiff half mile.

Appalachian led. Grimaldi trailed him. Ibn Saud was five lengths back as they swung round the bend . . .

But Ibn Saud had his ears pricked and was full of running.

"He's got it."

Maria simply said, "Yup."

The rain had thickened now into a sheet of white muslin. The crowd was hollering so loudly and raucously that the commentary was almost drowned out: ". . . come to the last . . . Appalachian . . . Grimaldi . . . strong challenge . . . Saud making up ground . . ."

There was a battle royal up front. Grimaldi nosed ahead. Appalachian, refusing to give up, came back. The whips were out. Both horses reeled. Neither would concede. But all this, I knew, was irrelevant. Ibn Saud, three lengths back, had the beating of them.

"Now," I murmured. Lenny scrubbed at him half-heartedly. Nothing happened. "Now!" I said out loud. "*Now!*" I shrieked. "Go, *now!*"

And only now did Lenny reach for his whip and give Ibn Saud a quick one. Only now did Ibn Saud shift easily into his wonderful, surging overdrive and come at the leaders at twice their speed. Only now.

"Oh, God!" I covered my face with my hands. All about me the crowd roared and jumped and stamped and the stands shook and buzzed. I stood in red darkness, trembling with fury and crying like a child.

It had to have been deliberate. Even I, who knew the horse's blinding turn of foot, would have initiated the challenge a good half furlong earlier. I wouldn't have asked Dancing Brave to do what Len had demanded of Ibn Saud. It had to have been deliberate.

"Couldn't shake him up in time," I heard Maria say. The clamor and the thudding subsided.

"Balls," I mumbled. "He hooked him. The horse wanted to win. He just needed —"

I raised my head then and gazed up at the roof of the stand. "The horse was betrayed," I said, "and I was betrayed. Oh, God almighty, what the hell is going on here?"

Maria was brisk and practical as ever. "What you need," she said, "is a stiff drink."

She was right, too.

Four large whiskies later, I was ready.

I knew where Dad would be. Richard Heron's box had been his base at Cheltenham for as long as I could remember.

Back in the fifties, Heron, now a multimillionaire and one of the biggest bloodstock owners in the world, had run illegal poker and chemmy games in London.

When gaming was legalized, Heron was ready. He already had the experience, the capital, and the punters. He founded two Mayfair casinos, Bentham's in Mount Street and Lucy's House in Shepherd Market.

Chris Wildman and Dad had been involved in the illegal gaming and had played hard, I gathered, at both Bentham's and Lucy's.

Some of that gang, like "poor old Johnny Lucan," had come an almighty cropper. Others had prospered. Heron had come out on top, plowing his money into diverse fields in the leisure market. Chris, a qualified solicitor, had ridden in Heron's slipstream and now had a formidable empire of his own. He owned or had interests in countless casinos, clubs, and restaurants. As for Dad, no businessman, he had landed on his feet when old Maud Gascoigne had developed a crush on the young gambler and bequeathed him Waylands.

So far as I could remember, I'd never seen Heron at Waylands, but Dad and Deirdre went to stay with him at his house in Jersey, attended his huge birthday parties, and had twice borrowed his yacht for holidays.

The Heron box at Cheltenham, like the Heron box at Ascot, saw an annual reunion of many of Heron's old cronies. I had been unofficial barman at both since I was seventeen.

The boxes stood on the right-hand side of a white concrete corridor. Each one comprised a long plain white room and a balcony from which to watch the races. I was perhaps five yards from the door of Heron's box when the door opened. A woman lurched out into the corridor. She bounced off the wall and into my path. Behind her there was a burst of laughter. It was snuffed as the door swung shut.

The woman stood stock still, her shoulders hunched. She faced me like a fighter. "Nick," she breathed. The husky sound seemed to creep slowly along the skirting board.

I stopped and frowned. Then I realized who she was. I took two involuntary steps backward.

"Eledi!" I frowned. I composed myself and stepped forward, hand outstretched.

She took my hand and rested her weight on my arm. That beautiful autumnal hair splashed onto my sleeve. Those once-beautiful green eyes flickered erratically over my face. They were yellowish now at the corners.

I remembered Eledi Donovan, the beautiful young actress. Five years of being the fourth Mrs. Heron had drawn those lines about her eyes, those broken kinks at the corners of her mouth. "Nick, you seen Charlie?" she drooled.

"Charlie who?"

"Charlie Vane, of course, silly."

"No. No, I haven't, love."

"Only decent man among the lot of them," she said meditatively. "And I had to kick him in the teeth. I want to see Charlie. Bastards did you, too, didn't they?"

"What are you on about, Eledi?"

"Did you." She pulled herself upright. "Jocked you off. Bastards. Cheats. You fight 'em, Nick. Don't let 'em bully you. You're a better man than any of 'em. So's Charlie." She gave a sudden deep giggle. "Want some coke?"

"No thanks, love." I took her hand. "Look, I think you

might, just *might,* have had one too many. Don't you think you'd be better off back in the box?"

"Back in the box," she hummed. "Back in your box. Back, Jack. . . . No." She was truculent. "I'll not go back in my little box, thank you, Nick. I want to find Charlie. I'm going to escape. Give him back his ring. . . ."

The door opened again. Richard Heron stepped out, sleek and plump as a seal. "Ah, Eledi," he said softly. "Wondered where you'd got to, darling. And Nick. Good to see you, old chap. Come along in." He scooped us up and shepherded us in with one broad sweep of his arm before Eledi even had a chance to protest. "Come on in," Heron murmured again. "I think you know everyone."

I did. A fair smattering of the nation's more distinguished trainers and richer owners turned to look at us as we entered. A lot of the cheeks were very red, and a lot of the eyes were glazed. Ravaged sides of salmon and marmalade-glazed hams sprawled amid champagne and whisky bottles on the white tablecloth.

Only my father, who sat out on the balcony, very deliberately did not look round.

Eledi reeled against the table and swung round to face the room, supporting her weight on her hands. "Oh," she sang on a wistful, childish descending scale. Her hair trickled down over her face like molten toffee.

"Drink, Nick?" Heron tipped up a champagne bottle. "So, how are things?"

"Oh, fine." I took the glass from his hand and drained it in one. "Just fine, thanks."

I started to walk toward the balcony.

Chris Wildman stood up. He blocked my way. "Uh-uh, Nick," that deep voice throbbed.

"I want to know what's going on."

"Of course you do. So do I. But this is neither the time nor the place. Hold hard. I understand how you feel, but not now, Nick. Take my word for it."

But the emotion had reached the boiling point. The whistle had to blow. "The bastard jocked me off!" I shouted. I pointed past Chris. "He said I was scared, for Christ's sake, and then, then . . . Ibn Saud was hooked, Chris. You saw it. He was fucking pulled!"

"Shh." Chris moved closer, as if to suffocate the sound with his bulk. "Jesus, Nick," he mumbled. "You go on speaking slander like that, you'll be bankrupt as well as out of a job. Hush up, will you, boy?"

"It's not slander," I said pathetically. "It's true. What the hell's going on? I'm not leaving till I know, till that bastard's explained."

"Nick." Heron plucked at my elbow. "Steady on. Not in here, please."

"Go it, Nick!" Eledi chortled. "They're all in it together. A little embarrassment won't do this mafia any harm."

The chatter had stopped, even out on the balcony. Everyone looked my way.

"I need to know," I said fiercely. I knew that I was being petulant and that I looked a damned fool, but every muscle in my body was cold and hard and trembling.

My father ducked as he came in through the door. He strolled over to the table and helped himself to champagne. He hummed. Then he turned and looked up. "Oh, hello, Nicholas," he said in his most infuriating conciliatory tone. The vowels were drawn out. The consonants hissed and crackled. It was a sound to make Saint Francis reach for a revolver.

"W-what the hell's happening?" I blurted out. "Come on. Explain."

"Nick." Chris sighed sorrowfully.

"Explain what, old boy?"

"Tell them. Come on. Why'd you do it? Why'd you jock me off? Why'd you get a jockey who . . . ?"

"Nicky . . ." Chris again, this time minatory.

"Okay, okay. No, but just explain, will you? I'm sure everyone's interested."

"Nick, old boy." My father sipped his champagne. He smacked his lips. "You really are making a terrible fool of yourself, you know. Still, since everyone has heard you ask for a public explanation, I shall explain. You are demonstrating quite clearly why I think that you are unfit to be my stable jockey. You are too inexperienced, too self-absorbed, too self-indulgent, and, frankly, I don't think you've got the guts for the job. There. I'm sorry, but you did force my hand, old boy."

"That's not the reason." Eledi giggled behind me. "That's not the reason at all. They're hiding something from you, Nick."

"That's enough, Eledi," Heron purred.

There was silence then, save for the shivering of the convector heater.

"It's a lie," I said at last, though my voice served me ill. I tried again. "It's a lie, and you know it. I've ridden bloody well, haven't I? Haven't I? Look at the papers. Look at what they say." I spun round in search of support. Everyone looked away in embarrassment.

Rashid appeared in the door to the balcony.

"Did you agree to this?" I called. "Did you think I rode badly? I won on your horse. Mr. Bloody Egan lost, didn't he? Well? Didn't he?"

"It was unfortunate." Rashid spoke very softly. "But your father is my trainer. He is a gentleman. I do as he advises."

"So, old boy," Dad droned, "don't you think you've done yourself enough damage? I really think you should apologize and leave, don't you?"

I swallowed three times, croaked "Sorry" to Heron, and turned to leave.

"Oh, and Nick . . ." Deirdre's voice. I did not trust myself to look at her. "We'll need the cottage by the end of the week."

The breath was forced out of my body. My eyes burned. My hand shook violently as I grasped the door handle and wrenched the door open. I slammed it hard behind me. I then spent a while beating up the wall.

I could not have done a better job of ensuring that my father's claims should be known throughout the kingdom.

It took just two weeks of toting for rides and favors and waiting by the telephone for me to realize that not only was I not the flavor of the month, but I was about as popular a feature on the menu as Thames mineral water.

53

All my friends and the owners I had ridden for said, "Of course we'll find you rides. Don't you worry. You'll be back in no time." But after I had rejected as being beneath my dignity a few small rides offered by small trainers, the telephone squatted silent as a stylite.

Dad was not done. He elaborated on his statement in the gutter racing press:

> I gave my son as much of a leg up as I reasonably could, given that I am first and foremost answerable to my owners. He knew from the outset that his position, like that of any other would-be professional, had to be subject to review.
>
> I cannot understand why he thinks he has any grounds for complaint. I am sorry for him, of course, but he just isn't disciplined enough, and for him to come charging into a friend's box stamping and shouting after all we've done for him was quite disgraceful.

Richard Heron was quoted, too:

> Everyone drinks a bit too much at the National Hunt Festival, and Nick is young and was obviously overwrought. I bear no grudge. It was just unfortunate.

Which was sweet of him.

There were two months of the season yet to run. I was becalmed amid trade winds.

I drank, of course, which served to ease the impotent anger that seared my brain; it permitted me to sleep but did nothing for my professional reputation. I tried to exist without whisky, but no sooner would I nod off than I would start up again, panic-stricken and groaning at the hurt.

The intensity of that hurt never diminished. I never became inured. Just let my mind wander for a second and the horror would dart in with a quick flurry of blows.

I had known its echo in sexual jealousy. That, too, tainted the entire galaxy by making the sufferer seem an ugly blot on his own landscape. But the disgusting projections and speculations of sexual jealousy in time faded and died; the memories were infinite. Here both speculations and memories were infinite. There would always be another lover. There would never be another father.

In selling me — for I knew with certainty that his treachery had had a price — my father had sold not just the few intimacies of a love affair but every moment of my life and everything that I had become. From the intimacies of nappy-changing to those of first-day-at-term tears, from the observation of my adolescent passions to the story-telling sessions in the pub, he had bundled up the whole package and hawked it for some petty advantage to himself.

Jasmine was the first innocent victim to get caught in the blast. At first she came round every night to the room that I took in a Newbury pub. She listened to me spitting out my half-digested thoughts in bitter chunks. She tried to bring some order to the room, which within a week became a ketchup-stained monument to my state of mind. She tried to console me with all the warm, soft gifts of her body. And I, now protective of my self-pity, resented her, as if she had been a charwoman who had tidied my chaotic desk.

"I understand, Nick, darling," she said, "but nothing's going to get better if you don't lay off that stuff."

"You understand?" I mocked in a voice made deep by whisky and tobacco. "You with your nice little daddy in his sailor hat . . . ?"

And so on, until one night, in tears, she bundled up her bag with trembling hands. "Okay, Nick," she said in a stiff tremolo. "Okay, so I don't understand. There are lots of things I don't understand, but I can still care for them."

"I saw that movie, thanks," I snarled. "*Some Came Running,* nineteen fifty-nine."

"One thing I understand," she said from the door, "is that you're set fair to become as self-centered a drunken shit as your father, and that's a pity, Nick. It really is." And the cold wind came into the room to take her place.

I acknowledged the truth of her words, but they did not help. That was just another factor in my indulgent agony. I knew, I thought, my father's faults, but there was much of him in me, much in him that I had admired. I was inescapably cursed by my genes.

It was Maria who kicked me into something approaching waking. She rang on a pewter Saturday evening a couple of weeks later to offer me a ride. Sure, I told her. If I could fit it in. Where and when?

Wetherby, she said, the day after tomorrow.

"Ah, come on, Maria. Wetherby? Go all that way for the chance of a brass pot and a hundred quid? No thanks."

"Funny," she said briskly. "It's what professionals do. Ah, well."

I was not so scornful when she rang again three days later, but I nonetheless turned down the offered ride at Hereford. It was for the day of the National. Surely someone must want me in that vast cavalry charge. Not only that, but I was damned if the papers and the television would record that I was scrubbing around Hereford while the rest of the steeplechasing world was at Liverpool.

On this occasion I was right. Trevor Brooke, the outspoken old-stager from Middleham, called. "Remember March Brown?" he yapped.

"Yes, sir." March Brown was a weary, honest old plodder who stayed forever and won races only by waiting for others to lose.

"You want the ride? Graham's gone and busted his elbow. And don't say no, because I know you're as much in demand as vaginal deodorants to skunks. So."

The storyboard was already sketched in my mind. The favorites fall. March Brown plods on to win. Adulation for boy jockey. *They said he'd lost his nerve, but only the brave get round Aintree, only the bravest win. . . .* Egg on Dad's face. Offers pour in. He begs forgiveness. I graciously grant it.

So I drove up to Aintree and strolled into the weighing room as casually as if this were any old race. That's okay. Everyone was doing that. We — Waylands, rather — had two runners, so Lenny was there, and Paul Martin, our — Waylands's — second rider. They were all there. Every jump jockey from the champion to the lowliest aspirant. I chatted a lot to the champions as we waited after weighing out. They did not talk back much.

It was a bright blue National day. Dad, of course, was in the paddock. He never once looked my way.

I mounted, paraded, cantered up to the start, lined up, and broke well. Let others hang cautiously back. I was brave.

We were right up there at the first, because I was brave. I adopted a forward seat because I was brave, sitting well into the horse as he surged upward, so that when his forelegs clipped the top of the fence and he pitched forward and stumbled, I found myself lifted as though by giant hands beneath my buttocks, and heaved forward. I heard myself moan "Oh?" and "Shit?" My forehead thumped hard into the horse's head. For a split second then I was upside down and gazing into his eyes.

Everything suddenly seemed to speed up. The other horses were all around us. One sideswiped March Brown with his shoulder, and I was rolling on the cold turf, clutching my head in my hands and cursing, cursing as the hooves squelched and puddered all around me.

I wanted the noise to go on forever. The silence afterward, I knew, would be cold and lonely.

I didn't know the half of it.

I opened smarting eyes. I wanted to see at least five or six other jockeys uncurling like hedgehogs.

There wasn't one.

I whipped my right boot so savagely that it hurt. Absurdly, I was convinced that the whole vast audience, prompted, no doubt, by Dad's glee, had eyes for nothing but my discomfiture as I ducked beneath the rails and nodded to the Saint John's ambulance man. No matter that they had come here and invested fortunes to see the world's greatest steeplechase. There was a better spectator sport now, a gladiatorial sport: Storr *v.* Storr. And I was the abject loser.

Trevor Brooke said, "You made a right balls up of that, lad." Then mercifully, "Don't worry. I did the same thing meself once, thought I was Roy Rogers. Mind, my dad gave me a thrashing so's I'd never forget. Still. Reckon as you can do without that just now. You're all right. Silly sod, but all right."

That night I crossed the Pennines and sought out High Rigg Grange, training establishment of one Maria Thornton and, so my *Horses in Training* informed me, of nine nags of more use to Pedigree Chum dog food than to the handicapper.

Maria greeted me at the door in the light from the carriage lamp. Her greeting was in execrable taste: "Hello, Humpty. Wondered when you'd show up."

I had thought at first to stay for a couple of days; I had been there now for eight weeks.

Headlight beams swung like lances beneath me. They picked out orange scabs of heather, suppurations of oily water in the peat. I walked on down toward them. The soughing of the wind turned imperceptibly into the groan of an engine. The beams now dueled way above my head.

For a moment I was dazzled. I raised my open hands before my eyes. The car passed me. And stopped.

I tensed. They — whoever they might be — had obviously come to finish me off after these extraordinary, inexplicable months of "softening up." I was ready for them, happy to have someone to fight at last. Only three months before, I had been fit and strong. I could take some mundane villain. Surely.

"Nick?" The door of the Mini Traveller swung open. "Nick, come on. This is getting bloody boring."

I slumped into the passenger seat. The Mini puffed. "Hello, Maria."

"Nick, you're drunk."

"No'm not. Three pints, couple Scotches. Nice of you to come out 'n' fetch us."

"God's sake, Nick." Maria sighed. She exhaled smoke through her nose. "Don't bullshit us, okay? You're pissed, lad. Nothing wrong with that once, twice a week, but Jesus, you're meant to be an athlete. You've got to get your act together. There's work to be done, and I'm not here to be your wet nurse. So." And she gunned the engine.

Hours passed behind my eyelids. I had to work hard to

remember what Maria had just said. "Just a few beers, for God's sake." I was truculent. "I'm a man, aren't I? I'm young and . . ." My words ran down.

The Mini hummed and hawed as it climbed the hill. It turned into the concealed drive. The headlight beams juddered as we crossed the cattle grid, sprang up and down as we passed over puddles and potholes. Suddenly they found what they were looking for and, for the last fifty yards, steadied.

They showed rough golden stone, deep mullioned windows, and a ravelment of wisteria and lilac. A fat black Labrador stood in the porch, blinking smoky blue eyes and wagging his cosh of a tail. Maria stopped the car, switched off the engine, pulled on the handbrake, and opened the door as if in a parade-ground drill. She was out of the car before I had unbuckled my seat belt. The door clunked shut.

I watched her stride briskly across the gravel. Her hair looked like something charred. She flung her cigarette hard at the ground, then smiled as she scratched the dog behind the ear. She led him into the house. The front door closed.

I sighed and pulled myself reluctantly from the car. If I had slept there, I reckoned that Maria might have locked me out for good. So I teetered a bit, then followed her.

I staggered through the boots and whips and crash helmets that littered the porch and crossed into the high, dark hall. Ocher walls spun about me, a fox's furious mask, foxed Herring horses, a gray marble fireplace filled with a blaze of dried flowers.

Maria was not there. I wandered through into the deep-red dining room. No one there, either. The table was covered with newspapers and form-books. I walked to the drinks table and poured myself a Smirnoff. The ice bucket was full of warm water. I took a couple of gulps of vodka, shuddered, and pulled out a dining chair. "Shit," I breathed.

I slid the nearest newspaper toward me. I thumbed through the pages fast. Somewhere below the level of consciousness I noticed that Rollo Northop was about to be divorced, that the Luxury of Pure Silk could be mine for as little as £23.95, that the England cricket team had been trounced by the Pakistanis, and that Thomas Rhymer, my father's little chestnut colt, was well in at the weights at Doncaster. My eyelids drooped. *Peanuts* blurred. Snoopy was underwater.

"Right, Nick. Wake up." Maria noisily dumped a tray on the table just where I had been thinking to lay my head.

"Mmm?" I blinked.

"Come on. Black coffee. Orange juice. You and I are going to talk. This can't go on."

"What? Dunno what you're on about, Maria." I smiled. "Nothing to worry about."

"Yes, there is. I'm giving you the boot is what there is to worry about. Sorry, Nick, but the season's damn near over, and I'm buggered if I'm going to be a boardinghouse landlady to any self-pitying piss-artist." She picked up my glass and put it on the mantel. "Okay, so you're feeling sorry for yourself. Don't blame you. That bastard's done for you, and it hurts like hell. 'Course it does. He had a part in making your standards. He condemns you, you have to doubt your whole identity. Can't stop him being your father, more's the pity. But you sit here and drink, you're letting the bugger win. It's the young should beat the old, Nick. So what are you going to do about it?"

I shrugged. "Nothing I *can* do."

"There's always something you can do. It's impotence makes the pain so bad, so do something, anything. You carry on like this, I'll have no use for you, nor'll anyone else. Maybe that's what you want — stack up the rejections, then you can sit there and say, 'The whole world's behaved like a shit to poor little undeserving me,' and drink yourself to death. Here. Coffee."

The coffee was black and so strong that it made me gag. "So." I cleared my throat. It sounded like something heavy being dragged over dirt. "So, fine. Exactly what am I meant to do?"

Maria sat on my left. She counted off suggestions on her fingers, though she got stuck on number one. "First, stop being so bloody high and mighty. So mine is a tatty little yard and half my horses are crap. So? What have you ever done to deserve better? You were born Perry Storr's son is all. Right. You're not Perry Storr's son anymore. So you're a professional jockey.

Know what professional jockeys do? They start at the bottom, scrubbing around Market Rasen and Sedgefield and Devon and Exeter, and if they're any bloody good, perhaps they get noticed and taken on by one of the bigger yards. So you started by shooting up a ladder. Lucky you. Now you've hit a snake. Tough shit. Doesn't entitle you to look down your nose at what we do. This is the bread and butter of racing, Nick. Novice hurdles and selling 'chases and easy races half the season so's to beat the handicapper once a term at Hamilton. Not glamorous, okay, but it's how we ordinary people have to do things. And we have to bet, because the average Shetland pony couldn't be kept on the prize money in these parts. Right?"

"Yeah, yeah, okay."

"Right. Oh, and while we're at it, Nick, I know your father's damn-fool attitudes toward women trainers, but if I were you, I'd forget them, because I'm all you've got."

I nodded slowly. Both her accusations, I knew, had some merit. Northern racing had frankly astonished me. The yard at High Rigg bore as much relation to Waylands as Dotheboys to Eton. Both schools sought to educate boys; both stables sought to train racehorses. There the resemblance ended. Scots Grey chickens pottered about High Rigg yard. Two of the stalls were filled with old furniture. Hay came from the local farmer, water from the tap. The gallops, so called, were no more than a strip of turf five yards wide encircling three fields on the side of a hill. The "schooling ground" consisted of one battered plain birch fence and one hurdle. Maria herself "did her two" — tended two horses — just like any stable-girl.

Three other people worked here: Hector, a venerable, taciturn old man with a permanent drip bejeweling his nose; Tom, his son, a flash Harry with long springs of dark hair and a mustache like a charred sausage; and Rachel, a neat little blonde who had come here on a Youth Training Scheme and stayed on because Maria had given her the means to keep her beloved Fleet. Fleet was an aged ex-racehorse who had never been fleet and could now barely manage a hack canter. She loved every mangy hair on that tired-out body.

I had seen the vet only twice since my arrival two months

back. For all the other cuts, bruises, swellings, and discharges that would have occasioned veterinary conventions at Waylands, Hector simply administered one of the nostrums that he kept in dark-brown bottles in the tack room.

I had had five rides and two winners in the past two months. The first winner was Maria's much-vaunted novice, Pipistrelle, who was, I had to admit, a very nice sort indeed. We had taken a £4,500 'chase at Sedgefield by just half a length. We could have won by twenty, but my instructions had been explicit.

The other winner had been a disaster.

It was at Uttoxeter in deep mud, and it wasn't meant to be a winner at all.

The horse was a hard and strong dapple gray named Ortolan. The trainer was a ponytailed, soft-spoken ex-actor named Corin Gilmour. He was a near neighbor, a nice guy with the face of an angel who'd done a bit of slumming in the basement.

"Don't bust a gut on this one, Nick," he instructed me. "Armchair ride, okay?"

"What if he looks like winning?"

"Have a word with him. Teach him modesty, patience, self-denial. He'll listen to you, Nick."

"Yeah." I nodded sadly. I had been hoping if not for a blaze, then at least for a soggy splutter of glory. "Okay."

But out there on the boggy track, it was all very different. The other runners slithered and sprawled in the hock-deep mud, while Ortolan's high action made light of it. We had lost three of our seven opponents by the end of the first circuit, and Ortolan was as fresh as if he had just started.

The galloping horses about me sounded like a machete massacre, and the mud spurted like blood from the kicking hooves ahead.

And Ortolan loved every sucking, squelching stride. That horse needed a psychiatrist.

I took him easy along the back straight. I tried to look as though I were nursing an inexperienced and erratic jumper, but our opponents were foundering and coming back to us willy-nilly. When we turned for home, there were three ahead of us.

I had just two choices: either take each fence as slowly and cautiously as a nervous pony-club camper or go for it.

I told myself that I had no choice.

I know now that my duty was to my paymaster. But my father's blasts had scorched my ego. I'd not have anyone call me a coward. So I let the rubber reins slip through my fingers, and I leaned forward and growled into the horse's bobbing ears, "Get on with you."

Ortolan struck out, and suddenly there was a wind.

My rectum began twitching just a split second after we passed the post. I could imagine what Corin was going to say.

It was worse than I had imagined. He said nothing.

Not then, that is, in the unsaddling enclosure. Later, in the Buller's Arms, he had plenty to say. He said it slowly, softly, so bloody *nicely* that I wished he'd just scream and stamp.

"Nick," he said, and his voice was baize, "you know what that heroic little performance cost us? I don't want to torment you, but you really must know. For your own sake. That horse has been improving all season, but he's consistently run down the field. Why? Because, at best, he could make us five grand a year in prize money if he was always up there fighting for a place in the frame. He'd just about pay his keep. Then the handicapper hits him, and it's another twelvemonth of scrubbing around before he even gets a chance to win, let alone win at long odds. So we wait. The handicapper relaxes. The bookies relax. He opens at thirty-three to one in a moderate contest and squeaks home by a length or two and we've all made a packet. . . ."

"I know, I know." I cringed.

"It's all very well saying 'I know,' but you've got to understand, Nick. All very well for the likes of your father, though I'd like to know how he's survived over the years in a place like that without hooking a few —"

"He doesn't need to do things like that," I said with an ill-judged flash of hauteur.

Corin's eyebrows rose. "*Really,*" he said, heavy on the wonderment. "Ah, well . . . you see, my way, we have a big punt, net say twenty grand; that could mean the difference between survival and going down the tubes by next year. That's what you've cost us today, Nick. Think about it. Now, as it happens, I have another animal who might see me clear before the season's done, and I'm lucky. I've got a little capital — a little, mind you — set by, but twenty grand still hurts like hell. You're in the real world now, Nick, not the nursery, not Perry Storr cloud-cuckoo-land. You could have bankrupted a good trainer today."

"Look, I'm *sorry.*"

"Sorry's very nice in the nursery, Nick. It doesn't pay the bills."

"It's just that it's a good horse, and I was brought up —"

"I know how you were brought up, Nick." For the first time, there was sharpness in his voice. "And believe it or not, I was brought up in much the same way, so don't quote high-flown principle to me. Principle, you will discover, relates directly to the fullness or otherwise of your stomach. Thou shalt not steal. Sure. Tell that to the starving as you sit down to a four-course meal. They'll steal and cut your throat into the bargain, and quite right, too. Oh, sure, there are one or two principles that are worth maintaining even unto death, but 'Thou shalt not give a horse an easy race' ain't one of them. We're in the entertainment business, and we don't entertain any the less because today a horse is a little slower than tomorrow. And if there's such a bloody fool that he'd put his fortune on an animal when he doesn't even know if it's off, I have yet to meet him. So. I might employ you again, Nick, because I think you're good, but when you ride for me, you're my servant. You understand?"

"Yeah, okay, Corin."

"Nick."

"Hmm?"

"You're a professional jockey. I'm a trainer. Let's put things on a proper footing, shall we?"

I gulped. Heat prickled up my throat and suffused my cheeks. "Yeah. Sorry. Right."

He just waited with eyebrows raised.

"Mr. Gilmour," I mumbled.

He nodded. He patted my arm. "Good. Now let me buy a drink for my winning jockey."

As to Maria's accusation now that I might regard women trainers as incompetent, my first response was angrily to reject it, but I was forced to acknowledge that I had adopted — often, perhaps, without conviction — many of my father's prejudices and postures simply because I had thought them easy or amusing. He had always maintained that a woman "couldn't train a bloody clematis," and the concept had lodged unchallenged in my brain.

". . . So do something, instead of being a drink-sodden pain in the rear end. You can only see motiveless malice, and you can't live with that, you can't defend yourself. You need to understand why he did what he did, right? *Tout comprendre, c'est tout pardonner,* all that. So. Find out."

"Oh yeah? And how am I to do that?"

"Oh, come on, Nick. Use your head. Go and talk to people. Do some research. There has to be a reason for unnatural behavior like that. You know the man is still going around justifying himself by saying you're a coward and all that, right? Why?"

"I dunno." I was sullen. "Nearest I've got is, he obviously wanted the horse stopped for some reason, knew he couldn't ask me to do it, and has to persuade himself and everyone else that he was in the right."

"Okay, so why does a trainer stop a Gold Cup contender?"

"Lots of money." I shrugged.

"Could be. Could be a stick rather than a carrot. Maybe someone put pressure on him."

"Maybe," I acknowledged, "but what the hell can I do? I've got what, four hundred in the bank? He's got hundreds of thousands, friends, contacts, the lot. I'd never get near . . . Anyhow, I don't know. Maybe he's right. Maybe I'm not good enough. Not for a yard like Waylands. I mean, trainers do sometimes have to jock off their riders. I'm not the first."

"Not like that we don't. Not without a word of warning or explanation. No, Nick, something stinks here, and I accept that okay, you have to find out the whys and wherefores. Fair enough. I would, too. So find out. You can do it. Why not?" Maria crushed her Marlboro packet and chucked it onto the table. "You're young. You've got some time on your hands. The season's as good as over. You're homeless and unemployed as of next week. Go for it. Damnation, Nick, you probably already know the answer, only it's been too close for you to see. Come on. Think. What do you know about the man? You may not be able to salvage your reputation with the world, but you can sure as hell salvage it with yourself. Stop licking your wounds, get up, and start delving. Start right now."

"Start where?"

"At the beginning," she hummed. She lit a cigarette and leaned back in her chair. She crossed her legs. "Tell me a story."

I was born in the Royal United Hospital in Bath in January 1964.

No, Maria insisted. Back. Further back.

Okay. My father missed the war. While his school heroes and prefects fought in North Africa or in Italy, he defended Lancaster Gate.

Further. Start at the beginning.

Okay, okay. (Damn it, can't a man have a drink for this sort of business?) The beginning. His father, my grandfather, was illegitimate, the by-blow of an Edwardian grandee and his courtesan. All very respectable, if demimondain. Great-granddad, a cotton millionaire, second-generation baronet, huge landowner, and personal friend of the king, would visit his second family from time to time. In later life they remembered the entourages, the carriages and teams, the tales of my chum His Majesty. Then this fairy-tale prince would return to his first family, leaving nothing in the Gloucestershire rectory to tell of his passing but cigar smoke, a few presents, a half-finished bottle of port, and a host of dreams and aspirations.

The old rogue paid for his bastards' schooling at Rugby. He found them good jobs in his various businesses.

Then he died.

"Poor sod." Maria looked up from a study of her clasped hands.

66

"Who? My great-grandfather?"

"No, no. He had the best of all worlds, didn't he? No, his son. Your granddad. Neither a gentleman nor not. You hear all these grand stories, see all the conspicuous trappings of wealth and know you're someone special, and then it's back to being nice respectable but not quite Master Storr in his country rectory. But you'd never shake off the idea that deep down you were better than everyone else. And then what? All the money and estates would go to the first crop, of course. You've got bugger all. Just a conviction that you're a changeling and the world owes you a living. Poor bastard. Literally."

"Yeah, well. He found himself a rich wife."

"He'd have had to. Were they happy?"

"Not very, I think. She was business. Her dad was just a shopkeeper. Brilliant shopkeeper, okay — Mr. Newby of Newby and Foster — but still trade. My granddad teased her constantly about her middle-class ways. Very smooth, very disdainful."

"Makes sense." Maria nodded. "I mean, he'd think — basis of his father's behavior as well — he's above petty things like the law, but there he is, dependent for money on a nice little law-abiding Anglican miss. So your dad will have grown up with that attitude for a model."

"Yes." I yawned. "I suppose so. Everything was 'common' when I was a child. There was next to no money left, of course, by the time my granddad had finished, but everything was 'common.' Never understood. I'd be sent off to stay at smart houses to contract measles or German measles or mumps or whatever, but if I wanted to go to the fair or the circus, no way. I might catch germs. From the common people, I suppose. Common germs rather than patrician germs."

"The same thing three generations on. Dear God. So. Okay. Your father. What clues can you find back there in the dim and dismal?"

"I don't know." I shook my head. I was weary. I laid my forehead in my hand. "Well, silly as it sounds, I know precious little about the man. I have only his own accounts of himself, really. You must understand. I saw him only rarely from the time he bolted, when I was two, till the time I came back at sixteen, seventeen, looking for a job. My grandmother seems to have wanted him to be a gentleman — expensive horses, a hussar regiment, all that. Making up for her husband's illegitimacy, I suppose. She didn't know about that until after they were married. Apparently it shocked her rigid.

"Anyhow, like I said, he missed out on the war. He always expected to follow his friends to death or glory. It must have been a bit of a shock when they called the whole thing off. And suddenly there were all these veterans, barely older than he, but men, returning to take the places in industry and the universities and so on.

"Only action he ever saw was when he was a recruit during the last few months of the war. One morning he's told, 'Storr, today you will defend Lancaster Gate.' Dad ups, says, 'Excuse us, sir, but it's Two Thousand Guineas day and I'm meant to be helping out.' Orders are gazetted: 'Lancaster Gate will not be defended today.' Not much to boast to the guys returning from El Alamein and D day and all that.

"Anyhow, so then as a regular cavalry officer he starts his gambling. Amateur rider, too. . . ."

"Yeah, I've read that. 'Amateur rider, former steeplechase jockey.' Check it out, shall we?"

"What?"

"Let's just check it out." She walked toward the parlor door, trailing a cavalier plume of smoke.

I took a quick swig from the vodka bottle and sank once more into my chair. I felt sober now, and wide awake.

"Right." Maria breezed back in. She laid a pile of leather-bound volumes on the table. "Nineteen forty-five through to nineteen fifty-two," she announced. "You start at the beginning, I'll start at the end. Let's see exactly what ex–steeplechase rider Storr actually did, shall we?"

I flicked through the first book slowly, the second faster, the third faster still. "But he's always said . . ." I frowned. "I mean, in all the published biogs . . ."

"It's the sort of lie no one bothers to check." Maria was dismissive. "Nothing here."

"But he always went on about how he and his generation were so bloody good and tough compared to us lot, told stories —"

"*Stories* is right, lad." Maria pulled out another cigarette. It waggled on her lower lip.

"But I've seen the photographs at Waylands!"

"Maybe a few point-to-points, that's all. We've all done that, and we don't call ourselves ex–steeplechase riders. So what's that tell you?"

It told me . . . a picture that I had had since early childhood now shivered into fragments. I had always thought that I had been following in my father's footsteps, that his approval or criticism was founded upon experience. "I don't know." I shook my head.

"It tells us he's got Walter Mitty tendencies, for one. It tells us the sort of person he would like to be. It tells us that, okay, he can fulfill some of his fantasies through you, even put some of your success down to heredity, claim the credit —"

"He did."

"But then you start doing really well, becoming the sort of person he always wanted to be. You're riding winners. He never has. You're getting the girls. He's not. Before, you were just a jump-jockey. He could say, 'like I used to be.' You become a good, a well-known, jump-jockey, and his fantasy crumbles to dust. So let's mark down jealousy as a motive."

"Yes." I nodded slowly. "For the nastiness at least, yes."

"I agree. Not the motive for the whole thing, but a factor in his unpleasantness. Right. Move on." She slammed a volume shut. "Just this next stage, the one the papers all talk about. London."

London In The Fifties: it had been in capitals for as long as I could remember. It possessed nigh-legendary status. Those were the days when young Captain Peregrine Storr, having resigned his commission, found his niche in life and made his friends.

There were countless stories, most of them centered upon money, the commodity that he affected most to despise. All the stories were about men. Women, when they were featured at all, were objects, not subjects, and each had a kennel-club name to go with her given one: Fiona, Hell of a Looker; Henrietta, Ghastly Lesbian Bitch; Margaret, Great Gas. Often, too, their pedigrees were alluded to *en passant,* so, "Diana, Strathburnham's oldest, Right Little Goer."

As for the men who did the doing in these anecdotes, they were all well educated but unfit or unwilling to take a job in this new, dour postwar world. They aspired, so it seemed, to create a new aristocracy, beyond or above the petty rules that governed rationed, bomb-bruised Britain.

Absurd though it seemed to those of us who grew up in later decades, these guys expressed their rebellion by aping their fathers' dress, manners, and opinions. Before the war, they believed, gentlemen had been gentlemen, not pinched, parsimonious, proper little businessmen and politicians.

The war had seen servants turned to soldiers, estates diminished, common people and foreigners clambering into positions of power while gentlemen were dispossessed. So these young gentlemen — most of whom, so far as I could see, had had precious little to lose before the war — dressed in suits and blazers and Lobbs shoes that they could not afford, they despised common people and foreigners, they drank whisky and soda in nightclubs, and, above all, they gambled.

Gambling was illegal, of course, but the laws were not for such as they. My father's nanny had left him a basement flat in Clapham, and somehow, by dint of loans from his aged mother, a small legacy from his father, and his winnings, he led the life of Riley.

Now that I sought to remember for Maria some of his many stories of that time, I found that not one of them remained. There was just a crazy expressionist collage called *London In The Fifties*. There were bow ties in there, and endless crystal tumblers, green baize tables and smoky bars at the dog track, villains named Al and Reg and smooth chums with smooth chops — Jimmy, Johnny, Quentin, Alexander, Chris, all purring away in their deep urbane drawls while the tables clicked and the dice burbled and the clocks ticked and whirred.

I think that my memory was so imprecise simply because

none of the stories of the time related to anything that I knew, cared about, or even understood. These people, so far as I could understand, had been motivated by snobbery, petty one-upmanship, and greed. I understood and remembered stories in which love and sex and sport were the principal causative strands. Greed was not alien to me, but greed that seemed to have no secondary ends beyond money was incomprehensible to me.

"So that's all I know, really," I finished weakly. "It's not much. I just know he was involved in that world."

"A world absolutely geared to his pretensions," Maria mused. She clattered behind me, picked up a decanter, and poured us both a shot of whisky. She leaned over my shoulder and thumped down the glass. "There. You've earned it. So then came Waylands?"

"Yes, and he sodded off and left me and my mum."

"So, let's start with her. Where's she now?"

"Somerset. Down near Taunton. Been in Scotland the last few months. Tried to get hold of her, but . . ."

"So call her. Tomorrow. Arrange to meet her. I bet she'll not approve of any of this, and I bet, too, that she knows a damn sight more than she's told you. Go and see her." She sighed and picked up her cigarettes. "It's got to be in there somewhere, Nick. It's got to be." She walked wearily to a spot behind me. She laid the hand with the cigarettes on my shoulder. "I'm sorry, Nick, to give you the boot. Second time this year and all. Come back next year, sure, if you've decided women and northerners are worthy of you. I like having you around, like to have you ride Pip. You're good for one another. But for God's sake, use this time. Sort yourself out. I ain't got time to pay Perry Storr's self-indulgence bills, nor, I'm sorry to say, his son's. Okay?" Her arm slid down my chest. Her mouth rested on my head. "Okay?" she asked into my hair.

"Yeah." I reached back and quickly squeezed her hand. I nodded. "Okay."

She kissed my crown. "Right. Come on. Bed. You should have been tucked up hours ago. Long day tomorrow."

*   *   *

71

The jackdaw stood on the rim of the stone manger. I made a face at it. It raised and lowered its feet in four quick stamps and croaked, "Fuck off, mate." I never got my O level in Jackdavian or anything, but some things need no translator.

I leaned against the door frame and watched. Rachel Davies wisped Pipistrelle's quarters until they glowed like mahogany bowls. "Don't understand why you put up with that creature," I said.

"Hmm?" Rachel looked up with those flashing blue eyes. She pushed blond hair from her brow with the side of her hand. She breathed heavily. She was getting her whole weight behind that wisp of hay. "Whosat, then? Oh, Jacky. Ah. He's rather sweet. No manners, but. He sits on Pip's back sometimes, you know. Pity it's not him up there this afternoon, hey? Probably do better than the lump who's meant to ride him."

"Sure. Ha ha. Seem well in himself? The horse, I mean."

"Great."

"Still no sign of the old problem?"

"Uh-uh." She reached up and tugged his ears. "Good as gold, aren't you, feller?"

"The old problem" was a puzzler.

The term *bolter* usually conjures pictures of breakneck (sometimes literally), terror-stricken huge rides cross-country. Pip's style of bolting was less dramatic. He bolted like Ben Gunn let loose in Harrods' cheese department. He wolfed his feed, he inhaled it, and then, with a deep grunt, he would sink into his straw like a clubman into his armchair after second helpings of spotted dick. There he would lie, moaning and sweating and glaring indignantly at the huge balloon that had mysteriously appeared beneath his ribs.

It was this habit above all that had kept Pipistrelle from a career on the flat and enabled Maria's husband to pick him up cheap at Doncaster. He was now owned in equal proportion by Maria, the local doctor, and the Rawcliffe Arms.

They had tried putting lumps of granite in the manger. To no avail. Still this beautiful beast had seemed fretful. Still he had weaved in his stall, swinging his head from side to side. Still he had given himself daily bouts of acute colic. At last Maria had resorted to the tedious expedient of feeding him six times a day. Thanks largely to old Hector's skill as a feeder, Pip had improved and found some sort of form.

Then last spring, Rachel had arrived on her Youth Training Scheme, bouncy, trim, all sparkling eyes and love and enthusiasm. Hector was having his once-monthly day off "under a doctor's care," with his back and a monster hangover. Rachel gave Pip a normal evening feed.

He ate it slowly, soberly, and with no ill effects.

There was rejoicing at the Grange that night, and the horse had eaten normally ever since. He had also been tranquil, happy, and ready to give of his best. Since no one knew, however, what had cured him — for her part, Maria thought that Rachel's presence was chiefly responsible — he was still closely watched.

I eyed him up and down now, this animal that Maria believed capable of taking on the likes of Ibn Saud. In the flat-race way of reckoning such things, Pip was actually better bred than Waylands's champion. His dam, Batravia, had won over ten and a half furlongs in France and was half-sister to stakes winners, including Fledermaus (second in the Poule d'Essai des Pouliches). His sire was a Grade III–winning son of Patch.

He looked class, too. Where Ibn Saud was big and rangy, Pip was compact as a pony. He threw to his sire's Hyperion line. You could have drawn a nigh perfect square from withers to quarters to hock to knee. He was a strangely dappled deep brown, like a biscuit cake. I liked the little fellow. He was an equine Cagney — agile, tough, ballsy, and really rather sweet under all that muscle and masculine swagger.

"You having a bet on him today, then?" I asked Rachel.

"You bet." She plucked hair from the dandy brush as she walked past me. "Or rather, I do. Buck up." I slouched out after her, appraising as if from habit that trim, tight, boyish little body in cowboy shirt and jeans. She shut the stable door. "Yup. Week's wages on you, Nick, so if you get left or half-lengthed, I'll be wanting sixty-four pounds of flesh, okay? You can spare it." She shot the bolts on the door to the next stall.

"I'll do my best." I sidestepped a guinea fowl and followed her in.

"Hello, boy," she cooed. "Hello, my darling, darling boy!" She stood on tiptoe, her arms about the aged Fleet's neck. She kissed his near eye. "Yes, it's odious Mr. Storr, but please don't savage him."

"Couldn't savage a cloverleaf, that old nag." I grinned. "God, poor old bugger."

"Just you wait." She tied the horse's head to the ring and bustled out for the pitchfork. "I hope I'll still be around when you're a clapped-out old bugger with prostate trouble and runny eyes and whatnot. And I'll come round the geriatric home and I'll say, 'Don't know why you bother to keep the old thing alive, myself. Feed him to the dogs, I would.' See how you feel about it. Fleet's a friend of mine, that's all. Aren't you, boy?"

The horse grunted and rubbed his eye on her chest.

"You so-called professionals" — she tossed the clean straw — "think being ruthless makes you a professional, don't you? Rest of us, bit of normal soppiness, we're automatically amateurs, right?"

"No, not necessarily," I objected. "I mean, sure, amateurs have a tendency to be silly about their animals, but it doesn't mean . . . I mean, okay, I've seen pros, old pros, crying their eyes out over animals with broken necks and so on. And trainers — an animal serves you well, you return the favor, see he gets a good home when he retires, that sort of thing. But you get a wrong'un, doesn't pay his way, it's off to the sausage factory. It's not callous. It's just that horses cost money, and money's food for children, money's more horses, money's fun and happiness and security. I mean, you can't just throw it away on the undeserving. Anyhow, you can't tell me this old crock actually enjoys life."

"'Course he does!" She was astounded. "Just because he's not a Derby winner doesn't mean he doesn't enjoy a roll in the paddock, a linseed mash, or whatever. Or his people. Of course he enjoys life, don't you, feller? Don't listen to the mean old sod."

"You're crazy," I said.

"No, I'm not." She handed me a muck bucket. "Here. Make yourself useful. Know something?" She looked up at me with those ridiculous wide eyes. Obvious. Infantile. She listened to pop records, for Christ's sake. She watched *Dallas*. She liked *The Mill on the Floss*.

"What?" I swallowed. "What?"

She touched the tip of my nose with her forefinger. "I don't believe a single word of all this 'I'm such a tough professional' macho stuff. Babe in arms, you."

And after this incredible impertinence, she turned back to her horse, humming some dippy ditty.

"'Lo, Nick, mate. 'Ow're ye doin', then?" Len Egan swaggered into the Market Rasen changing room after the second. He wore Costas Theodolou's pale-blue and white colors — colors I had worn once. Worse, he had just worn them to victory.

"Oh, fine, thanks, Len." I slipped off my camel-hair. I had already changed into Maria's red and green. "Just fine." I sighed.

"'Ear as you've got yourself a nice little retainer, that right? That Maria, eh? Tasty. Wouldn't mind doing a bit of hard riding for 'er an' all."

He looked around for agreement or applause. None came. The rest of the lads — northerners, for the most part — just sat on the benches in companionable silence or bustled about their business. Dudley Knox, the big blond teddy bear who had taken more crashing falls than any three of the rest of us put together, sat gape-legged beneath Len. He pursed his lips and examined the stitching at the thong of his whip. Beside me, Tommy Phelan, who looked for all the world like a timorous middle-aged bank clerk, yawned noisily.

Len didn't give a damn. He pulled the sweater up over his head. Scarred white ribs emerged, then nipples — large flat brown disks surrounded by four or five wiry curls apiece — then a neck stretched like a chicken's in the butcher's window, then that gray, gaunt, grinning face. "By the by, gather your dad 'ad a brief riding engagement there an' all, eh? Smart girl. Trade in the old model for the new, eh?"

All I could manage by way of witty retort was "Balls." I wanted to belt the little shit, but he hadn't exceeded the limits of barely acceptable changing-room conduct, and if I hit him

I'd only draw attention to his slander and make myself look a resentful jerk into the bargain.

"Gawd, mate, that cottage of yours was a dump." Len pulled down his breeches. Flaccid off-white underwear. Scrawny white legs, snarled with black hair.

"Yeah?" I smiled faintly. I looked up at the overhead light, down at my boots. I shrugged.

"Yeah, I says to your old man, 'That kid of yourn —'"

His words stopped with a noise like a giant hiccup. There were two padded thumps. I looked up. Dudley was standing now. Still he examined his whip. Lenny sat on the floor, his clean breeches around his ankles. He clutched his left shin.

"Oh, sorry, Lenny." Dudley's voice thudded like a snare drum. "Here, look, everyone, our southern friend Mr. Egan's fallen over. Anyone want to kick 'im, seeing as 'e's down? That's what they do down where 'e comes from, isn't that right, Lenny?"

There was a deep rumble of laughter. "Nah," Tommy Phelan growled. "Like to keep my boots clean, me."

No one looked at me. I was grateful for that. I saw like an impressionist just then. There were teasels where there should have been lights.

Sing hey for the life of the steeplechase jockey, that glamorous, amorous, colorful life.

At the very peak of the profession, you drive forty thousand miles a year through snow and rain and fog and ice in order to ride through snow and rain and fog and ice, just occasionally breaking the odd bone or dislocating the odd joint for variety's sake. And when you get home, you can reward yourself with a nice hot — well — baked potato, perhaps, or cup of tea, something lavish like that.

All in all, days like this were, for us, as rare as condoms in a nunnery. Today we got to know how those flat-racing boys felt. The sunlight was heavy on our shoulders. The sky was blue. The birds twittered like rain.

We were walking and trotting up to the start of a two-and-a-half-miler, £5,400 added to stakes. I had been in bigger contests, but none more important. On this little animal's performance today rode not just Rachel's sixty-four quid but four hundred of Maria's, a hundred of mine — not that jockeys bet, of course — and the hopes of High Rigg Grange, not to mention those of the Rawcliffe Arms regulars. Should we lose here, we'd be living on muesli made of horse feed and last year's apples for the rest of the summer. Should we lose because Pip proved inadequate, the cost would be still higher. We would have to resign ourselves to enduring mediocrity. We would never be able to afford another live prospect like this one. He might be mad, but he was hot.

From outside, I suppose, we must have looked like some complex automaton. We sat rigidly upright. We moved forward, ever faster. The starter's hand reached. We rocked forward as one and were away, a homogeneous mass of horses and men flowing round the track as though borne by a current.

From inside, it was a whole lot different. There were the sounds, to start off with — the cries of "No, sir!" "Please, sir!" "Fuck it, come *back,* will you?," the soothing *whoa*s and *easy*s, the complaints of the saddles, the loose-change clinking of harness, the rub-a-dub of hooves on the hard ground. Then the gates thud up and your horse is striking out as though kicking a ball and you veer toward the rails.

And someone else swerves in ahead of you and you take a pull, and your boy's ears are bobbing up and down because he's straining to take control. This, no less than war for the soldier, is what all those months of training have been about. Nothing should curb him now that the time has come.

There are the heels ahead of you to think of, the rails hard at your right, the horse close at hand at your left (and the jockey, Dudley, was pom-pomming a Mozart horn concerto, for God's sake), and the fence up ahead.

And the colors are splitting and re-forming and blurring all the time — the pale gray shifts up on the left beneath scarlet and silver, the bay heels ahead kick up a spray of black tail and a spurt of divots beneath yellow and blue, the green of the turf rushes back beneath you, spattered and scarred with the pink of clay. There is the white slash of the wings, the brown of the looming birch fence.

And you're over.

No problems there. My lad saw it clearly, got back on his hocks, and cleared it with a foot or more to spare. There are advantages to being small, such as having to make that much more effort.

We were comfortably tucked in on the rails in fourth or fifth place as we took the plain fence on the bend beyond the stands and headed out into the country. Pip was enjoying himself. Dudley's gray, Snow Bunting, matched us stride for stride. Beyond them, and three quarters of a length up on us, Len crouched low on Asteroid, a promising brown mare. A Way-lands mare. Ahead of us, Tommy Phelan's legs and bum were steady as a keyhole above a bay back so pale as almost to be dun. The horse was a veteran northern campaigner called Humoresque.

My mind, as ever, was doing its own thing as I took in a reef to give Pip a clear view of the open ditch. "Jean Negulesco, nineteen forty-seven," I murmured. I exerted slow, steady pressure to give us some space. "John Garfield . . ." and I shoved forward two strides off. Pip put his head down and charged at the fence like a bull. I gave him a quick tap on takeoff. "Joan Crawford . . . gwarn!"

We ripped through the top of the fence. Down to our right, Snow Bunting, who had thought to fly, crash-landed with a great clattering and plowed a deep, straight furrow fit for Campus Martius market-gardening. Dudley was still sitting bolt upright as his mount slid. He had time to utter a despairing bellow of "Bugger-ation!" before tumbling forward and disappearing in the pell-mell maelstrom of flesh and wool and bone.

The gods go steeplechasing from time to time. We call it a thunderstorm.

Pipistrelle saw open space ahead. He bounded like a puppy.

"Screenwriter Clifford Odets, for Christ's sake," I muttered as I sat into him again. "Bloody awful film." I was pushed back in the saddle as Pip landed. I had to scramble to regain the reins.

"I mean, Odets did *The General Died at Dawn*, nineteen thirty-six. . . ."

My horses get to learn a lot about movies. They never complain, which makes a pleasant change. Some of them even respond quite well.

About this movie thing: it just sort of happened to me. I had a movie-buff Latin teacher at school. I used to try to catch him out. And one day I was so convinced that Ginger Rogers had played the lead in *Ball of Fire* that I took a fifty-pound bet with a schoolmate. I lost, of course. It was Stanwyck. I was mortified until Mr. Johnson said, "Funny, that. Matter of fact, the part was written for Rogers." Then I saw *Pretty Poison* one week, and was entranced, and *Double Indemnity* the next, and was awed. I wanted to know what else the directors had done. The answers, to my astonishment, were respectively "nothing" and "just about everything." I got hooked on the manifold inter-relations of movie history, and my brain just seemed to absorb the flood of data like a sponge. I know it's annoying. I just can't help it.

We were in second as we took the turn from the back straight. Tommy still set the pace. Len was upsides, on our outside. Pip was still full of running. He felt good — even, perhaps, very good. Maybe Maria's dreams of glory with this one were not so far-fetched after all. Pip was that most desirable yet most dangerous of animals, a natural. His talents needed direction and discipline. It would be so darned easy, however, to smother by training this natural joy in jumping, this urgent, eager need to win.

We leaned into the bend. Suddenly the world lurched. Something hit us, savage as an air pocket.

I gasped "Shit!" Pip made a sound like a fighter hit deep and hard in the gut. He swerved into the rails. For a second I hung out at an absurd angle, clawing for handholds in the air. Then Pip bounced back beneath me. I gulped down my terror. A cackle from Len Egan told me that the vicious barge had been no accident.

At this sort of speed, such antics were no prank. In the old days the wooden rails would have broken beneath our weight, and the horse — or even the rider — might have been staked on the splintered shards. Even without that danger, though, a loss of footing on such a bend could have proved lethal. "What the fuck are you doing?" I shrieked.

I knew now that I was in danger.

Out there on the racecourse, there is precious little law and next to no law enforcement. The stewards can see little more than the movements of the automaton and the occasional tactless move that interfered with its smooth, preordained operation.

When an old pro like Len moves in on you out in the country, the stewards have about as much power over your fate as the police on a Soho street at four in the morning.

Len did not even look my way. His lips were pulled back in a ghastly rictus. "Fucking whining baby," he said as though clearing his throat. "Say up front I pulled that fucking dago horse, huh? See how you like playing games with the real professionals. Bit rough for us, is it?"

And on that "is it?" he swung across again, just three strides off the open ditch. He hit us hard, then kicked on. Pipistrelle reeled and staggered sideways.

The ditch shrieked beneath us. We were slithering rather than galloping toward it.

I did the only thing possible. I told Pip that he was to blame. I sat down, gave him a hard smack, and howled, "Go on!"

The little horse climbed that fence. Somehow he contrived to tense those sinews like springs. Somehow he managed to fling his bulk upward. Somehow he managed to corkscrew, all volition gone, through the top of the fence. I scaled his neck. It was like a slide show. One moment everything was blue. The next, with a fierce jolt that rattled my brain, the slide had changed and I was looking almost vertically down at green turf pocked by hooves. I leaned way back and clutched the saddle-tree so as not to yank Pip in the mouth. He landed, stumbled, pecked — literally pecked, just like a chicken — and staggered five or six sprawling yards.

Then he raised his head, and suddenly he had started all over again. He was racing hard and fast, and to hell with this cumbersome creature on his back.

If horses could shout, Pipistrelle would have been hollering, "Come back here and say that, cull!"

My heart beat faster than the hooves about me. That moment of terror had been transmuted into simple blind fury. I was angry that Len was riding my horse and living in my house. I was angry that he had endangered a mare that I had known and cared for. I was angry that he had endangered Pip and me and the future of High Rigg Grange in the cause of some petty vindictiveness.

Did I infect the horse with my fury, or did the horse infect me? I only know that, in that moment, Pipistrelle discovered that he had ancestors who had served at Waterloo, and I that there were genes in me that far predated the Global Village and Universal Brotherhood. Give me a donkey's jawbone and a sufficient stock of Philistines just then, and I'd have given David a run for his money as champion smiter and circumciser.

Not, of course, that I had a chance against Len. Old pros are mightier smiters than young aspirants.

Tell that to Jack the giant-slayer, said Pip.

We were just one length behind him as we took the next.

I had to collect Pip. He had his ears back. He wanted to show his assailant who was boss.

We moved upsides. "Huh," Len spoke out of the corner of his mouth. "Thought you were down." He was pushing the poor mare out now. His chin was thrust forward.

"You're a pathetic little abortion of a man, Egan," I panted. "A dirty, jumped-up little crook."

Hardly eloquent stuff, perhaps, but the best I could manage at the time. My only aim was to annoy him, and I fancy that my sneering tone succeeded. Such color as he could muster rose in his cheeks. We were headed for the last plain fence before the home turn. We were in full view of the crowd. He could not attack me here, so he made a noise like a puking lion and clicked on.

I shouldn't have done it. I liked that mare.

Pip wasn't flat-bred for nothing. I kicked. I clicked. He put on a spurt. We swept past Len in three strides and were just half a length up on him when we took off.

Len took off, too.

It's the oldest trick in the book. Had he not been agitated, Len would have seen it a mile off.

As it was, I called, "Yeah!" and we flew.

Asteroid heard, saw, and tried to fly, too.

Half a length off.

She found a fence in the way.

She hit it, I assume, amidships and hard. Certainly as Pip's forefeet cleaved the turf, I heard a loud crash from behind us, a shrill "Faaaah" from Len, and then a heavy thump and a bit of rattling.

I wish I'd never had to do it.

We could have won that race by thirty lengths. Instead we sneaked in to pip Humoresque by half a length in the last strides. I was riding for a betting stable now. When at last Pipistrelle came out in high society, we intended to catch the crown prince and dance all night.

Daybreak was no more than a rumor when I awoke on my last morning at High Rigg. A blackbird hesitantly hypothesized its coming. A faint silver flush at the horizon gave the idea some substance. The wind scampered about the house, trying all the doors and windows, then suddenly dropped back and whined a bit before renewing its onslaught.

I awoke instantly and, I thought, totally. I knew that I was going somewhere today, though I could not remember where or why. Then it came to me. I was going on a quest for my father, a quest for the truth of my past. Suddenly the prospect terrified me. Perhaps, after all, the dead should remain buried.

If, as Maria supposed, the explanation lay somewhere in the past, somewhere back in those mysterious years that had seen my father's transition from soldier to gambler to man of substance, my mother above all others should be able to enlighten me.

I had said all along that knowledge, whatever that knowledge might be, would satisfy me, that if once I could understand the malicious ghost that haunted me, it could be laid to rest. Only now did I consider with a shudder that other ghosts, too, might be awakened by my digging. I would have to live with the inheritance of whatever I discovered about my father.

Every Adam, I suppose, hesitates before taking the apple. As often as not, he prefers to use his will and his wiles to persuade Eve to press it on him. I had cast Maria in that role.

I should have listened to the warning murmurings in my head that morning. I would have saved two human lives.

My mother had croaked "Darling!" and then, "Hello? Hello? Oh, there you are. Where are you?"

I had told her and she had said, as though buying time, that I must go and see a whole host of dear friends who happened to have estates in Yorkshire. Then, "Why didn't you call sooner, darling?"

"Yeah. Sorry. Not an easy time. I rang when, well, when the mess happened, and you were off in Mull or wherever, and then things just got — I don't know — a bit sort of chaotic."

"Well, I wasn't going to stick my nose in where it wasn't wanted. Of course I saw that you had a few rides in the north, but I know how unpopular I become whenever I try to help."

"That's not fair. I just . . . I prefer to lick my wounds on my own."

"I know, I know, darling. Don't be so defensive. Poor you. What that man can have been thinking of. . . . Typical shit's trick, the whole thing, and shouting it from the rooftops. God, darling, I am so sorry."

"Well." I had shrugged and spoken a bromide: "There you go."

And then there had been an interruption while the dogs barked at the postman and her husband, Guy, my stepfather, brought her a portable electric fan, which she said was a god-send with these infernal hot flashes. And she had given the electric fan's provenance ("that little shop, what's it called, next to Lloyd's Bank in Crewkerne") and explained about the batteries' running out. And finally she had said, "So, darling, why don't you come and stay? It would be good to see you."

It would have been good to accept, too, to have gone down

there, stayed a while, settled in, been the son of the house, fed, indulged, protected, and introduced to nice girls. But not yet. There were things to be done first.

"Just for now, can we meet up somewhere, have a chat? I want — I just want to sort out a few of the whys and where-fores, you know? Pick your brain."

"Bit like picking the carcass after the vultures have gone, but of course, darling, where?"

"Are you going up to London sometime soon?"

"Not if I can help it. I'll be at Ascot, of course. Tuesday and Thursday. Any good?"

It was good.

"Perfect," I had told her. "Just perfect."

Now I arose and packed my sponge bag and my jeans and loaded up the jeep with my few worldly goods. And Maria came out in lime silk to help, and then to lay her hat on top of my suitcases, and Rachel arrived with cups of tea to admire our finery and quickly to tell me, "See you around, Nick," before returning to the yard.

I was itching and twitching until we set off. Then I was itchy, angry. Up here I had a bed, a home, and relative anonymity. Down there I had nothing but a name.

Maria, however, was fizzing. "Do you know? All these years, I've never once done this? Ridiculous, isn't it? I mean, York, sure, but basically racing for me means sheepskins and quilted jackets and thick boots, not the full vestments. God, I feel like a June bride togged up like this. You're sure no one's going to say I shouldn't be there? Big joke that would be. All the way to bloody Royal Ascot and I get turfed out at the gate. Great."

"Nah," I reassured her. She would be entering on a pass that I had obtained for Jasmine. "Precious few people there'll know who you're meant to be. It'll be okay."

"So." She rocked forward as we reached the crossroads. But there was no traffic. There was nothing to be seen on any side of us, just twisted clasping junipers and the occasional mammoth-dropping of granite in the heather. "So, prepare me. What do I expect?"

"You've seen it on television, haven't you?"

"Not Ascot. Your mum. What's her story?"

"Oh." I sighed. "Anglo-Irish and a bit of Almanach zu Gotha. A thousand quarterings, a few red hands, and bugger all cash. I mean, okay. By today's standards, her family wasn't badly off. Her dad had a few acres and a burned-down mansion in Waterford, her mother had a flat in London, a little manor in Devon, that sort of thing; but Mum was the youngest girl. She rode well, hunted, looked the part, was elegant and innocent. She was only nineteen when she married Dad. He was thirty or more. Lamb to the slaughter, I'd say. He was experienced and charming; she was young and looking for something a bit more exciting than stuttering old Etonians. Dad is bloody funny, and although I'd bet she'd never admit it — no, she'd not even have been aware of such a factor — sexy. Bedroom eyes, lots of silly jokes, all the obnoxiousness and lechery barely concealed beneath a naughty-little-boy manner."

"I know the type," Maria said out of the corner of her mouth. "So, the perfect girl to show off in his gambling clubs. And?"

"I don't know. We lived in a cottage with a small yard down near Devizes and — I don't know. They were married in 'fifty-nine. A lot of small trainers were going to the wall. My father spent precious little time down there — he was still playing the tables up in London — but we survived. Don't know how.

"And then in, I don't know, 'sixty-five or so, when I was nearly two, apparently Dad comes back one evening and says, not to worry, we've inherited Waylands. Some old dear thinks he's the bee's knees. She has no heirs, bequeaths him the lot. Whoopee. Everything looks great. I mean, Waylands, one of the, what, three, four most famous National Hunt stables in the land? Next thing, just as we're about to move in, Dad runs off with Deirdre."

"So that's got to be one of the first questions." Maria tapped a cigarette on the dashboard. "How in hell did a gambler get his hands on a great yard?"

I considered the problem seriously before realizing that I already knew the answer. "Oh, that's easy. He met the old girl at the club in Mount Street. She was a compulsive gambler, apparently. Losing thousands. He took her in hand. He saved the last few thousand or whatever of her capital by breaking her of the habit. No heirs, time came, she thought, This guy's saved the estate for me. He's into horses. Who else deserves it? So she left it to him. She was genuinely fond of him, I believe."

"You believe?" I swear I heard those thick black eyebrows rise.

"Well, all the evidence . . ."

"Cite."

"Cite. My father, obviously, for one. Chris Wildman. Richard Heron. Basically, he'd saved the estate so he deserved to get it. That was the idea."

"Hold up, Nick." Her voice was sharp. "You're telling me Chris Wildman and Richard Heron were happy that your father should stop this old dear — what was her name?"

"Gascoigne. Maud Gascoigne."

"You're telling me they were grateful to him for stopping the good Mrs. Gascoigne from losing her all in their casinos? Nice guys. Part-time Salvation Army volunteers, I suppose?"

"No." I was irritated. "Of course not. But these guys weren't out-and-out villains, either. Perhaps it was, you know, a temporary sentimental aberration on Dad's part. He was a free agent. Why shouldn't he help her? You've got some sort of obsession here, Maria. Just 'cause the guy, according to you, made some sort of pass at you, you've got it into your head that he's some sort of monster. What? Feminist stuff, is it? I mean, why shouldn't the guy try his luck if he sees you smile nicely and misunderstands? He didn't rape you, did he? I mean, sure, I'm the last person to claim he's perfect, but that's no bloody reason to make him out to be — I don't know. He's a nice guy, for God's sake. Oh, hell." I shook my head. "I'm not sure I can see the point in all this."

"Okay, Nick," Maria sang. "You just go on believing that. Fine by me. Let the man destroy you. Remote control. He launched you. Now, from a million miles away, he presses a button, activates a system that he planted way back when: self-destruct. Abort mission. Great."

I sulked. It was ten minutes before I spoke again. The morning had turned as gaudy as cheap china. "No, so anyhow, in those days I didn't see much of him. Alternate Christmases I'd go to Waylands, and every year I'd get dragged up to Sutherland with him. He was a fanatical stalker. Still is. I didn't take to it. I liked birds, hawking, fishing, but those weren't men's sports. Stalking was what men did. Otherwise there were just occasional visits on high days and holidays or when he happened to be down in our part of the world."

"Easy for those buggers, isn't it?" Maria leaned forward to pick up a cellophane-wrapped lozenge of barley sugar from the dashboard. "Men can always buy affection. Women have to sell."

"S'pose. Anyhow, yes. There were always lots of presents, and endless cream cakes and records and Hermès ties. And outings to London. Lunch at the Berkeley, tea at Fortnum's, you know? He always made things seem glamorous and fun. Lots of jokes, silly songs, easy affection, oh, and the occasional tantrums. He'd . . . one example I remember. He'd bought some sirloin somewhere, gone off for the afternoon. Meanwhile the washing machine floods the kitchen, so Deirdre only has time to grill some fish fingers or something. So my father comes in. Where's his sirloin? Deirdre explains, but he goes on, rubs his hands with glee. 'Oh, good-oh, we're going to have sirloin. Butcher says it's a wonderful bit of meat. Hung for three weeks. Said to make sure it was eaten today. I've been looking forward to it all day. Can't wait. Nothing like a lovely bit of beef.' And he gets the horseradish out, puts it on the table, opens a bottle of red, sits down still blustering about how he's longing for this bit of cow.

"So Deirdre sighs and serves up fish fingers and frozen peas and says, 'Don't be silly, darling. I've told you, we've been worked off our feet all afternoon cleaning up the flood.'

"And all this time he's getting noisier and his color's rising. He did not want crap like this. He wanted beef. Beef that made England great. Beef without which no man could live. And *this,* this red stuff was beef, and *these,* these yellow sticks, were not. And he flung the plate to the floor. And as for floods, he liked floods. Always had done. His father had always liked floods. A house wasn't a house without six inches of water on the floor and a large joint of beef on the table, that's what he always said. So he turns on all the taps, fills the washing-up bowl, and chucks it all over the kitchen floor. 'Ah, that's better. Now all we need is beef,' he says, and dear little Deirdre's patience snaps and the shouting match gets obscene and my father storms out and vanishes to the pub with a roar and a screech of brakes."

"Spoiled brat," said Maria. "I'd have slapped his silly face."

"Yeah, but that's the thing. Spoiled brat. He was childlike, absurd, so he always got away with it because his antics seemed funny in retrospect, and he'd come back with a meek little grin and a present and he'd always be forgiven. Naughty-little-boy stuff."

"He'd not have bloody got away with it with me. How come your mother stayed with this would-be eccentric maniac as long as she did? Bidding for sainthood, or what?"

"No. You can ask her, but I think she was just old-fashioned — and she loved him. I know you find it difficult to believe, at this distance, and from your perspective, but he really was lovable. Most of the time. She'll probably tell you otherwise now, though. She was bitter, you know, after he absconded with Deirdre."

"One is," Maria pronounced dryly. "Undeserved rejection hurts like hell. You may have noticed." She blew twin columns of smoke that exploded on the windscreen. She pushed a tape into the machine.

There was never any question as to custody. Dad had left us, my mother and me, for this woman, apparently a former dealer at Bentham's, even as the builders worked to prepare Waylands for our coming. It was as if, now that he owned a new house, a gentleman's house, he had no further need of us. I would live with my mother as a matter of course.

I was confused, I think, particularly by the intensity of my mother's emotions. Mothers were not meant to cry, nor seek shelter from their anguish in their growing sons' arms. Other-wise, I believed (and continued to believe for several more years), the breakup had little effect on me. I returned to Thunderstone Cottage during the school holidays but eagerly accepted invitations to stay with school friends. In term-time my mother lived alone, working all the hours that God gave. She sculpted animal figures in terra-cotta and wood.

Guy Cullinan became an ever more regular visitor. Guy had proposed to my mother many years before; now, tentatively and gently, he paid court to her once more. Guy was a nice man with a nice Somerset rectory. He was unambitious, conservative, and kind. He had a military pension and a small private income.

My mother resisted his suit for a long time because she believed the marriage vows to be singular and absolute. In the end, however, a priest friend persuaded her that God would not wish her to be enslaved for life to a renegade husband. Eight years after Dad's desertion, she consulted me, received my gracious if precocious blessing, and became Mrs. Cullinan.

Sound and *trustworthy* may not have been my favorite epithets, but I am sure that after all those years with Dad, my mother thrilled to such words. As for me, Guy generously and courteously accepted me as a member of his household, but by the time I was fifteen, I was already spending more and more of my holidays at Waylands.

It started with long weekends. I would ride out. My father would give dinner parties on the Saturday evenings, and I would be presented to famous jockeys and trainers, the occasional millionaire owner, and the occasional trainer's or owner's beautiful daughter, with whom I would fall instantly, blushingly in love.

My father sang my praises embarrassingly loudly at these gatherings: "Got a scholarship, you know. Damn near won the national public-schools debating thing. Bloody good draftsman, too. Quite incredible. Lord knows where he gets it from." He would press drink on me, and me on the unfortunate girls, with advice that revolted my romantic sensibilities. "For Christ's sake, old boy, stop mooning about, and get your hand on it."

But aside from such violations of my dreams, he was splendid. Oh, I could see the comical nature of his pretensions. At times I cringed as he held forth about vintages that he had drunk, dukes whom he had met, and so on. But he was generous and sporting and fun, and he gave me a flattering sense of companionship and fellowship in gender. This was refreshing after the claustrophobia of my mother's home, where, despite the fact that I was an adolescent, I was treated only as a child ("I see the lawn still hasn't been mowed").

"He's buying you, that's all," my mother would say. But she saw only the half of it. "Just like he always did. When you were small, you remember? You can't imagine how hurtful it was. I'd save a bob or two for a trip to the pantomime, or the ice rink, but it would always be, 'It's so much more fun with Daddy.'" Thanks a lot. Of course it was more fun with Daddy. He'd buy expensive lunches, the royal box at the theater, all that.

But adolescence was driving me. I had specific ambitions. I wanted to fuck twenty-three thousand women with impeccable bone structure, perfect skin, and the morals of frogs. In the brief interintercourse intervals, I wanted to drink every fine drink and ride every fast horse. That was what young gentlemen did. My father had even told me of an old cavalry wager that perfectly matched my aspirations. The challenge, he related, was to drink three bottles of champagne, fuck three women, and ride nine miles cross-country in three hours. I thought that eminently admirable. Let others put shots or engage in synchronized swimming. I knew with the assurance of the prodigy that this triathlon was my sort of sport.

At Guy Cullinan's, however, girls had thick ankles and suffered from a curious psychological quirk whereby the mention of sex instantly prompted thoughts of Mummy. Drink consisted in Tio Pepe or Bulgarian Cabernet squeezed from the bottle, and the only two horses were sturdy hunters more noted for standing up than for running.

No contest.

My mother wanted me to stay on at school and try for Oxbridge. I wanted to leave. That dispute served as my pretext. One week after my seventeenth birthday, I moved into Waylands. I found it only convenient to call it home. At nineteen I did the Jackeroo bit in Australia. At twenty, at Dad's insistence, I enrolled in an accountancy course. I had my first winners as an amateur two years later. It all seemed to be mapped out. I turned professional and became second stable jockey to Way-lands at twenty-four. Then success and succession to Stan Doyle. So easy. And now, just as easily, it was all gone.

The people were bright in their hats and their fluttering silks. Golds, pinks, blues and yellows, spots, stripes, flowers, berries and birds, all gleamed the brighter for the black and gray morn-ing coats against which they were set. But the whole gaudy flag of the Royal Enclosure seemed in the end just a small dull patch on the vast expanse of brilliant green.

The Royal Procession had flowed straight as mercury down the straight and been absorbed in the molten crown. The crowd had turned its thoughts from history and loyalty to the serious business of the day, swimming against the tide of barathea and silk in hope of a drink, looking for odds against any horse known to be able to run, and looking one's best when the TV cameras swung one's way.

The first race was under way when I spotted my mother and Guy. They stood near the top of the stands. Guy wore a black silk topper and a Guards' Club tie. Otherwise I could see noth-ing of him but a shiny pink nose bulging out between the eye-pieces of his binoculars. My mother wore a black wide-brimmed hat dressed with the same black-spotted sapphire silk as her bod-ice. Her husband's regimental crest, rendered in diamonds, glit-tered on her left shoulder.

"Sure is one elegant lady," said Maria. She pulled out her binoculars and turned to watch the race.

I was a little surprised to acknowledge that she was right. My mother's hair was now eels of midnight and her skin a neurotic's doodle-pad of little wrinkles, but her features were large and strong, her wrists and ankles were fine, and her ability to wear clothes (which had earned her a lot of free dresses from couture houses in the hard days) was as impressive as ever.

"Nicky." A rumble at my shoulder. "Good to see you. How are things? Where have you been hiding?"

I did not turn. "Up on the wild and windswept moors" — I nodded toward Maria, standing six feet away — "giving her a hand."

"All going well, then?"

"Not exactly, Chris," I mumbled through a sigh. "Eight animals in North Yorkshire is hardly Waylands." I turned to face him. "And I still don't know why all this has happened. That's why I'm here."

"Uh-oh." Chris was waggish. "Now I hope that doesn't mean you're here to make trouble, Nick. Cheltenham is understandable, but I reckon Cheltenham and Ascot in one year will render you definitely persona non grata. You've got to learn some diplomacy, old chap. Never get results charging around like a demented billy goat, you know."

"Has he said anything to you?"

"Whozat? Oh, Perry. No, not really. You know what he's like. Gets a bee in his bonnet, you'll never shake him till he calms down. No, I think he just suddenly . . . I mean, look at his position, Nicky. Suppose he really does think you're not good enough yet. I mean, he's got to do the right thing by his owners, right? But the trouble is, he doesn't know how to tell you, doesn't want to hurt you. Net result, of course, is that it all comes out suddenly like that, and it hurts you ten times as much. But that's Perry for you. Lovely chap, but a terrible moral coward. You know that."

It all sounded horribly persuasive. Dad *was* a moral coward. He would do anything, no matter how hurtful, if it caused pleasure and won him a grateful smile, and he would hide anything, no matter how sure it was to come out, in order to avoid resentment or pain — or rather, the perceptible manifestations of resentment and pain. But somehow I remained obscurely convinced that though this might explain the manner of my rejection, it did not explain the deed itself.

"No, there'll be no more trouble." I sighed. "Don't you worry, Chris. No more scenes. It's just that I know there's got to be a good reason, and we've decided to find out what it is. Do some digging, you know?"

"We?"

92

"Well, me. Maria's been helping, that's all."

"Hm. Well, okay, but just one thing. Don't let's have some sort of bloody vendetta, okay, old chap? Things are messy enough without that."

"No vendettas, Chris," I assured him. "Matter of fact —" I stopped because the horses were in the straight and for a minute or two it was like trying to be heard above Atlantic surf. The sound subsided. Like a parade dismissed, the straining, alert figures of the watchers slouched and turned away.

Maria, too, turned toward us. I introduced her. Chris touched his hat brim. He said, "Ah, of course. Maria Wyatt in the old-fashioned way of things, right? Poor old Mike. That's right, and you used to work for Perry, didn't you?"

"For my sins." Maria grimaced.

"No, listen, Chris," I said. "Matter of fact, you could probably help us on this one. Wanted to ask you about those days back in London, how Dad got hold of Waylands, all that. Mind if I come to see you sometime?"

"Nick, you're always welcome, you know that. But you must be feeling the pinch a bit, hmmm?"

"A bit." I nodded.

"Yes, well. Look, I've been wanting a word with you. Got a job for you, if you want it. Tell you what. Why don't you come and have lunch, hmm? Tomorrow, why not? Chance to discuss it." He had pulled out his wallet and was picking through its stuffing. "Here, old chap. See you over." He doubled over a sheaf of twenties and stuffed them into my breast pocket. "Okay?"

"Sure. Fine. Yes, thanks, Chris." I beamed. "Sorry —" I saw my mother gliding by. "Mum!" I called.

She turned. She smiled. "Darling!" She hugged me. Her cheek gave like a half-deflated balloon. "I am so sorry about all this beastly business. Have you seen Benet? I'm sure he'll give you rides. Oh, no, he only has flat horses, doesn't he? Oh, hello," she said as she noticed Chris and Maria. "Hello, Chris," she said stiffly, then to Maria, "I'm sure I know you. Sorry. My memory." She squinted at Maria's badge. "Jasmine, is it?"

"Maria," said Maria and I at once.

93

"Oh, yes. Now. You want to tax my memory. I've got to meet up with Polly and Jakey Verulam after the third, I think, but otherwise I'm — oh, look, there's old Gwen Masterson. Incredible. Must be a hundred, and still looks fit as a fiddle. It's that coloring. All the Mastersons had —"

"Look, Nick." Chris jostled forward. "I really can't see the point in all this grubbing around digging up the past. It's not going to help. I mean, what the hell d'you think all that ancient history's got to do with whether you ride Perry's horses or not, for Christ's sake? Damn it, Fiona, Nick can't have been more than what, two, three when Perry got lucky? No point in stuffing his head with all that old stuff. I really do think you'd be well advised to leave well enough alone, Nick. Don't want to see you getting all bitter and twisted, chip on your shoulder, all that. Plenty of life ahead. Don't you agree, Fiona?"

"Mmmm?" My mother was magnificently vague. "No. Very good for him, learn a few home truths, I'd have thought. Too many lies. That's the trouble with Perry. Always was. Doesn't even know when he's lying these days."

"Oh, come on," Chris drawled, "leave it be, for God's sake. Serving up last night's hot dinners cold?"

"No, but there are some fascinating mysteries," my mum insisted. "Some things I've never understood. Waylands and the boy and —"

"What on earth's the point?" Chris snapped. "What's done is done. Couple of years, Perry'll have forgotten all about this. Nick'll be the favorite again. Meanwhile, I've got a bloody good job for him. I mean, why get him all worked up?"

"I should think he already is. Worked up, I mean. Aren't you, Nick? I know I would be if my father had behaved like that. Anyhow, Chris, I really think you can leave this sort of thing to me and my son, don't you? I mean, it's very kind of you and all that. . . ."

"He is my godson too, you know, Fiona."

"And we're very grateful, but I reckon Nick needs protection from that madman Peregrine Storr, and knowledge might help. So. Where should we go, do you think?" She turned back to Maria and me. She excluded Chris. "The crowds here — I don't know. . . . In the old days Queen Mary would just say, 'We do not know that woman,' and that woman would be out on her . . . Nowadays, what with pop stars and used-car salesmen . . . Did you see that dreadful blousy starlet whatshername — legs like egg timers — making an ass of herself yet again? Now, what was I saying? Oh, yes. There's that bar down by the paddock. At least it's shady. What do you think? Come along, then. So, Maria, I hope he's been behaving himself . . ."

I hung back. I said, "Hey, look, I'm sorry, Chris. Don't worry. There'll be no vindictiveness, no scenes."

"Oh, it's not that. No skin off my nose. Just thinking of you, old chap." Chris spoke airily. He was looking now at the crowd on the lawn. "Just take everything your dear mother says with a large pinch of salt, all right? Dear woman, but . . . Ah." He caught sight of a tall, dark woman with legs from here to there and a nose to match. "Melissa! See you tomorrow, Nick. Office. Twelve-thirty? Good. . . ."

I caught up with my mother and Maria. We made our way on a needle's course through the stuff of the crowd. My mother chatted all the way. Maria answered as best she could. She looked as if she were having some difficulty in keeping up and in retaining a straight face. She evidently liked my mother. I was used to this. Others, it seemed, did not share my exasperation at the hither-and-yon scudding of her mind.

We providentially found a table outside the bar. I battled inside and joined the ranks of men doing semaphore with ten-, twenty-, and fifty-pound notes. It took me just five minutes to get a trayful of Pimm's (at the cost of a tankerful), and half of the liquid was still in the glasses when I emerged again in the sunlight. My mother sat with Maria beneath bellowing drinkers.

"So." Maria offered us both cigarettes as I sat. "You got any bright ideas as to why your ex might be behaving like this? Any grisly secrets that might explain it all?"

"I wish there were." My mother shook her head at the cigarette. "No, not for me. Disgusting things. How do you manage it? I always think it's so clever, sucking all that smoke into your head and then puffing it out without coughing. Bit like fire-eating, really." She pulled the umbrella from her drink. "Ridiculous things."

"Do you reckon he'll have done it off his own bat, or he was pushed?"

"Oh, pushed, for certain. You know, if you use double sec and sweet Martini and gin, it's just as good and a lot cheaper. Angus told me that. Quite true. That reminds me, darling. You must send Constance a postcard or something. She's always asking about you. No, I mean, it's always been the same. Perry, at least in my day, always dodged things, ducked things, wriggled, looked for the easy answer, the instant result, then tried to justify his actions. That's why he's so busy compounding his crime by running around saying that you were a coward and a drunk and all that. Has to persuade himself that he was right. Why do they have to put half of Kew Gardens in these drinks? No, I wish I could help, but really, I can't think of a single skeleton in the cupboard that might explain things."

"Nary the one?" Maria said sadly.

My mother shook her head. "I mean, there was a lot of unpleasantness back then, bills unpaid, the odd bit of shady dealing. Sold an animal for Boy Maitland. Two grand. A lot of money in those days. Ivor never got the cash. All gambled away. That sort of thing. Poor Boy still scowls at me to this day, not that I had anything to do with it. Not that I blame him. I mean, I was brought up to be loyal, so I was loyal, though I did everything in my power to get the money paid. That was always the problem, really. I lost respect for Perry very early on. You can never re-create that, never replace it. I think by the time he left, I was pretty foul, really. Protecting you, darling, me, the standards I was brought up with. Now here's something I never told you. For your christening, Benet Kilcannon gave you three silver decanter labels by your namesake, Paul Storr, and a couple of cases of rather beautiful port — 'forty-seven, I think it was. And suddenly the labels were missing from the sideboard, and the port from the cellar. Perry claimed to have taken the silver to the bank and the wine up to London for safekeeping at one of his clubs. Rubbish, of course. The silver turned up at Sotheby's a year or two later, and I assume the wine either settled a debt or just got guzzled by Perry and his friends. Anyhow, yes, I suppose I can't really blame him in the end for running off with that funny little woman. Unchallenging. Though it was bloody galling after all those years to have him walk out just as he hit easy street. Bugger."

"Yes." Maria pulled a folded envelope from her bag. "Nick and I were talking about it all. I scribbled down some questions. I suppose the major one is, how in God's name did a gambler and small-time trainer get hold of Waylands? I mean, that must count as the most phenomenal stroke of luck, mustn't it?"

"Oh, it was, it was. Will you look at that hat? They get weirder and more ridiculous every year. The fact of the matter is, I really don't know. I mean, as Nick probably told you, Perry was away most of the time in those days. Stupid thing is, I'd known that it would be like that, but I'd still married him. It all seemed so glamorous, you know? So different from the norm. Of course, if I'd had any sense, I'd have had an affair with him and that would have been that, but I was not brought up to have affairs with people. So along comes this faintly disreputable ball of fire, and I go and marry him. Idiot, idiot, *idiot!* Anyhow, no, where was I? Yes, so I had no idea what went on up there in town. I had my hands full with you, Nicky, and with helping Conor — Conor Lecky was our headman, Jasmine — helping him run the yard. Sorry. It's Maria, isn't it? Your badge is *most* confusing. *West Side Story.* That'll remind me. No. It was in the middle of a row — Nicky was just toddling. I can't think what the row was about. Probably just the fact that Perry thought a job too menial to contemplate while I was apologizing to all the tradesmen in town for his bouncing checks. That sort of thing does wear one down in the end, you know. I really wasn't a nag when we started. Anyhow, suddenly he says, 'Well, it so happens I'm inheriting Waylands,' and I say, 'What?' and he says, 'Oh, yes, it's all very well for you with your high and mighty aristocratic tone' and so on, 'but it so happens that Maud Gascoigne has named me as her heir.' Something like that. So I said don't be ridiculous, you know. Just another lie

97

like all the others. Soon afterward, down he comes, all triumphant, clutching the deed in his warm and sticky. What won that race, by the way?"

I shrugged. I hadn't been listening to the commentary. Maria said, "Sorry. No idea."

My mother hailed a passing punter with an imperious wave. "Hello," she said, almost yawning, "what won that race?"

"Er . . ." The pippin-cheeked young man was taken by surprise. "Um, Trevor Elm's thing. What's it called?" He removed his hat and scratched his terraced hair, which faintly steamed.

"Accipiter," supplied Maria briskly. She smiled at the boy. Eton had prepared him for many things, but to be assailed at once by a pretty young woman who smiled at him and a grande dame who valued his opinion was altogether too much. He flushed and nodded to me as though I were his ally. He said, "Well, jolly good," and plunged into the bar.

"Sweet!" squeaked Maria.

"And that," said my mother, smiling, "is why I married the old bugger. No, anyhow, so. No, so Perry was going to inherit Waylands. Still seemed to me like a fairy tale spun for the creditors. I mean, he was always coming up with letters from his friends to satisfy the duns. 'Dear Mr. Storr, I have always wanted to own a residence called Thunderstone Cottage and am happy to pay up to thirty-five thousand pounds for the privilege.' I thought it was that sort of thing.

"I only met Mrs. Gascoigne once. Oh, for God's sake!" She spun round, and her eyes were ice. "What the hell do you think you're doing?"

I had seen it happen, seen it about to happen. The burly man now blinking foolishly behind her had wandered toward our table. He had looked above the crowd as though in search of an airborne friend. His crotch had hit the back of my mother's chair. He had said, "Oh, sorry," even as the wine jerked from his glass, split into strings of glass beads, and smashed on her hat, her hair, the shoulder of her dress.

We were all standing now. My mother was not appeased by her assailant's appearance. "You ridiculous person!" She spoke like a lepidopterist identifying a specimen. "Are you blind or just bloody stupid?"

The man said "Sorry" again, and then, "Barged me arm, didn't they?" He wore a plain dark suit, a scarlet tie, and very square black shoes with dentate flaps, like a golfer's.

"Man," I said. In fact, he put me in mind of a root, a mandrake root, all brown and bulbous and knobbly. If his jacket could have buttoned at all over the hard swell of his belly, it would only have been with a giant asterisk of welts. He had thin black hair cropped high up on his neck. His left hand pushed down hard in his jacket pocket.

My mother turned back to us, evidently satisfied that the mandrake was sufficiently cowed. She wiped an eye with the back of one long hand. "I *am* sorry," she announced, "but this absurd creature's conviction that he is in the taproom of his local inn means that I'll have to go and clean up. I won't be long. God. *Royal* Ascot. Hold the fort, will you? This is quite ridiculous. Excuse me."

The mandrake had retreated into the bar. For the next few minutes, Maria and I once more sat and watched the world go by. She surprised me by identifying outfits. "Valentino," she said, or "Oldfield, I bet."

"I thought such things were beneath you, Maria." I smiled.

"You thought wrong, didn't you? Preconceptions, Nick. I like this." She scanned the crowd. "Hell, beats Ripon in the mud, doesn't it? You know these people?"

"Fair number." I nodded. "Yeah."

"It's a bit like does the queen have clean sheets every day. Do these guys — are they like this all the time? Do they ever take off their fancy clothes and —"

"Oh, do they ever. Designer labels on their tucks, but sure. This is just the old school's Sports Day." I looked down at the race card in my hand and wondered, not for the first time, why I always had to roll the damned things up. I frowned. "Strange about that guy."

"Hmmm?" Maria's mind was elsewhere.

"Mandrake, as I think of him. Sort of knobbly root, you

know? I saw him. Just came up, spilled his drink. Said 'Sorry' even as he did it, maybe before."

"Weird. Pissed, probably, or just blew his fortune on a handicapped handicapper. You think she's all right?"

"Mum? Oh, she'll be fine. She's always fine."

"Don't you think I'd better go and find her? She's vague, isn't she?"

"Vaguely. Think she's forgotten all about us? Possible."

"No, but . . ." Maria roused herself. "No, I think I'll just see how she's getting on." She stood. "Back in a minute."

I nodded. The sun and the Pimm's and the burbling of the crowd were having their effect. I saw people whom I would normally hail, but I let them pass. I did not want to meet anyone from that life. Not yet.

"Quite incredible." My mother's voice snapped me out of it. It was almost shrill. "The whole thing must have been planned. I really . . . I mean, if you hadn't found me . . ."

Her voice seemed to come from a young man with buffed cheeks and a Belly Liberation Front beneath his Jermyn Street stripe. "Excuse me," said my mother's voice. Champagne trickled down the man's chin as he shuffled sideways and my mother emerged from behind his bulk. There were still damp patches on her hat and her shoulder, damp spots on her breast.

Maria followed, shaking her head. "Oh, just you wait till you hear this, Nick. Did you see that guy leave here?"

"What guy?"

"Mandrake."

"No."

"Mandrake. Yes, I like that." My mother sat. She mopped the table with a paper napkin. "Bastard. Really."

"So what happened?"

"What happened — if Jasmine here hadn't come to find me . . . Our friend Mandrake was waiting for me when I came out of the ladies'. Quite extraordinary. Said 'Terribly sorry' again, but happy that he could make it up to me by bringing Madam a message from her son. Knew my name, ever so respectful suddenly. According to him, the two of you had met up with some friends and gone off, and could I meet you at the

100

Castle Hotel after the last. Well, I thought 'odd' and 'a bit rude,' but all right. I was heading off to the stands when by pure good fortune I bumped into — um . . ."

"So someone," Maria pronounced portentously, "doesn't want us talking."

"No prizes for guessing who that someone might be," I mused. "Long arm. Pretty hamfisted, but it could have worked. He's not here, is he? No one's seen him?"

"Who, Perry?" Mum shrugged. "No. Doesn't mean he's not around, though. Or dreary Deirdre. It's all quite extraordinary. The worst of it is, I can't think what priceless secrets they think I'm going to reveal to you. As far as I know, you know as much as I. Or as little."

"There has to be something." Maria leaned forward. "About Waylands? You said you'd met the old girl."

"Yes. Only once. Oh, look, there's Henry Royston. I thought he was dead. Oh, no. That was his brother."

"And?" Maria prompted.

"What? Oh, yes. La Gascoigne. Yes. Just months before she died. What? 'Sixty-six, would it be? It has to be said that she was a particularly hideous old girl. Looked like a peasant, if you know what I mean. Short fringe, heavy features, heavy bones, dark, suspicious little eyes, knees broad as her thighs. A beast of burden. She lived by night mostly, I gathered. Her butler clocked in at nine in the evening and stayed on duty till six. She was whatshisname's daughter, famous trainer back then at the turn of the century."

"Dick Dawson?" suggested Maria. "Day? Darling?"

"No, no."

"Butler." I sighed. "Victor Butler."

"Oh, of course." Maria closed her eyes. "Lupine, right? Bra-ganza. Wasn't Parisina his?"

"That's right." I nodded. "Moody old sod, they say. Got his biography somewhere. First trainer really to set up as an inde-pendent on the open market. Before him, a trainer was as much a member of staff as a cook. He and Dawson changed all that. His son died at Verdun, and the old boy got bloodier and bloodier. Only talked to horses by the end. Slept in the yard.

One night went up on the gallops and shot himself. So the daughter copped the lot. The stables folded."

"Yes, well, that's as may be," my mother said briskly. "Whole place was running to rack and ruin by the time we went to see her. I felt rather sorry for the poor old thing. When we were shown into her drawing room that day, we caught her trying desperately to get up off the floor, all blushing and angry and pretending that she'd taken a tumble. It was quite obvious that she'd been playing with her poor little grandson, who was still at the crawling stage. We'd heard her clucking and cooing from the other side of the door. When we came in, she glared, defying us even to suggest such a thing. I suppose it was her looks. She must have thought she'd look grotesque doing anything so — am I still allowed to say 'anything so feminine,' or will battalions of dykes in fatigues descend upon me and shoot me for treason? I don't know. I'm sure we were allowed to say anything we felt like when I was a girl. Except 'effing' and 'blinding,' of course, but I never had any great need to do that. Nowadays you're allowed to say 'fuck' but not to say what you think. Anyhow, yes. There you are. Somewhere inside that hideous, rude old frog there was rather a sweet old dear."

"So who was her husband?" asked Maria.

"Haven't the faintest." My mother shrugged. "Fortune hunter is all I was told. God knows, she must have been easy meat. Stinking rich and ugly. Lamb to the slaughter. I think that's where most of the money went. Gascoigne, whoever he was, spent just about every penny on whores and yachts on the Riviera and horses and whatever before leaving her. That's right. I believe he ended up somewhere up the Amazon with a large stock of whisky and a bevy of dusky maidens. That was the story. And all poor old Mrs. Gascoigne had left was the house and yard. Well, she must have had some sort of income, but not much. Her only daughter died some time, back in the early sixties. Drugs, I think. Something shady like that. Unlucky family, one way or another. You look terrible, Nick, darling. All puffy and yellow. Should take some exercise."

"So she took to gambling?" I snapped.

"No, no. That was long before. That's how your father met her. She'd always gambled a bit. Quite successful. Unlucky in love, I suppose. Only fair."

"Until?" I prompted.

My mother looked surprised. "Until nothing. She used to play blackjack quite successfully. All I know."

"No," I persisted, "I'm sure . . . I was always given to understand that she got hooked and was pouring her fortune into Heron's places, and then Dad saw her and sort of stopped her."

My mother whooped. She threw back her head and laughed uproariously. "Oh, darling, darling," she gurgled and blinked at last, "you are sweet. Why on earth would a shill stop a punter?"

"A shill?"

"You don't even know the word? Oh, how delightful to find innocence in youth. What the hell d'you think Perry was living on all those years after he left the army?"

"I don't know." I shrugged, resentful. "His private income, gambling . . ."

"Gambling is right, but it wasn't he who did the gambling. Look, darling, I hate to disillusion you, but it's about time you faced the facts about your heroic papa. Oh, he's very lovable, but the fact is, he's a thief. They all were at that time, mind you. Know what they'd do, those smart young men about town? They'd get lists from the smarter schools — Heathfield, Queen Anne's, and so on, and they'd race to catch the richest of the rich young ladies before they appeared in London. They'd escort the poor little impressionable creatures everywhere, swank and slumming both. Go out to Esmerelda's Barn, run into the Kray twins, point out Bud Flanagan at the dogs', Al Burnett at the Stork Rooms. Dinner at A L'Ecu or Quags or Pruniers and find they'd lost their wallets, then on to one of dear Richard's games. God, the little darlings were impressed. Invite them up to Daddy's flat. My nice young man, was in the army, Daddy, says the same things as you about wogs. Days before Daddy misses the silver snuffbox or the enamel clock. There was a pub just off Sloane Street where the cream of British youth fenced all this stuff."

I stared. "Dad did this?"

"Oh, they all did. It was a game to them. You survived by whatever means. Except getting a job."

"Jesus," I breathed. "Oh, holy Jesus."

"No, your father was one of Richard's shills. Which means, simply, that he played for the house, same as lots of those chaps. If you had the accent, the clothes, and the contacts, you were in. Do stop catching flies, Nick. You look idiotic. Look. You've got a poker game. You all sit down, and the chosen punter starts to win. Maybe it's a one-night hit. Maybe he's allowed to come out a little bit on top tonight and he comes back next week. Either way, he wins a good deal. He doesn't know that at least two of the charming young men losing to him are employed by the house. The cards are never high. He wins on two pairs. A moderate full house is a world-beater tonight. So the mark is feeling well pleased with himself. Bit of luck — and encouragement — and he orders a drink or two. Toward the end of the evening, he's dealt a high full house — queens over tens, say. He bets high. So do the shills. The other punters drop out. There's no limit to the pot. The shills force him up and up. All drop out save one. He turns up kings over deuces. Thank you, Mr. Punter. Jolly bad luck. You just need two hits like that and he'll be into you for thousands. He'll still come back for more. After all, he's been winning most of the evening. Next time he'll be luckier. Blackjack, roulette, same thing. The bank has the edge in any case. You have a shill or two at the table, the odds swing drastically in the house's favor. Anyhow, according to your father, a shoe and a wheel can both be fixed. And then if you do win big, you'd better have some burly friends. If you carry the cash away, you'll get turned over before you reach home. If you win on credit, a couple of big men will come round to your hotel room the next day. You'll settle."

"God in heaven." I was as much shocked by my mother's words as by their import. Such words, so blithely used, seemed especially incongruous on her aristocratic lips. I would never have thought that my mother knew what a full house was. "And — and you knew about all this?" I asked her.

104

"Oh, not when I married him, no. I just knew that he was a bounder and a cad, but that was all right. Sort of glamorous, really. No. All that came out years later, when he was in his cups. Oh, my God. Is that another race over? It's always the same at Ascot. Don't know why they bother with the races. I must go. Listen, darling, I'll try to think of anything else, but I don't think it'll help much. I'll keep having a go at Perry, too, if I can get past that bitch Deirdre. Last time I spoke to her, she told me it looked like rain, so I said, 'Yes, dear, shouldn't you have a little lie-down?' It took her time, but she got there in the end. She didn't like it. No, I never knew why old Maud left the place to Perry. Maybe he closed his eyes and stuffed her. I wouldn't put it past him. I instantly suspected something fishy at the time, demanded that he tell me the truth, but he dodged the issue. That was just before he buggered off. Strange, the whole business." For a moment she was pensive, then she blinked and snapped out of it. "Right," she said, gathering up her bag and her binoculars. "I'm so glad to have seen you, darling." She bent and kissed me. "Lovely surprise. I wish you'd come and see us. Still. Jas— Maria, dear. Nice to meet you. Do make Nick ring me from time to time. No, don't get up, Nick. Bye!"

Maria and I watched her go. My mother breezed into the crowd, and the crowd made way. "That's one hell of a lady," Maria murmured. As though she had heard her, my mother, now twenty yards away, stopped. She stood stock still for a moment amid a swirl of morning coats and frocks. Then she turned and started back fast. She was frowning.

I stood as she came near. "Hi. Forget something?" I scanned the ground around her chair.

"No. I've just thought . . . it's probably wholly irrelevant, but —"

"Go on."

"It's a story your father used to tell about old Clem Hedges. You remember. Trained in the Midlands. Had that National winner. Thingy. Now, let's see if I've got this right. Perry jocks you off without explanation, and the horse loses. If I can still read a race, which I can, the horse could have won, right? So the reason he wanted you off must be that he wanted the horse pulled and either he knew you wouldn't do it or he was ashamed to ask you to do it. Right?"

"That's what I assumed," I agreed, "though I can't see why any trainer would want to lose a Gold Cup. A jockey, perhaps, if there was enough money in it, but . . ." I shook my head.

"No. That's what I thought, but then . . . Listen. I must be quick. Clem Hedges trained for a stinking-rich, profligate chap called George Torvill. Big, big punter. They say he used to spoof for a thousand pounds a time. Anyhow, Torvill had a fling with Clem's wife, Pam. Clem said, 'Right. He stuffed my wife. I'll stuff him.' He did, too. Every time a horse was off form, he'd tell Torvill it was going to win, and Torvill would lose thousands. Every time he had a surefire winner, he'd put Torvill away. He bankrupted him in three years. Torvill died on skid row. Don't know whether this has anything to do with what Perry's up to now, but it's a thought, isn't it? Must fly."

"It is indeed," Maria murmured as my mother once more sailed away, "a thought."

"So, where to now?" Maria slurped at the French onion soup she had insisted on ordering as a postrace restorative. She looked up with a blond mandarin mustache of molten cheese. "I'm enjoying this," she mumbled into her napkin.

"Evidently."

"No, not the soup, twit. The quest. The chase. We're on the right track, lad, no question."

"How d'ye make that out?" I tapped sugar from a screw of paper into my *citron pressé*.

"Ah, come on, Nick, you can feel it. They just have to see us and they're shitting themselves. I mean, look at your godfather. Wildman is harmless enough, but he's trying to warn you off. He knows that something stinks not very far beneath the surface. I think your mum's got to be right. The only possible reason for jocking you off is that your dad wanted that animal stopped. Big rich trainer doesn't stop a potential Gold Cup winner for any amount of money, so it follows he's got it in for the owner. The rest of the nastiness is just his self-justifying temperament — and, of course, he's got to persuade Rashid and the rest of the world that he's got a genuine reason for getting rid of you. As a matter of interest, what would you have done if he'd asked you to pull that horse?"

"Told him to sod off. Said he was crazy." I shrugged. "Damn it, it was he who taught me to say 'sod off' in those circumstances!"

"Exactly. So. Query: why should your old man have it in for an Arab to the extent of losing a Gold Cup?"

"No bloody reason." I was depressed and surly. I was acutely aware that every cell in my body contained the pattern of my father's genes. I wanted to know no more of that squalid legacy of which I had once been so proud. When I thought how I had boasted about him at school, in the weighing room . . . Suddenly a lot of knowing glances and indulgent smiles were explained. No one was going to say, "But didn't you know? Your father is in fact a second-rate shit." They would just smile and smile and pity my puerile pride. I felt physically violated. I wanted to bathe in some acid that would strip me clean to the bone. "No bloody reason at all," I repeated.

Hats and coats now discarded, we sat in a bistro halfway up Windsor's steep high street. Through the smoked glass of the windows, the castle's masonry looked like an old woman's skin caked with makeup. The sun still shone, but it was dirtied now by evening.

"Well, don't know about you, but I reckon you should warn him. Poor bugger trusts his trainer. God, he could — guys like that bet seventy, eighty grand a time. How many horses has he got with your dad?"

"I don't know," I said for no reason. "Sixteen."

"Shit. He could be down millions already. Someone's got to tell him."

"Oh, sure. I roll up, say, 'My dad's trying to bankrupt you by having your horses pulled. He's a crook. Len Egan's a crook.' Why should he believe me, for Christ's sake? He'll just put it down to sour grapes."

"You still ought to try."

"Yeah, well, maybe." I sighed. The sentry in his box stood

like a man in a faded photograph. "I've had enough of this," I announced. "I wish I'd never come back."

"Back?"

"Yup. The north was a different world. Up there, no one gives a damn who your father is, who your friends are. You're good company, they'll give you the time of day. But this — Ascot, all those people — I used to come here for the panto-mime. Tea at Fuller's. Show Queen Mary's dollhouse to foreign friends. It's all bloody haunted. Oh, stuff it." I shook my head. I reached across to take Maria's hand. "I'm just being wet. Ghosts crowding around, you know?"

"Sure I know, Nick." Maria's hand twisted to cover mine. "And in some ways you've had a good education; in some ways, like your dad, you've been allowed to feel the world owes you a living. Now the old sod's turned against you, and unless you're prepared to fight like a guttersnipe, he'll ruin you for good and all. He's already done his best to bugger up your riding career. Think you're going to get a lot of good owners if you ever set up as a trainer? Shit, racing spans everything — show business, the City, the lot. That man can screw you up pretty thoroughly, and unless you find out the truth about all this and, if necessary, publicly rub his nose in it, that's what he's going to do. So, what do you reckon is the next stop?"

"I dunno." I shook myself awake. "I mean, there are still some questions . . . I still don't understand this Waylands business."

"Me either. So find out. Me, I'll have to get the train back tomorrow night, but —" she broke off as an aproned waitress leaned between us to jangle silverware in an officious manner. The woman removed our plates with a sniff. Maria leaned forward again. "I mean, where are wills kept? Somerset House, is it?" She picked up a toothpick and studied it wistfully. "And go back to Uffington. The locals must remember something about —" Maria's eyebrows suddenly jumped. Her lower jaw dropped. "Bloody hell," she breathed.

"Whassat?"

"Your mum . . . What she said . . ."

"Yes?"

"Mrs. Gascoigne . . ." She stabbed the tablecloth with the toothpick. "Mrs. Gascoigne was down on her hands and knees, talking — playing . . ."

I leaned forward. Suddenly my heart upped its tempo. Funeral march turned to carnival. "With her grandson. Dear God. With her grandson. And heir."

That night we dined at an esperanto restaurant in South Kensington and shared a twin room in a Select Family Hovel in Victoria.

That night, too, Guy Cullinan's stableyard in Somerset was burned to the ground. The fire brigade and the villagers managed to douse the flames before they reached the house. They did not manage to save Guy's old hunter, Trafalgar, or his two English setters, who died respectively trumpeting and howling amid falling, flaming rafters. There was no question, my mother said, but that it was arson. Kerosene had been sprinkled in one of the stalls, and a candle left to burn down. I had wanted to ask her about the mysterious grandchild, but this was not the time.

Chris's offices were impressive. That depressed me. They were designed to be impressive. I resented the designer's success. Hell, Wildfire Leisure Corp. (the sixties origins were evident in the name) comprised twelve stories of open-plan lime and white offices surrounding a Roger Barr fountain of stainless steel. The lift was a bulimic's pill-capsule.

How did people work in places like this, I wanted to know. You couldn't scratch yourself without seeing it on tomorrow's city pages. But it wasn't like that on the twelfth floor. There all was *luxe, calme, et volupte*.

It was a bit like finding sleek cattle in a Japanese garden. There were plenty of contentedly fat things in here, yet somehow you found yourself looking about at the sofas and the armchairs, the plump books (not the usual books by the yard, but the latest hardback best-sellers), the flabby gladioli and the overblown Peploe flowers above the fireplace, and wondering on just what they might have fed in these sparse surroundings. Not on the adzed oak panels or the fudge-colored carpet, nor on the huge *pietro duro* catafalque of a coffee-table — flowers again, of amethyst, lapis, and rhodochrosite in a field of cloudy gray marble — nor on the plate-glass windows flanked on either side by large Skeaping bronzes of racing horses. Sybaritism did its best to live with stark elegance. It has to be said that it did a fair job.

Chris wasn't at his desk — a beautiful Irish Chippendale library table. "Ah, Nicky." His voice came to me from the balcony, and then his dark bulk emerged at the window. "Good to see you. Come on out here and join me. Got a bottle of Gewurz out here. Do you?"

"Sure. Great." I ambled across the office. I felt faintly uncomfortable in my one dark summer suit. His hand engulfed mine. I followed him out onto a balcony as big as the average director's office. "Bloody hell," I said, gazing admiringly around, and that's when I became annoyed. The whole setup had been calculated to make me gaze around and say, "Bloody hell." I had obeyed an unheard order, a sort of universal posthypnotic suggestion. I resented it, but I stayed impressed nonetheless.

From here, high above Leicester Square, I could see a huge area of London. At my right were Piccadilly, Green Park, Buckingham Palace, Westminster Cathedral, and the glint of the river, with mile upon mile of office blocks and houses in between and beyond. At my left, though the view was obscured in part by our equally tall neighbor on the other side of the street, were Covent Garden, the Strand, and the City. It was a cliché, this opulent aerie, and it worked, damn it.

"This is outrageous, Chris." I took the glass he offered. "It steps straight out of a thousand movies. Sinatra and Holden in *Sabrina,* and I scoffed at it then. Goes with a secretary with legs up to her neck, or yours, depending on the scene and the movie. It's — yeah, *outrageous* will do."

"Thought you'd enjoy it." His eyes twinkled. "As for the secretary — well, you'll meet her. She'll do as well, I think."

He nodded slowly. He frowned. He swilled the wine round in his glass before looking up with a smile. "Now look, what I wanted to talk to you about is this: I think you should be thinking of something long-term in the leisure business. Between us, you know — me and Richard — we ought to be able to find you something pretty good, something with serious prospects. Just say the word." He rested his forearms on the parapet. He narrowed his eyes as though sighting over the rim of his glass. "You're bloody well placed, you know, Nicky. More than we poor beggars ever were."

"Yeah, thanks, Chris." I looked down. This was brave of me. Heights horrify me so much that I long to throw myself off them simply to stop them from doing it, whatever it is. People moved beneath us like the last grains at the bottom of a coffee jar. The odd taxi shuddered and creaked, slow when fed, quick and fierce as a shark when hungry. Once its belly was full of human, it slowed again, and lurked. "One day I'll think about it. Not now. I don't think I could cope with the restraints of this city just now."

"Restraints! Ha!" Chris murmured. "I don't notice any restraints."

"Oh, sure, for you. I'm like, I'm still at university, if you see what I mean. I mean, this riding business, suppose I stick with it for a decade or so, do okay, then I can make decisions. Be worth a lot more to you if I do well. I've started, so I'll finish. Make a go of it."

"You remind me of your dad. He was the same. Buggered if he'd give in, yield to the demands of commerce, become a good boy. The world would come to him or he'd end up a tramp. That was his attitude. Mind, he was lucky."

"You?"

"No. I always knew where I wanted to go, me. Probably didn't enjoy myself half as much as old Perry as a result. I ended up in that set because I wanted the good games, the lovely women, so on. But I always knew what I was really after. All those years gambling and all that, in a funny way I was just researching human weakness, learning my trade. Oh, and enjoying myself, of course, but . . ."

"And did you get it? What you wanted? Is this it?"

"Oh, who ever gets it?" Chris sighed. Intercostal-diaphragmatically. "I had fun. I have fun now. This isn't bad. Put it this way: we all wade through sewage, but I get to decide who shits in my sewer. I can go where I like when I like. It's not bad. We weren't hippies in my day. Too busy sweeping up the mess of the war. It was different. That's all."

"So, I never really knew. So how'd you start building this little empire?"

He shrugged. "Right place, right time, same as anyone. I was in with the in-crowd, and I was a solicitor. Likes of Richard needed quite a lot of legal advice when they were setting up, you know. I got a couple of directorships, started from there. Obvious, really. Then, you know, someone was needed to organize the Nassau setup, then Jo'burg, and I picked up a few cinemas and things on the way. You know how it is. Been lucky, that's all."

"Must've been rough times, those early days."

"Oh, I don't know. No room for bleeding hearts, sure, but basically just gas. Got quite hairy on occasions, particularly before we went legit. You should try having one of the bigger East End firms take a swing at your neck with a broadsword."

"You *what*?"

"Yup." He laughed. "They'd been trying to get protection money from us. I was sent out as a sort of front man, you know, calm things down, give 'em a bit of the verbals, put the fear of God into them. Great, only I got this huge coon high on black bombers or whatever. Grabbed this bloody great claymore hanging on the wall, swiped with all his might at my neck. Lucky he was only using the flat of the blade, but know what? I sat down hard, and I actually found myself looking for my head. Seriously. Thought I'd see it rolling across the floor."

"Jesus." I whistled. "And?"

"Well, it was pretty obvious that the softly, softly approach wasn't going to work, so — I can't remember. We'd have put some pressure on them somehow. I mean, we had some clout in those days because we were establishment. MPs, peers of the realm. There was no real point in tangling with us. The mobsters went back to their gutters, and we stayed where we belonged."

"Mum said Dad worked as a — shill, was it?"

112

"Hmmm? Oh, well, yes. We all did when we were down on our luck, you know. Well, not me. As a solicitor, I had to keep my nose clean. But everyone else did. You know, put yourself in poor old Perry's position. He'd play with his own money, lose, pile up a bit of a debt. Richard likes him, I like him, none of us wants any nastiness, anything like that. Fine. Perry plays for the house for a bit, does what he enjoys best and makes sure we get our money back. Nothing wrong with that, hmm?" His voice wore kid gloves.

"No . . ." I was dubious. "But isn't it cheating? Playing for the house, I mean?"

"Why on earth?" Chris was affronted. "I mean, sure, it increases the house's chance of winning, but it makes no difference to the punter's chances whether you're playing for yourself or the house, does it?"

"S'pose not." I frowned. I wished I were better at this sort of thing. I had an obscure feeling that there was something wrong with Chris's reasoning.

"Anyhow, just you remember, Nicky. It's all very well for you to be all ethical, brought up in the lap of luxury, denied nothing. We had to struggle and hustle for a living. Ethics are a luxury that the less fortunate can't always afford. We sure as hell couldn't afford to be sorry for the jumped-up little oiks and dagos who came in and flashed their money about. Just you remember that, and don't be too quick to judge your poor old man. All right? Now" — he was a cheery, chubby chum once more — "we should be thinking about lunch, hmm?"

Chris knew a little place. Give Chris five minutes anywhere in the world and he would know a little place. He might even own it.

This was a good little place, as London little places go. It had fewer pretensions than most, either to grandeur or to ethnic simplicity. The linen was linen, the flowers were fresh, the plates were of plain white porcelain, and each bread-roll was a little daybreak. The butter was unsalted, iced, and curled, and had never in its worst nightmares conceived of such horrors as foil wrappers. Such pleasure did these erstwhile commonplaces afford me that I would have thought it the best London lunch that I had had in years even had we left after olives, bread, and negronis.

The waiters knew Chris, of course. They flapped our napkins for us and changed the ashtrays every two minutes, although neither of us smoked.

I ordered Carne alla Zingara and John Dory, Chris, Gnocchi alla Romana and Dover sole. He nodded to two or three people as they entered.

"No, but I really think you should consider what I was saying. About finding work in this business, I mean. I mean, you say you'd be worth a lot more on the open market if you'd done well as a jockey. I'm not so sure. The days of sporting heroes' being eagerly sought as executives are gone now, partly because most of them today are spotty kids or the most godawful thugs, and partly because they come and go so fast nowadays. Heroes don't become legends anymore. They become answers to questions on radio quizzes. People clutch their brows and say 'Oh, what was his name?' when only twelve months ago they were cheering you to hell and back. I mean, okay, say you spend ten years getting to the top, win the Gold Cup, something like that — sure, I'd still be delighted to have you, but you'd be a darned sight higher up the ladder if you started work right now. Start, say, at thirty k. Ten years under your belt and you could be running a major chunk of this business."

"God." I laughed on one side of my face. "I suppose I actually have to start thinking about things like this. The future, I mean. I'd always assumed . . ."

"Hmm?"

"Well, that I'd take over from Dad in the end. Sure, five years perhaps learning about finance, five years in Chantilly, say, and then come back as Dad's assistant."

"Well, why not?" Chris hummed. His blond eyebrows jerked up and down in time with his chewing.

"Oh, come on, Chris."

"No, seriously, old chap, why not? I mean, okay, so he jocked you off. Doesn't mean he's disinherited you or anything. I have

114

that from his own lips. Come on. You'll make it up. Few years, the whole thing'll be forgotten. You know Perry and his towering passions. Still, I really think you should be thinking about a career in the straight world right now. Lord, man, what's the point in smashing yourself up, risking your neck, all that? Not going to make your fortune that way, and you're letting all the opportunities in the world pass you by. Why bother?"

"If you don't know, Chris," I sighed sorrowfully down at my raw beef, "I'm afraid I can't explain."

"Oh, sure, sure, soulless man of business, me. I get all that from Louise."

"Louise?"

"Yes. You remember. Bloody daughter of mine."

I thought back. I vaguely recalled a pretty blond girl who had insisted on showing me her bottom at a children's party. It had been a nice bottom. "Long time ago," I mumbled.

"Druggy tart now. She blames me for what she's become. God, I don't know. Thank God for La Thatcher. At least she had the guts to stand up and tell the proles success isn't a sin. It's about — it's like bloody Vietnam. We do our best, work like slaves, and then we're meant to feel guilty because we've got a bit of cash. I don't know."

I waited until the debris of Chris's tiramisu had been removed and coffee and brandy were on their way.

"Look, Chris." I was easy. "What do you remember about old Maud Gascoigne?"

He eyed me quickly. I wondered if he would lie. He turned back to the napkin that he was crumpling between his powerful hands. "Oh, God," he said at last. "Why'd you want to know?"

"Hell, I'm meant to be heir to her property. I'm interested, that's all."

Again I felt that mental searchlight flash quickly over me. This time it was I who turned away. "Not much, actually, old mate," Chris said. "Sorry. I mean, I met her, what? Twice? Once when Perry introduced us up at Bentham's — just struck me as a dotty old bird who liked to play the tables and had a bit of a thing about your old dad. Next time Perry came to me, said she wanted to draw up a new will. Could I help? Simple enough job. I said sure, went down to Waylands, she left the lot to him. I tied it all up. That was that. She died a couple of years later. Weird old biddy."

"What about her grandchild? Just cut out with nothing?"

"Grandchild?" Chris was vague.

"Yeah. My mum said she was there one day, found Mrs. Gascoigne playing with her grandchild."

"Oh, no." Chris shook his head fast, and his dewlaps wobbled. "No, no, no. Don't think you'll find a grandchild. The old girl had no heirs. I remember that. No, there was a daughter — Amanda, Annabel, something. Died at eighteen, nineteen. Tragedy. Yes."

"Died of what?"

"Nick, what's with you?" Chris met my gaze and held it with eyes that looked quizzically into the middle distance. He wasn't looking at me. Not really. I was just a face in the center stalls. "I mean, this is all a long time back. Are you out to crucify your old dad because he annoyed you? If so, you'll not get help from me. He may be all sorts of idiot, but I like the guy, and he's never set out to hurt a soul. Made mistakes, sure. Who hasn't? But there's not an ounce of malice in him, and I'd not be pleased to see you getting all vindictive. You have your family squabbles, Nick, but don't try to involve me."

"This is no squabble," I told him. "I'm just interested. How did she die?"

Chris had gained time. He had needed it. I could see that in the briskness with which he answered, "Okay, okay. Old story. She suffocated on her own vomit. Pretty girl. Got caught up with a bad set, got pissed. Probably drugs as well. I don't know. Jesus, Nick!" The table suddenly vibrated. "You haven't got a clue what it was like in those days, have you? Listen. You want to screw someone, she wants to screw you, you just do it, right? You've grown up rich and bloody spoiled in the age of the Pill, the age of feminism, all that. We — we couldn't do that. We had no bloody money, were made to feel like infants because there were all these boring old farts coming back with their fucking war stories, and we couldn't screw anyone. We lived in terror of pregnancy. You know that? Bloody terror." The brandy slopped in his glass as he twirled it. "An abortion was the worst — well, no, the worst was a respectable girl, sister or daughter of a friend, says she's in pup and you've got to marry her or you're stuffed. And you *were* stuffed, dear God. No drugs like your lot — well, maybe a few pills, black bombers, purple hearts — and no fucking money. And always that terrible threat — that you could end up a respectable little Mr. Pooter in a suburban home with net curtains. Jesus. Life was passing us by, Nicky. We made a stand, and there were casualties. There are casualties today, aren't there? Drugs, AIDS . . . There were casualties then, too. Impressionable girls who knew no better. Fellows who blew their patrimony in a couple of years and ended up with bugger-all. On the streets. And what we had, we lucky few, was the equivalent of marijuana today — the pardon-able crime, did no one any harm, had always been done, our link between ourselves and the real criminals, established us as rebels, outlaws, gave us kicks. That so wrong, was it? What we had was gambling.

"Some of us — me, your father, Richard Heron — we did well in that little world. Others went down. Okay. Is that any different from the bloody dope dealers who now own shipping lines and hotel groups and so on? Some of us didn't play just for the fun of the game, okay? And at least we didn't prey on the weaknesses of people better than ourselves, at least in gen-eral we treated women with respect. So leave it out, Nick. Just leave it out. You've fed too damned much off our earnings to start getting all holier than thou, okay? So . . ." He exhaled. It was astonishing how rapidly he could shift from one gear to another. Now he smiled as sheepishly as one who resembled a prize Wessex saddleback hog could smile. "Oh, hell." He wiped his brow with his blazer's sleeve. "Sorry, Nick. I'm tired. But sometimes, you know, it really gets my goat, the young being so bloody sanctimonious. Must be getting old, eh?"

"Sorry, Chris." I shook my head, bemused. "I didn't mean . . ."

"I know you didn't. No, you're okay, Nick. My fault." And suddenly he was standing, shooting his cuffs, saying, "Ah," grinning at someone behind me. "Here we are. . . ."

And I stood, too, half turned, caught a glimpse of a lot of shadowy leg. I pushed my chair back.

"Sorry I'm late," the girl was saying, and she looked me full in the eyes and gave me a smile that I had to swallow. "You must be Nick."

I think I said, "Um."

Chris's voice was telling me that this was Deborah. She was saying that these documents needed his urgent attention as they had to go off immediately, if that was okay, but the words were just background babble because I was taking her in, inch by inch.

It was as though they had set out to make an African beauty, had sketched big black eyes, broad pink lips, short torso, and long, sinuous limbs, and had then changed their minds, thought, Why not? and given her long, straight, glossy dark hair and white skin, as smooth and thickly textured as rose petals.

She walked round the table like a naked woman, unabashed, unafraid, everything on offer. She seemed fluid as she curled into her chair, tucked those endless legs beneath her, that black miniskirt stroking her thighs way up there, and Jesus, I thought, I will not lick my lips, but it was like a child trying to eat a jam doughnut while keeping his tongue in his mouth. My tongue had a will of its own, and she saw and she smiled. Chris was talking as he scanned and signed, scanned and signed. ". . . trying to persuade Nick here that he's got a future in our business, Debby, love. Sooner break his neck with the nags."

"No," I said, "it's just . . ."

She seemed fluid as she placed her elbow on the table and her chin on her hand, her long, long-nailed fingers spreading out like a fan. She said, "Oh, come on, Nick. Give it a try. Be fun, have someone young about the place." There was a trace of smoky Midlands in her voice.

"Look, Nick." Chris replaced the gold cap on his pen. He was still reading. "Tell you what. All right, so you don't want to give up riding. Fair enough, but at the moment at least you've got nothing to ride, right?"

"S'pose." I nodded down at the table. "Next season, maybe."

"Sure. Maybe. But at the moment you're broke, so . . ." He drank his coffee. His tongue slithered quickly about his lips. "What about this. You come and give me a hand, see how you like it. No commitment either way. I need someone I can trust. In this business, the help are up to all the dodges. I can't be everywhere making sure standards are maintained. Now, no one knows you. You go round the clubs and restaurants and all that — Debby could give you a hand, show you the ropes — and you report back direct to me. Say — what'll we say? Three hundred a week, cash in hand? Do you? Expenses paid, of course, and you can doss in the flat above mine in Holland Park. Pretty basic, but I'll not interfere, you can take girls back, whatever. At least until Perry reconsiders, it should do you. What d'ye say?"

"Come on, Nick." Debby touched my sleeve. "Give it a try. What's to lose?"

Money, position, women: for the second time in my life, this intoxicating cocktail proved too strong for me. I shrugged. I smiled. I held out my hand. I said, "Thanks, mate. You got a deal."

"Hell," he rumbled, "what are godfathers for?"

Maria was waiting eagerly for me and for a table. She was full to bursting with discoveries. She shifted from foot to foot like a circus elephant between Fortnum's food hall and the Fountain restaurant.

"Come on, then," I told her. "Shoot."

"Not till we can sit down. I have been yomping about this bloody town all day, and I would kill for a cup of tea. They said five minutes five minutes ago. My money's on the blue rinse and ranch mink over there on the right. She polished off her chicken and bacon stack and Mont Blanc ten minutes ago, and her son or toy-boy has had lobster bisque and cucumber sandwiches and —"

"Shut up, Maria," I said cheerfully. "Anyhow, you lose." I nodded toward a designer family now gathering together its coats and carrier bags. Even the smallest of them, a boy who could not have been more than five, had three bags of his own.

"Oh, thank God." Maria was off and almost trotting over to the table. She sat before the family had finished collecting itself. She pushed aside plates streaked with jam and cream. She pulled cigarettes, lighter, and a sheaf of papers from her handbag. She lit a cigarette and kicked off her shoes.

I waded between the tables after her. "They've ruined this place," I protested. I pulled back a chair and looked round at the dull-brown, dirty-protest walls of what had once been a sugary confection of pistachio and cream.

"Don't give a bugger." Maria puffed out smoke like a dragon who'd just come. "They can paint it pink and purple for all I care, as long as they clear up this mess and bring us a gallon of Lapsang."

It took a further five minutes for the waitress to deign to notice us, but at last Maria was equipped with the necessaries of life: an ashtray, a pot of tea, and a rich chocolate cake.

"Now," she said like a conjurer, "take a look at this." She pushed a large folded sheet of paper across to me.

It was a photocopy of a standard will form. Maud Butler Gascoigne bequeathed the manor of Waylands in the county of Royal Berkshire and all and any monies, goods, and chattels whereof she died possessed to her dear friend Captain Peregrine Raymond Storr. The will was dated 14 November 1964.

"Look at the witnesses," Maria was urging as I read. "Just look at the witnesses. And the lawyer."

"Lawyer was Chris," I murmured. "He told me."

"Oh, did he? And the other witness?"

The other witness's signature was in a familiar hand: Deirdre Samson, soon to save on customized luggage by becoming Deirdre Storr.

"So?"

"Well, think, for God's sake. What is your dear stepmother doing witnessing Maud Gascoigne's will?"

"Presumably she was already Dad's mistress." I shrugged. "Mrs. Gascoigne tells Dad, 'I want to make a will.' He says, 'Okay, I've got a friend who's a solicitor. I'll get him down.' And then they need a witness. Deirdre just happens to be with Dad, or she's outside in the car or something. Not surprising, when you think about it."

"Oh, thanks, you appreciative audience you. Thanks a lot. More likely they all got together to put pressure on the poor old bat. Still, okay, get a load of this."

She tossed two more sheets of photocopy across the table. One landed on my hot chocolate and perched there, seesawing. The other swooped to the carpet. "Okay, okay," I soothed. "Steady. So where did these come from, then?"

"Colindale. The newspaper library. God, you should try getting out there. It's hell."

I bent to pick up the fallen sheet. There were two cuttings on it. The first was marked, in blue ballpoint, *Daily Sketch, 3 October 1964.*

SOUTHWARK CORPSE MYSTERY

The body of a young woman was found in Bittern Street, Southwark, yesterday morning. Police say that foul play is not suspected. Her identity has yet to be established.

She is described as being in her late teens or early twenties, with brown eyes and short brunette hair. She was expensively dressed in a maroon silk dress with a large black bow at the waist and black patent-leather high-heeled shoes. "We are anxious to find out who this poor girl was and what she was doing in this area late at night," said a police spokesman. "Anyone who might have seen her is requested to contact us."

The second cutting was longer. It came from the *Daily Express* of 6 October.

TEENAGE HEIRESS FOUND DEAD

The body found on Wednesday night in Bittern Street, Southwark, has been identified as that of Alison Mary Gascoigne, 19, granddaughter of famous racehorse trainer Victor Butler and heiress to his fortune and the great Waylands training-stables in Berkshire. Miss Gascoigne, an art student and well-known member of the Chelsea set, was seen at Lucy's gaming-club in Shepherd Market, Mayfair, earlier in the evening. "She was a good-time girl," remembered fellow student Frances Macdonald, "a great partygoer, always laughing."

Police believe Miss Gascoigne's death to have been accidental, but are still anxious to know what took her on her final journey to a narrow dark street on the South Bank. "There are no residences or places of entertainment on Bittern Street," said Chief Inspector David Tate. "Someone must know what drew this well-brought-up, attractive young woman to a deserted alleyway where she met her tragic death."

"Well?" Maria was smiling triumphantly at me.

"Well?"

"Come on, Nick, what's with you today? She was at one of Heron's clubs the night she died. Jesus!"

"Yes, and?"

"It stinks, Nick!" she squeaked. "She's at Lucy's the night she dies, and just a couple of years later, your dad, one of Heron's shills, inherits her fortune."

"Yeah, so we knew the Gascoignes hung out with that set. Mrs. Gascoigne says, 'My daughter's up in town, show her a good time, introduce her to some interesting people.' So Dad introduces her to his crowd. One night she drinks too much, suffocates on her own sick. Dad starts thinking, Who else is going to inherit Waylands? and sets out to charm the old girl. Greedy, perhaps, but not criminal. So she decides to leave the place to him. He thinks, If the family solicitor is used, he'll try to dissuade her. Better keep it among friends. So he calls Chris. Shitty, okay, but we know he's a shit. Some would just call it opportunism, good old Thatcherite business."

"And the grandson?"

"There wasn't a grandson. I asked Chris. God knows, it's not the first time my mother's got her wires crossed. They don't mention a child here, do they?"

"No, but they wouldn't, would they?" Maria's color had risen. "In those days, when a respectable girl died, they weren't going to say, 'By the way, she had a bastard.'"

"Maria, it was an accidental death. That much is established.

There is no evidence that there was a child. Dad played up to La Gascoigne, and he inherited. That's all we've got."

Maria breathed noisily through her nose. I turned back to the second sheet. The third cutting was a report of the inquest two weeks later. By this time the papers had stocked up their armory of information and buffed their speculatory adjectives. The *Sketch* again:

Poor little rich girl Alison Gascoigne gambled at Lucy's in Mayfair. She won £40. She drank vodka and took pep pills. That was a bigger gamble. She lost her life.

Heiress Alison, whose grandfather, trainer Victor Butler, counted royalty among his friends and trained two Epsom Derby winners, was found dead in a lonely South London alley only hours after she left the luxurious gaming club in the notorious Shepherd Market, a coroner's court was told yesterday.

Dressed in crimson silk, dashing brunette Alison started the evening beneath glittering chandeliers. She laughed with millionaires. She ate smoked-salmon sandwiches. She carelessly tossed £5 chips onto the green baize tables. By three o'clock in the morning, she was lying in a damp, unlit street on the other side of the Thames in a drink- and drug-induced stupor, suffocating on her own vomit.

The nature of that night reflected Alison's strange double life. The court heard how Alison, a gifted student at the Chelsea School of Art, liked to glitter at high-society balls and cocktail parties but also enjoyed the low life in the cafés and public houses frequented by the immigrant population. "She was a great girl," recalled Euclid Lucas, an unemployed West Indian. "No side to her. Always ready with a sub [loan] when us was down on our luck. She'd come down the clubs and jive the night away, or she'd call on us at our digs just for a chat. I have never known her to smoke ganja [marijuana]. She was a decent girl."

Richard Heron, owner of Lucy's, remembered a very different Alison. "She would come in perhaps twice, three times a week. She bet £40 every time. Never more, never less. She was very popular, very smart. She always drank a lot but was never out of control. It is all very sad. She will be missed. I had no idea that she took pills."

Neither Alison's father, who lives in South America, nor her mother, eccentric racehorse owner Maud Gascoigne, was in court.

The coroner recorded a verdict of Death by Misadventure.

I laid the paper down. I felt very cold. Maria was glaring at me. "You've made up your mind, haven't you?" she asked.

"Made up mind about what?"

"What did that Chris say? You've decided to join them, haven't you? Take the money and run."

"No! Come on, don't be ridiculous, Maria. It's just that there's no evidence here that anything was wrong. Sure, if I can find out why Dad fired me, I'll be happy, but it hasn't got anything to do with this lot, whatever else it may be about. Anyhow, what's it to you? Why the vindictiveness? That's what gets me. I'm the one who got hurt, and you know, yes, I'd love to get back at the sod, but it's you who's doing all the pushing, you who wants to read the worst into everything. Just because Dad tried it on with you —"

"Tried it on and, when I refused, not only booted me out but spread the rumor throughout racing that I was in the habit of being gang-banged by the lads. Thanks. Know why I was working as a stable-girl, Nick?" She was becoming shrill. "Do you? Because I had a little bastard myself, name of Lucy, and my parents didn't want to know, and I had to support her somehow. So what it came down to was this: either let Captain fucking Perry Storr screw you or lose your job and any chance of keeping your daughter. And he knew that. And he knew it even as he was spreading his oh-so-amusing rumors and making sure I'd never get a job in racing again."

I flinched. "Oh, Christ, I'm sorry, Maria. Oh, dear God, I am sorry."

"So I ended up living on the dole in a council flat in York. Two and a half years of temporary typing and cleaning jobs when I could have been doing what I do best."

"And Lucy?" I did not want to know the answer.

Maria blew out smoke and concentrated very hard on stubbing out her cigarette. "Died," she said. "Menin— meningitis." She blinked, looked up. "Ah, well, can't lay that at Perry Storr's door. But the missed years . . ."

"Christ," I said again, stupidly. Her pain and my inherited part in it half blinded me. "You should've told me, love."

"I try not to think about it. All gone." She smiled. The echo of a child's phrase hit her, and she looked quickly back at her cigarettes. "But . . . so . . . well, I meet another victim of that bastard's greed and vanity, I think, he's part of the club. Help if I can."

"Of course. Sure. And I'm grateful, Maria. But you can't keep me through the summer months, and we've come up against a dead end, and Chris has offered me a decent summer job — what am I meant to do?"

"Oh, God." Maria's voice was deep. "I don't know. Got nothing against Chris, just that he's a bloated bastard who makes money out of other people's misery."

"Oh, come on," I said. "And pleasure. They're not forced —"

She gave no sign of hearing me. "And he's a friend of that shit, but . . . I suppose you couldn't just go and live on the dole and take temporary jobs, take a job in a shop, work in the fields . . . ? No," she answered her own question sadly, "not you. Not with all Wildman must have offered. Easy street. Ah, well." She snapped out of it. "Fun while it lasted. I still think you ought to warn Rashid. He's a member of the club, too. Have to give it a go. Well, suppose that's it." She was gathering together her bits and pieces. "You pay the bill, Nick?" Her voice was light. She looked anywhere but at me.

"Sure, but —"

She stood. She stuffed cigarettes and lighter fiercely into her pockets. "Give us a call, hmm? See you." And she walked briskly away.

I sighed very deeply. I looked at the half-finished chocolate cake, which only minutes ago had been a childish treat. I said, "Oh, bugger it all!" and clicked my fingers for the waitress, who didn't like it.

Book Two

"NO, NICK," Deborah whimpered, and then, from somewhere in the vicinity of my left hand, another, deeper voice moaned, "Oh, God," and her lips again slithered across my cheek and engulfed mine, and my hand was suffered to slip once more into the center and source of the heat down there where I could feel her frantic pulse through the nylon.

And Redcliffe Square drifted by, and the lights of Earls Court Road, and the taxi driver hummed.

"Nooo!" She raised her head. I nuzzled her throat. "No, Nick, honestly." She pushed at me. "No."

She backed into the corner of the taxi and sat up straight. She flung back her hair. A few strands remained glued by saliva across her cheek. She plucked them away. Her voice shook. "Come on. Not now, Nick." My hand still stroked her thigh. She picked it up and placed it carefully on my own. "Down, boy," she said. "Look. I like you, I'm attracted to you, that's obvious enough, but I'm not just going to hop into bed with you straight off."

"No, okay." I swallowed down my heaving breath. "But God almighty, I want you every minute of the day."

"I know, I know." She touched my hand as though testing the temperature of an iron. "And I want you. Don't bulldoze me, that's all. Just wait, okay?"

I nodded, though God knows why.

"Okay?" she said again. "It won't be long, Nick. I'm as bad as you."

"God." I met her eyes, then my gaze wandered down to those now crossed legs and the darkness in between. "God, I hope so."

Life should have been so *sweet*. It was all being organized for me, after all, by a high priest of fun and games, a man who had made a fortune by anticipating and fulfilling fantasies.

The flat: there was a bedroom with a double bed like a gilded barge, a large, dark-green tiled bathroom full of diamantine bottles and potted plants, and a cork-lined listening room in which the only decorations were four huge speakers and a massive Francis Bacon of a naked figure crouched in blue grass on a dark-blue field. The carpets were the color of oatmeal, and the fireplace, in which dried flowers blazed, was of dun marble.

Here I started each day with a bath fragrant with Trumper's or Floris oil, dried myself with a towel like a cloud, and dressed in one of the two suits that had been bought for me against my future earnings. If I was bound for the office that day and Chris was in town, I could share a ride in his black Citroën DS. Otherwise I would take a taxi or drive the jeep to one of the countless businesses in which Wildfire had a share.

This was one of the things about Wildfire. I had run through the interminable list of the company's interests on the computer screen, and I'd marveled at the spread of its portfolio. It owned 100 percent of very little — only the Golden Grange in Shepherd's Bush, Rio's Club on the Fulham Road, the Renaissance in Johannesburg, the Silver Star in Sydney, a roller rink and disco in Swindon, a hotel/conference center near Sunningdale — and 10 or 20 percent of a vast range of concerns. Restaurants, hotels, casinos, discos, bookmakers, high-class strip joints, even musical shows had all benefited at one time or another from an injection of Wildfire cash, and were now owned in part by Chris. We — he — had also backed thirty would-be franchise owners in a worldwide Tex-Mex chain to the tune of 40 percent. Chris even owned his horses in partnership.

130

None ran or stood in his name, but his total share of the better end of the bloodstock market must, in all, have comprised sixty-three lovely legs or more. As often as not, Richard Heron was a co-owner both of horses and businesses, but here were plenty of other names as well, many of them better known than Chris's. Occasionally (as with a Chinese restaurant in Suffolk and a chain of four launderettes in and around Reading), I felt sure that Chris had not sought out his share but had accepted it in payment of a gambling debt.

My job, it seemed, was simply to visit some of these places and have a good time. I lunched and dined at the restaurants, gambled at the clubs, watched the strip shows and drank at the discos. I then wrote up reports: "Salade de foie de volailles posing as salade de foie gras," "Wiener Schnitzel pork not veal," "Leonie Lamont listless, plainly bored, out of keeping," or "Teacher's here sold as Glenmorangie." Chris was gratifyingly impressed — if, it seemed to me, somewhat ungratifyingly surprised — by my acumen. I was, in short, a sybaritic spy. It should have been fun, but it did not make up for the mornings that I spent groaning at the white face and tobacco-stained eyes in the mirror, with a mouth that felt like I'd eaten the fishery cat the night before.

My other role, I suppose, was that of surrogate son. I picked up visiting Arabs or Americans at the airport and guided them, to the changing of the Guard in the daytime, to brothels and Chris's casinos at night.

I was selling not me but the part of my father that existed in me. It seemed to be a salable commodity.

And Chris was — what? Affable, cheerful, frequently drunk, always approving, always dismissive of any problems.

It was on a night in early July that I saw Rashid and Moran.

I was visiting Rollers, one of the smaller and more select casinos, in upper rooms on Half Moon Street. Rollers was to old-fashioned, serious casinos what steakhouses are to restaurants. Everything was plush, unimaginative, predictable.

The serious gambler likes to see his opponents and the dealer's hand on the shoe. To him, the burble of dice and the smack and hiss of cards are music enough. Here the lights were low and a pianist tinkled and trilled "Satin Doll" and "L'Hymne à l'Amour" and "Corcovado" as though Ellington, Piaf, and Jobim had all sprung — nay, slithered — from the same sterilized test tube.

Unsurprisingly, such consoling comforts drew punters. The richer Hong Kong Chinese lost their money here. Television people, inexperienced and insecure young gents with their hearts and their bimbos on their sleeves, minor Arab billionaires and Ruhr valley nouveau Eurotrash — the Gstaad crowd, in short — forgathered here. They could eat well and eye the waitresses' fishnetted buttocks and play the tables, much as one may swim in the Mediterranean and imagine all the challenges of the real sea without ever having to face the true terrors relished by the big boys — the great rip, the great buzz, the great wave, the great white.

So I sat there at the bar, and a girl dressed as a French maid had just served me a champagne cocktail, a bowl of olives, a smile, and a bill (the smile must have cost six pounds) when I heard a moan like wind in a corrugated-iron shed.

I swiveled round. A crowd had gathered about a chemmy game at the far end of the room. "High rollers?" I asked the girl.

"Losing big," she said, nodding. "Still, they've got it to lose, haven't they?"

When a rider takes a big fall, the ghouls gather fast to goggle and to gasp, so it was with something of a feeling of guilt that I slid from the stool and wandered over to the table. Although Moran stood tall in the crowd, I did not recognize him at first because his head was bowed. He was looking down at Rashid where he sat at the table. Both men were in dinner jackets.

"What's happening?" I murmured to my neighbor, a smooth-looking, tall young man with terraced blond hair.

"The Ayrab. Won three in a row. Fifty grand. Passes the bank. Strolls away, but he doesn't want to. You could see. Bank's going begging. Only covered for twelve. He turns round, breaks free of his minder, says *banco prime*. Shit. Draws a five and a three, lovely, only it's *neuf à la banque*. Your man calls *banco suivi*. Same thing happens, only this time he gets two queens,

132

calls for a card, gets a seven. Bank turns up an ace and a seven. Man's got *suivi* mania."

Rashid looked calm enough, though a pulse beat at his temple. Moran, however, was pale. His teeth were gritted. His huge, freckled hand clasped the back of Rashid's chair as though to squeeze juice from the wood. I could see only the crown of the man who held the bank, but the hair was glossy brown and beautifully cut. Gold gleamed at the double cuffs, on the little finger of the left hand, and about the left wrist.

The croupier, a snooty-looking young man with a long, flat face, flicked the cards from the shoe. Two to Rashid, two to the middle of the table. Rashid studied his cards, laid them faceup on the baize. An ace and a deuce. He made an impatient little gesture to the croupier. The third card skidded toward him, the card on which £200,000 depended. The watchers groaned. Ten of spades.

The dealer flicked over the bank cards with his spatula. "*Huit à la banque,*" he announced smugly.

There was a moment's silence. Every eye was on Rashid now. Would he — could he — call *banco suivi* yet again, at a risk of £400,000?

Would he — could he — walk away? I did not envy him his Hobson's choice.

His only reaction was to clasp his hands before him and to straighten his fingers twice. He gave a little shrug. He looked defiantly up at Moran. Then he pushed back his chair. The crowd sighed.

Rashid stalked across the room to a table by the wall. He sat down hard. Moran followed. He perched opposite him, leaning forward on the edge of the seat like a jockey in a finish. He talked. He wasn't telling jokes.

I gave them five minutes. By then Rashid had leaned back sulkily in his chair and Moran was sipping Guinness and scanning the club. I stood.

He clocked me at once. He frowned quickly, then nodded. Rashid's gaze locked into his like a bomb sighter. He leaned on the table again, clasping his fingers.

I strolled toward them. Moran stood. His expression was

neither admonitory nor welcoming. He did not know whether I approached as a friend or a foe. If foe, he was ready for me.

"Mr. Rashid, Mr. Moran," I said.

"It's all right," Rashid told Moran's back. He caught my eye. "It is all right, isn't it, Nick?"

"Sure!" I laughed. "God, what is this? I just wondered — I mean, finding you here just by chance, I just thought — I wondered if I could have a quick word, that's all."

"Of course." Rashid gave me a little smile. "Please sit."

"So, Nick." Moran was effusive. "How're you doing, then? Looking pretty much the city slicker, eh?"

"Yeah. Well. Look, I don't want to disturb you —"

"No, no," they said in chorus.

"It's just . . . ," I said, and my words evaporated. I suddenly felt faintly absurd. We were a world away from the things that I wanted to talk about, the things that had seemed so urgent, so momentous back there in the mud and mist and rain. Only the echo of Maria's urgings forced me to persist. "Look, I was just wondering . . . You mustn't take this wrong. It's just — well, I still don't understand why what happened did happen, and" — I took a deep breath — "well, every time that Ibn Saud won, I rode him, and then I was sacked and he's lost twice. Okay, you've had outsiders run well, but your favorites have been getting stuffed, and I'll bet you've lost a lot of cash, and I was wondering, have you done anything, anything at all, that might make Dad want to hurt you? Because that's what I reckon he's doing for some reason. He knew I wouldn't hook a horse, so he got rid of me . . ."

Rashid was shaking his head, Moran frowning indulgently. I was gabbling, I knew, but it had to come out.

". . . and if I'm right, it could cost you millions in the long run. You think Dad's so marvelous, and, well, he is in some ways, but watch it, okay? And I'm not trying to get back at him or anything. It's just . . ." My voice trailed off. "Well, I had to warn you, that's all."

Rashid looked at me for a very long time. At length he put out a hand and laid it on my forearm. "I believe you are sincere,

Nick," he said softly, "but I think your father, too, is sincere. No father would do such a thing unless he had to. It must hurt him. This is why I think he is sincere. He is a gentleman, and he would not break his word. You, too, are a gentleman, but it is natural for a son to challenge his father. It is not *natural* for a father to challenge his son. That is why I believe both of you. But no, to answer your question, I know of no reason why your father would wish to hurt me. On the contrary, he has always been generous and considerate, is that not so, Frank?"

"Pretty much," Moran mumbled. He was taking shorthand notes on his napkin.

"Certainly we have had a run of bad luck. But then I have had a run of bad luck at the tables, too. Your father does not control the cards. These things happen. After all, I have had seven or eight years of good luck. And yes, maybe your father is mistaken about you, but he is my trainer, and I must trust his judgment, and I know his decision has made him suffer much. Still, thank you for your concern, Nick." And he held out his hand.

I took it and stood. "Well, just bear it in mind," I said sadly. "I've done what I can. See you, Mr. Moran. Sorry to bother you."

I returned to the bar. The reality of defeat slowly sank in. That, then, was that. This — the bar, the chatter, the gaming tables, the smell of cigar smoke, whisky, and Chanel, the practiced smiles of the girls in their winking fishnet stockings — this, then, was the future, not dung and piss and straw, cold mornings, broken limbs, and battles in the mud.

Looked at like that, it should have made me happy. Looked at like that, it failed to do so.

I ordered some spare ribs and made a fair crack at looking suave. Then I gave that up and slumped. I gazed down into the beaded gold in my glass.

Ex–steeplechase jockey. Man-about-town . . .

Was that what Dad had wanted? To ensure that I should not excel him in any regard? That I should never have an identity more substantial or more autonomous than that of a chip off

135

the old block? If so, it had not been difficult to arrange. I possessed much of his vanity, his snobbery, and his sybaritism. I was thus easily seduced by this, the world in which he had strutted for so long.

Ex–steeplechase jockey. Man-about-town. Trainer. A consoling replica of a man and a life . . .

"Nick." Moran gave a sort of extended grunt as he climbed onto the bar stool beside me. He slouched in order to appear smaller than he was. His hands were joined on the bar as though for prayer.

"Oh, hello." I was careless. Me? Care? I glanced over at Rashid's table. The Arab was no longer there.

"Listen," he said, and then he stopped to think. A long, low growl like a cello note oozed from him. "Rashid's off in the john. Quick word. What you were saying. I think you may just have a point. All that stuff about 'He is a gentleman,' eh? God, if he knew what we know about English feckin gentlemen. Fact is, I've been vexed about this whole business. Drink?"

"No," I said, because the outboard of hope was just chugging and choking again. No suppressors. Not yet, anyway. "No, I'm all right, thanks. Go on."

"Well, all very well for Rashid to say, 'A father wouldn't do that without good reason.' In my book, a father wouldn't do that period. Not the way your dad did. And you're right. Rashid's been losing all the way down the line. Fortunes. Fortune to you and me, at any rate. Sod's law, he hits a run of bad luck at the tables at the same time. Couldn't win a split with two twenties as things are. Jesus. Fact is, the betting's not the thing for these guys. All they want's to have the fastest horse, fastest saluki, best peregrine. Pure sportsmen, you might say. Must make life difficult for trainers, I can see that, have to try to live on your slice of the prize money without the punting." Moran shuffled his bulk forward on the bar stool, ham to ham. He addressed me over his shoulder like a cyclist. "I mean, I'd like to know how in hell your old man keeps up a place like Waylands, for Christ's sake? Jesus, must cost a packet. What? Fifty, sixty grand a year? Easy, and that's before you've so much as employed the boot boy." He shook his head. His hair, in need of a cut, swished along his cotton shirt collar. "Look, have you any . . . any evidence of what you were saying?"

"Nah," I said sadly, "just — it's the only explanation I can see, the only one that makes any sense of this whole upside-down business. All right. I hate to have to say this, I — I can't even understand it — but it's my belief that that horse was pulled in the Gold Cup."

"I am" — Moran spoke precisely — "inclined to agree, though I can't make nor head or tails of it, either, and maybe I'm just being paranoid. No. Okay. Look, keep an eye out, would you, Nick? Find out what you can, and keep me posted. The old feller may have money coming out of his ears, but it's my job to look after him — Jaysus, it's the Moor in Venice all over, isn't it? An innocent abroad . . . and I'll not see him ripped off. You need help any time, just let us know, okay?" He slapped my shoulder and glanced quickly over his.

"Okay." I nodded. "Sure. Glad to hear that someone's prepared to take me seriously."

"More than can be said for your dad, Nick, boy." Moran slapped my shoulder. "See?" He shrugged. "Maybe there *is* such a thing as progress, despite the available evidence. Come on. Cheer up. You'll be back, Nick. If you've got the balls for it, if you want it bad enough, you'll be back. You mark my words." He looked over his shoulder again. Rashid was studying the carpet as he returned to the table. "Ah, well." Moran grinned, a nice, boyish grin. He cocked his head toward the barmaid. "Could do worse than that to take you out of it. God, if I were in your shoes. Be in touch, huh, Nick?"

I nodded to an empty bar stool. The pianist trilled and shrilled "Help Me Make It through the Night."

Forget *Bolero,* accelerating like an overheated engine until the whole thing blows up and that's your lot. Strictly for Spanish jackrabbits, that. No, Brahms 4 was right, was good, on Chris's Bang and Olufsen quadrophonic, for which the flat had been bought. All that slow mounting stuff dissolving into shimmering haze, reforming, mounting again . . .

And she was sleek and warm as a puppy tucked in there

between my legs, all that glossy dark hair splashing over my lap and her fingers with their maroon talons so stiff that they curled upward on my thighs.

Sensation.

She was a luxury, Deborah. You came back and there she was, sprawled on the sofa flicking through a magazine, *Vogue* or porn, whichever. Or already in bed, iced Smirnoff Blue and lipstick-stained filter-tips on the table. "Here. Show you something. Something nice." No hassles, no anxiety, no "don't" or hiss of pain if you got it wrong, just limber limbs looping about you, and sweet slippery heat.

God, get home, pour a drink, switch on some music, run a bath, sink your muzzle into the oblivious darkness there, feel her bucking like a colt on your tongue. That first night, that crisp hair split my lip.

And now she moved up, sank onto me, breath plush in my ear, and she was riding hard, shuttling back and forth, squeaking encouragement to herself, not to me. "Yes . . . go . . . fuck it . . . harder . . ." When her mouth sought and hungrily pasted itself to mine, she was just seeking a mouth. She'd remember me afterward. She always did. For now it was just "Go, go . . . ," riding a winner right to the post.

And afterward, stock compliments, purrs, and moans, "God, that was good" and shivering "Mmmmah" and "Cuddle me," in a little voice.

I half sat, half lay there then, with her head on my shoulder. Her hair irritated my nostrils, and I wanted to be up and doing — something, anything, so long as it was clean and vigorous and constructive, anything aside from lying there, drinking another vodka, strolling down to yet another Thai or Italian restaurant and back here for more of this and restless sleep.

Jesus, suppose I said, "See, there's *Fedora* on BBCTwo tonight. Reckon I'll stay in." Then it was, "Ah, come on, Nick, I want to go out. You can tape it, can't you?" Whining like a musical saw. Or "Like to go to the Clapton concert?" and suddenly she was the Birmingham duchess: "God, all those smelly oiks in cheap jeans and Old Spice. Thanks a lot, but no thanks." She said "Yuck" when I suggested fish and chips, pointedly slouched and sighed through a Peter Curling exhibition, disdained sport and film, theater and pubs, but she was the cultural expert when it came to cosmetics, clothes, and restaurants.

But by six o'clock every evening, I was thinking of her again, dreaming of how it would be that night. I just had to see her, touch her, and the werewolf in me would take over once more.

God, and I was complaining?

I mean, that month I had everything that I could have wanted in terms of the *Playboy* life-style dreams of my adolescence, the dreams my father had passed on like some cigarette-card collection of supposed but untested value, and at first I hoarded each new experience with avidity and glee. Soon the dreams, when realized, seemed tawdry. The prized collection proved counterfeit.

It was a bit like the man who said you should never go back to Ireland because then you'd no longer have Ireland to go back to. I had my own flat in London. I had money. I had wheels. I had Deborah. It had looked so damned good in the shop window, but now that I had got it home, it seemed cheap and garish.

I was anesthetized, I suppose, all through June and the early days of July. There was always the memory of the night before, the prospect of the night ahead, to banish any thought that might batter at the gate. There was always music or whispered endearments, promises or lies, the roar of traffic or the rush of alcohol in my temples to drown out the still small voice of reason, the sweet, stern, stimulating whisper of anger.

But Moran's faith had started my awakening. The gods now completed the job by haphazard means.

Deborah was wriggling and stirring. She kissed me absently. Her right arm extended for a cigarette, shook off the packet. "Mmm," she said as she reached for the lighter and lit the cigarette over my shoulder. "Good." She exhaled.

She dismounted. A good sight, this. She sauntered over to the mantelpiece, where her drink stood. She flung back her hair with one hand. A great gesture, but heedless of the Gallé cameo-glass vase, one of my few remaining treasures. "Jesus!" I was up out of that chair and diving forward, all dignity long forgotten.

The vase was toppling forward. It tangled for a second in her hair, dragged sideways as she started, then broke free, a soft Vaseline glow in the flicker of the gas flames, plummeting now.

My right hand grabbed at it. My left stopped my headlong dive into the fireplace by hitting her stomach. She yelped. Vodka splashed on my arm, but I had the vase by its neck.

"Goddamm it, woman!" I panted. I straightened and cautiously replaced the vase. "That's about the last two grand I've got in the world. Be careful, would you?"

"Be careful, would you?" she mimicked. "Come on, Nick. What's two grand? Anyhow, it's a hideous thing. Where'd you pick up a thing like that?"

"I bought it," I snapped. "I won a race, went to an auction, bought it. I like it."

She shrugged. She sang, "Oh, well." She sauntered over to the director's chair where her black tights hung. She sat and slowly pulled them on. I turned away from her to pull on underpants and jeans together. Brahms had become a stately mockery. I turned it angrily down.

"Oh, by the way, darling." Debby's voice seemed very loud. "Someone rang. Ever so high and mighty: 'Just kindly inform Nick that I rang and would like to speak to him. As soon as possible.' Sounded like she thought she was the queen."

"What was her name?"

"Collins, or something. *Mrs.* — no Christian name. . . . No, Cullins, Cunningham . . ."

"Cullinan?"

"Assit."

I strode across the room to the desk, picked up the telephone, and tapped out the familiar number. Deborah was reaching behind her to fasten her black bra. The effort proved too much for her. She slumped back in the chair, sprawled, and smoked.

"Hello, Mum?"

Deborah covered her mouth. She gave a muffled giggle.

I walked toward the bedroom. "Hi. Gather you called."

"Yes, darling. I am sorry to bother you. Listen, is there any chance you could get down here for a couple of days? Give me

140

a hand? Guy's in hospital, and I have to visit, and there's no one to mind the shop, and . . ."

"Sure, sure. I'll come right now." The anxiety in my mother's voice would, I think, have been audible to no one else, save perhaps Guy. But the faintest tremor, that rabbit-thump on the emotional seismograph, told me that things must be badly wrong. I reached for a shirt from a hanger.

"What's up with Guy?"

"Stroke, I'm afraid."

"Oh, bugger. Bad?"

"Not good, darling."

"So what time are the trains?" I looked at my watch. Twenty past six.

"This evening?"

"Yes, this evening."

"Nick . . ." from behind me in the doorway.

"There's a seven nineteen or a nine nineteen."

"I'll try to make the first one. Call you from the train . . ."

"Nick!"

". . . or the station if I miss it. See you."

I pressed CLEAR. The phone squeaked. "Right," I told Deborah, "I've got to get down to Somerset. You throw a few shirts and a toothbrush in a bag for us?"

"Hey, come on. Who the fuck do you think I am?"

"My assistant, I thought." I fastened a cufflink. I reached into the wardrobe for a grip and flung it on the bed. "So assist me."

"Silly sod," said my mother, sitting on the edge of a chintz armchair, in jeans and a cream silk shirt that sagged on her narrow frame. "Didn't like to tell me. Grossly underinsured. Wouldn't have paid for a new dog kennel, let alone a yard. As if it mattered, but what with the dogs and Trafalgar — he *loved* that horse — and he's only got his pension — I mean, no one's seen a dividend this year — well, you can see. We haven't even been able to clean up, still less replace anything. God, gloom and doom and I hadn't a clue why. Anyway, suddenly — I mean it probably . . . maybe it isn't connected, but he's just been so

141

disconsolate since the fire, and then I come down and there he is at his desk. Beastly. I thought he was a goner at first, but he sort of moaned at me, and . . ."

"What's the prognosis?"

"Not brilliant." Her hands trembled until they were wrapped around a mug of tea. "Pretty bloody, matter of fact. All to do with hemispheres, left-hand side, right-hand side. . . . His speech will be affected, though how badly . . ." She shrugged. "And a degree of paralysis is all they'd say. Oh, sod it. Poor Guy."

"Poor you."

"Oh, I'll be fine." She looked up with a weary smile. "No, I mean, if I can keep you just for a couple of days. I am sorry, I know it's a bore, but —"

"Don't worry, Mum. Honest."

"No, but just till — who was that girl on the telephone? — oh, never mind. No, I've got Angus to advance some cash on a couple of pictures that he'll sell for me. Sorry, darling. Bit less patrimony or matrimony for you. The Pryde and the Orpen, I'm afraid . . ."

I nodded. I had already seen the blank patches in the hall and in the corner here.

"So there's a nurse coming down — probably a ghastly battle-ax, but they say she's good. She's coming down on Monday and can get things organized. It's just after that beastly fire — incredible how these things knock the stuffing out of you, you know — I don't like to leave the place empty and —"

"No worry." I fetched the whisky bottle from the half-moon table. "Here. Shot in that tea'll do you good. You can relax now. Take it easy."

She looked up at me. She blinked once. I bent and kissed her.

"I'll stay as long as you need me, see the battle-ax settled in. Have a go at cleaning up that mess out there. God," I thought out loud, "if people ever saw the consequences . . . you start a chain reaction and . . . shit, Perry Storr strikes again."

And out in the yard, where I wrestled with black and sodden laths and rafters and made cairns of lime-washed plaster, I wondered, had my father really brought about this last blow to such a modest, middle-class life?

The yard had been a luxury, like the occasional bottle of port, proudly proffered and carefully recorked, like the occasional day at the races or out shooting with which my mother and Guy marked out the passage of the days. Dogs and horses, beloved friends and mementos of good and grander times, had simply been destroyed, and with them so much of happiness and innocence, by a man with power, a man with a firebrand, a man to whom they were "only" dogs and horses, a means to his ends. Guy had seen his little luxury destroyed and, worse, irretrievably polluted. And he had given up.

Was that my father's work? Absurdly, and knowing well that it was absurd, I was driven by guilt as much as by pity to get this job done. Some almost biblical hangover told me that I was somehow responsible for the sins of my blood. So when the hail came, I worked on, when my hands bled, I worked on, and when at last I returned to London on the Monday evening, I quietly asked a sullen, incredulous Deborah to leave, please. I wanted some time on my own.

It was surely by chance that on that evening I picked from Chris's library a copy of *Weir of Hermiston,* and the "Introductory" caught me by the throat, as it must catch anyone who knows English from Serbo-Croat, and I read:

> He lay and moaned in the Hunter's Bog, and the heavens were dark about him and the grass of the field an offence. "This is my father" he said. "I draw my life from him; the flesh of my bones is his, the bread I am fed on the wages of these horrors. . . ."

It was surely chance, too, that led me the following night to an NFT showing of *Invasion of the Body Snatchers.* Not even my type of movie, though I admired the sparseness and economy with which its paranoid terrors were induced — or evoked. And I found myself that night, tired and sated, a susceptible convert to the idea of bodies' being taken over by other, soulless souls. It was happening to me.

For once, the conviction of an evening survived a night.

The fallow period was done. Slowly, self-mockingly, I started once more to ask questions. To which, God save me, I already had the answers.

"Do you mind *terribly?* This bit always takes me a minute or two, but you see, it is *so* important to get every one." Andrew Linton stepped into the road to touch a grid with his left foot, then back up onto the pavement to touch each of the eight or nine patches of iron in the stones. "Compulsive neurosis, they call it. It can take me a frightfully long time to get from one end of a street to the other, but you *see,* I just know if I miss one, something *too* ghastly's going to happen, and" — he took the last step in an intricate dance — "we *can't* risk that, can we? People just don't *understand*. They tell me to go home and sleep it off. I've had my foot run over twice, but it's quite necessary. I take *taxis* everywhere. *Fearfully* expensive, but it *does* save me this duty. Now. Yes. Oh, dear, you really are asking me to *rack* my poor overwrought brain. Let's sit down. I cannot think perpendicular. I think best in the *bath,* but I don't think you'd be eager to join me there, so this will have to do. There." He hopped up onto a bench by the Old Brompton Road, extended his little legs along its seat, and crossed his hands in his lap. "Room for you at the end?" He blinked. "Good. Cozy."

He was a plump little man who looked as though someone had scrubbed him, buffed him, and dipped him in oil. His cheeks were pink, his eyes were bright, and his hands flickered with his every exuberant phrase.

He was a painter of surprisingly bold, even aggressive landscapes. I had seen them back in his studio in Roland Gardens. He had proposed a "breath of fetid air." He spoke like a granny's letter.

He had been at Chelsea Art School in 1964.

"So," he said smugly, "of course one *remembers* La Gascoigne, though no longer in *intimate* detail. By the way, how on earth does a nice boy like you get to *know* that silly old stick Lady Edward Bayer BF, RA?"

"He knows my mother," I shouted above the shuddering roar of a passing bus. "He painted me as a child."

"Oh, he would. He knows everyone's mother, old Teddy Bayer. *Ghastly* dauber. Society portraits, but my dear, what a society! Who on earth wants to paint beastly bloated burghers and their doxies? Oh, dear. No. Yes. Alison Gascoigne. What the DJs call a Blast from the Past. I mean, one *was* aware of her. Pretty little thing. Pots of money. Liked to go slumming. Never much *good* technically. Always coming to me for help with her etching, but talent, I think. Quite a lot actually for a little rich bitch. And really *quite* jolly. Went in for witticisms a little much. Seriously, you know, ponderously, like Dorothy Parker. One feels that a witticism should be a quick-flash of silver in the water. It bites and is lost. She favored them mounted and cased and *imposing*. You know the sort of thing.

"Nowadays, of course, everyone would sing her praises for being a good little liberal, but in those days it was too *risqué* to consort with our swarthier brethren like little Alison did. Except for buggers. They did, but of course they could do anything because they were *outlaws* anyhow. I don't think she'd have *screwed* them, do you? Mind, one can't be *sure,* but we didn't do much of that sort of thing then. Well, she obviously screwed *someone,* anyhow, of whatever hue and tone. The poor little bastard came out white. At least, I *assume* so. Nobody ever *told* me that it was dusky. On the other hand, I don't know that anyone ever actually *saw* the little mite."

"There was a bastard, then?"

"Oh, yes, my dear. Either that or the most *ghastly* colic. *Huge,* she was, all fecund and flowering and *quite* brazen about it. I think she went back to Mummy Gascoigne's seat to *have* the little brute. Anyhow, she vanished for a while. There'd been a tiff with Mummy Gascoigne, who, as I recall, was a very odd old bat. Ali had been all rebellious and so on. We all were, you know. They must have made it up when the bairn was on its way. Anyhow, yes, she was away for six months or so — winter and spring of 'sixty-three–'sixty-four, that would be — and then she was *back,* bouncy as ever, living just down the road in Onslow Gardens with the infant. Started painting things that looked *suspiciously* like nappies. Went all abstract expressionist on us, poor dear. Anyhow, *next* thing we knew, she was dead as a dodo. Great pity. The art world lost a most *promising* hausfrau.

"About her *death,* well, one doesn't *know,* but there was a lot of talk. A *lot* of it. I mean, *really,* my dear, what on *earth* would she have been doing in some *insalubrious* little alley *on the wrong side of the river?* I mean, she *wouldn't,* would she? Even if she *wanted* a quick dog-rig with one of her pet jungle bunnies, which is unlikely if she was as inebriated as they say, why on earth down there in *Balham* or whatever dreadful social-realism borough it was? *No one* went south of the river for *anything* in those days. Except to go to hospital. No, no. We all reckoned she had died somewhere *fearfully* embarrassing and was transported there and, well, *dumped.*"

I nodded. The thought had crossed my mind as well. "So if *you* could work it out," I said softly, "why didn't the police?"

"Oh, they *would* have done, my dear. Come along," he said, swinging his legs from the bench, "I feel ready to face the next hundred yards." He pulled the dark-blue gabardine tighter about him and lowered his head as though the damp breeze were a gale. "They would have done, of course. Even Mr. Plod can work out the very basics if given sufficient time. But you're out of period. You don't understand how things were. *No one* was going to listen to *students* in those days. We were a negligible joke. It was another four years before we had a voice, and another ten before anyone *listened.* No, it was a little like college servants, you know? Turn a blind eye to Mr. Pratt-Smyth's indiscretion *provided* that he doesn't embarrass us by being too obvious. What harm does it do? The girl's *dead,* after all, and we can't do much about *that,* and there's obviously no crime per *se,* so why kick up a hullabaloo? I mean, the people involved were basically nice chaps, paid their taxes, donated to police balls. They didn't make a *habit* of this sort of thing. And the press in those days were an obedient lot. Investigative journalism meant curates and choirboys, not our noble rulers. Must say, there's a lot to be said for a system like that. Civilized. Sensible. Only *trouble* is, the common man can't see why the Pratt-Smyths should be allowed to get away with it while he isn't. You and I know why, but he has a horribly insistent, if inaccurate, conviction that he's as good as the next man. So there you are. One can't even kill one's cook these days. Whoops." He scuttled out into the middle of the road in order to step on a manhole cover. He scuttled back again, pursued by the wail of a Jaguar's horn. "Phew!" he panted. "Nearly missed that one."

"Car bloody nearly hit you," I pointed out.

"Oh, yes. Mine is a perilous duty. The police don't understand that, either, *always* telling me not to tread on metal bits. I give them rather a *good* lecture about freedom of religion, and they don't seem to like it. This world is not fit for heroes." He shook his little head sadly.

"Did Alison drink a lot?" I resumed.

"Mmm?" Andrew was dragged back from his musings on his high and lonely destiny. "No, not so far as I know. I mean, she went to *parties,* but she wasn't a louche lush or anything. Normal, really."

"Drugs?"

"Hoo! We should have been so lucky! Though I don't *know* . . . maybe Ali, because of her *associations* with the coloreds. They had some nasty potions down in their jazz clubs, of course. But a *stick of pot* was rare in those days. You barely saw it. Damn it, I mean, *rationing* had only just ended. No, no. The *press* made much of the decadent, drunken life she had led, but that was all so much gibberish. She was just a normal, healthy girl full of silly opinions and ideas and so on. Be a pillar of the church in *Haslemere* by now if she'd lived. No. A feminist photographer in Islington, that's it. Now, let us dive into this pub and into a pint."

A spray of horns on "Hey, Big Spender" projected me up the steps from the basement club in Dean Street. The door swung shut behind me, and the brass became paper and comb, the frenzied drumming as muffled and regular as the churning of a washing machine. I turned toward Shaftesbury Avenue.

"Well, Nick Storr." A slow frog's croak behind me. "Peddling smut, are we? Or buying?"

I did not recognize the voice. I swung around but made no

147

move toward the speaker. It was only early evening, but he or she stood in the deep shadow of a doorway. I could see only the lower half of a slim pair of legs in pale jeans. The fabric at the left knee was frayed to reveal bare skin.

"Who's that?" I murmured.

There was a low laugh. "Aha. A ghost. A spirit from the distant past." She — for it was a she — made a childish ghost noise. She stepped forward onto the pavement.

She was very pale and painfully thin, though her cheeks were still chubby enough to make her eyes seem narrow. Those eyes were lusterless. They absorbed rather than spat back light. She wore an old tweed jacket over a cheesecloth shirt. Her shoulders were hunched, her hands pushed deep into her jacket pockets. Her hair was lank and wet-beach blond. It was cut short but styled long, as though Rapunzel had suddenly turned gay and reached for the kitchen scissors.

"Come to haunt you in your evildoing." She half smiled, half sneered. "Miss Marley, clanking chains. Remember me?"

"Er —"

"No, 'course you don't. Never one of us, were you?" She walked around me like a prospective buyer. "Paid-up member of the Society of Exploitative Arseholes, you. Daddy put us down at birth, right? Fancy suit. Like it. Striped tie, like I'm not a member of a regiment or a club but I can pretend, can't I? Proper little Thatcherite hero, you. Got some money?"

"Some." I frowned.

"Want to buy us a drink?"

"Now hold up." I laughed. "I mean, okay, so you know my name, but who are you? I know the face, but . . ."

"It's all right, Nick." She soothed me as she might a dying dog. "It's all right. You don't know the face. Resemblance to another face, perhaps?"

"Resemblance . . ." Then it hit me. I took a step backward and found that the pavement had run out. "God." I recovered my balance. "Louise!" She said nothing, just watched me sardonically until doubts crept in. "Louise?"

"That's right, Nick. Your sainted master's disgraceful daughter. So, are you going to buy this pariah a drink, or what?"

"I . . . sure." I nodded like an idiot. "Yup. Right . . ."

"It's all right. Come on."

She led me down the street, over the spangled strip of Shaftesbury Avenue, and into a shorter, darker little street. There was a pub at our left, but she led me past it, past a porno cinema and a closed-down barber's shop, past a Chinese restaurant with glazed orange ducks hanging in the window. She walked briskly and with a swagger in her step, yet her muscles seemed curiously flaccid, and her shoulders drooped like those of a drunk. She kept her head down.

She swung so swiftly to her left that I damn near walked right into her. We were on a sparsely carpeted staircase then, between a newsagent's and a Chinese souvenir shop. We were halfway up the second flight when I heard someone else coming in through the door, someone else climbing the staircase behind me at a run. Suddenly I was scared.

Louise opened a door on the landing just as our pursuer caught up with us and I pressed myself against the wall. He was a Hamlet, tall and thin, with honey-colored hair flopping over a long, angular face. He did not look up at us, just mumbled "Hi" and brushed past me into the room.

It was a sitting room of sorts. A thick gray veil of smoke floated above assorted sofas and armchairs and scuffed Bokharas on bare white boards. Miles Davis was working out his neuroses in free association on an incongruously expensive-looking stereo. There were six or seven people in here. None, save for two girls squatting beneath the window, was talking. Two or three people were arguing in a kitchen visible through a door in the corner.

"Hi, Lou," a young man with a bloated face and an autocratic voice greeted Louise from the sofa. He laid a Márquez paperback facedown on his knee and then frowned down at it as though wondering what it was doing there, changed his mind, and resumed his reading.

"Joe here?" Louise scanned the room.

"Through there." A tiny blond girl in a sweatband and a voluminous T-shirt nodded toward a closed door. "Hey, you carrying?"

"Not yet," Louise droned. "Hasn't William . . . ?" She looked at the Márquez reader.

"Uh-uh." The girl in the sweatband looked sad. "You know him. Gets a hit, and the rest of the world can go fuck itself. Shit. Clive due round?"

"Said so. Christ knows when." Louise turned to me. She was curt. "Come on."

A man in a striped shirt and pin-striped trousers and a girl dressed as a tart lay listlessly entwined in our path. Louise stepped over them. She pushed the door open.

We were in a little bedroom. Here too the smoke was thick. Louise's head displaced smoke as she moved. It cast a shadow on the air. A woman lay asleep on a bed that ran along the right-hand wall. She wore fishnets on her chubby legs, a leather mini-skirt that had ridden up above her crotch, and a black angora tank top that revealed a lot of blancmange cleavage. Her black hair was lifeless. It looked like coagulated juice seeping from her skull. The tall man who had pursued us up the stairs sat by her head. The snuff handkerchief was already tied tight about his left arm. The needle was just sliding in.

He looked up as we entered, and his smile was beatific. I knew him. His father was a big flat-horse owner. Our fathers had been to school together; our families had shared a lodge in Scotland for the stalking for six or seven seasons, and he had been with me when I killed my first stag. He now drove Formula Ford race cars.

Louise strode over to where a dark, bearded man sat on the floor watching a Mad Max video. "Joe. Scotch, please. We got money."

Joe flicked off the video. He clambered to his feet. "Shit," he said, and then, "Okay, sure. So where's the bread?"

"Nick?" Louise held out a hand.

"Right. How much?"

"Twelve." Joe wiped his hands on his buttocks.

"Stiff."

"Fine." Joe turned away. He switched on the television again. "Shit. You go out there, see if you can do any better."

"Nick . . ."

"No, look, I'm sorry." I pulled out a twenty. "Look, that's fine. Twelve's fine."

Joe snatched the note from my hand and slouched to the door.

"Jesus!" Louise's voice, when unaffected, was unbroken and girlish. "You have to argue every penny? Shit. I mean, know how much Joe'll be screwing them for down Great Windmill Street for that bottle later tonight?" she was saying. "Say four, five in the morning? It's his job. Sells booze out of hours at the top of Great Windmill Street. Sixty quid a bottle, he can get late enough."

"Dear God," I muttered. "Life expectancy is not exactly high in that business, I'd think."

"Fuck life expectancy." Louise had turned to watch the jacked-up Formula Ford, by now curling contentedly up with the chubby sleeping girl. "You can keep expectancy. At least we have life."

"Oh, leave it out, Louise." I sighed. "This is tedious stuff."

"'Oh, leave it out, Louise,'" she mimicked. "'This is tedious stuff.' Christ, what an ass."

Joe shambled back in with a bottle of Red Label. I held out my hand. He gave the bottle to Louise. She said, "Thank you," like a well-mannered child.

Joe touched her shoulder and once more sank to the floor. He flicked on Mad Max again and was at once lost in it.

The acquisition of the bottle was, it seemed, the cue for a party. People came in and with "Hey!" and "Thanks, Lou," held out their mugs or their cheap glasses and drifted away again. I managed to take one swig from the bottle. Louise drew on it constantly. After ten minutes of standing there feeling lost, I said, "I've got to be going, Louise. Sorry."

"No," she yapped, then softly said, "No, don't go, Nick. I want to talk to you."

"Yeah, well. Can hardly talk here."

"No, come on. Christ!" She slammed down the bottle and threw herself into a red vinyl armchair. "I want to talk to you,

151

okay? Fuck it, who d'you think you are? My daddy's little gofer, hey? Oh, well done, Nick. Height of your ambitions. And you only, what? Same age as me, right? Twenty-eight?"

"Twenty-six."

"Oh, well done, well fucking done."

"Right, then. See you, Louise."

"No!" She gulped. "No, please, Nick." She had reached up and grasped my arm in panic. Her eyes were positively puppy-like in their plaintiveness. "Please. Seriously."

"For God's sake, what's the point?" I was irritated. I squatted at her feet. "What is there to talk about, anyhow? This scene — okay, you've chosen it for yourself. I think that's a pity, but what's it got to do with me? Just let it go, will you? Your dad works, what? Just a quarter of a mile down the road. You want to make contact —"

"Sure, I've seen him. I've stood just ten yards away as you and he arrived at that high-rise mortuary, and you think he saw me? Shit, Christopher Wildman sees nothing he doesn't want to see. First time I ever got busted, I was in New York, and so was he. So I use my statutory telephone call, right? Ring the bastard. Get his secretary. Great. I say, okay, I'm in stir, come and bail me out. Know what? He had a dinner engagement that night, so he couldn't make it. Twenty-four hours later, he's flown back to London, one of Richard fucking Heron's young executives turns up and pays the ante. Thanks a fucking ton, Dad." She dragged a hand absentmindedly through her hair. "Mind, he had time to make sure the newspapers didn't touch it. Oh, sure, spent half the night doing that, but couldn't get down to the cells. Sure, like you say, he's just down the road. He wanted to contact me, he'd just have to dispatch one of his minions. I tried to go straight, clean up my act last year, right? Eventually plucked up the courage, gave him a call. Terribly sorry, he is rather busy, perhaps next month. I said 'And fuck you, too.' I mean, it's not as if I ever had a row with him, anything like that. I was a nice little girl till I started chasing the dragon."

"How old?" I asked.

"Nineteen, twenty, and even then I didn't rip him off or anything like that. If I was hurting anyone, I was hurting me, right? But no, I was letting him down, endangering his reputation. Know the worst? One day, I've been going to meetings for six months or so, this guy gets up to do a share, right? And he confesses, terribly sorry but I have been breaching the secrecy and anonymity of this group, right? I've been accepting money to report back everything Louise Wildman says or does here. Jesus, I mean, can you imagine? I've been sharing with these guys, spilling out my guts about all the things I did when I wasn't sober, really revolting stuff, and this guy's been writing it all down and passing it to my father, for fuck's sake."

"You're sure it was your dad?"

"Oh, sure, the FBI would really want to know who I screwed when I was out of my head, right?" She threw back a spray of hair. "No, the guy said it was a man he met in a pub. Never knew his name, but of course it was my father. I know how he works. Knowledge is power, right? His motto. Has files on everyone, *everyone,* so he can put pressure on them. You know that chest in his drawing room at home, the Wellington? You look in there. I did once when it was left open. Jesus, it's a fucking porno collection, only the actors didn't know they were being shot. Your dad's even in there — apparently he was responsible for some poor girl's death way back when." Something squirmed very swiftly up my backbone. She went bitterly on. "Accident, but he got away with it. I'm in there, too, and I should think you've got a file by now."

I stood. "Look, okay, so you've had a bad time at the man's hands." I tried to be firm, but my voice trembled. I swallowed. "But he's been good to me, okay? I don't know what you want, what you think I can do . . ."

"Nothing." She shrugged and sneered, then changed her mind. Her expression softened. "It's just — I always liked you, Nick, felt sorry for you, and then I saw you —"

"You want money."

"No! Well, yeah, sure, I need cash. Sure. Why not? Who doesn't?" She was fierce again. "Shit, you sell yourself, don't you? Okay, so I see a guy I know, sure I say, 'Can you help?'"

"You hustle?"

"Fuck off."

"No, I just mean, how bad's the need? I mean . . ."

She stood and barged past me. "You don't know anything, do you?"

"Probably not," I admitted.

"Shit, you're a bore."

And she walked off with my whisky bottle, topping up glasses and, like a nurse, touching everyone, here speaking a few words and laughing, here stroking and soothing a somnolent figure, here touching a knee and sharing a silent smile. I walked over to her, tapped her shoulder, and, as she straightened, pushed a fifty-pound note into her back pocket. "See you," I said, nodding.

"Yeah." She smiled. Her childish voice followed me to the door. "See you, Nick. Thanks, okay?"

I wandered like the Ancient Mariner, seabird pendant and all, looking and barely seeing. I wandered about Soho, everywhere opportuned by garish posters for sex films and topless basement bars, scents of salami and garlic from the delicatessens, and bored girls who called to me from street corners. Most appetites were catered to in these parts, but not the fierce, undefined hunger that I had in me now.

I dodged through Rupert Street market. I tossed coins to a giant reddish trout-fly that sprawled in a doorway loving a bottle of British sherry. I stepped over the legs of an apparently dead junkie who lay flat on his face in Archer Street. Well-tailored trousers and polished brogues climbed rickety stairs, lured by a pink light on a doorbell. A clockmaker, loupe to eye, talked to some minute mechanism through pursed lips as one might coax a kitten, while, next door, a chubby leg beckoned from the shadows. All around, slogans leapt out at me like angry dogs bounding off wire netting, yapping Three In A Bed! Live Sex Act! They Are Naked And They Dance! Aphrodite, Goddess of Love . . .

What?

And so over Eros's island into Piccadilly and its great gaunt gray palaces. Great-aunts of buildings, these emporia and hotels, yet even these discreetly indicated that if you behaved yourself nicely and had a suitably upholstered wallet, even you might enter their warm and fragrant nethers.

I sidestepped clumps of gawping Japanese and gabbling Italians and raced my shadow past Fortnum's, the Royal Academy, and the Ritz, and continued down to Green Park, littered with lovers.

I had not shaken off my shadow.

Shepherd Market lay to my right. Only now did I realize that I had been heading there all along.

I crossed Piccadilly and strode up White Horse Street, still feeling that something was pulling or pushing me. The ghosts of past revelers, in knee-length silk skirts or dark suits and regimental ties, jostled me. Their heels clicked or clattered. The men barked. The women giggled like rivulets. Their feet and their voices said that they were secure. This was their patch, their territory.

They lied, of course, those steel-capped soles. Their wearers were just playing "Rule Britannia" very loud within the Pale.

It was not my father's immorality that dismayed me. It was the squalid, mean nature of his crimes, the transparent vanity of his pretensions, the high, smug moralism of his manner.

Alison Gascoigne, too, watched from the shadows with an archaic smile. It had been an accidental death. Misadventure, the papers said. There had been no question, no speculation as to crime. No. What worried me was that Alison Gascoigne had not been a stranger, that Dad had, however indirectly, been involved in her death and would have been immediately aware of it. Had he then started a campaign to wrest Waylands from a grief-stricken, reclusive old woman? Was that the nature of my inheritance?

And where in hell was this grandchild?

If Andrew was right, the boy would have been two and a half, a little bastard without protectors, when his grandmother died. He was almost exactly my contemporary. So who had tended him in the two years between his mother's death and his grandmother's? Had his father — whoever he was — taken him in? If so, the boy would have taken his unknown father's name and would by now be untraceable. And was it possible that old Mrs. Gascoigne could have fallen so completely beneath the spell of Captain Perry Storr and his pet solicitor Chris Wildman as wholly to disinherit her own infant, orphan grandchild?

Sod it, the questions kept flooding in.

And preeminent among them was this: what the hell had the death of a nineteen-year-old unmarried mother back in the year of my birth to do with my father's attempt to destroy me?

I did not know the answers. I did not want to know them. But I knew that I must either seek them or rely on whisky and pills for sleep for the rest of my days.

Chris had been an effective Mephistopheles; I could see the option that he offered clearly enough. Why should I not take over Wildfire? Who else was to do so? In time, I, already the master of Waylands, might have thousands, not just tens, loving me for the magic that, with a wave of a pen above a checkbook, I could do. I, like Chris, could be a fairy godfather. But my mother — and to some extent also my father, slavishly aping her lady's ways and lady's words — had not versed me in this role. I could claim no moral merit in my drive to uncover the sins of my father. It was a self-interested, reluctant resolve. I could not live with the facts as nightmares, but I just might be able to cope with the nightmares as facts.

The Market was no longer a market, just a colorful little village of shops and pubs and cafés with pavement tables. A stunning black girl with legs that turned my mind at once to higher things greeted me as I entered Shepherd Street. "Hi. You want a good time?" she asked.

"Now there's a lovely old line. Yeah, I want a good time, but not that sort. Not just now. Hey, you must be sweltering."

She looked down at her body. I wished that I had something like that to look down at. She wore a short pink leather jacket, a gray T-shirt, and a short brown leather skirt. "Nah, 's all right." She smiled slyly. "Not much of it, is there?"

"True. Generous of you."

"That's me all over. You sure you don't want a bit of fun?"

"I told you: sure I want some fun, love, but not the bouncing and squelching variety. Look. Tell you what. You want, say" —

I glanced at my diminishing wad of money — "you want a thirty? Okay, so maybe some punter picks you up in the meantime, forget it. I want to know, where was Lucy's Club back in the sixties? Right? It was somewhere in the Market, I know."

"Come on," she trilled.

I shrugged. "Worth thirty quid."

"Okay, okay, I'll find it. Me a private detective. Great. Lucy's, right? What was it? Cathouse?"

"No. Casino. I'll be over there." I pointed to an empty gingham-covered table.

My new friend teetered away. I sat at the table and ordered espresso and a glass of milk. They still hadn't arrived when she returned with an I-don't-care slouch. "I sit down?"

"Sure." I stood. I pushed a plastic chair out for her. She folded herself into it. "So, God, this is easy money," she said. "Wish there were more like you. Right. That were Lucy's." She pointed at a four-story redbrick Georgian house immediately opposite.

"Sure?"

"Yup. First and second floors where they played, 'parently. Top floor sort of offices, manager's room, all that. Real posh, they say. Gone downhill, eh?"

"Seems so. What is it now?"

"Rooms."

"Rooms?"

"Yeah, for the girls. Netta, Orla, Sandra . . ."

"Who owns it, you know?"

"Nah. Some company or other owned by some company or other owned by the Church of England or something. That's the usual way. Guys actually own it are too far away to get a sniff of it. Just get the rent. Built a disco in the basement before it closed, sometime in the early seventies. Flopped. Well, it's not the place for that sort of thing, is it?"

"No," I agreed, with an acute sense that I hadn't a clue as to why. "Right. Thanks, love." I fished money from my back pocket. I had no tenners, so I handed her two twenties. She shoved them into a pocket in her jacket.

"Ta," she said, grinning. I saw the white purse of her knickers as she unfolded. "Never made forty quid in five minutes standing up. Have a wish." She waved with waggling fingers. "God. Bouncing and squelching. That's really revolting."

"Thanks," I said. She paraded away.

NANETTE, said one. MICHELLE another. The top bell told of a somewhat more self-effacing FRENCH MODEL. I glanced over my shoulder because that's what you do in those circumstances. I ducked in like a vole into his hole.

There must have been a hall here where people checked their coats, a desk where someone sat to check your bona fides. Not now. The rooms on either side of the door had been blocked off, and a narrow pine staircase put in.

I climbed up slowly. There was a barely open door to the right of the landing. I knocked and pushed. It was very quiet in here. Hard to believe I was at the heart of one of the world's great cities. The door moaned.

A little old lady with a wig of red-squirrel fur and a face like a punched pillow sat knitting something purple by a table. "That's it. Come on in, dear. She's busy at the moment, but just you come in and have a nice cup of tea, eh?"

I faintly smiled. I wandered in. The woman busied herself with a kettle and a teabag that looked as though it had been worn next to her skin for a few weeks. She rustled with every last movement.

There was a television on the table. Roadrunner was taking a hairpin bend above a towering precipice.

"Nice day, isn't it?" The woman rustled back to her chair. She sank into it, and her body made a sound like a sigh. She had thick legs riddled with black veins.

"Lovely."

I looked about the room. The utility armchairs, the squat square table, and the little electric stove made it seem small, but there were good moldings at the cornices and about the bare light that hung from the center of the ceiling, and an incongruously big sash window looked down on Trebeck Street. Imagine it thickly carpeted and furnished with delicate gilt chairs. Guess, then. This might have been where the poker games were played. Probably the bar was in the corner — or did they merely help themselves from a sideboard? The walls were now papered in the color of wet sand, but the paper had peeled back to make a map of Sierra Leone by the outlet for the stove. The map was in some fabric of a deep kingfisher blue.

"Been here long?" I sat at the table. I picked up the steaming mug in a companionable sort of way. I did not drink.

"Who? Oh, Michelle. No, she's new, from France. Lovely girl."

"No. You."

"Me?" She touched her nose as if to define the pronoun for herself. "Oh, me. No. Well, three years."

"Know anything about the building?"

"Building?" She frowned as though I had spoken an obscenity. "Building? Here, you been drinking?"

There was a click behind me on the landing. I heard a man's heavy, slow, scuffling footfalls, his heavy, slow, puffing breaths. A voice like a parrot's called, "Bye, then, love."

"She'll be tidying up. Just be a mo," the old woman croaked. Roadrunner went "Beep-beep."

I stood and left the room. I pushed open the door opposite. Michelle, New, Lovely, from France, was smoothing the bed. She held a ball of tissue paper in her left hand. She looked up — thin, blond, forty. She said, "'Ere, 'old on."

The room smelled of Youth Dew and dental hygiene. It was perhaps twice the size of its neighbor. There were the same moldings and the same big window, though here there were two of them, and they were dimmed with blinds. The walls were orange. A mirror ran the length of a bed deeply littered with cushions. The soft light made it easy to imagine how the room must have been once, filled with people, rattling and buzzing.

Michelle threw the tissue paper in the wastebasket. Her glossy rose dressing gown could have been a hostess's ballgown, the way it shimmered as she came toward me. "You're impatient, aren't you?" she said with the briskness of a matron. "Well, seein' as you're 'ere, it's twenty-five, and a fiver for the maid."

159

She came very close to me. She reached past me to push the door shut. I checked her hand. It felt like warm chips in oily paper.

"No," I said simply. "Sorry. Here. Changed my mind. Fiver for your trouble. See you."

I backed out. I ran up the stairs two at a time. The next floor was laid out like the one below. I did not bother to stop. Swung round the banister rail. Ran on up, drawn by an urgent and ghostly siren song.

And here on the top floor, things were different. I was in a dark corridor. Five doors gave onto it. I tried the first on my left: a broom closet. Dark old bottles of cleaning fluids lurked on the shelves; on the floor were a few wine bottles, empty and dusty now. I picked one up. Lafitte '47. I was holding an Aladdin's lamp from which the genie had fled. I sniffed at the neck in hopes of an echo. Nothing.

I opened the next door. A kitchen, long abandoned. Black tiles, an aged gas stove freckled with rust, a fat Kenwood mixer wrought in butter.

The next was a plain, bare, greenish room with built-in white cupboards along one wall. I opened one. An old sheepskin coat hung there, heavily molded, and a pair of dusty blue suede high-heeled shoes.

The final door was at the end of the corridor. I pushed it open with my chest.

There was a gilt mirror on the wall. I saw my face as I entered.

I saw the resemblance to my father in the bronzed glass.

There was a marble fireplace. There were pink rosebuds on the white walls. There was a bed beneath the window. The girl who sat on it turned slowly. Her eyes were wide. Her lips were parted.

I knew with certainty what had happened here.

The girl was Alison Gascoigne.

I lay on my back beneath the huge Francis Bacon. Outside, rain alternately flapped and fluttered. I stared up at the shifting watery shadows on the ceiling. Far below, cars hushed and rushed like surf. Their headlights made rectangles of yellow that scudded like sails about the walls. Worse still, the window seat was bobbing.

It had been hard explaining to a perfectly respectable whore going about her business just why I had subjected her to a positively scandalous assault upon her person.

To barge in as I had done might have been permissible. Sex was routine. But seizing her and pressing her to me and kissing her fiercely, kissing her lips, her eyes, and drooling, "Alison, thank God," was little short of violation. Barbara Cartland memories are not welcome in whorehouses.

My subsequent attempt to make her understand that I had momentarily cracked beneath the strain and mistaken her for a girl who had died twenty-six years earlier was not successful. Fifty pounds had proved more eloquent. She had even smiled and suggested that I should "relax," but for all the wide eyes and the glossy brown hair, she looked nothing like Alison by then. She was just another girl whom a few years of tobacco and booze and weary sex had eroded. I had smiled and made my excuses, thus confirming in her the firm conviction that I was cracked, gay, or both.

But in that moment when I entered that room and saw it faded but unaltered since Alison Gascoigne's eyes had ceased to see pink rosebuds on the walls, in that moment I knew what had happened there. The months of hurt had sensitized me. A thousand word-associations and avoidances, elisions and allusions in my father's talk suddenly crystallized in a picture clear as now.

The vehemence with which he had so often asserted when hearing of a rape case, "Silly bitch asked for it," the viciousness with which he spoke of those who died of drugs, the certainty with which he maintained that casualties "had to be responsible for their own actions," these were all explained, but they were just a minute part of the amalgam of impressions that now became images.

We had lived just half an hour from Waylands. My father had

known it and coveted it. He had met Alison in London and discovered that she was the sole heiress. He had set his sights on her.

He would have assumed, no doubt, that an eighteen-year-old from the country would yield before his glamour like a flame before a gale. I mean, for God's sake, a well-dressed gambler, officer of hussars, smooth, good-looking, knew about racing, knew her home. Easy. What he hadn't banked on was that she was in fact a bright, independent girl with ideas of her own — liberal, modern, infantile ideas.

She would have laughed at him.

But she'd have been flattered and charmed, a bit, all the same. She'd have enjoyed this new raffish world. It was a laugh, and older, more sophisticated men offered something different. She'd have strung him along, as eighteen-year-olds must and should.

So that night my father had taken her to Lucy's. With Chris's connivance, he had spiked her drinks. The purpose: to seduce her, if possible to impregnate her. According to his mores, she would then have to marry him — this despite the fact that he was already married. Even if he failed to get her with child, she would feel committed to him, and marriage would soon follow. Waylands, wealth, and status would be won at a stroke.

When she sagged or talked of going home, there had been pills to keep her going, keep her drinking. And at last he had supported her, singing and giggling, up the stairs to that bedroom.

I was a mewling infant down in a Wiltshire cottage when he fucked her in what was now the attic of a brothel.

Then she had passed out.

My father, triumphant, would have come down to the gaming rooms again, probably with a quick wink or a thumbs-up sign to Chris. As the tables spun below and the decks of cards thumped and scraped on the baize and the dice burbled and the voices twanged ever louder, Alison Gascoigne's body, poisoned and raped and abandoned by its captain, had desperately sucked and heaved for air and found only acid, viscous liquid. Her heart had raced. And stopped.

My father would have panicked when he found her in the early hours. No doubt about that. Chris would have taken charge. He would probably have called Heron. The chaps did not let their own down. It was part of the code.

Chris would have known how to do it. He was the solicitor. He would have scraped the vomit from her cheeks and the pillow, to be spread on her face again when they found her resting place. He would have dressed her and somehow loaded her into an unobtrusive car. He and my father, sleek, privileged young men, would have driven south and arranged the body artfully in a dark, unused alley.

And then? Then back to the club for a well-deserved cognac.

Once the danger was past and the inquest over, my father would have justified the whole business to himself. Her fault. One was responsible for one's own actions. She had been willing, hadn't she? In a very short time he would have been telling himself that she had talked of his living with her at Waylands. He would have persuaded himself that he was the natural heir.

Dear God. I knew the shit so well.

So then what? Wooing the desolate mother — surely an easy enough task.

But what of that nameless child who wailed and waited for his mother that night and the following morning, and who had waited in vain ever since? Where was this child whose mother my father had killed and whose place I had usurped?

The child had been, what? Something between eight months and a year old when he lost his mother. He was almost exactly my contemporary, God save him. My mother had seen him when he was "somewhere about a year old" at Uffington, playing with his grandmother.

Then he had disappeared.

I had never realized just how easy it was for a human being to disappear.

I rang High Rigg the following morning, as soon as I was sure that Chris's flat was empty.

"Nick. Hi."

I said, "Don't give up on us."

"Ah, Nick." Maria sighed. "You do what you like. Your life, your father. All very well me being a crusader. Can't expect you to take up arms."

"Yeah, no, look. I think you're right. I think there is a rat here. A monster rat. I'm not giving up. I'm . . . they bloody nearly succeeded, but I'm not taking their Valium anymore. I got a little lost there for a while. Still. Listen. I'll be up at York next week. You be there?"

"Oh, hell, no, sorry. I'm off to Alnwick on Friday."

"Alnwick?" I grinned. "There are only two reasons for going to Alnwick. One, you're a medieval historian; two, you're off on a very secret dirty weekend."

"You know me and medieval history, Nick."

"Yeah, sure. Bugger. I've got something to show you."

"Show Rachel. Give her dinner. She deserves it, and she knows all about this business anyhow."

"She bright enough?"

There was a long pause, then, while Maria sucked her teeth. "Nick . . . ?" she said at last.

"Mmm?"

"How many A levels you got?"

"Three, why?"

"Rachel's got four: Biology, Chemistry, English, and Maths. She's going to train as a vet once she's saved the money. Buy her a bloody good dinner and eat humble pie yourself. And behave yourself, or you'll have me to deal with."

"Mother hen," I said, and wished that I hadn't.

"And the familiar colors of Richard Heron surge to the front," called the television commentator, "and it's Melincourt three lengths clear and drawing away, Melincourt . . ."

I heard no more, because the suite at the York races was full of cheering and whooping. Glasses were raised, bursting the membrane of cigar smoke above our heads. A champagne cork spat and sighed at my right.

"Well done, Richard!"

"Nice one, Richard!"

"Well done! Well done!"

They gathered around Heron where he stood at the window, while the more intelligent freeloaders made a dive for the drinks table or the buffet.

Chris had brought me here as his assistant — principally, I thought, in order to establish me once more as persona grata, at least with the flat-race crowd. Many of the people here were just faces in the newspapers to me — trainers and owners and businessmen. I had been introduced to many of them and had nodded politely. Yes, old Perry's son. And I had seen their eyes flickering over me, amused, appraising, greedy for anything that would make a good phrase.

Now, thank God, I was an acknowledged part of the furniture. The winning owner and the crab claws and the dim sum were altogether more interesting than I. Chris was somewhere up there in the crowd. He owned, I think, 12½ percent of the winning animal. I could sidle away, lose myself for a while among ordinary people down there on the course.

I was just yards from the door when a chestnut-haired girl barged past me, rocking me off balance. She said, "Sorry." She flung the door open. Eledi Heron scampered after her, one long hand extended as though to draw her back.

"Angela, *please,*" her pleading voice echoed as I stepped out onto the tiled landing. The chestnut girl was already trotting down the stairs with a lot of clatter. "I need you," Eledi whispered urgently. "You can't . . . I can't cope without you. I love —"

At the bottom of the stairs the girl turned back. "Oh, for God's sake," she said, sneering. She tossed her head and clasped her Aigner handbag to her hip. She swung round and strutted disdainfully to the next flight. She clattered into darkness.

Eledi stood stock still, just three steps beneath me. Something deep inside her groaned, "Oh, God." Her shoulders drooped and then started jerking. She half turned to lean against the tiled wall, and sobs shuddered out of her. Slowly she sank and curled like a comma. Now her "Oh, God, oh, God, oh, God" emerged as a squeak.

I turned back. I thought of tiptoeing back to the suite, but I looked at the shrunken, sobbing figure there and knew that I could not leave her to be found by a journalist or by one of Heron's chums.

I walked down to her. I tentatively laid my hand on her hair. I said, "Eledi."

She turned her head further toward the wall.

I squatted down beside her. I put my arm about her shoulder, my lips to her ear. God, me and the great Richard Heron's wife. But she was still really only a girl, though perhaps ten, twelve years older than I. I said, "Eledi, come on. You can't stay here. Let's go somewhere quiet."

She leaned her weight against me for a second, and for a second I thought that it would be all right, but suddenly she jerked away from me with a yelp. "No! You're another of those bastards. Get away from me!"

"Easy," I soothed. "Look, let's go somewhere, have a talk."

"No." She sucked in a deep breath. Her voice moaned like a wind in the tiles. "No. You sold out. Chris fucking Wildman's little spy. Perry fucking Storr's offshoot. Fuck off. Get away from me. Don't touch me!" she yapped. She struck out at my hand and then turned back to moaning "Oh, God" to the tiles.

"Look, Eledi, I am no one's bloody spy," I said harshly, "and my bloody father's no friend of mine, either. And any minute now someone's going to come out of that suite and drag you back and lock you away again. So if you want to escape for a while, get up and let's get moving. Now. Right now."

She turned to me then, with puzzled green eyes. Suddenly she nodded twice. She put her left hand on my arm and pulled herself up. Now all was bustle. She wiped her eyes and bit her lip as we hurried down the steps. By the time we emerged into the sunshine, though her eyes were still red, her tawny hair was once more ordered, and her face composed. She had not been an actress for nothing.

"God," she said, "I'll get hell for this."

She stood blinking at the light. Confused, she looked to the left and the right, like a released prisoner who cannot make a move without being ordered. "Come on," I said, and I took her elbow and steered her through the gate into the ring, where we might pass unnoticed among the hollering bookies, and then quickly to the Tattersalls gate onto the street. The old man on duty at the gate directed us to a taxi stand. "Oh, Lord," Eledi said again as she clambered into the cab, "I'm going to get hell for this."

"Somewhere," I told the driver. "A café. Somewhere we can get ham, egg, and chips."

"Oh, God." Eledi hugged herself. She half laughed, half sobbed. "That sounds good."

I rejected two chichi teashops, which the garrulous driver obviously thought better suited to "the likes of us," before at last he delivered us, with much tutting and shaking of his head, to a place called Enzo's, which was just perfect. There were only two customers, both busy with the *Sun* crossword in the corner, and a woman who must have been Mrs. Enzo. Two like her standing immobile, and Italy would never concede another goal. She shouted up the lift shaft, "Two hameggachis!" I took the two cups of coffee — cappuccino for Eledi, *all'americano* for me — over to the table where Eledi sat trying to make Paul Costelloe look like Marks and Spencer.

"So," I said, and I sat down. "What's up?"

"Oh, leave it." She scowled.

"Okay, okay. I'll leave it."

"You'll only go back and tell dear Mr. Wildman."

"No, I won't, but okay, leave it. I work for Chris because he was the only guy who offered me a job. My dad jocked me off, remember? Chris is just helping. He's my godfather."

"Bollocks."

"I beg your pardon?"

"I said, bollocks. He's employing you to keep you quiet. You had to go, but they don't want you kicking up a stink or looking too closely at their affairs. That crowd never did anything altruistic. They cheat from habit. They cheat because it gives 'em a kick. They could manage well enough, but they like cheating. Why I'm where I am, bloody fool."

"Look, if things are so bad, for God's sake, why don't you get out?"

She rapped out a laugh like a hammer striking marble. "Because they're cheats, Nick! Because they have to possess, hold, never be denied, so they cover themselves, cheat, cheat, cheat. Listen." She clasped her hands and rested her weight on her elbows. "You know I *believed* that Sabrina, Richard's ex, was a lesbian? He had pictures, made sure she didn't look for alimony, for fear the pictures would be brought out in court. Only what no one knew was that those were the pictures that didn't have dear grubby Richard in them. He was always there, it was he who set the whole thing up, he who persuaded her, he who couldn't cope with just one girl at a time. So he just keeps the pictures in which he just happens not to be in the bed. She got off lightly, but me, I'm a prize. He stole me from poor Charlie Viscount Vane, Steward. I walked out on him. Jesus, think what it would do to my parents, to Charlie. No. I can't go, not till Richard finds a better prize or goes down. He's actually threatened — would you believe it? — he's actually threatened to send pictures anonymously to my dad, distribute them round the racecourse, if I don't do as he says. God, I am a *fool!* Such a total bloody fool." She gritted her teeth and closed her eyes. Her hand shook as she raised it to her brow.

"And that girl?" I said softly.

She did not open her eyes. She gave a little laugh through her nose. "Angela?" she said vaguely. "Oh, God. All I have, I suppose. God, Nick, I am confused. You watch it, in ten minutes I'll be in love with *you*." She laughed again, without humor. She opened her eyes.

"Hameggachis twi," announced Mrs. Enzo at my shoulder. Eledi smiled, and the world lit up. I had not seen her do that before. It was a good trick.

She tucked into her illicit meal with enthusiasm. Every time she stopped to drink coffee or dab egg yolk from her lips, she said "Mmm," and those eyes danced.

"What you said . . . ," I said slowly, "about Chris."

"Chris shithead Wildman." She nodded. Her eyebrows curled. "Look, you won't mention —"

"I swear, Eledi. I won't mention anything."

"Well, just you ask yourself, how's your dad manage to sustain a place like Waylands on a trainer's ten percent of the winnings, hmm?" She emptied her coffee cup and nodded to Mrs. Enzo for more. "He bloody doesn't. There's better money available from bookies for *losing,* isn't there? And who that we know has interests in bookmakers?"

"But he doesn't." I frowned. "Jesus, I rode for him for three years."

"Sure, and maybe he thought he could afford to go straight. But Chris was out of the country then, wasn't he? Your father probably quite likes you, far as he's capable of liking anyone. So fine, those years. But then Chris comes back. The pressure's on again. Perry's getting jealous. You're expendable."

"Thanks a lot."

She shook her head. She twiddled the diamond stud in her left earlobe. "Look, Nick, you don't know these guys. Gambling debts aren't legally enforceable, right? So how come people pay them or top themselves because of them? Because these guys are experts at the pressure business. Not violence; no need. Intelligence. Blackmail. You should see the muck your friend Mr. Wildman keeps on file. He and Richard swap information. I've heard them, seen them. You know, Richard wants to force through a deal but he's got nothing on whoever's resisting him. So he rings Chris. Chris gives him the dirt on whoever, the deal goes through. The worst sort of force, same as Richard's got me trapped. You're the nigger in the woodpile, you. I had high hopes for you. Honorary member of the set, but getting in the way. Not brought up like them. So first they chuck you out and then they buy you back. Stick and carrot. You don't want to cause grief to your old dad, do you? And you've got a nice cushy job. Why should you kick up? Couple of years, you'll be one of them. Shit." She sighed and pushed her plate away. "All the decent people corrupted or ruined by those bastards. You don't do what I did, Nick." She took my fingertips and shook them. "Just don't bloody do what I did. Hell" — she pushed back imaginary hair — "what's the time?" She looked at her watch. "God, four-twenty. We've got to get back."

It took ten minutes to get a taxi, ten minutes in which Eledi flapped and fluttered and cursed. I tried to calm her, but she snapped at me and whined, "We've got to go. God, we've got to go."

In the car she sighed and muttered, "Come on, come on," and her fingers scrabbled at her skirt. The taxi drew up at the racecourse gates. She put one hand on either side of my face. She said, "Thanks, Nick," and kissed my lips. She threw open the car door and bounced herself out. She ran to the gate.

I climbed out and paid the driver. I turned.

Just inside the gate, Richard Heron stood with his arm around Eledi's shoulders. The chestnut girl stood on Eledi's other side. She was very beautiful. She smiled with the smugness of possession.

"Ah, Nick." Heron smiled. "Glad to see you've been looking after Eledi. We were worried, weren't we, Angela?"

His smile vanished suddenly. He seemed to study me. "Now," he said. He turned Eledi about, and the three of them walked back toward the stands without another word.

"Richard was not best pleased," Chris said stiffly as we entered the lobby of the Chase Hotel. "Eledi is not well, old boy. Wrong in the head, you know. Hysterical. Mustn't encourage her."

"She seemed coherent enough to me."

"Nick, a lot of seriously ill people *seem* coherent. Just take it from me, Eledi is seriously unbalanced. Developed a ridiculous crush on one of the girls who works for Richard."

"You're saying she's a dyke?"

"I'm not saying anything, Nick, and nor will you." A slight growl had entered his soft voice. "Order tea for us, would you? I'm going to make a couple of telephone calls." He pulled himself up the first three carpeted stairs. "Just remember, old chap, will you? It is not a good idea to upset Richard. I'd stay well clear of Mrs. Heron if I were you."

I walked straight past Rachel in the bar of the Tricoleur, perched myself on a stool, and ordered a dry martini. The barman walked up to the carousel of bottles and poured me a jigger of vermouth.

"No," I said, "a dry martini. That means gin, ice, and a sliver of onion or an olive with just a touch of French."

"Oh, you mean a martini drah!" The Brylcreemed barman thrust out his bustle.

"No, I mean a dry martini. And I am the customer. Know what they say about customers? Make the Pope look erratic, customers do."

"I *am* a barman." He looked at me out of the corners of his eyes.

"Then you know how to make a dry martini. Set to."

"Nick . . ." A hand touched my upper arm. I turned.

And damned near fell off my stool. Oh, she had not turned into Hedy Lamarr. She was still Rachel, with those big eyes and those long eyelashes and that pale-pink mouth that revealed a secret grotto of gleaming teeth. But after the girls in Chris's restaurants and clubs, she seemed to glow with her own light, like a gem. Her blond hair gave off a pink glint. Her tight skin seemed to pulse with radiant life. And God almighty, the dark-blue silk-jersey dress fondled and fingered and clung to her every contour. I swallowed because my tonsils were tickling. I said, "Er, hi." I said, "Sorry." I said, "Wow."

She smiled. She looked down. "Sorry 'bout this. Maria insisted I get all togged up. Old thing, hand-me-down. Yuki, which shows how old it is, because now he calls himself Yamamoto or something. My sister's."

I kissed her cheek. "You look bloody wonderful."

"Makes a change from breeches. Forgotten how to walk." She sat on a stool. The jersey slid affectionately up her thighs and gathered in a deep, inviting pool of ripples. "So why are you making trouble?"

"Sorry. Habit."

"Yeah, well, break it. Now, can I have a drink?"

"Um, yup. Sure. What'll it be?"

She smiled at the barman. "Do you sell champagne by the glass?"

He said, "Um," too, then, "Yes. Surely. No problem."

"Great."

He eyed me much as the other son must have eyed the prodigal.

". . . so I've been through the computer files at the Wildfire offices. Nothing. At least not under any obvious file names. And all the real dirt, apparently, is kept in this cabinet at Chris's flat. No way I can get in there. But Chris has got a personal computer on his desk in there, too, right? And one day I'm at the flat having a drink with him when a messenger comes to the door. Something about redirecting a parcel, I don't know. So while he's off there chattering away at the door I sort of casually type in STORR, P., and up comes STORR, CAPTAIN PEREGRINE, and then just this list of figures, that's all. Far as I can see, they make no sense. Then back comes Chris, so I quickly switch back to the original file and pretend I was engrossed in the erotic subplot of the telephone directory. Now" — I clicked my ballpoint, opened up a table napkin — "up till now, it never crossed my mind. Couldn't see any significance at all. What we've got is two columns of figures. Look." I wrote fast.

"You've got all this in your head?"

"Mm-hm. Memories like mine have uses beyond annoying Trivial Pursuit opponents. Yup. Been carrying them around wondering what they meant. I think I've got it now. Here. Notice anything odd?"

She quickly perused the two columns. She said, "Hmm," and her tongue appeared at the corner of her mouth. The figures on the left, I knew, seemed to be dates. There were never more than four entries and never less than three in any year in the past two decades. The only break in the sequence occurred in the season when I had become Waylands's stable jockey, with the entries resuming again only on 31 July of this year, a date still in the future. I had thought when first I found these figures that the entries relating to those missing years might have been obliterated simply for fear that I might see them and that they might mean something to me, but Eledi's words this afternoon had given me the clue that I needed.

"Okay." Rachel put her tongue away. "Let's assume that the figures on the left represent dates and the ones on the right, what? Payments of some sort. At first sight, then, 1,234 somethings — pounds, dollars, whatever — were paid one way or another on the third of January 1976, 993 somethings on the sixteenth of April '76, and 1,747 on the eighteenth of March. Small sums, and apparently nothing to do with your father's horses, because often more payments are logged in the summer months than in the 'chasing season. But start with the premise that these guys don't mess with small sums and that these do relate to racing, and there are various things that suggest that the dates just might not be dates. I mean, real dates are listed in order, right? But here you've got several out of sequence. Look, 12.6.69 comes before 27.3.69, and 2.9.70 before 20.4.70. And then, too, how come occasionally you get two or three separate payments on the same date? This last one — the thirty-first of July — we've got two entries of 1,935. Surely you'd normally record a single payment of 3,870, right?"

"Right," I agreed, a little shell-shocked.

She popped an olive into her mouth and chewed as she went on. "Okay, so suppose that the last payment has to do with Ibn Saud's last race, which was on the fourteenth of March, right? So the payment — yes, that's reasonable — the payment was made on the nineteenth! Not exactly subtle, is it?" She spat out the olive pit and chuckled. I was affronted. In five minutes, this girl whom I had taken for a pretty little thing had synthesized material that I had been trying to make sense of for more than a month.

She took another olive to aid thought. "So what we're doing is moving the first two, three, or four figures of the date — the day and month — to the second column, and using the corresponding figures from the right-hand side to make a confusing date. . . . Yes, they all work, and every date, so far as I can see, falls in the season. Add a nought for certain to our eventual payment, and there you have it! But you can't have a sixty-second of the month, so you have two payments on the thirty-first. Grand total of 63,500 pounds for Ibn Saud, paid five days after the race. Simple."

"Oh," I said sadly. "Yeah. What I reckoned. Only it took me about a thousand times longer."

"Different sorts of brains." She smiled and touched my hand. "What I wouldn't give for a memory like yours. Mine's like a sieve."

"Sure, but that's just like a certain shape of nose or something. It's an accident of birth. It's not creative, not analytical."

"Cleopatra's nose changed the course of history. It's how you carry the accidents of birth that counts. I reckon you're just learning to carry some big weights lightly. God, just think of a child with your memory and gumption and my — I don't know — my burrowing, holding, jumping, terrier sort of brain. No one would be . . ." And her voice dwindled as she realized what she was saying. She almost whispered, ". . . safe.

"Anyhow. Right." She sat up straight and looked again at the napkin. "Yes. God, slightly different from easy races for novice hurdlers up here, isn't it? Gold Cups. Millions of pounds. Sods, aren't they?"

"Yup. Listen. It's not exactly evidence, but would either you or Maria show it to Rashid or Moran? I've got work to do. . . ."

"And we haven't?"

"Yes, yes, of course you have, but I'm going to wrap this fucking thing up. Please, love. One of you — preferably you, you can explain it better — put the case to Moran. Please. I'll fax you a clean copy and a note of explanation the day after tomorrow."

"Okay. I'll try. Poor sod. Rashid. Comes over here all innocence, just likes horses, trusts the nice English gentlemen, and gets done."

"That's right. And we should be able to trace some other beaten favorites from this lot. Have to go easy with the information, though. Mention it to the wrong person, we'll end up in trouble."

"Sure, Nick." Her eyes were sad and alarmed. "But you. What are you going to do?"

"Me?" I shrugged. "Me, I'm going to do what I should have done ages ago. Oedipus, me. I'm going to meet my father at a suitable crossroads, sort this out for once and for all."

"I think you'd better tread carefully, Nick. We're talking about — God knows what these guys' motives are — but we're talking about the sort of sums people will do most anything for."

"Yeah," I said glumly. "Worst of it is . . . hell, I'm working against myself, aren't I? I stand to inherit Waylands. I love the place."

"Sure, but if it's not yours —"

"Oh, fine, in principle, but look, it's mine by birth. I was brought up to inherit it. This grandson — I mean, assuming that he's still alive, assuming that there's something wrong with the will and Dad wasn't meant to inherit, I mean, I know what the rules say, but morals are more than just rules . . . you've got to consider the consequences. . . ."

Rachel watched me.

Rachel smiled.

Rachel nodded very slowly.

She said nothing.

Eloquent bitch.

"So!" Chris appeared at the door of his hotel room as I tiptoed past. He was in shirt sleeves and had removed his starched collar. His cheeks were flushed, his hair awry. "Good evening?"

"Yup, yup. Fun."

"Good! Good! Come on in!"

He stood back. I walked in. He shut the door carefully behind me. "Drink?"

"No. No thanks, Chris. Thought I'd turn in early."

"You didn't tell me you were going out."

"No. Sorry. It was sort of sudden."

"Pretty girl." Chris sat on the sofa. He poured himself a triple whisky. He looked up at me suddenly. "Oh, yes." He was roguish. "I saw you, Nicky! Can't put anything over on me. Think I was just going to sit here, poor old chap, on my own? No, no. Decided, Nicky's not the only one to have a bit of fun. Happened to enter this restaurant recommended. Pretty girl. Left you to it. Good to see you enjoying yourself. Get in her knickers, did you?"

"No."

"Oh, frigid little thing, eh? You get 'em. Often the prettiest. Still. Glad to see . . . thought you might be out with that Thornton cow. I don't want you mixing with her. She's trouble."

"She's just a small-time trainer."

"Allow me to be the judge, Nicky." Chris was bullish. "She's trouble. You've got to tread carefully in this business, Nicky. Got to learn that. Today, Mrs. Heron. Must keep your nose clean, okay? Must stick to the rules. Proper way to behave and wrong way, you know? Stick to the rules, Nicky. Makes life easier. Remember that."

"Yes, Chris."

"Good. Good chap. Fine. Right, then. Damn pretty girl. Pity. Still."

"Yes, Chris."

"So just watch yourself, okay?"

"Yes, Chris."

He drained his drink in one. He laid his glass down on the table. And very suddenly his hands dropped and hung loose between his thighs, his eyelids fell, and his head dropped onto his chest. A snore rattled his frame.

"Yes, Chris," I said again softly, and I tiptoed to my room.

The rain wriggled from my cap-brim. Our old vicar was on holiday. A locum was in residence. I introduced myself.

"Nick! Nick! Right! Hi!"

Oh, God.

That sort of vicar. Every vowel flattened by an unctuous smile. Thou Shalt Not Unless Thou Really Wantest To, and All Persons Are Brothers Like Man. *Hoc est enim,* prithee take my body risen in a Kipling cake. Oh, God. And he was forty-five if he was a day, with thinning black hair and ice cubes for glasses.

"Right. So. Nick. What can we do for you?"

"I'm looking for a record of a christening." People like that bring out the stern side in me. "Back in the sixties."

"Right! That should be easy enough. Great. That'll be in the vestry, right?"

I shrugged. I'm the sort that if you tell me to make the

sign of peace to my neighbor, I nod. Unless she's very, very pretty.

"Okay, so!" He was beginning to get the idea that I entertained no fraternal feelings toward him and that I did not like standing in the rain. "Right. I'll just get my mac."

"Do," I said.

It was a transparent plastic mac, a full-length French letter. Which I considered suitable. It swooshed as he walked. What with the squelching of his galoshes he sounded like soup course in a Trappist dining room.

Uffington is a little church but a great church, a serious church. Early English. Cruciform. Octagonal tower. Lovely two-storied south porch, gabled east doorway. That's it. Austere. Holy.

Reared a Catholic, I had never worshipped here. I resented that fact. Perhaps when the Greeks get back their marbles, we can have Uffington back. And Durham, while we're at it.

I followed the slurping cleric up the nave. The tiger light from the paired lancets fell on a marble plaque at my left. "Hold on," I said. "Just a second."

I sidestepped along the pew. I had seen the plaque before but had never considered it. "SACRED TO THE MEMORY," it said in pedestrian Roman gilt, "of Victor Delaunay Butler, master of Waylands, beloved husband and father, born 4 May 1847, depd. this life 21 August 1932. *'Let us lay aside every weight, and the sin which doth so easily beset us, and let us run with patience the race that is set before us.'* Hebrews 12:1."

I didn't know what the handicapper would have had to say about "laying aside every weight," but the bit about "the sin which doth so easily beset us" hinted that Butler had been no angel. And here came his accuser: "also of Isobel Gwendolen, relict of the same 1874–1944." Not, plainly, a popular woman. There was no mention of her daughter, Maud, but then who had there been to erect a memorial to her? Only my father, who had had other things on his mind.

"Lovely old thing," said the vicar from the aisle.

"Hmm." It was neither lovely nor old, but the man had stock responses.

An actress I once knew had a faintly dippy contemporary at drama school. This other girl had been rehearsing some Jagged Slice of Life piece for two weeks before her colleagues asked her just what she thought she was doing in act 2, scene 4, or whatever. All that time they had been a trifle confused to see her striding back and forth upstage making curious pushing and pulling gestures while puffing air through vibrating lips. In explanation, she drew their attention to a stage direction: ". . . while Elaine hovers distractedly in the background."

There was a pause. "Oh," she said at last with a wriggle and a giggle, "'*hovers,*' is it? I thought it said 'hoovers'!"

My cicerone, whom by now I hated cordially, both hovered and mimed hoovering in the background as I turned the heavy pages of the folio volume in which a million passions were distilled to their enduring manifestations: hatches, matches, and dispatches.

I had thought a parish register to be a commonplace thing. The words had seemed redolent only of dust and cobwebs and Miss Marple, but what I found here was a blockbuster. Sex, violence, grief, elation, tenderness, devotion, and above all disappointment filled every millimeter of blank space surrounding the formal entries. The book seemed as potent as that famous single ham prepared for the Prince de Soubise at the expense of forty-nine others.

I could have sat for days enjoying these unwritten stories, but the vicar sighed and hummed and paced and said "Brr" and "Jolly cold" and "Any luck, then?" and "Bells. Huh." He leaned over the back of my chair. His condom coat snuffled at my back.

I hated him very much.

So I found what I was looking for within six minutes. First came the baptism of Dennis Niall Gascoigne on 2 March 1964. No mention was made of his father, nor of any godparents.

The funeral of Alison Mary Delaunay Gascoigne, only daughter of Maud, widow of this parish, took place on 10 October 1964.

And last, an entry beautifully inscribed in black copper plate: "14 October 1966. Laid to rest Maud Frances Gascoigne, dear friend of this church and this parish."

So old Maud had died on or about the second anniversary of her daughter's death. Another puzzle. Did rich old widows particularly designated "dear friend of this church and of this parish" not commonly remember church and parish in their wills?

I regretfully slammed the book shut and pushed back my chair. I told the vicar "Thank you," and he said, "Family matters, mmm?" I said, "No. Curiosity." He said, "Oh, jolly good. By all means." I said, "Well, bye, then," and he said, "Oh, yes, do come back. Lovely. Always welcome."

The subtitles in the ether were obscene.

I wandered out. The rain had stopped now. The thrushes were following up their advantage, pecking and tugging pink entrails from the grave mounds. The familiar sight of the spangled cottages beneath the green downs induced instant dysentery in me.

My home and presumably my father were only yards away. Everyone in the village knew me, had known me since I was a child. Everyone, too, would have heard and read my father's explanation of my sudden departure. I was a coward. I was a crook. A father would never do a thing like that to his son without good reason. No smoke without fire. . . .

I had to gulp a bit before climbing back into the car.

I drove to Joey's cottage. His wife, Doreen, greeted me on the porch. Her blond-gray hair hung in springy tendrils about her face. She dried her hands by twisting up an apron on which Snoopy danced. "'Allo, Nicky!" she said, and she smiled wearily. Her North London accent had not been eroded by the years.

"Hello, Doreen, love. How're you doing?"

"Gawd." She flapped the apron. She turned and led me through the living room. "Chaos, as usual." I was honored. I had not been asked to remove my shoes.

The house was a temple to Joey and Doreen's twin religions. A madonna stood in a scallop shell on the mantelpiece. A crucifix, complete with gore, hung above a burning nightlight in the corner. Holman Hunt's *The Light of the World* hung beside plastic gladioli on the windowsill.

But as if these were not graven images enough, there was

179

another shrine beneath the stairs. Here, in dim red light, Elvis sneered or smiled from every wall — Elvis glossy as a new-made waxwork, Elvis a bloated waxwork melting down. A tasseled, rhinestone-studded jacket had pride of place. There were statuettes and pennants and magazines and a framed silk scarf that bore the regal signature. Hundreds, maybe thousands, of records lined one wall, and beneath them, side by side, there were two red crushed-velvet cinema seats. Here Joey and Doreen sat hand in hand to hear the commandments of their Memphis paraclete.

Doreen bustled past this sanctum and into the kitchen. "Where'd I start?" she was saying. "I mean, Kevin's been nicking things in Swindon, little b., Sharon's being all broody and bad-tempered about some boy who rides a motorbike, and her little one — lor', well, look, I mean, getting about like a blue-arsed fly now, aren't you?" She bent to coo at a baby boy who looked like an uncooked loaf. "Fingers in everything, i'n'it?"

The child squawked.

"So how're you, then, Nicky? Joey an' I've thought a lot about you. Prayed for you. Joey got into a right barney with your old man. Spoke his mind, he did. No good, but." She shrugged and opened the frosted-glass door. "Joey," she shrilled, "Nicky's 'ere! No" — she knelt and shouldered the child — "still don't understand it, we don't. You di'n't do nuffin' to offend 'im, did you?"

"Just grew up." I grinned.

"What Joey reckoned. Jealousy, he says. You getting winners. The girls like you. Pathetic, that's what it is. Pathetic."

Joey limped in. He folded his *Daily Mirror* and threw it down on the table. He shook my hand with both of his. "Nicky," he said. There were tears in his eyes. "Good to see you. Saw you had a nice winner up Market Rasen back end of last season. Good lad. Looks a likely sort, that Pipistrelly. Your dad wasn't best pleased about that. Specially you half-lengthing our Lenny. Gawd, silly ass, thumb in bum, mind in neutral. Says to the Captain, I do, all cheerful like, 'See young Master Nick had a nice one yesterday. Rough race, too.' He says, 'Keep your mouth shut, Beale,' like I was some sort of lift-boy or something. 'I know your views on my son, but I'd remind you that he is my son, thank you.' I says, 'You'd never know it.' God, he's had a cob on him ever since he blew you out. Growling and yelling and, not that I like to say it, hitting the bottle quite hard. Atmosphere's bad, Nick. Worst I've ever known it. And that woman — well, you know, we've never exactly seen eye to eye. Hard, she seems to me. Gets what she wants and to hell with anyone in the way. I know I shouldn't say it, but . . ."

"Yes, listen." I frowned. I had been wondering about this ever since I saw Deirdre's name on Maud Gascoigne's will. "Exactly when did she turn up? I mean, you were working for Dad, traveling around with him. When'd you first know she existed?"

"Hmm." Joey screwed up his eyes to think. "Come on through, Nick. Let's sit down. Tea? Glass of home-made wine?"

"Not for me, thanks." I strolled back to the living room and perched carefully on a pristine armchair, complete with antimacassar.

Joey changed into his slippers and followed me in. "No, well, I'll tell you." He sat on the other side of the gas fire. "It was before you were born, anyhow."

"Before?"

"Yes, Nick. 'Fraid so. I remember I was shocked. Your mum with child, and him visiting this woman up in London. She was a dealer at a big club up there. You knew that?"

"Yes." I nodded.

"Then he must've brought her down here — I shouldn't be telling you all this, but it's only fair — he brought her down here about, what? Two years before he moved in?"

"Here?" I was startled. "She actually lived here in Uffington while we were in Wiltshire?"

"Yeah. Didn't you know? Yeah. He got her a job as private secretary at Waylands. Couldn't have been more convenient for him. I mean, he was helping the old girl out regular, and, you want to know the truth, I reckon as he was working at getting her to leave him the place. So she needs a secretary, he moves his, er —"

"Mistress," I supplied.

181

"Yeah, well. He moves her in. Two birds with one stone, see."

The import of the words dripped into my consciousness. *Deirdre had been Maud Gascoigne's private secretary.* My father's mistress and my father's oldest friend had been the only witnesses to a will in which a reclusive old woman left him everything. The horror lay in the sense that I had, however imprecisely, known all these things all along but had locked them out. Now they stormed in and demanded an audience.

"Why'd no one tell me?" I asked lamely.

"Not a lot of people knew," Doreen sang from the kitchen. "Gather they never came out of the 'ouse, last two years of the old biddy's life, i'n' that right, Joey?"

"'Sright. And, see, one doesn't say like to a son, you know, 'All this time your dad was . . . misbehaving . . . with someone right here in your home,' does one? God, I did feel sorry for your mum. Last one to know anything about it, and her with an infant and all."

"You ever meet Mrs. Gascoigne?"

"Me?" Joey looked guiltily down at the empty pipe that he had drawn from his coat pocket. He pulled out the tobacco tin, too, and balanced it on his knee. "No. That is . . . not to say met her, no. Saw her, yeah. See . . . thing is, your dad took a tumble once, on the gallops down Devizes. Broke his leg. He — he got me to drive him up to Uffington. He'd give me a fiver, tell me to have lunch in the pub."

"Joey!" Doreen appeared in the doorway. Behind her the child started to cry. "You never. And Mrs. Storr and the baby?"

"Yeah, yeah, I know." Joey nodded sadly. He pressed Gold Flake into his pipe. "It was a long time ago, and . . . before I was born again in the Lord. I didn't like it even then, but I was young and foolish and I just said, 'Well, the boss says do it, it's not for me to judge,' right?"

"You and the Nazis both," Doreen snapped.

"Yeah, well, I know that now. There." Joey popped the pipe between his teeth. It wagged as he patted his pockets for matches. "Anyhow, so I'd sit in the pub or drive up on the downs, come back again a few hours later. I'd see your stepmum saying hello and goodbye, and a couple times I seen the old girl in the big window, you know, the drawing room. Very old, she looked, very weak. Hair dyed black, pudding-bowl cut, very white, very wrinkled face. Looked like whatsisname — Friar Tuck, sort of, only not fat."

"Know anything about her grandson?" I said casually.

"Grandson?" Joey lit the pipe and puffed. He narrowed his eyes against the smoke. The match burned down. Joey conducted *The Flight of the Bumblebee* for a bar or two. "Grandson? No. Don't know nothing about that."

"If there'd been a grandson, he'd have got the place, wouldn't he?" said Doreen with simple certainty.

"There was a grandson." I resolved to trust them. "An illegitimate grandson, but the old woman acknowledged him. I don't know where he was between his mother's death and his grandmother's, but he was here at least once. Then he vanished. Vanished completely. Now, of course, maybe his mum put him up for adoption. Maybe he died. I can check both of those things. But there are a lot of lies being told, and I have a sort of feeling — I don't know. Listen. You arrived in Uffington when? 'Sixty-six?"

"May thirteenth 'sixty-seven," rapped Doreen.

"Okay. Probably too late, but did you hear anything around that time? Anyone say anything about an unexpected boy child having suddenly turned up in the area a few months before? Orphaned grandson suddenly presented to grandparents, estranged wife suddenly pops up with a three-year-old, that sort of thing?"

"Um," said Doreen.

"Nnnn," said Joey.

"Nothing? Try an infertile woman goes away for a while, comes back with a boy. Or someone suddenly announces they've adopted a child. Any baby, one, two years old, and no one's witnessed the pregnancy or the birth. Or even — I don't know — a seriously ill infant suddenly gets better. . . ."

"There was 'at girl worked down the Cross Keys," said

Doreen. She sat on the arm of her husband's chair. She twiddled his hair as absentmindedly as a picnicker twiddles grass. "You remember? You thought she was a bit of all right. Skirt up around 'er armpits. What was 'er name?"

"Nnn." Joey shook his head.

"Ah, go on with yer. You was down there every night trying to get an eyeful of her Berkshire 'unt! Every bloody stray dachshund in the village trying to get in through her cat-flap. You remember, Maureen, Maisie . . . *Maeve*. 'Ass it. Maeve Cummings. Turned up with a boy round that time."

"Nah. That was late sixties," Joey corrected solemnly. "'Sixty-nine, something."

"No, it wasn't."

"Was."

"Much earlier."

"She was there the night of the party after Damozel won the Mackeson. Right or wrong? Puked on your shoes. Right?"

"Mmmyeah."

"'Sixty-eight, that was, and she was new. So."

"Awright. Awbleedinright. Always right, aren't you?" She blipped him across his crown. "Racing as does it, Nick. Ask him what year he was married. He'd say, 'Um . . . ,' then, 'Oh, yeah, year Big Bertha won the Derby and Brown Betty took the Futurity. 'Sixty-six, that'd be.'"

"Yeah, well, think on." I slapped my knees. "It's a long shot, but . . ."

"Bloody 'ell." Doreen had been thinking. Now she shuddered. "He wouldn't. He couldn't. Could he?"

"No, no," I reassured her. I stood. I plucked the twill from my knees. "Come on. It doesn't have to follow. There are other explanations."

Joey also stood. He looked from me to Doreen and back again. "What are you two on about?"

"That poor old woman." Doreen was all dreamy. "That Deirdre keeping an eye on 'er. . . . Gawd, he could have done it easy. Little boy . . ."

"Yeah. From what I can gather, she saw no one those last

two years except Deirdre and Dad and the solicitor, who happens to be Dad's oldest friend."

"And no relatives to ask questions."

"Except a toddler."

"You can't just *disappear* someone like that. You *can't*."

I caught her anguished look. I smiled. I shrugged. I said sadly, "Seems you can."

It took my father just fourteen minutes. I know because I timed it by the great oak tax-clock behind the bar.

There had been five people in the Cross Keys when I swaggered in. I had swaggered because why not, and because anything else might have been seen as skulking.

Every eye had briefly turned. I had called to two of our lads by the fire, "'Lo, Chalkie, Kevin," and they had mumbled, "M'Storr," and turned back to their pints and lunches.

They say that when the aborigines first saw Cook's ships, they just sort of hummed a bit and looked the other way and carried on doing whatever they were doing. They chose not to see those massive, intricate machines.

Cook, as an Englishman, probably approved. You can see Ulysses returning to Ilford rather than Ithaca. Strolls into his local after twenty years of wandering. "Hello, old girl. Suitors, eh? Jolly good." And the landlord would simply say, "Evening, colonel. The usual? Lovely day. . . ."

No one had looked surprised to see me. No one had expressed curiosity or concern. I had just walked up to the bar and ordered a pint, and Terry had said, "Afternoon, Nick. All well?" and I had answered, "Fine," and he had said, "Warmer tomorrow, they say," and I, "'Bout time." Then I had sat down at a table, opened the *Times*. And waited.

Various people had entered the pub during that time. My back had been to the door, but I had not turned. I would know when my father came in. That he would come in I did not doubt. My action in coming here when exiled was outright lèse majesté. He would fear that I was lampooning him among his own, or attempting to defend myself from his accusations. He would fear, too, if he had talked to Chris, that I might be learning too much from the locals, or spreading rumor and suspicion. He would not want to confront me, but he would be unable to stay away.

When he did come, every head in the pub rose and stayed raised. I heard the rattle of his boots on the hearth, then the rustling of his tweed coat as he passed me on the way to the bar. For a second I wanted to giggle. It was so absurdly like those moments in Westerns when the gunman enters and everyone ducks down behind bars and tables.

He strode up to the bar and nodded to Terry. "Afternoon."

"Afternoon, Cap'n."

"Large Scotch, would you?"

"Coming up."

My father drummed the bar with flat, straight fingers. He looked at the Schweppes calendar. He turned to lean on his right elbow. He called, "Hello, Adrian, all right?" Adrian, the racing-mad owner of the local garden center, called back, "Doing well, Perry," and turned back to his wife.

The glass of Scotch was placed at my father's elbow. He swung back to pay for it. "Have one yourself," he said, and he tossed a note onto the bar.

"Cheers. Thanks, Cap'n."

"Good luck to you."

He swung round and leaned back against the bar. God, he was a ham. He sipped. He caught my eyes over the rim of his glass. His eyes widened. He raised a hand to push back the wing of hair at his right temple. He strolled over to me. "Well, hello, old boy. Nice to see you."

"No, it isn't." I kicked a chair back with my foot. "Sit down."

"Now, steady on, old boy —"

"Sit down," I said in a monotone, "or I'll have to speak loudly."

"You can speak as loudly as you like, old chap." He feigned amused astonishment. "Shout and scream if you bloody like. Makes not the slightest difference to me. Getting used to your histrionics."

"You want me to shout and scream about Alison Gascoigne?" I raised my voice but kept it level.

"Alison Gascoigne?" Still that snide small smile. "Certainly, if you think you know anything about Alison Gascoigne. Bit before your time, I'd have thought. Still, yes. You have a good scream about her if it makes you feel better. Why not?"

"And about how once you'd fixed up her corpse, you disinherited her son, Dennis?"

He dropped into a chair as though shot. "Shit," he hissed. "Shut your bloody stupid mouth, will you? What the hell do you know about anything?"

"Just about everything," I lied.

"So?" He recovered his poise. "So? Exactly what *are* you talking about?"

"Alison Gascoigne. You got her drunk and screwed her, and she died."

"You really are absurd, old chap. Just because I decided you weren't good enough to ride for me —"

"You then battened onto Maud Gascoigne and planted your whore in her house. You tried to make yourself indispensable. You dropped hints. You put pressure on her. So did Deirdre. You got her to sign —" I stopped. *She had not made provision for her grandson or her church.* "No, you bloody didn't. You *faked* a will, dear God. You and Chris faked her fucking will, didn't you? There was no one to complain but an infant. No one checks a will unless it's challenged. You . . . yes, it's obvious. You got her to make a will, right? 'My nice friend Chris will help you.' Everything to her grandson except, what? Five hundred to the church, five hundred to the butler? Yes. Captain Peregrine Storr to be regent, right? Bring up the little boy as his own, run Waylands for him until his majority. But Captain Storr and his lawyer are greedy. They want more. So you take the will back and you draw up another one, only this time everything — the land, the house, the money, everything — goes to Captain Storr. This will's dated on the same day, right? Of course, so the butler and everyone else'll remember that yes, Mrs. Gascoigne voluntarily made a will that day. And then there's just one small problem. What do we do with the grandson? So. What *did* you do with Dennis Gascoigne, Dad? Hey?"

He had lit a cigar as I spoke. He had watched me with pity-ing eyes and a small, thin-lipped smile. He had slowly shaken his head. At last, as I raised my voice, I managed to rattle him. "Shut up!" he hissed. "For Christ's sake, what crap has Chris been telling you? You're bloody mad."

"No, I'm not. I'm so certain that I'm right, in fact, that I have every intention of ringing the police as soon as I leave here. There must be other people who know about the Gascoigne child. There must be other documents carrying Mrs. Gas-coigne's signature. So?"

"So ring them." He oozed calm and charm. "Be lucky if you're not locked up in Broadmoor for your pains, but it's entirely up to you."

"Okay." Echoes from schoolground arguments here — dare and double dare. He had the upper hand. "Okay, I will."

I got to my feet and walked quickly round the bar to the dark corner where the telephone hung. I struggled through a much-ripped directory to find the number of the local police station. I fumbled in my jeans pockets and found nothing smaller than a pound coin. I wasn't going to give my father the satisfaction of seeing me ask for change. I fed the coin in. I tapped out the number.

"Hello," I said fast, "I want to report a case of massive fraud —" And then my father's breath was hot on my face, his gut shoved at the small of my back, and his cigar smoke wrapped around me like a baby's blanket. The side of his hand came down hard on the cradle.

"What the fuck do you think you're *doing?*" He spun me round so that my back hit the wall and made my teeth jolt together. His teeth were gritted. His gray irises darted from one side to another between narrowed lids, like animals looking for escape from a cage. "Jesus! Who the hell d'you think you are, Nick? Standing in judgment on me and Chris and . . . How dare you? How bloody dare you?"

I pushed him aside with a straight arm. "That approach won't work," I said. I sounded cooler than I felt. I headed back to the table. "I've had it from Chris. Okay, so we've had condescension and aggrieved pomposity. What's the next psychological power trip? I think, you know, I'm immune to them all now. I wasn't, but you've taught me these past few months. In March I'd have collapsed. Not now. It's like a mother's used every inducement to get a child to suckle, then she weans him overnight. Now she's got mastitis and she's trying to get him suckling again. Know what I see?" I sat and crossed my legs. "I see a frightened, pathetic, strutting, social-climbing old fart. No more secretaries to screw. No love to sustain you. Only decline and death ahead. Rage, rage against the dying of the light. That's all. So leave out the mind-fuck games, okay? They don't work anymore. I'm a big boy now."

It struck me as I spoke that paternity gives nigh irresistible advantages when it comes to battle. A father can break his child with ease because he knows, and when challenged will use, things about that child that the child does not even know about himself. Unconsciously, as a hunter amasses a million unspoken murmurs from the wind and the fields, a parent stores up the hints of a child's gestures and words and moments of pain and joy until he knows, should the child revolt against nature's imperative, precisely where to strike to cause the maximum injury. Think how much more effectively an ex-lover can hurt than an enemy who has never seen your nakedness. How much better armed is a parent who has been trusted with every frailty and folly, when he elects to break that sacred trust?

An example. I was thirteen. My father and Deirdre had taken me out from school for the weekend. They were staying at the Viking Hotel in York, a mere half hour from my school on the moors.

On the Saturday morning, after breakfast in bed, I wandered into their room and sat on the double bed. It was covered with newspapers. Deirdre must have been in the bath. My father was shaving. He popped his head around the door. He said good morning. I sat on the bed and riffled through the papers.

I came upon an article about Tommy Steele, a cockney entertainer of some sort. The article said that Steele's birth was by

cesarean section, which "might explain his regular good looks."
I called through to the bathroom, "Dad, what's Cesar Ian?"

My father stopped singing. He said, "Mmm?"

"Cesar Ian section."

"Cesarean," he corrected. "It's when they cut the baby out
'cause it can't get out the normal way. Pull it out through the
sunroof. Why?"

"Why's it make someone good-looking, then? It says here
'which might explain his regular good looks.'"

"Oh, well, yes. It's just that cesarean babies don't have to go
through the business of being born. It's a big effort. Can twist
your face all up, you know?" he said blithely. Water lapped. I
could tell from the tightness of his vowels that he was shaving
his throat. He said, "Which explains your problems."

I did not cry. I just sat there gazing down at the papers. The
awareness sank in like cold water into dry soil. It penetrated my
every cell. It became part of me, permanent fact because stated
by my father. I was ugly.

I know now that it was a lie, or a joke, but I can never really
know it. My awareness of myself is of one "all twisted up." It is
still a sweet surprise that any girl should kiss me.

If you want your son or daughter to be promiscuous, that's
the tried technique.

My father now sank heavily into the chair opposite me. He was
not the lithe, blithe stalker of my childhood, but nor was he
quite broken yet. He still tried the superior smile, the stock "I
really have never heard anything so ridiculous," but there was
bemusement in his eyes. He had the look of a spinster when
Woofypoo turns rabid. The smell of defeat was on him.

"I hope you know what you're doing," he grunted. "I'm sick,
you know. Pancreas shot to hell and back."

"So stop drinking. It's very simple," I told him. "You tell me
where Dennis Gascoigne is, or I call the police and they can find
out for me instead."

"What the hell d'you want to go disturbing things for,
for Christ's sake?" he mumbled. "Everyone was perfectly
happy —"

190

"I wasn't."

"For . . . why d'you think . . . ?" He found a good one amid the flotsam. "Jesus, the whole thing's just for you."

"Bollocks. It's for you, just like everything else you've ever done."

"Oh, thanks. Great. So why d'ye think I'm so keen to hold on to Waylands, then? I haven't got that long. It's for you, isn't it? The whole thing. All for you. Fine thanks. Blow the whole thing up. I've only worked all my adult life to make sure . . . Oh, the hell with it. I'm going to get a drink."

Deeply wounded, this improbable Lear grunted and puffed as he pulled himself up and lumbered to the bar.

"The whole thing's for you": could it be true?

No. Because Deirdre had had a hand in all this. And Deirdre hated me.

No. No doubt amid the impulses of greed and personal ambition, he had found consolation in the idea that he was doing all of this for his "family." But that "family" was an imper-sonal concept, a totem like "the church" or "the regiment." It had nothing to do with the infant son whom he had abandoned.

More probably — and this was far more consistent with Deirdre's collusion — his "family" at that point was not thought to include me at all. I belonged to the bad old days. He was thinking, rather, of a very posh little family of Waylands Storrs got on Deirdre.

But Deirdre had proved barren, so he had wooed me back.

"Look, for God's sake, old chap," he said as he placed a pint in front of me. He sat. His body sighed like a slow puncture. "Just let it lie, will you? It's history. We don't want to kick up a hell of a fuss, undo all the good we've done, hurt a whole load of people, do we?"

"Take three generations of the Gascoigne family," I said. "You kill a woman, you cheat her poor old mother, and you disinherit her son, and then you ask me to forget it. Christ, man, don't they haunt you? They sure as hell haunt me already."

"I didn't fucking kill —" He looked quickly around and low-ered his voice. The preliminary crackles were now as loud as the words that they enclosed. His aftershave was Givenchy. "Listen.

I don't know what Chris has been telling you, but I didn't kill the bloody girl. She took a drink too many, that's all. She was an adult. She was responsible. We are all responsible for our actions, whatever the whiners might say. Jesus, potty training, broken homes. You can't go on like that. Misadventure. That's exactly what it was."

"She knew what she was drinking?"

"What? Of course she did. She was famous as a drunk. Ask anyone." He spoke quickly, and drank quickly afterward. I knew he was lying.

"I *have* asked," I murmured. "She wasn't."

He ignored me. He was busy trying to put Humpty together again, trying this bit here, that bit there. He knew that once I had respected him; he had once even respected himself. He just could not at the moment remember how the trick worked.

"And anyhow, come on. It was perfectly decent and normal. I felt sorry for the old girl. Sure I loved Waylands, but I mean . . . I wanted to help her. She was old and frail and . . . okay. All right. I did feel a little guilty about the girl. I mean . . . And just you remember, if the girl hadn't died, I'd have had Waylands anyhow. She'd have married me, so it all —"

"You were already married." I shook my head, stunned by his speciousness. "And you had a mistress."

"Don't be naive, Nick. Please. Anyhow, so I visited old Maudie, helped her to train the few remaining animals and sell them. What was wrong with that? And sure, I hoped she might leave me the place. Natural enough."

"You told me she gambled. She never did, did she?"

"She . . . no. Okay, so what was I meant to say? No. All right. That was a fib. A white lie, if you like."

"And the child?"

"Oh, for Christ's sake stop harping on about the bloody child, will you?" He licked his lips noisily. "What's the little bastard to you anyway? He was adopted. He'd have been adopted anyhow, wouldn't he? He had no one else, did he?"

"Who adopted him?"

"None of your bloody business. Stupid, immoral, arty-farty

girl. No bloody use anyhow. Always hanging about with blacks. I'm meant to weep for her and her bastard brat? Don't be fucking ridiculous."

"Who adopted him?"

"Listen." He slapped the table. "Just listen. Bloody self-righteous . . . It wasn't my idea. It was Chris's idea. Okay, so I was making up to the old girl. Like I said, I felt a little guilty, and anyway, why not? Had to have someone to run the place. Bloody child was being looked after by Barnes and his wife . . ."

"Barnes?"

"Yes, dammit. Her butler. Bloody sharp, Barnes. Knew which side his bread was buttered on. He was furious when she didn't leave him anything. Twenty-four years of service. So, old Maudie wants to make a new will. Me as guardian. She doesn't trust solicitors, doesn't trust anybody much. Just me."

She only trusted the man who had killed her daughter. Sweet Jesus.

"So I say all right, my friend Chris'll do the business. So he comes down, draws up the will, goes away again. Next thing I know, he calls me, says, 'You'd best come up to London, Perry, old boy. Got something rather important to show you.' And he shows me this will that says she leaves the whole damn shooting match to me. He'll square Barnes, he says — and he does, too. Makes him manager of a club in Sydney. Everybody's happy. So what's wrong with that?

"He says — Chris says — 'Come on, Perry. You'll never have another opportunity like this. Eccentric old bat, keeps herself to herself, no one to ask any questions, and you get one of the greatest yards in the country. Poetic justice.' Bloody good of him. I mean, just think of the risk he was taking. Solicitor. Well, all right, I argued a bit, but come on. You tell me. Come on. You're all holier-than-thou. Just tell me. What'd you have done? New son, not a bean to your name, heavy gambling debts, and there's everything you ever wanted within reach. You're not hurting anyone, are you? I mean, the brat, what he doesn't know, he can't miss, right? So who's it hurt? All very well for you, brought up in the lap of effing luxury, but you just think about it. You just bloody well think about it, hmm?" He raised his eyebrows and hummed on a rising note. He had his confidence back. "Well?"

I tried not to let him see my amazement and disgust. "I don't know," I said huskily. "It — the whole thing, the whole idea would just never have crossed my mind."

"Exactly!" My father slapped his thigh. He rocked back in his chair. "Like it would never cross the queen's mind to nick a packet of burgers from Safeway's. Does that make her any better than the poor penniless sod who does because his family's got to eat? Or is he the brave one, the survivor, the one who deserves to succeed? Well?"

He had a point. A hateful one. Perfectibility and natural selection cannot coexist, because it's the cheat and the coward who survive to pass on their genes, while the saint and the hero go down at the first volley.

"And why are you able to be so high and mighty?" He was smiling now, and excited. "What bought you the luxury of a clear conscience? The fact that Chris and I did the necessary, that's what, and you grew up without a care in the world as a result. If we hadn't done it, you'd've been brought up poor. Son of a bankrupt. A chance like that came your way, you'd snap it up, and well you know it. Oh, yes. So." He folded his hands in his lap and looked smug. "Just don't you start criticizing your old dad. Just you be jolly glad and grateful that he did his best for you."

I stared. The man was incredible. He had quite seriously played defense counsel, judge, and jury and had not only found himself not guilty but had even awarded himself a special commendation from the bench. Now he sat there like Jack Horner, thumb in plum.

I wondered, did all perpetrators of evil have this ability to persuade themselves of the justice of their deeds? Were all villains so commonplace and so silly? Did any truly evil man ever think of himself as evil, or was that just for harmless poseurs like Alistair Crowley or Alice Cooper? You could see it. The Moors murderers over the fried eggs and Newcastle Brown ale complacently discussing just why the slow dissection of whimpering,

194

pleading children was the consequence of a moral or existentialist imperative, and pass the ketchup, please.

The worst of it was that three or four months earlier, I reckon I'd have swallowed my father's tawdry tale. I'd have convinced myself, too, that a nineteen-year-old girl was just naive and unlucky to drink herself to death, that the rewriting of Maud Gascoigne's will was a sporting opportunist scheme. Not now. Now I saw squalid manslaughter and more squalid fraud, self-aggrandisement, self-deception, arrogant idleness, and bullying.

I needed more information, however, so I jollied the bastard along. "Makes sense," I said at last. "So why'd I get booted out, then?"

"Oh, God," he just flapped my torment away. "Just wait a year, maybe less, then you can come back and everything'll be back to normal. Just a year. I mean, God. Provided you don't rock the boat, you get Waylands, all the cash, the lot. Just keep quiet for now, okay? Chris has called in a small favor, that's all. Won't take long. Just stop making waves."

"He's blackmailing you," I said simply.

"Don't be ridiculous. He's a chum." My father was pompous. "He did me a favor, now he's asking me to do one for him, that's all. We're friends."

And he's a skilled and unscrupulous businessman, I thought, and you're just a venal self-important mug.

I said, "Has he still got the real will?"

"Oh, God, I don't know." My father was impatient. "But that's got nothing to do with it. He just . . . for God's sake, gentlemen stick together, help one another when it's needed."

"So why's he want to break Rashid?"

My father growled from deep in his belly. He leaned forward. He beckoned. He said, "Listen. All right. Keep you quiet. This must go no further. Understood?"

I leaned forward, too. The smell of his aftershave was strong. "Strictly hush-hush" — a crackle — "family honor, all that. Dago bastard . . ." He shuffled further forward. "Dago *bastard* stuffed his daughter. You believe that?"

I was at a loss. "Whose daughter?"

195

"Chris's. Poor bloody girl. On drugs. Needed the money. Filthy bloody Arab. Two girls."

"You mean Louise Wildman was hawking her fanny for drugs?" I laughed.

"I don't see anything bloody funny about that," my father intoned stiffly.

"No, no." I swallowed my words. "Nothing. But I mean, what are you saying? That Rashid raped her, or what?"

"As good as. I mean, she was so desperate for the cash. Chris had cut off her allowance. It all came out when she dried out."

"And Rashid knew who she was?"

"I wouldn't be in the least surprised. Devious little buggers, those dagos. Always have been. But that's not the point."

"No, no. Of course not." I could just about resist the temptation to burst out laughing, but I could not control the quaver in my voice. So Rashid had summoned in good faith a couple of call girls, and one of them had turned out by chance to be Chris Wildman's junkie daughter. For that these two English gentlemen, puffed up with righteous indignation, intended to ruin him. This despite the fact that twenty-five years earlier, these same two English gentlemen had perpetrated the rape and manslaughter of a nineteen-year-old girl who wasn't in the retail business.

I could not believe that my father remained blind to the irony, but he just watched me gravely, one eyebrow cocked, as though he were awaiting a suitably weighty judgment from me.

I said, "Tut tut."

"Anyhow, Richard's sick and tired of all these chaps' coming and lording it over British racing. We all are. Teach the buggers a lesson."

"So" — I was as casual as I could manage — "where's young Dennis now?"

My father's eyes narrowed and swiveled quickly toward me. "I don't think you need bother yourself about that, old boy," he snapped. "Leave him alone. He's happy, you're happy, we're all happy. Leave it at that, okay?"

"I want to know."

"Nick, you've created trouble enough." His chumminess was

gone. "You make any move, you're going to get into very serious trouble. The Establishment . . ." He spat the word out in soft chunks. He liked the effect. "The Establishment does not like disturbance, and the Establishment is very, very powerful. You don't mess with us. Remember that."

I shook my head. I pushed back my chair. "You know something, Dad?" I stood. I leaned forward and rested my weight on my bunched fists. He raised those wet gray eyes to me. "I'd get a mouth guard if I were you. You'll need it for the boxing come March. You are mad. Not just you, the whole damn lot of you. Gibbering and squeaking, drooling and driveling mad."

"Oh," he chortled, though his fingers scrabbled at his thighs, "so you're better, are you? Shrieking scenes at Cheltenham? I don't see you being welcomed at the Athenaeum. You're a mess, Nick. A failure. A total cunt. You and that bitch, that — what's her name? — that Thornton cow. Frigid little bitch. Okay. That's what you want, you've got it. Live with it. And just you think, Waylands and gracious living and . . . all that could have been yours."

"Where's Dennis Gascoigne?" I demanded loudly.

He raised two thick, shivering fingers and gestured at me. "Go to hell."

This, then, at last was it. I had broken cover. For the moment I could crouch and creep. Within hours, the View Halloo would ring out. From then on it would be headlong running all the way.

I reached Central London just before four o'clock. I drove straight to the Holland Park flat, changed into jeans, a white shirt, and a waxed sweater and packed with shaking hands. Chris was a guest at the Lord's cricket match, and since mobile phones are forbidden in the stands, my father would not be able to reach him until he returned either to the office or to his flat.

When that happened, Chris would very urgently wish to find me. He would know, I supposed, that I was short of evidence, but he would know, too, that I could now make some dangerous and damaging assertions about matters that he would sooner leave undiscussed. My father was a weak and venal man.

Chris was strong, and accustomed to making and implementing unpleasant decisions. I did not fancy being the object of one of them.

I needed the files on Waylands and Alison's death. Unfortunately, having been educated in a system so short-sighted as to omit Breaking, Entering, and Allied Studies, I needed a key to the flat downstairs, and the only person who I knew had a key was Chris himself. I had to confront him, then, even though I was unsure as to whether he already knew that I had ceased to be his docile and obedient servant.

When my two suitcases were packed, I ran rapidly down the stairs and loaded them into the jeep. I wanted to be ready for a quick and untrameled departure.

Back in the now stripped flat, I sat on the bed, where I could see the street through the window. I picked up the telephone and dialed High Rigg. My heart was railing against confinement.

"Maria?"

"Nick. Good. Listen —"

"I've got nearly all of it. It's a pretty disgusting sort of story. All I've got to do now is find evidence and the poor dispossessed bastard."

"Look, we've talked to Moran, faxed him the figures. He's convinced. Rashid's horses are going elsewhere, but they don't want a fuss. Make Rashid look like a patsy, and anyhow there's no real evidence."

"I'm going to get evidence of a lot more than some race fixing. I —"

"Nick?" Rachel's voice broke in. "Hi. Thanks for dinner." There was some amplified breathing and clattering, some muffled giggling.

"Hey, what's going on there?"

"Nothing," Maria panted. In the distance, Rachel called, "She's pissed!"

"You having a party up there?"

"No — stop it — no, it's just pissing with rain, and Rachel bought a bottle of champagne. . . . Hush up, will you? So, listen, Nick, can we expect you soon?"

"Very soon, if this works out." The laughter of women always makes men feel isolated and alien. Sometimes it makes us resentful, but on this occasion I felt only lonely and envious. "If not, I'll be in jail."

"Oh, for God's sake, be careful, Nick."

"I've been careful for too damned long, love. No, if all works out, I could be up there tonight."

"Please, Nick." She was suddenly serious. "Make it as quick as you can."

"There a problem?"

"No, everything's fine . . ."

"What?"

"No, nothing."

"Come on, Maria. Not that bloody routine. What's up? Pip okay?"

"Oh, fine, fine. No problems. Eating up like a good 'un and looking like a million dollars. No, I don't want to stop you from ferreting. Just get here as soon as you can. That's all."

"I told you I would."

"Only I've only got Hector and Rachel here . . ."

"Okay, okay. I'll be there tonight, though God knows what hour."

"Thanks."

"Shh! Hold on," I whispered suddenly, and illogically covered the mouthpiece with my hand. I thought I had heard a soft thud from downstairs. I listened for a few seconds. "No. It's okay," I told Maria. "Thought someone was there. Listen, I've got to go. See you later, and love to Rachel."

"Send him my love," Rachel hollered in the background.

I frowned as I put the receiver down. I knew that there was nothing more that I needed to say, but I nonetheless had an obscure conviction that I had forgotten something of great importance.

He returned in a taxi. I watched as three stories below, he stepped out onto the pavement and unhurriedly paid the driver. He wore a Panama and two-tone shoes of tan leather and fawn canvas. I was reassured — a little — by the relaxed ease with which he stretched and looked up at the building. His cheeks still glowed from the afternoon's sunshine and the booze.

I turned away and walked out of the flat. I tiptoed down the stairs to the landing above Chris's door. Beneath, the front door swung shut. The lift clanked above me and wheezed down. The clatter of the door sliding open echoed in the stairwell. The rising lift keened like a hungry dog. I set off down the final flight, so that I just happened to be passing as Chris's head appeared above the tiled floor.

"Oh, hello, Chris." It was hammy, but it would do.

"Nicky!" He beamed amiably enough through the bars. No suspicions, then, as yet. "Good day?"

"Yes. Constructive. Just been writing up my report."

"Good, good." The lift door slid open.

"You? How was the cricket?"

"Oh, splendid, splendid. English seamers getting hit all over the ground. I knew we should have played the spinner. Indians had us tied up in knots." He stepped out. He removed his Panama and combed his flattened blond hair with his fingers. "Well, if you've got a moment, come on in, have a quick drink."

Whenever Chris steered me anywhere, I was again made aware of his formidable bulk and of the weight of his will. He made me feel like a child. His breath smelled of peppermint and cigars. He unlocked the outer door and then swiveled the heavy bunch of keys on his key ring with a swift, impatient, practiced movement. He pushed open the inner door. He stood back to allow me to pass.

I knew my way around. All the rooms gave onto this cream-carpeted corridor with its straw-colored walls. There was a broom closet immediately at my left, into which Chris now plunged in order to switch off the alarms, then, beyond a marble-topped console table borne by an ebony and gilt blackamoor, the drawing room, the other table of the pair, and finally Chris's bedroom, an opulent room lined with hand-printed gold and verdigris Chinese paper, a lonely man's room. At my right were a small, smug virgin of a kitchen, the dining room, and the spare bedroom and bathroom. Chris stopped at the first console table to open his mail. "You go on in," he droned. "Make the drinks, would you? Be in in a second."

I walked reluctantly on. The drawing room was, in the common way of reckoning such things, a peculiarly masculine room. The walls were papered in vertical stripes in two tones of mossy green. There was a beautiful Lucien Freud nude above the marble fireplace on which a battalion of invitations drilled, and a cloudy Wilson landscape at the other end of the room, above the demilune card table where the drinks stood. Otherwise there were only drawings — Tiepolo, Stubbs, Boucher, Monet, Picasso, even (and God, how I coveted my neighbor's goods) a little Goya of two laborers wielding picks and spades. The sofa and the armchairs were burly and covered with some rich crimson stuff, and between the two great windows opposite the door, the personal computer stood on a surprisingly delicate kneehole writing desk inlaid with silver and mother-of-pearl. At its right was the burr walnut Wellington chest where, so Louise had said, Chris Wildman kept the details of my father's crimes.

It was possible, of course, that Chris had since moved his incriminating files, in which case I was shortly going to be in considerable trouble, as well as looking a right fool. On balance, I doubted it. You could not keep such material in an office, for fear of industrial espionage and the curiosity of secretaries. Then, too, there were no alarms in Chris's offices, for the simple reason that the building was almost never empty. When the last of the workers left in the evening, the security men and the cleaners moved in. Here, however, there were alarms on the doors and windows, and pressure pads beneath the carpets. For a while I had considered the possibility that he might have transferred these documents, whatever they might be, to a safe-deposit box, but Eledi had stated that he often had cause to consult them. He could surely trust no one else to go down to the bank to pick up the desired file and to return it once it had been used, and I could not see Chris himself rooting about in a safe-deposit box every time he or Richard Heron needed information.

There, then, I was sure, lay the material I needed, just feet away from me, though I had not the faintest clue as to how I was going to get it. I could not overpower Chris, nor was I sufficiently acquainted with relative skull thicknesses to ambush him with a silver candlestick or a bottle as he entered. I knew nothing of lock picking, chloroform, carotid pressure points, or any of the other commonplaces of my film heroes. I possessed neither Bowie, Derringer, Browning, nor handy surface-to-air missile. I was, in short, stymied by a nineteenth-century lock and a millimeter or two of timber.

The telephone shrieked. I damn near shrieked back at it.

I dived for it. I raised the cordless receiver. My breath sounded like amplified butterfly wings. I held it.

"Hello, Chris?" My father's voice. "Have you found him? We've got to do something, and fast. I can't just sit here wondering what's . . ."

"Who is it?" Chris's footfalls were soft on the corridor carpet.

I quickly laid the receiver down. "Who was it?" Chris strolled into the room. He threw the letters down on the table.

"Dunno." I shrugged. "Went dead."

"Oh, one of those. So, where are those drinks, then?"

"Sorry." I walked over to the drinks table and slopped out two enormous whiskies. I kept glancing over my shoulder at the telephone and willing it not to ring. It seemed to vibrate with frustrated malicious intent. How long could it take my father to call back, for God's sake?

"No water," I mumbled. I picked up the jug and headed for the door. Chris sat at his desk. When I heard the click as he picked up the telephone, relief almost made my knees give way. I reached the kitchen, leaned on the work surface, closed my eyes, and muttered a fervent prayer to any god who might be listening.

"No, here, damn it, at home," I heard Chris insisting. "Right now. Don't piss me about. Yes, I'll manage. Right. Good."

For a second I thought he was summoning someone to deal with the problem of me. I shuddered, then gulped down the panic and told myself not to be so fanciful and self-absorbed. God, this was a civilized Holland Park flat, not a Transylvanian dungeon. This was ridiculous. I filled the jug and carried it back to the drawing room. Chris was no longer at his desk. He had taken the telephone across the room and laid it on the mantelpiece. "So." He removed his blazer and flung it onto the sofa. "Where were you today, then? Can't remember."

"Mmm?" I poured water into his glass. "Er, Hampshire. The Nore Valley Club, you know." I carried the drink over to him. He was undoing his cufflinks, so I had to wait for a minute as he rolled back his sleeves.

"Ah, yes. I must give young Robert a ring. So, everything okay?" He took the chuckling drink, sipped it, and made a noise like a spent astronaut.

"Yes, yes." I turned back toward the drinks table. "Fine. I've written you a report."

"Got it here in the flat? I'd like to have a look at that."

Dear God, he knew. He must know. I grabbed the heavy Waterford tumbler and took two huge gulps of neat Scotch. The heat shuddered through me. "Yeah, but not in fair copy."

I turned to face him. I perched on the arm of an armchair and tried to look casual.

"Fair enough. Okay." Chris glanced at his twinkling chunky watch. "Well, now, hold on here. Won't be a second. I'm just going out tonight. Tasty little number, meant to be a Sicilian princess or something, met her at Annabel's couple of nights ago. Husband's in New York. So. Thought I'd take a quick bath, scrub off the grime of the day. But you hang around. Chat to me. Please."

"Yes. Sure, Chris." A momentary flash of triumph. With Chris in the bathroom and the telephone in my control, I could pry that bloody chest open and . . .

Chris had taken just two steps away from the fireplace when the telephone rang.

He turned and picked it up. He pressed TALK and said, "Wildman . . . Yes . . . What the hell are you talking about?" He took a quick gulp from the glass. He frowned. His eyes flickered quickly over me, then he swiveled back toward the fireplace and made as if to stir the artificial logs of the gas fire with his two-tone shoes. "Yes, all right, all right, calm down. What the hell d'ye want to do that for? Bloody hell. Look, I've told you . . ."

I knew from Chris's tone, and from the quacking coming from the mouthpiece, that it was my father on the line. I took one wistful look at the chest as I edged toward the door. Chris turned and rumbled, "Hold it, Nick."

I bolted.

I bounced off the corridor wall and threw myself toward the door at the end. Behind me, Chris shouted, "Nicky?" and then said to the caller, "Shit, man. What d'ye want to ring for? I had it all sorted . . ." I pulled open the inner door, fumbled at the latch on the outer, heard the clatter as the telephone was thrown down, and the hissing of Chris's breath, and then I had an idea. Or rather, I acted on an idea before I was even aware that I had it. I turned back, shoved open the broom-closet door, and slid around it into the darkness. I had the door shut a scant second before Chris brushed against it and the ghosts of his feet appeared in the crack of light below.

"Nicky!" he roared. "Nicky!" The second cry pursued the first, caught up with it, and tangled with it somewhere halfway up the stairwell, and together they ran on squabbling to the high ceiling. I stood there in the darkness and tried not to breathe, tried not to think, even, for fear that a telepathic whisper might reach the mind of the man just a foot away. I had given up trying to do anything with my heart, which seemed to me to be thudding loud enough to cause the neighbors to complain, or my stomach, which was squirting out jazz clarinet squeals. I stood to attention, not daring so much as to twitch.

Chris breathed, "Shit!" His feet rapped and clanged on the landing. "Nicky!" he bellowed again. This time it echoed downstairs. "Come on. It's all right."

"Go on." I clenched my fists and willed it. "Go on, *go on*." Upstairs or downstairs, I did not care. Just let him set off in pursuit of me. Just let him give me two minutes here on my own.

Very suddenly and very loudly, a constipated cow complained in my right ear. The doorbell. I ducked down. A barely damp cloth flapped against my right eye and cheek. Chris's footfalls returned fast. "Yes?"

"Macinerney." A broad, rough Ulster voice.

"'Bout bloody time, too. See a bloke running out just now?"

"No."

"Good. Come on up, fast, by the stairs, but one of you hold the door. Don't let anyone out. Hear me?" Chris pressed the buzzer to let them in.

Way below, I heard the door click open and then slam shut again. Four feet made a sound like a concert audience of two trying to provoke another encore. They stopped as they reached a landing, then started again, still louder. "Where is the bastard?" the Ulster voice demanded before the echoes had died.

"I don't fucking know," Chris said through clenched teeth. "I had him, could have held him. Goddammit, he ran out, what? Two, three minutes ago. He could have gone up or down. He's got the flat up there. Could be on the roof, in the basement, anywhere. You're sure you didn't see him leave?"

"Sure I'm sure."

"And you've got a man on the door? And the lift is still here. I don't think he can have . . . Come on, come on. You, whatever your name is, wake up. We'll work down from the top."

They were all moving fast, so I moved fast. I'd have liked to stay in there breathing ammonia and lavender wax until I was certain that they were all well scattered, but time was too short for caution. I pushed open the door and tiptoed back to the drawing room.

So my father had managed to talk to Chris, either at Lord's or in the office. . . .

The Wellington was cold, though the bobbing and wavering gas flames were reflected on its polished surface.

. . . and Chris, for all his apparent cool, had already summoned Macinerney, whoever Macinerney might be, before returning here all smiles and Jolly Good Chaps. Purpose — what? To intimidate me with a beating, or simply to get rid of the problem for once and for all?

There were no separate locks on the drawers, just a single vertical plank of wood with a keyhole at its center, which effectively locked them all.

Bastard, I thought, and I grasped that plank in my right hand and pushed the chest away with my left. It did not yield to steady pressure. Above me, doors slammed. Chris barked out something.

I looked quickly around. I pounced on the thick silver letter opener on the desk. The pommel was of jade. Good jade. Waxy and virgin-cool. I set my jaw, thrust the blade into the gap, and, with two sharp jerks, splintered the wood about the lock. The wood groaned and spat. I grunted. I just had to pray that they were making too much noise upstairs to hear me. This was a time for butchery, not microsurgery.

I pulled out the entire top drawer and laid it on the desk's tooled and gilt leather surface. It appeared to contain nothing but loose receipts or invoices. I laid the second drawer beside the first. I pulled out a green cardboard wallet-type folder. In the flickering light, I made out the words in Chris's tiny, cramped hand: *Kellow Hoyle,* <u>*CONFIDENTIAL.*</u> Hoyle headed the youngest of the big bookmaking businesses. Then a pink folder: *Stratton, Marquess of (and Marchioness of),* <u>*CONFIDEN-TIAL.*</u> And a blue: *Gordon Welby, MP,* <u>*CONFIDENTIAL.*</u>

There were more — five or six more in this one shallow drawer. I dealt them out like cards but found no reference to *Storr, Captain Perry.* I found that file, a pink one, only at the bottom of the third drawer.

The footfalls were loud and clipped again upstairs. It was time for me to be going.

I was halfway across the room when I turned back. Jesus, if that chest contained half of the muck that Chris had amassed in all those years running casinos and clubs, it must be worth millions.

I do not know — I honestly do not know — whether my decision to return and gather up the other files was motivated by curiosity, greed, death wish, or altruism. Later I persuaded myself that it was altruism. Chris, like any casino owner, was in the blackmail business. Not every gaming debt would be paid in money. To draw an extortionist's teeth gave me pleasure.

So I was heavily laden as I walked out of the flat and onto the landing.

I walked back again considerably faster.

I had caught a glimpse of the man leaping up the stairs. He

looked like van Gogh in jet-black glasses. The Creator of All Things had done only some preliminary molding. He had shoved his two middle fingers in the clay to make eye sockets, used both thumbs to hollow out the cheeks, one to hollow out the chest, tugged at the legs until they were long and tapering, and then had got called away for a drink. The man had a bleached skull for a face, and ginger pubic hair on his head and his chin. "Mr. Wildman," he panted as he climbed the next flight, "Mr. Wildman . . ."

This, then, was Macinerney. I reemerged on the landing and started down the stairs. Above me, Chris sounded like grumbling thunder. "Of course I bloody do . . ." At least two sets of feet flapped on the steps above me. I started to run.

The man at the foot of the stairs was bigger than I, taller than I, older than I. His dark hair was painted on his cranium with a broad, dry brush. He turned as I swung round on the landing above him. I lobbed the files at him.

Then, for good measure, I threw myself.

The files confused him. He flapped at them. He closed his eyes. Then Superman flew into him at speed, grabbed his coat, and took him on what remained of the flight.

There wasn't much of it. Gravity was being its predictable self that day. I kept my head up; he had no such choice. His head was the first thing to hit the hall tiles, and it hit them hard. The jerk on landing made my head, too, snap forward. The floor hit my right temple, but I was used to this, as to the headlong slithering and tumbling forward when my mount stopped dead. I rolled and picked myself up. Very dark blood was seeping from the right ear of the man beneath me. Otherwise he looked quite rosy, if uninterested now in what was going on around him.

I gathered up the files. The descending feet above me were raucous as rattles. I reached for the door. Even as my hand touched the cold steel of the latch, the three men appeared at the top of the final flight. Chris, in the middle, pointed. His pink face split in three. A gleaming crimson fruit grew, ripened, and rotted at the center. "Theeeeeeargh!" he yelled.

The men at his either hand actually snarled like hounds

before running on down, but I had the front door open and was jumping down the stoop and running, running, dodging couples on the pavement, leaping in and out of the gutter, nipping between cars and across the road into the tree-shattered light of the square. I vaulted into the jeep and did a lot of things proscribed by the Highway Code, but the car was free and clearing its throat to sing.

It was to have a lot of singing to do that night.

I saw the flush of orange sparks bobbing like midges above the yard, and my first thought was *Rebecca,* Hitchcock, 1940, and my second, So Rashid has already removed his horses from Waylands; this is Dad's price for the favor that I asked of Maria and Rachel. My third thought was to gun the engine.

I took that downhill moorland road fast. Any sheep that happened to be on the road would be seriously and instantly tenderized. I did not care. I had to get there. Maria would be down there amid the flames, and Rachel above the old coach house, and Pipistrelle, and it was all because of me, and I had not even been there to protect them.

I was five hundred yards from the gateway when I passed the parked car, and a further hundred yards on before I realized what I had seen. I braked hard and spun the wheel.

Although I hadn't seen what sort of car it was, I knew it wasn't a High Rigg car, and why would anyone choose to sit out on the moors in the small hours while nearby a stable burned?

By dint of climbing the bank, I had the car turned in two points rather than three. But the sightseer had realized that it was time to move on. His headlight beams bobbed out onto the road and scanned the heather. By then I was heading for him fast.

In a second I saw eyes white as spit-gobs and a mouth open wide to snarl or shout.

Mandrake, lurching against the dashboard, back against the upholstery, spinning the wheel hand over hand, and off now down the narrow lane. I would have recognized that ugly face anywhere. Silver-birch trunks leapt out of the darkness and back again, and I shouted something like "Gah!" as if I were urging a tiring horse at a big fence. I settled forward, into it.

We were out in open moorland now, and climbing. There was little moon. There were no stars. The sky was lighter than the moor. That was all. The sky was pinkish at its edges, like black felt-tip smudged with water. Otherwise there were just Mandrake's headlight beams above me, whipping at the heather and the rocks. He was moving at — what? — forty on the bend, well over sixty on the straight. He had the beating of me — but I knew the moor.

Over the crest with a leap then, and down, on a long, narrow hook of road, the sky now big. We were headed southward. In two miles, down there in the valley, the narrow stone bridge spanned Little Beck where it ran into the Lusk.

I murmured to myself, "Come on. Come on." Moths spun at me like scraps of silver paper hoovered up by the headlight beams. Beneath me Mandrake was already at the apex of the bend. I said, "Fuck it." I would have to cut him off. I switched off the headlights. I swung off the road. The jeep bucked beneath me as we hit rough ground.

But now the race was on.

Mandrake's car was still down at my left, heading fast across the valley. The road was almost straight down there, and but for a few teeth-clunking potholes, smooth.

I, on the other hand, was on a moorland track that ran straight enough but was anything but smooth. It was like traveling on a trampoline that in turn was being carried by some very unsteady porters. The roof hit my head. The seat kicked my arse. Suddenly one of those porters would stumble, and the whole world would tilt at an absurd angle. I could see almost nothing beyond the fringe of heather at the edge of the track, the white snow posts, the vague glimmer of sandy soil ahead, and Mandrake's headlights, at every second cutting the angle of that goddamned hypotenuse.

The car complained like a man with a hangover beneath the goad. It groaned. It grumbled. It roared.

I gave the accelerator one last despairing kick, and the jeep bellowed, "All bloody riiiight!" It shot forward and jumped the final ridge, wheezing at the exertion. I wrestled with the wheel and spun the jeep to the left, and we were back on the road, heading back the other way.

And Mandrake was almost upon us. His lights were now dazzling — not two shafts but one huge bright sea urchin with a million spikes. I flicked on my own lights and drove straight for Little Beck Bridge.

I had not thought it out. I had merely wanted to get him; I had not cared how, nor what the consequences might be. Perhaps one day I will rue those consequences. I am told that it is likely. I drove at him, accelerating all the while.

And he — he must have seen the lights appearing from a vast dark waste. He must have cursed and raised a hand as much against the shock as against the light. He must have swerved instinctively. Had he been thinking — and had he been wearing a seat belt — he would have done better to withstand my charge. But he swerved, and the car lurched against the bridge's low stone wall. There was a lot of shrieking — stone on metal, I suppose. I cannot think — I would sooner not think — that his shriek was audible in there, too.

Then my left side was hit, and I had problems of my own as I fought to control the spinning jeep, as it, too, lurched against the right-hand wall, as I was slammed forward against the belt, back against the seat. I tasted blood on my tongue. My vision was smeared. But then I saw the raised arm, the hand that scrabbled at nothing, the wheels rising as the car, like some great animal dying, rose belly up and flipped over the rubble of the wall.

The shrieking, the crashing, the splashing and patter of falling debris seemed to go on for a long time afterward.

Then there was just the twittering of the water.

Perhaps even then I could have done something. I could have scrambled down the steep bank. But there was not time, and I did not care. Mandrake could live or die. I had no preferences in the matter.

The jeep said, "What, *again?*" like certain unfit horses as you turn out into the country for another circuit, but it made it back to High Rigg in five minutes.

The house, thank God, appeared to be untouched, but the stables were well away. The bright orange light wavered like satin, sequined with rising sparks.

I jumped out and ran through the archway into the yard. Suddenly I was in the midst of it: the crackle and roar of it, the crashing as beams gave way, the sound of running feet, the dragon's breath that damn near knocked me over.

Rachel emerged from the tack room dressed in nothing but a man's shirt. She carried a fire bucket. She looked magnificent in that flickering psychedelic light. She charged across the yard and into one of the blazing stalls without seeing me. I ran to the back door of the house and shoved open the door. I dragged the heavy, old-fashioned extinguisher from the kitchen. All six wooden stalls along one side of the yard were filled with flames; there was no saving them. The creosote on the doors at the top of the yard was already being licked by flames, but the old stone stalls had not caught. I ran up there. I drove the plunger hard down on the extinguisher, and for once (they had always failed me at parties) it worked. It fired a jet of foam over my legs and feet and then, when I had it under control, over the door of the first stall and the bedding inside.

"Nick!" Rachel was back. She panted. Sooty sweat beaded her brow. Straw zigzagged from her hair.

"Hi!" I yelled. "Where's Maria?"

"Gone to get the extinguisher from the horse box!"

"Where are the horses?"

"Out. She put them out last night!"

"No point in trying to save those!" I shouted into her mouth, indicating the wooden stalls. I pointed. "Best hold it back here and down there!"

She nodded. "I've got all the taps on full!"

"Great!"

The extinguisher sputtered, spent. I followed Rachel to the tack room. "You fill, I'll chuck!" I called.

Maria was back in the yard when I returned with the first sloshing bucket. She was spraying the stalls at the bottom of the yard. I saw her shoulders leap as one of the blazing stalls at her right crashed to the ground.

211

"Fire brigade on the way?" I shouted. I flung water where she was spraying.

"Yup. And the village. Oh, Christ, if only they'd hurry up. The whole shooting match is going, and my life with it. Come on, come *on*."

"This is because of me."

"Fuck off," she shrieked, and her pointing finger shook. "Get water."

For what seemed an age but was probably only three or four minutes, we worked without speaking. I ran to the tack room, flung the empty bucket at Rachel, picked up the full one, and ran to any spot where I saw the fire advancing.

Then cars from the village started to arrive. Joe came from the pub with his two sons, armed with axes and hoses. Major Halstead came from the manor with orders that nobody needed or heeded. Nice Nora from the Post Office and Nice Nora's Next-door Neighbor came with a tea urn.

Billy, hothead and moralist, arrived later, but he came on his father's snow plow. Without a word to anyone, he drove in, hosed himself down with water, hopped back into the cab, and simply drove straight through the topmost of the blazing stalls, bringing it smashing down about his ears and emerging blackened but, incredibly, unharmed. It was another five minutes before the two fire engines arrived. By then the four bottom stalls and the beams in the coach-house were burning merrily.

Maria sat on the wet cobbles and watched as the power hoses drove jets of white water like battering rams into the stone and wood of her stables, gradually dousing the light. Two tears had left trails down her cheeks and now shone like pellets of amber on her jawbone. "Shit," she said. "So much work. So much time. I can't . . . Fuckers!"

I slumped down beside her. I said, "You knew this would happen?"

She nodded and stared ahead, transfixed by the destruction. "I guessed. That bastard at Ascot —"

"Mandrake?"

"Yup. Saw him in the village. Or thought I did. Then he

vanished. And after what happened at your mum's . . . not very imaginative, is he?"

"No, he's fucking not. You'll be pleased to hear that I got him."

"*What?*"

"I got him. His car was leaving as I arrived. It's upside down in the river now. He won't be holding any more fireworks parties for a while."

She sighed and leaned back against me. I kissed the top of her head.

Major Halstead squatted in front of us and held out a silver hip flask. Maria shook her head. So did I.

"Did anyone think of getting an ambulance up here?" I asked.

"Haven't seen one. Can get one easy enough, though. Got one of those telephone thingies in the barouche. Command module's convinced I'm going to have a coronary. Do we need one?"

"Not me." I sighed. "Chap who started this. Car crash. He's under Little Beck Bridge."

"Good place for him, you ask me." He stood. "Still, I suppose I'd better. Yes. Do that. Surely."

Rachel came and sat on my other side. I put an arm round her shoulders and hugged her. I kissed her, too. I said, "Hey, where'd you get that shirt? It's mine."

"*Was* yours." She shivered and pushed harder against me. "You may be able to chuck away pure cotton shirts just because the collar's frayed. I can't."

"Your old boy safe?"

"Fleet? Yup. He's over at the major's."

"Thank God."

The police took statements. The crowds dispersed. The birds slowly started up. I answered a lot of questions. I had pursued Mandrake. He had driven too fast on the bridge. The inspector said, "Thank you, sir. If it wasn't like that, it should have been," and snapped his notebook shut. "Any idea why he'd want to do this?"

Maria looked at me.

I shrugged. "Not a clue."

Maria said, "Hmmm."

There were eggs, there was bacon, there was tea, there were tears. Everything that we touched was smudged with soot, no matter how often we washed. Everything bore the foul scent of burning. Rachel bustled and jollied. Maria alternately kicked inanimate objects and chided herself for doing so.

We were alone. It was all as normal. We felt ridiculous.

"And we can't hit back." Maria shook her head angrily. "That's the bugger. All that destruction, all that evil. We know who did it. We can't hit back."

And only then did I remember, and I grinned. "You reckon?" I stood. "Just you wait here."

I walked out through the blackened skeleton of a stables to the jeep. When I returned, I dumped the pile of Chris's files on the table in front of Maria. "Read 'em," I told her, "and weep."

"Dear God in heaven," Maria said as she closed the file on the Strattons. "First thing we have to do is get these bloody things out of here. A lot of people would kill to get their hands on these. And on you. Those pictures are revolting. God, next time I see that fat old cow standing in the paddock with royalty . . ."

Kellow Hoyle had been photographed with rent-boys. The Marquess of Stratton and Kilkhampton owed Chris's casinos more than £100,000, and his wife was — or had been — a ravenous dyke with a penchant for the African and Asian branches of gastronomy. A certain junior minister owed nearly £80,000. The bloody fool had even written letters: "This cannot go on forever. My influence re Harrow must have been worth 50K. . . ." A well-known cabaret chanteuse had fucked three of Chris's clients in payment of her debt, unaware that a camera had double-crossed her. Kevin Sharkey, who rode for Richard Heron on the flat, was Chris's property, if only because of a number of IOUs and a communal approach to copulation. . . .

"I was researching human weakness," Chris had told me. He had graduated summa cum laude. Solicitors, councilors, a major general, a deputy chief commissioner, and a television news-reader were all in Chris's net. He specialized in the double bind. He would get your mark to do something unethical in payment, then glean evidence of that something unethical, and so on ad infinitum.

And then, of course, there was the little matter of Peregrine Storr.

Chris had been careful there.

First there was the will, the long and complex document with which my father had been held in thrall. It, like the one at Somerset House, was dated 14 November 1964. It left everything whereof Maud Gascoigne died possessed (less £1,000 to the church and £1,000 and her Daimler to her butler, Barnes) to "my only beloved grandson, Dennis Niall Gascoigne." The witnesses were Chris and Deirdre. My father was to be the executor. Chris had stapled to the will a chit signed by my father, authorizing Messrs. Coutts of the Strand to pay the sum of £140 per calendar month to a Mr. Clifford Roche of Worcester Terrace, Clifton, Bristol, until further notice.

"And that, I rather think," Rachel pronounced, "is where we'll find Dennis Gascoigne. Thirty-five quid a week. Not bad just for raising a child in those days."

"Not bad at all." Maria was remembering. She blinked.

"Tell you something else," I said. "I'll warrant Chris's signature on this will ain't the same as it is on the fake one. He'll have done the fake one left-handed or something, or got someone else to do it. That way, he's in the clear. 'Me? I only drew up the one will. I was astonished to learn that she'd drawn up another on the same day. Now, of course, I realize that she did nothing of the sort. A blatant forgery. Just look at my supposed signature. . . .' Christ, the man may stir shit, but always in surgical gloves. So. What do you reckon? Take this lot to the bank?"

"No way," Rachel croaked from the sofa where she lay. "Nick, love, you've got to get going."

"She's right." Maria stacked the files. "You vanish right now. Okay, so you left Wildman with some cleaning up to do, but it's not going to take long for him to work out or hear that you've come up here and smashed up his henchman; and it's not going to take long for him to get some of his friends together. Then what? It'll take 'em three, four hours to get here? You've got to get out. Return these things to their rightful owners."

"Oh, God." I closed my eyes and concentrated on breathing for a while. It had been a long day, and a longer night. "Yup. I suppose I bloody must, though at this moment I'd sooner burn the lot and curl up with Rachel on that sofa. Still, a lot of sinners are going to be very happy."

"And grateful, Nick."

"Yup, she's right," Rachel purred into a cushion. "Yucky, I know, but might be the best chance we've got, that gratitude."

"You don't reckon I should do it anonymously?"

"What the hell for?" Maria was now pushing me toward the hall. "What's with the white knight bit? You need all the help you can get, and this little lot should buy you a deal of goodwill. Play your aces, lad."

"All right, all right. Always getting shoved out of this place. Bye, Rachel!" I stopped on the porch. "What about you two?"

"What about us? We'll be fine. We'll have half the village round here after tonight. And anyhow, I don't know where you are, so we can't tell them. Just take the jeep and sod off. And stay sodded off till you've sorted all this out. Here. Coat. Get lost."

She gave me her cheek to kiss. She waved from the porch.

I got lost.

RIPON

An isinglass curtain of rain. Extracted four hundred quid from the cash dispenser. Ate a steak pie and chips in a greasy spoon. Planned my itinerary.

For the next two days I was going to be Father Christmas. With the Hounds of Spring hot on my tail.

LEEDS

Councilor Bruce, a gray little man in a gray little suit that cracked rather than creased at the elbows and the knees, looked furious when he saw what I had brought. He resented his nakedness in the face of the photographs, resented being forced to thank me. His wife, however, a blowsy blonde of forty or so, showed me out to the hall. She ran her fingers, itsy-bitsy-spider, along my elbows. She said, "We don't get to swing anymore. I miss it."

"Yes." I nodded. "I can understand that. Er, look, be careful, will you? Don't hold on to any of that stuff for kicks. Burn the lot. And now you're free of this thing, I want you to think very hard about whether you know anyone or anything we can use against this bastard, okay?"

"Nothing, I told you." She leaned back against the umbrella stand and showed me a lot of tanned leg. "I don't even know the guy. Look, I mean, I used to do a lot of swinging, right? We both did. Stopped it — officially — when Donald started getting all political. Then Donald started gambling. This Volare place gives him credit, more credit, enough rope to hang himself. So he comes to me eventually and says, 'Look, Luce, I'm in shit, and the guy runs the place says it's pay up, lose my legs, or open yours. Not that I'd think of letting you,' he says. So I say, 'Well, Christ, why'd you bother to tell me, then?' Well, I didn't mind, to tell you the truth. Exhibitionist, me. Got a kick out of it. Go down to town, all expenses paid. Private parties at these casinos, right? Champagne, gentlemen, no one to recognize us. Do what looks like a straight strip, then me an' this other girl come down off stage, pick out the stuffiest true blue, and go down on him. Make 'em feel better. Make 'em feel good enough.

"Next thing I know, the debt's all paid, or nearly, only a) someone's been snapping us all this time, and b) someone's been showing the pictures to Donald and saying, 'Bitch enjoys this. Why should she have fun while you sit at home?' Drags him out to the clubs, loses more money. Brilliant. We're worse off than when we started, and now this guy's got evidence on me, too. Fucking marvelous. So I say enough, and what the hell. One good spread in the *News of the World,* every porn magazine in the country'd be paying me to open Sesame, right? Blow for freedom. But Donald says, 'No, no. The cause of freedom is the cause of the left-wing. We mustn't betray the party,' all that crap. So, great. I go on strike, I mean, there's AIDS and all that anyway. He starts to pay his debt with little favors. Green belt becomes building land, that sort of thing. Blow for freedom. Great. *I* was blowing for freedom, if you ask me. He was farting for favors. No, but there was never a name or a face. Just the manager of the Volare first, these clubs in town, nothing written, then telephone calls, 'You'll vote against this, for this.' That's it."

"So. Why don't you leave the arsehole?"

She said, "Oh, I couldn't, you know? I mean — fuck it — I'm a Catholic."

MANCHESTER

The Pennines were cloaked in inky black. The jeep veered beneath me like a green horse in the buffeting, rain-speckled wind.

The deputy chief constable was brisk and savage, a terrier in uniform, snuffling and snapping at the documents and at his wife.

At last he said, "So, what do you want, son?"

"Nothing." I shrugged.

"Don't be ridiculous."

"Wish you were a picture dealer."

"What?"

"Nothing. Listen, I want nothing, okay? I'm giving this stuff to you. A *gift,* understand?"

"Don't be bloody impertinent, *son.*"

"Sorry, do you want it or do you want me to send it to the *Police Gazette?*"

"You can do what you like."

"Okay." I stood. I reached for the file of papers on the desk.

"Don't touch it!"

"Learn humility, little man," I barked back at him like an Alsatian. "Learn contrition. Say 'Please' and 'Thank you.' You think you're so goddamned superior because you're older than me and you wear a uniform and you roll up your left trouser leg from time to time with a load of good old boys who call themselves Freemasons? But remember, *son.* I've seen you. I don't see a uniform or a thirteen-year-old pubis mustache. I see a man who has allowed criminals back onto the streets to bully and wound and con other cunts like you because you were too shit-scared for your own hide. I have brought you your salvation, and I can, if I choose, damn you. Unlock all those little closed cubicles in your third-rate museum of a brain, man, smash the display cases, let air reach the specimens. Now, you tell me about Chris Wildman, or I'll take *this* to the highest bidder."

"That's black—"

"Shut up!" I shouted so loud that the figurines danced on the smoked-glass table between us. "Shut up, Mr. Walford. I've done my bit for you. You just speak. Quietly. Logically. Cogently. Now."

He started, "I never so much as met the man, damn it. I've heard his name, of course, but I had no idea that he had anything to do with this business. . . ."

LEOMINSTER, HEREFORDSHIRE
"Oh, you darling!" Mrs. Reeves-Curtis popped a sugar cube into the mouth of each spaniel in turn. "Oh, this is good news. I can't tell you."

She wore a gray silk flapper-style bandeau about her head. It was fastened on one side with a scab of jet, then flowed down over her low-hanging dugs. She wore a dress of Liberty peacock pattern. She lived in a large white cottage in which everything was covered in paisley cashmere or Chinese silk, much of it frayed, all of it fringed. Such light as there was crept guiltily through heavy velvet drapes and skulked in corners.

"No, we are terribly, terribly grateful to you. Really. Could you give me my bag, please? Because I need my engagement diary, as it gives me all the details. I find it so hard to remember details. I've been doing my story, such as it is, and of course I'm trying to recall all this beastly stuff one had tried so hard to *forget,* don't ye know? You know — no, why should you? — that I have written a little story or two? Oh, yes. Nostalgic smut, really, but terribly popular. Anyhow, no, we had to stay so quiet about poor Reeves's gambling. Silly fellow, but it was the plague of the time, you know. No Visa or Access or anything then. Only way you could play at having money you hadn't got was to go down to one of that dreadful little wide-boy Heron's clubs. I mean, Reeves was a very, very silly boy. Waiting to inherit all those years, and the old Methodist bugger — old Larne — positively refusing to die. Ridiculous behavior. No, thirty-five thousand pounds, for heaven's sake, and that was worth five times as much as it is today, but we weren't too worried. I mean, Larne had millions to leave. But then up pops that bastard Wildman, and he says to Reeves, I get the money now or I go to Larne, tell him the whole story.

"Well, I mean, *unheard-of!* But as I say, clever. All right. Wildman goes to old Larne, he kills the goose that lays the egg, right? But at the same time, of course, we couldn't have Larne cut us off without a penny. And he would have done. We'd have been bankrupted by Wildman and Heron *and* cut off by Larne. Instead, they agreed to give us extended credit, and interest-free, but only if Reeves brings punters in.

"Poor Reeves. Meek and mild, and a gentleman, really, but, I mean, sunk, completely *sunk*. So he lures in his little friends — oh, dear — and they're even *more* susceptible. I mean, provincial peers and poets and shooting people and so on — hardly MENSA, are they, nor what do they call it? Street crud?"

"It'll do." I smiled. "Streetwise."

"Well, yes. Something. I mean, old Percy Keightley, streetwise? So Reeves brings these stuffy old sods in. They get flattered, and they lose lots of money, oh, dear, lots and lots. Tom Partridge tried to blow his brains out, you know. Oh, yes. Made a balls-up of it, but then he blinded my cocker once, too. All very traditional and splendid, put 'self' in the game-book, all that, but too shaming to go and miss. Anyone'd think he was trying to exaggerate the bag. Still alive, I believe, a-babbling of green fields. Well, no. He'd say 'hee-hee.' Completely gone. Plastic skull. It killed poor Reeves. When his heart attacked, he was so depressed he hadn't the will to fight back. Just gave up. Probably the best thing."

"You never thought to leave him?" I asked.

"Oh, no. My dear, one has one's friends and one's lovers and so on, but one doesn't go round leaving husbands like litter. It's messy. It's . . . American."

I said, "Will you give evidence against Chris Wildman? It'll mean revealing your husband's peccadilloes."

"Oh, that's all right. Yes, yes, of course one would. But it's only hearsay, of course. There's nothing in black and white . . ."

Brakes whined in the street outside. Feet clicked on the pavement. I moved to the window and pulled aside the faded velvet curtains. Two men had already pushed open the garden gate and were walking fast toward the front door. I did not know them. I did not want to.

"Oh, bugger," I groaned. "I don't think you're going to be able to keep those documents, Mrs. Reeves-Curtis. I advise that you fling them on the fire. Meanwhile" — I started as the doorbell trilled — "where's the back door?"

The tragedies, the comedies, were recounted in houses and apartments great and small. I earned grudging goodwill. Lady Stratton, she of the voluminous body and the voracious appetites, promised me lots and lots of rides, which sounded odd, while her husband puffed and stomped and grumbled like a walrus who had just got the bill from the carpenter. The chanteuse sobbed on my shoulder and pressed a Lalique yellow opalescent perch car mascot on me. I was receiving a crash course in human weakness and a vivid history lesson, but I was no closer to disposing of the threat from Chris. He had ensured that his victims had no evidence of his requests for favors or services. And while Chris remained in business, I was under threat. Constant, physical, and very possibly terminal.

Things improved when I came to the men of action. A famous Queen's counselor calmly scanned the folder and its contents, calmly shredded them, and said, "Thank you. Lunch?"

We ate oysters and sea trout at Bentley's. His flue-brush black eyebrows bobbed up and down with every swallow. He said, "Wildman know you took this stuff?"

I nodded.

"I'd say you're in danger, then? Hmm?"

"I'd say yes. I think he's got people on the lookout for me."

"Well, we'd better do something. Leave it to me, and keep me posted as to your whereabouts."

"We've got no evidence," I objected.

"Mr. Storr," he said slowly and heavily, "the law is a dinosaur that evolves slower than its environment, but it has reflexes. Stick a pin in its right foot and it strikes quite devastatingly fast and hard, and that slow old brain isn't even aware that anything has happened."

Kellow Hoyle, the bearded millionaire bookmaker, said, "Great, right. Now let's fit the fucker up good and proper. Been looking forward to this for years."

I gave him the number of my solicitor friend. He said, "Watch your back, Nick. If Wildman's using strong-arm boys from any of the firms I know, I'll neutralize them. Oh, and by the way, I'll see you right for this."

And so I came at last to Bristol, and to the changeling boy whom I had dispossessed.

Dennis Roche jumped up the steps from the basement two at a time. He turned to his right, shoved his hands hard into the pockets of his leather jacket, and set off down Worcester Terrace. It was thick dusk, and the roads and high pavements shone brighter than the sky.

Roche was short and strong. His neck was thick, his head round and carpeted with cropped black hair. His step had the fuck-you spring of the weight-trained fighter.

I followed him.

I could, of course, have walked straight into the Clifton basement and handed over my birthright — "Excuse me, Mr. Roche, but your real name is Gascoigne, and you own property worth five or six million" — but I was still uncertain as to the moral rights and wrongs of the case.

Technically, of course, it was cut and dried. Waylands, its contents, and the gallops were this man's rightful property. But just to hand it to him — would it make him happy? He was unprepared for wealth, unaccustomed to responsibility, uneducated to appreciate the beauty of the place, whereas I . . .

Oh, sure. If it hadn't been for Chris's and my father's villainy, he would have been brought up the young gentleman, and I the poor but refined neighbor, but Chris and my father had done what they had done, and things now were as they were. Was the *status quo ante* necessarily the right thing? To turn Dennis's life upside down, to deprive me of everything I had loved, to threaten Waylands and the people who worked there . . . Was it morally braver to resign personal responsibility to the letter of the law or to consider the greater good of all concerned?

Dennis Roche had been a "bad boy." I had it on the authority of the grocer on the corner. He still lived with his "parents" on the ground floor and in the basement. As a kid he had been "away — bit of trouble," for eighteen months. A pub fight. Possession of drugs. He hung out with the blacks down St. Paul's, just as his mother had hung out with the blacks in London years before. Now he had cleaned up his act, was working as an electrician's assistant. But was it fair to Waylands that such a man should be foisted on it? Was it fair to anyone?

The will — the real will — in my breast pocket said yes.

He walked to a smoky, poky pub: engraved glass partitions, naval hat-bands, and ghostly photographs above the bar. He was already at the bar when I pushed open the door.

And an arm shot over my right shoulder to keep the door open. And something very sharp punctured my skin just above my kidneys. And an Ulster voice that I knew growled, "Back up or I gut you." And a smooth-looking dark man in a dark suit squeezed past me through the doorway and turned to face me with a small smile and, like a host guiding a guest in to dinner, gently pushed me back out the door.

We were on the pavement now. Cars occasionally crashed through the puddles in the road as though hitting tissue paper. The two men were huddled about me, blocking my vision. It felt like an automatic car wash of worsted and tweed. I pushed at the dark man. He pushed back. I tried to break to my left, but a hand grabbed my right arm and held, a leg arose to trip me. For a while it was all rustling and grunting and heavy breathing, and then the dark man said, "Now, now. You're coming with us."

"Who the hell are you?" I panted.

"None of your business. Where's the stuff?"

"None of your business."

The knife twisted. Its point penetrated my shirt and pushed at my skin. I yelped. There was a quick flicker at the level of my stomach, and the fist drove into my gut, hard and low. I tried to double up, but the dark man pressed hard up against me. I wheezed Stockhausen chords and screwed my eyes up tight and saw a lot of fragments of bright burning paper rising against the darkness.

"Now, you're going to behave, aren't you?" said the dark man.

"You'd better," growled the Ulster voice in my ear.

Suddenly a human figure that seemed totally black dislodged itself from the shadows and rushed at us with what seemed to me to be terrifying speed. There was air behind me where the warmth of the knifeman had been. There was a violent choking sound. The dark man clung tighter to me and tried to pull me fast down the pavement. I pulled back. I yelled, "Roche! Dennis Roche!" and hit the dark man hard but essentially ineffectually on the shoulder. I tried for the jaw then. The blow just glanced off his left cheek. I'd had precious little practice at this.

The pub doors swung open behind us. "Dennis!" I yelled again, "Help!"

I was dimly aware of Macinerney dragging himself along the gutter down at my right. A figure turned his attention to the man who held me. Dennis Roche said "'Ere, you!" and his sneakers squeaked on the pavement.

My captor had released me. He was running. Dennis ran after him. I saw the sneakers flashing, the hands flailing. I sank to my knees. A large black man was leaning over me. He said in a Caribbean squeak, "You awright, man?"

I gasped, "Yeah," and it came out falsetto. "Er, yeah. I'm fine. Thanks."

There was the clunk of a car door, then a loud smashing sound from down the road where Dennis had run.

"Who — where are you from?" I asked the black man. I pulled myself slowly to my feet.

He grinned. "Angel. From heaven, me. Nah. Kellow Hoyle tells us you're 'ere, someone's gonna do you. You follow that guy, these fuckpigs follow you, I follow all of you. Grandma's footsteps, hey?"

Dennis emerged from the shadows of the street. The dark man's suit was stained and damp. His shirt was torn. His lower lip was puffed up and seeping dark blood. His right cheek was livid. Dennis held him up easily by his collar. He dropped his burden in the gutter at our feet, kicked him hard in the ribs, and dusted off his hands. "Had to drag him out through the windscreen," he told the black man. "Hi, Mo. So, what's 'is all about, then?"

Mo shrugged.

"Well, you, then," he said, stabbing at my chest with a thick finger. "And how come you know my name?"

"Oh, Dennis." I blinked at his wrinkled face, at the tell-tale oblique scar above his upper lip where a cleft palate had been patched. "You don't know the half of it."

We left our attackers snuffling and swearing; we thought it as well to move to another pub. We drank Guinness. I was a hesitant, weary fairy godmother to this unlikely Cinderella. I told the tale as briefly as I could.

After I'd finished, Cinderella gazed at me and then said, "You're doolally, you. Me, Gascoigne? Like the footballer who cries all the time?"

"Yup." I presented him with the will.

"Fahkin' Ada!" He glanced at it. He tossed it down onto the table. "Come on. This is some sort of joke."

"I should listen to the man, I was you, Denny." Mo nodded as though his head were attached to his neck by a spring. "I mean, this guy's a swell, i'n't he, and you don't get Kellow Hoyle takin' a personal interest in yer 'less you're someone. Why'd he want to have you on for?"

"I don't know." Dennis frowned. He flicked the will. "But it's got to be . . . I mean, this is crazy. I mean, me, a bleedin' millionaire? Don't make me laugh."

"It's true, Dennis."

"So who's my dad in all this, 'cording to you?"

I shrugged. "Nobody seems to know."

"I mean, anyhow, what'd I want with some bleeding great pile in the country? Jesus."

"Yeah, well, I want to talk to you about that."

"Only one way to sort this out." Dennis tipped up his glass and smacked his lips. "Come on. Drink up. Let's go back and see the old folks. Bleedin' crazy, this. I still don't believe it. Big joke."

It took just under an hour to extract the truth from the good Mrs. Roche. At first she swore that it was all nonsense. Denny was her little lad and always had been, always would be. Who the hell did I think I was, coming in and putting ideas in his head?

I told her. Then she had to spend twenty minutes apologizing to him for not telling him the truth sooner, but she could never find the right time, and it made no difference, really, did it? She hugged him. She begged his forgiveness. He wriggled a lot and mimed desperation over her head.

I sat in the little basement that smelled of gas and stale smoke and artificial honeysuckle. I yawned noisily.

"Well, of course, we just didn't ask, did we?" she twanged at me like a broken string. "I mean, you wouldn't, in the circumstances, would you? Lovely little baby, and I couldn't — well, *we* couldn't — have one, could we?" She turned to her husband in the corner. "And the money — well, it was very generous, wasn't it, Cliff? Thirty-five quid a week in those days — worth well over a hundred now. So the thing was, everyone was happy, way I looked at it. We didn't know anything 'bout the real parents. Nothing, did we? Only the mother had died. Just Barnes — the butler, that is, used to work with Cliff on the boats, that right, Cliff? Stewards for P and O together, weren't you? Well, Barnes says, 'You'd never be wanting a sweet little baby boy has no mam or da, would you?' Well, what are you, what is a person to say to the likes of that? You don't ask, do you? Gift from heaven."

The gift from heaven, the sweet little boy, muttered, "Gor, fuck me sideways." Then, "It's true, then?"

"Well, I don't know. I suppose so. I mean, if this gentleman says as it is, well . . . Isn't that right, Cliff? I always knew you were something special, didn't I? Always said it."

Mrs. Roche was a robust woman with pink balloons for cheeks and short mousy hair. She could have been in her early fifties. Her strong arms were always working. The husband whom she so constantly consulted, however, could as easily have been ninety. He said nothing, just sat in the corner in tartan slippers and enormous cords, smoking Navy Cut after Navy Cut, eyeing the silent darts on the television with yellow-edged eyes and occasionally, for variety's sake, coughing like a hatchet until those eyes streamed.

"Now, listen." I stood to command some attention. "I don't know, but I don't reckon you'd much want a place like Waylands, Denny. Am I right?"

"Too bleeding right." Denny shuddered. "Flog it. Set up in my own business. Buy us a yacht, Porsche, the works."

"Exactly. But I *do* like the place. I was brought up to it. *I'd* like to keep it. Now, you can prosecute my father, prove — possibly — that the will he has is a fake, and maybe in the end you'll get the whole darned lot and he'll get sent to jail. That's option one. He'll have the expensive lawyers, and the whole thing will take a lot of time, a lot of money, a lot of hassle. Option two is, you decide how much you want, how much you need — cash — and we go to my father and say, 'Okay, we can screw you, but we're prepared to burn the real will in exchange for compensation.' That way you get the cash straightaway, and I have a chance — just a slim chance — of holding on to Waylands. I know it means that the criminal benefits from his crime, but it might just work out a damn sight easier for all of us."

"Yeah, yeah." Denny was the businessman now. "All very well, but . . . Yeah, okay, makes sense to get the lot now."

"What you've got to decide is, how much?"

"Well, five million, I'd say." Denny shrugged as though he'd been saying such things all his life.

"Denny, Denny." I sighed. "There's no way my dad could start to pay you that."

"Yeah, but if that's what it's worth . . ."

"Listen, Denny. An hour back you'd have been grateful if someone had bought you a pint. Now we're talking millions, and you're not prepared to let a penny go. Okay, you're entitled. Far as I'm concerned, it's all yours, but you'll have to fight for it, and you may well lose. Let me put it in some sort of proportion. You get a million now. Invest it. You get a guaranteed income of over a hundred grand a year, for the rest of your life. That's a rich man, Denny."

"Yeah, but . . ." He was sulky. "All right. Say half."

"What?"

"Three mil."

"Three years in court. Maybe five."

"Two, then."

"One million five. I think he can make that at a push. The five'll buy you the car, the boat, a house, and you've still got the million to live off. Better than the pools, Denny."

"Well . . . what you think, Mum?"

"Ooh, I don't know. It's all too much for me." She wriggled. "Someone gives me a few hundred, I'd be happy. Cliff?" She turned to the compost heap in the corner.

The compost heap stirred. It rumbled sooth. "Go near a lawyer," it pronounced in Donegal Bristolean, "you're stuffed, win or lose. Like that show. Take the money, open the box thing." And it vomited air.

Dennis cocked his head. He screwed up his face in an agony of indecision. "Mmmm — okay!" He jumped to his feet. "You got a deal, Nick. Let's go see this sod. Sorry, your dad. I don't mean . . . Hey, Mum." He hugged her to him. "Me, eh? A bleeding millionaire!"

She said, "Go on."

I rang Maria from the Roches' hallway. She said, "Hi, Nick. Get off the line. Someone could be listening."

"Everything okay?"

"Sure. No problems. Horses well. You?"

"I think we've got it sorted out. Lot of people sleeping tighter today. Found the heir. No visitors?"

"Oh, yes. They were dealt with."

"Me too."

"You'd better go, Nick. We'll talk when it's all cleared up."

"Maria . . ."

"Yup? Quick."

"Oh, hell. Miss you. Both of you."

"That's nice. Sod off, Nick."

I rang my new solicitor friend at his home number. He sounded pleased to hear from me. "Ah, Mr. Storr. Is all well?"

"So far. I was attacked this evening, but Kellow's man happened to be on hand."

"Nasty. Yes. I wouldn't worry too much if I were you. I rather appreciated your friend Mr. Hoyle's completely unethical vigor. He should have been one of those sobbing evangelists. He'd have made even more money. No. We've cooked up a bit of this and that. A salmagundi, if you will. After tomorrow morning, I think you can sleep easy. Listen out for the news. Christopher Wildman is a spent force, I am delighted to say."

"What charges?"

"Oh, a variety, a variety. Ranging from fraud to a plethora of misappropriating and malfeasance counts, you know?" He sounded like a proud cook unwilling to yield the precise recipe. "With the right word in the right ear, I'd say eight, nine years. You should be all right."

"Great," I said, and I meant it. I felt muscles that I did not even know I owned relaxing in my neck and shoulders. "Thanks."

"Thank *you*, Mr. Storr. It is a pleasure. But — how shall I put this? — you really must remain discreet. You know about a lot of things that, if I may say so, are not your concern. You take my point?"

"I'd rather have known about none of them."

"Yes, well. You stick to that attitude, and you'll have earned a large debt of thanks from — well — from a number of people well able to pay that debt. And it will be paid," he said ponderously. "I give you my assurance on that."

I thought of my father's absurd "The Establishment does not like disturbance." I said, "I'm going to see my father tomorrow. You've heard what he's been saying about me?"

"I have been apprised. Vaguely."

"This isn't vengeful," I told him. "This is no domestic squabble, okay? He had no argument with me. He acted out of greed and jealousy, at Chris Wildman's behest. Thing is, my reputation now stinks. I want it to smell of roses, and I want him to know that the world does not think much of the way he's been behaving. He values the world's opinion."

"Understood. So you want me to get the word about before tomorrow?"

"A few indications, if possible, yes. Before tomorrow lunchtime, say. That possible?"

"Oh, I think so. Yes, I think so. Leave it to me."

It was the second time in thirty-six hours that he had said, "Leave it to me." I was tired. I was tense. I suddenly wanted to be a fluffy, kittenish little blonde. I just loved powerful people who said, "Leave it to me."

And last, I rang Waylands. It was a quarter to midnight. Deirdre was gracious. "Who the hell . . . ?" she snapped. "Do you know what the time is?"

"Deirdre? Nick. I'm coming up tomorrow."

"I wouldn't." She was brisk and breezy.

"Well, I am. I'm coming with Dennis Gascoigne, aka Roche, Master of Waylands." I pressed on. "And an exceptionally genuine will. We won't come to the house. We'll be up at Wayland's Smithy at one o'clock. We want to discuss the past. And the future."

"I wouldn't waste your time, Nick. We won't be there. You caused your father profound distress the other day."

"Funny thing," I hummed as though reading. "Your signature on both wills is identical, but Chris's signature on this will is not the same as the one on the Somerset House will. No resemblance. You see, he covered himself, Deirdre. It's you who carries the can."

That silenced her for a while. There was some rustling of bedclothes. At last she muttered, "Bastard," then, "Just dream on, Nick. We won't be there. We're really not interested in your sick fantasies." Her tone was all airy, like that of a taunting schoolgirl.

"Oh, you'll come, Deirdre. Because if you don't, you'll be living in a prison cell by tomorrow evening, and in a cardboard box if ever they let you out. You'll come. See you."

I slammed the receiver down before she could cut me off, with a savagery that the instrument had done nothing to deserve.

It struck me as I walked back to the B and B where I was to stay the night that in the past few weeks I had learned to judge those to whom I had once deferred, to give orders to those whom I had addressed as "Sir." I was frankly sick and tired of these posturing con men who clung to an illusion of class as though class were a uniform rather than a culture. My classical British education had at every point tended to make me deferential to authority, with a view to assuming it gradually, gradually, as of right. My father's rejection and my recent discoveries had taken a bolt cutter to the chains that had protected and bound me. I was neither gentleman nor "common," neither rich nor poor, southerner nor northerner. All badges were scrapped. I had but one name left to me, Nicholas Storr, and one set of convictions, my own.

The British have a way with sources of embarrassment. They lose them. The Radio 4 news the following morning told me that millionaire Christopher Wildman, managing director of Wildfire Leisure Corp., had disappeared, owing shareholders several millions of pounds. The fraud squad had been looking into irregularities in the running of Wildfire for some time, the newsreader informed us, and it was thought that they had been poised to make an arrest.

Yeah. And Shergar's door is being bolted.

The Establishment did not want Chris revealing all in the dock. Sooner have him retire to a villa in South America, where he could pass the evening of his years drinking cocoa and fulminating about wogs with Martin Bormann and Lord Lucan. And if there was so much as a murmur about memoirs, an ambiguous word or two would no doubt be spoken in a Pall Mall club as the Sheffield knives cleaved partridge breasts, and thousands of miles away a rusty *navaja* blade would find its way to Chris's iliac spine.

That is the polite way of doing things.

"Bloody Nora!" Dennis leaned forward in the passenger seat. "You mean that's . . . that'd 'ave been . . ." He gaped at Waylands from the end of the drive.

"Yup. That's the place you should have inherited. And four hundred acres, cottages, a pub. . . . Sure you don't want it?"

"Gor," he gulped. "Nah. Wouldn't mind the pub, but shit, must cost a bomb just to heat a bleedin' great pile like that."

"Does."

"Hassles I can live without. You're welcome to it, Nick, boy. Pretty, though, I grant you." He sat back. "Bloody Nora, I still can't get used to all this."

"Yeah, well, just stay cool, Denny. No excitement, no anger, nothing. You may want to belt my dad, but don't. And don't accept any offers without checking with me first. Right?" I started the engine again and drove toward the downs. Denny saluted. He said, "Yes, sir."

"I can't see 'em trying anything, but keep your eyes open. They're crazy enough."

"Gor." Denny looked around him at the downs. He shuddered. "I'm not very good at this country lark. Gives me the heebie-jeebies."

I gave him my well-practiced lecture on the Ridgeway and the Smithy, but I don't think he was listening. We reached the old tomb at ten to one. We climbed down from the jeep. I dropped a pound coin for the elfin swordsmith and led Denny up onto the plateau.

The wind hit us in big muffled punches. It was like swimming through surf. One moment all was still, and the next a cold gray wave crashed over you. Denny sat on a boulder and tugged at his fingers. I paced backward and forward. I wanted to see the car. I wanted to get this over with, whatever it might be.

"You know, Nick, I think maybe I do remember something like this. A dream, you know? And the house."

"Yeah?"

"May be imagining things, but yeah. And a big green carpet, pale green, and a lot of gold. Blue room."

"We'll find out. Ah," I said softly as I saw the big black Citroën Safari creeping like a gleaming cockroach up the track. "Here they come."

And suddenly I needed to pee very badly. My hands started to flap of their own accord. I could not stand still. I could not be comfortable. My clothes seemed to be scrabbling at my skin. "Shit," I breathed, for I knew that the moment that I dreaded but had labored to bring about was now just minutes away. I could have taken a cushy job with Wildfire. I could have returned to Waylands in a year's time, but I had insisted like a maniac on the truth. And here the truth came, in a car like a cockroach on the lonely downs above my home.

Denny came to stand at my side as the car drew up beneath us. The twelve-bore lay loose on the backseat. "Get that gun as soon as they stop," I said.

Denny nodded. He jumped down. He had the back door open and the gun out before my father and Deirdre had even managed to unclip their seat belts. He threw it up to me. I caught it by the breech and broke it. Jesus. It was loaded, and it was not on safety. And I had just caught it. They evidently did not teach the shooter's code among the villains of Bristol.

My father clambered from the car. He looked weary. There were bags as wrinkled as scrotal sacs beneath his eyes. His gray skin hung looser than ever.

Deirdre was as brisk and expressionless as ever. She said hello to Denny with regal disdain. She wore a Hermès headscarf with a pattern of bits and bridles. She reached back into the car for her handbag. Denny said, "Leave it, please, Mrs." She sniffed. Her eyes shifted heavenward, but she obeyed.

My father waited for her to come round the car. He stooped slightly. He offered her his hand. Together they climbed up

233

onto the Smithy. At one point my father slipped and sprawled on the slope. He grunted but pulled himself quickly up. There was a streak of green on the right leg of his fawn trousers. My heart ached, but I stood still.

"Well." He sighed and blinked. "Hello, old boy."

"Hello, Dad." The wind pounced.

"Well, here we are."

"Yup. Come on, let's sit down."

"I don't know what we're doing here," Deirdre snapped. "You've damn near killed your father. What the hell have you been doing? It's just pure vindictive spite. God."

"What are you talking about, Deirdre?"

"You, poisoning, telling lies. Four owners have rung up this morning to say that they want to take their horses away. The Turf Club and the Cavalry Club . . . I don't know how you did it, but it's just vicious and cruel and destructive."

"It's nothing to do with me, Deirdre," I said. "It's simply that people don't actually like to see a father behaving like this to his son. It's not 'done,' in case you didn't know. Now. You haven't met Dennis Gascoigne, or not for a long time. Deirdre, Captain Storr, Denny."

Denny said, "Hi."

My father's eyes rested on his face for a moment and then, infinitely sad, returned to me. "So," he said. He dragged himself over to the boulder where Denny had been sitting. He sank slowly onto it.

"Well, I'm not sitting, I can tell you that," Deirdre held her head on with one hand and gabbled on, but the wind snatched up her words and whisked them off over the downs. The bushes kicked up their skirts like can-can dancers. ". . . father and ruined your godfather," she finished. "God. Bloody ingrate."

"Dad." I sat down opposite him. Denny squatted at my right. "You know what I've got to say. This is a photocopy of Maud Gascoigne's *real* will. Chris's signature here is his real signature. The one on the will at Somerset House is a fake, probably done by some employee who didn't know or care what he was signing. Also, a court would know bloody well that a woman who has left her all to her infant grandson does not, within twelve hours, cut out the grandson, the church, and her butler and name a totally unrelated beneficiary."

"She did!" Deirdre was shrill.

"No, she didn't," I said gently. "Waylands belongs to Denny. Isn't that right?"

My father's tongue crackled. "I improved the place. It's worth more now."

"Sure. Sure. We'll discuss all that. Now. Denny's agreed to accept compensation and leave Waylands to the Storrs. That right, Denny?"

My father's eyes rose at the word *compensation*. He turned to Denny again. "How much?"

"One point five mil." Denny smiled.

"One point five . . . !" Deirdre shrieked. She started to laugh. The rooks hoarsely aped her. "Oh, that is too ridiculous! That is too . . . I don't believe it!" Her laughter subsided. The silence blushed for her.

"Don't see the joke myself, Mrs." Denny looked up at her, questioning.

"No. No, you wouldn't," she said, dismissing him. "You just snatch figures out of the air. They mean nothing to you. A fiver, a tenner, a million. . . . Where on earth will we find one and a half million? It's too absurd. Tell him, Perry."

"It's not negotiable, I'm afraid," I told my father. "The estate's worth five or six. It's good of him. As to where you'll find it, that's your problem. Sell shares, sell land, sell some furniture. It's just got to be raised. If it's not, Denny will go to the police and very publicly get the lot, and you two will end up in jail. For a long time, I'd say."

My father let out a deep, low grunt that went on for a long, long time. Suddenly Deirdre was above me, her hand swinging stiff-fingered at my face. I had time to tilt my face away, but she still slapped my cheek hard enough to shake my brains. I saw my father wince as the blow landed. "You little *bastard!*" Deirdre shrilled. "*Bastard!* After all we've done for you!" Her hand rose again. I gritted my teeth. I grabbed her arm as it descended. I stood. I gave as good as I had got. Better.

Her head jerked sideways. She staggered, her hand to her livid cheek. She collapsed onto the grass. She wailed.

Nobody moved. She wailed some more.

Sobs shook her body. It still had no effect, so she took to keening, "Bastard, bastard, bastard!" and she covered her face with her hands.

"Shut up!" I bellowed above her whimpers. To my astonishment, she almost did.

I sat down again. I said to my father, "I know, I know. Gentlemen don't hit women. So rule me out. They hit me, I hit them. Now. Okay, Dad? One and a half million. Cash. How long'd it take you?"

"Oh, God." He shook his head. He looked up at the sky. "Oh, God! Oh, God! You've made a right fuck-up of this, haven't you, old boy? Bull in a bloody china-shop." His voice cracked. He pulled himself to his feet. He sighed and sorrowfully shook his head. "I wanted to avoid this. God, I wanted to avoid this. Still. On your own head be it." Suddenly he pointed at me. A fist tightened about my heart. "All this belongs to Dennis Gascoigne, you say? Quite right, old boy, quite right. You" — he gulped — "you . . . oh, for Christ's sake! You *are* Dennis bloody Gascoigne!" He waved toward Denny. "And this is Nicholas Storr."

I looked at Denny. I thought, No. You can't be Nick Storr, because I am. It was the one sure fact left in my life. Nick Storr did not have a harelip. Nick Storr hadn't been to borstal. Dennis Gascoigne didn't know about horses or movies or anything. I knew about all those things. . . .

"No, come on." I laughed uncertainly. "That's nonsense. Mum would have known. When she told me she'd seen Denny here as an infant, she said, 'Poor child,' and now I realize she meant the — the lip. Sorry, Denny."

"Your mother didn't see you until late the morning after the birth. You ask her. She didn't know why you were taken away as though there were something wrong. She didn't know why she had to wait till she got home to see you. Perfect baby. You see" — he raised his head and gave Dennis a proud little

236

smile — "it was your mother's blood. Storrs do not have deformities."

I saw Dennis flinch as hard as I had from Deirdre's blow. He hissed, "You filthy fucker, you mean . . . ?"

"So you see" — my father had recovered his drawl — "I have abided by the terms of the original will. Except that I got to own Waylands, which was right and proper . . ."

Dennis's voice came from deep, deep within him. "You dirty, cowardly fucker."

"No," I said sharply. The panic drained away. "No, Denny. He's lying. A last, crazy, devious, hurtful lie. It's crap. Dennis Gascoigne must have been a month or two older than Nicholas Storr. My mother may be a bit dotty, but she's not so bloody dumb as to confuse a month-old child with a newborn baby, and she would know her own child."

"Are you sure, Nick? Hmm?" My father had one eyebrow raised. He looked down his nose at me with a supercilious smile. "Are you that certain that your dear mother wouldn't trade a healthy child for a sick one, hmm? Do you know her that well? Well, well."

"Yes, I bloody do!" I was shaking now with fury. "If for no other reason than that she derived no benefit from it and she quite reasonably hates your guts. As far as I can see, you hadn't even met Alison when Dennis was born. But we're dealing with a particularly devious sort of madness, Denny. He shook us, both of us. He got us to resent one another. He got us to think, What if I'd had his advantages? or What would I have been if I'd been in his place? It was a gambler's move, a last throw that would have been transparent if we hadn't been all wound up."

My father was still smiling.

"So. One and a half million," I said, standing up. "By — what shall we say? First October? No. Michaelmas will do nicely. When tenants pay their rents. Twenty-ninth September. That's settled."

"And this place goes to Nick," Denny added.

"Thanks, mate. And a deed of gift, please, Dad, by next week, giving Waylands to me. Don't worry. I'll not kick you out.

I just don't want to see you leaving the place to a cats' home out of spite. Right. That's it." I pocketed the cartridges and tossed the gun down on the grass. "Ready, Denny?"

"Stay any longer," he said, sneering, "I think I'd puke. Christ, what a pair."

"Greedy little crooks." I nodded.

We strode side by side to the car without looking back.

"Hold it," said Denny as I climbed into the driver's seat. He trotted across to the Citroën. He pulled something black from his leather jacket. There was a click, a quick flash. He stabbed the rear tires with the switchblade.

"Exercise'll do 'em good," he cackled as he climbed in beside me.

I let out the hand brake. The car jerked forward. I had to bump onto the wide grass verge to maneuver around the Citroën.

My father had stood and walked to the edge of the tomb. He stood there, a monumental figure beneath the crown of trees, and the wind shook his brown tweed ulster. He watched us with the dull immobility of a drunk.

It was not over. It was only nearly over. I suppose, save in fairy stories, that it never is. There had been no rapiers drawn to conclude matters in a convenient welter of gore. No wedding bells had rung to mark the end of one state of being and the beginning of another. There had been no Worker State, no New Jerusalem, no Happy Ever After. Time had just gone on, as is its wont.

I had proved, perhaps, the victor, in that I had survived while my enemies now suffered. But they lived on, I lived on, and the scent of victory was not one pheromone different from that of defeat. Either way, it seemed, strife, like sweat, was sweet when fresh but stank when stale.

The reckoning: I had killed one man whom I had never known. Mandrake (Gordon Timothy Walker) had been taken off life support in late August. I had destroyed the Tinker Bells of childhood by refusing to believe. I had lost my father. I had lost — but no, to talk of innocence is absurd. I had lost all the reassuring structures from which I had derived security and identity. I felt like a blind man when the interior designers have moved in unbidden. Before, I had known where the furniture was; now I had to feel my own way.

On the profit side of the ledger — oh, there was no end to the profits. I had the deed of gift that made Waylands inalienably mine. From the first day of the season, I had been inundated with offers of rides. Lady Stratton and Kellow Hoyle had been as good as their word. Their friends now knew that Nick Storr on their horses was as much an essential fashion accessory as this year's designer label on their dresses. After a month I was leading the championship table, but I wasn't good enough to sustain that. By the end of October I was second, and by November, after ten days off with a broken collarbone and three ribs, third. Now, in early March, I was still third, though I was registered as stable jockey only to Maria's yard.

I rode well enough, and could lose myself well enough in the shouting and the thunder of racing, but I found no more joy in the game. When I read the reports of my triumphs in the papers, my father's envy outweighed my pride. When I set off for work in the morning, I felt tired. The whole business seemed trivial in relation to the pain it had caused.

And I saw that pain daily. Daily my father, pale and stooped like a sheet frozen on the line, stood in the paddock and watched me with sagging eyes.

He had spoken to me only twice until the day before. At the beginning of November, at Chepstow, he had called up to me as I shortened my leathers, "Every bloody stolen penny. Satisfied?" In the middle of December he had caught me as I emerged from the weighing room at Doncaster. "Louise Wildman, old boy. Thought you and your dago friend might be interested. Died of an overdose in New York last week. Hope you're satisfied."

I did not mark Louise Wildman down in the debit column.

The more my father was cut by those whom he so desperately admired, the more he was ignored and lampooned by the young Turks of the turf, the louder he blustered and bluffed. The more races I won, the more he slandered me. He claimed to have laid a hundred thousand against my winning the next Gold Cup, because that was where one "told the men from the boys."

If I had been a gloater, I would have had plenty to gloat about, but I did not find it in me. You may beat cancer by having a limb amputated, but the victory is no cause for celebration.

As for High Rigg, it really felt very much like Happy Ever After. The Strattons had sent four good handicap 'chasers. The insurance company had paid up. Soon the swank new yard would be complete. In the meantime, Maria's animals occupied empty stalls in Corin Gilmour's yard, just two miles away. In gratitude and in a bid at reparation, Rashid had sent us six of his horses.

One of them was Ibn Saud.

"I really think . . . ," said Maria, and then all pretense at really thinking fled. She hit her forehead with the heel of her hand. Her fingers raked twice through her hair. "Look, go, will you? Just take him and go."

"Come on, Maria," I protested. "This is melodramatic."

"Maybe. I don't care. I just . . . we just can't take the risk." She picked up the telephone in Corin's office. She tapped out a number. As she waited for an answer, she pulled a cigarette from the packet on the table. She irritably shook the packet off the cigarette. "The old stone stalls at High Rigg are a damn sight safer. And yes, I know it's crazy, but . . ." Her lighter clicked. She blinked against the smoke. "Okay, maybe I'll look like a damned fool and you can all have a bloody good laugh, but . . . Hello? Is Major Halstead about, please? *No,* don't bother. This is Maria Thornton. Listen. Bit of a crisis here. Could you ask Rachel Leigh to get over here with the box right now? Urgent. Okay? I'm — sorry — I'm at Mr. Gilmour's. Right now, okay?" She replaced the receiver, then had to replace it again.

"God," she said, and she puffed out smoke and sat like a wary dysentery sufferer on the edge of a chair. "God." She got up again and walked to the window. "What's the bastard doing out there?"

"Trying to scare you," I told her.

"And doing a bloody good job. Jesus, Nick, you should have told me."

240

I nodded. I should have told her of my father's visit the evening before, and I was at a loss to understand why I had not done so.

It was the Saturday before Cheltenham. I had been riding at Doncaster and so had returned early to High Rigg, only mildly bruised by a slithering fall on a clumsy novice of Corin's in the fourth. Maria had been out and Rachel in the yard when the telephone rang.

My first impulse was to slam the telephone down, but Dad had sounded meek. "Hello, old boy, how are things?"

"Fine, thanks."

"I was wondering . . . Look, I wanted to let bygones be bygones. I — I mean, we've both been bloody fools in some ways. No need to be lonely the rest of our days, eh? I just . . . I was hoping we could have a chat. Just like to see you, you know?"

"Yup?"

"It's just, I'm on my own and I'm on my way down from Ayr, you know? You at Doncaster today, bad luck. No bruises?"

"Nothing much."

"Well, I mean, I'm almost going past your door, so I wondered, do you think we could meet? Just for a few minutes."

"When?"

"Well, an hour? Two? Something like that."

I had an acute feeling that he and I still had unfinished business. I wanted an end, a resolution. Now, of course, I realize that parenthood is forever unfinished business. I said, "Okay, but it'll have to be here. I can't go out. Have to be quick, too. I don't think Maria's exactly going to be glad to see you here."

"Oh, dear. No. Okay. I'll be as quick as I can. Thanks, old boy. You don't know what it means."

He turned up just over an hour later. It took him a long time and a lot of effort to pull himself up out of his car. He limped to the front door. I said nothing, just led him to the drawing room and indicated a chair. He sat down with a lot of geriatric business.

"So." I perched on the corner of Maria's desk. "How are things?" I asked.

241

"Bloody awful, old chap, you'll be glad to hear. Any chance of a drink?"

"You know bloody well you shouldn't be drinking," I said, and instantly regretted the intimacy. "Still, okay. What?"

"Scotch?"

"Okay." I walked over to the drinks table beneath the window. "So what dosage are you on now?"

"Forty Actrapid, sixty Monotard."

"Jesus!"

"Oh, well, what the hell." He sighed.

He had almost tripled his cocktail of insulin since last I lived at Waylands. He must be hitting the bottle hard.

He took the glass. He swilled its contents around, then gulped and gasped. "Horses well?"

"Fine."

"Ibn Saud, now. Done well there. Lovely ride at Kempton. Reckon you're going to win on Thursday?"

"I gather you don't."

"Look, yes. Thing is, I've been rather silly there. I admit it. You know, the stress of all that business last year, having to sell all that stuff — you know. Stress. Thing is, old boy, I think you ought to know — not that it should make any difference to you, obviously, but . . ."

"Come on. Come on, for God's sake."

"Well, I'm afraid I can only hope you lose. I sort of went for broke on my chap and laying against yours. You know?"

"Silly of you."

"It'll finish me if you win," he bleated. "Still."

"What d'ye mean, finish you?"

"Well, can't see me going publicly bust, warned off, selling up, going to live in Budleigh Salterton or something, can you?"

"Why not? Better men than you have."

"Yes, well, they must be better. No. It'd simply be the end. I've thought a lot about it. Of course, it may not happen. We win, Waylands'll be back to the good old days. Retrieve, oh, half the money I gave away last year. More. But if not . . ."

"I'm not going to stop Ibn Saud for you, Dad. Jesus. You never fucking give up, do you?"

242

"Oh, no. No, you shouldn't." He was wide-eyed. That crackle. "Absolutely not. It's just — it's only a race, isn't it, for you? For me . . . Oh, well, it's my fault. I should never have taught you to be so bloody high-principled, should I? Always brought you up to be straight as a die, and look where it's got me. Flat broke and dependent on you for my life because you're so bloody straight now, you'd kill your old dad sooner than stop a bloody horse. Irony, eh?" He laughed. "My fault. My bloody fool fault."

"I think you'd better leave, Dad." I stood.

"Yes, yes. Well, all I can say is, I'm jolly proud of you. Damn glad I could give you the start I did, the education, the training, and now here you are, making a fortune, eh?" He drank. "Funny the way things go," he said vaguely. He stood. "I really am very glad for you, Nick." He smiled, reached across, and tweaked my cheek. "Very glad. I wish you well. Come on. Don't look so gloomy! I knew what I was doing, and I've had a damn good time. It's not your fault — I taught you to be this way!"

On the doorstep, he stopped to pull on his gloves. He looked up at me. "Haven't got a hug for your old dad?" he asked. The tears were brimming in his eyes. "Wouldn't blame you."

"Dad," I wailed, exasperated. I really did not know if I was taken in or no. I just knew that I could not let him go like that. "Come here, you old bastard."

I felt his arms around me, and the waxy warmth of his cheek against mine, and God damn me, my eyes, too, filled with tears. Home is a time, not a place. I was glad for a second to be back there.

When I released him, I turned away fast and pushed the door shut hard behind me.

Was it shame that kept me silent when Maria came home, or simply the desire to deny all unpleasantness? The wicked uncle has no place polluting the Happy Ever After. Or was it that I did not want her even to consider that I might be ambivalent about the forthcoming race? Because I wasn't. We were going to win on Thursday.

243

Ibn Saud was the favorite after our victory in the race at Kempton. Pip was something like 50 to 1.

It was not surprising. Ever since the fire, Pip had been back to his old tricks. None of us had been able to work out why.

He had been on Major Halstead's land at the time, four miles away, so he had known nothing of the blaze, yet from the following day he had weaved and bolted his food once more. He had put on no condition. When I had ridden him at Worcester in December, he had run listlessly, jumped carelessly, and finished tailed off.

It had taken Rachel to find the answer. "Look, I know this'll sound ridiculous," she had said suddenly in January, "and Nick will just scoff, but I want a tape for Pip's stall."

"A *what?*"

It was one of our Sunday-evening meetings in the dining room.

"A tape. A recording, you know."

"Great." I had nodded. "Sure. *Champion the Wonder Horse,* is it?"

"No, Nick." She had tapped her ballpoint on the pad before her as though driving a stake through someone's heart. "Jackdaws," she told Maria. "I want the sound of jackdaws."

I had swallowed my smile.

It was so obvious that I wouldn't have thought of it in ten years. It was the only thing that the fire had changed for Pip. Whether Jacky had been roasted or had simply decided to move somewhere safer, Pip had lost his friend. Now, with the sound of jackdaws once more about him, he recovered condition and placidity. He slept as soon as he came in from exercise. He ate as though nanny were watching. We had not raced him, just schooled him once to jog his memory. He was our ace in the hole.

So, for whatever reason, I had kept my own counsel, and this morning, as every morning, we had driven over to Corin's to exercise our horses and his. It was afterward, when we were bedding down our mounts and Rachel had set off to attend to Fleet (now a lodger at Major Halstead's), that the news came in.

244

Corin, Maria, and I were sitting in the office, drinking coffee and trying hard not to speculate about the week to come, when Jimmy, Corin's head lad, walked in.

"Just going up on Hagg's Point," he announced. "Seems as there's a queer fellow up there was watching the string through field glasses. Ted saw him. Rang just now to tell us."

"Touts," Maria said, and she grinned. "What fun. He won't have seen anything anyhow."

"No, but we'll go and kick his arse for him." Corin stood. He strode over to the hooks where the coats hung.

"Any description?" I asked casually, but my voice betrayed me.

"Nope." Jimmy stood with his fingertips in his jeans pockets. "Just gray-haired is all Ted says. In a Citroën, with a bloody great rifle."

I gulped. I said, "Oh, God." It came out as a hoarse little croak, but Maria shot me a frowning glance.

"Camouflage," Corin mused. He shrugged on his leather jacket. "Bloody typical. Bookie doesn't know you can't shoot on a Sunday. Come on, Jim."

They strode out like heroes. A minute later, car doors thumped and an engine grumbled. Gravel spat.

"Oh, God almighty!" I covered my face with my hands.

"What is it, Nick?" Maria demanded. "Come on. What's up?"

"That wasn't a tout," I groaned.

"What?"

I pulled down my hands and blinked up at her. "It was Dad."

Maria looked as though she had died on her feet. Color and animation left her cheeks. Her eyes widened. Her jaw dropped. "You . . . you mean . . . ?" Her fingers rose to touch her lower lip. "What's he doing . . . ? Oh, no. Oh, no, Nick. No, he can't be that mad." She slumped and stared straight ahead of her. "Can he?"

"No," I sang consolingly. "'Course not! He's just trying to put the wind up us, that's all."

"What for, Nick? Why bother? There's no point. There's only one thing he wants — no, two: he wants to stop Ibn Saud, and he wants revenge."

"He wants to stop the horse, all right," I admitted. "He even tried to get me to hook him, but —"

"What?" Maria started to her feet. She came at me with fury in her eyes. "You've seen him?" she shrieked. "And you didn't tell me?"

So then it all had to come out, peppered with my apologies and Maria's recriminations, and at last she hugged herself and shivered and said, "God, Nick, I'm scared."

And then it came — the mighty crack of a rifle, the ringing, singing wave of sound playing tag across the moors.

Maria yelped. She was at the door and out of it before I could reach her. I followed her into the yard. She was running round the stalls, peering into those where a horse's head did not show.

I stood defiant at the center of the yard, gazing up at the basin of moorland that surrounded us. I pictured him lying somewhere up there in the heather, watching me through the telescopic sights. The walnut stock of his old Winchester .308 would push into his cheek. A small smile would tug at those thin lips.

"Breathe in gently, old boy . . . squeeze, don't pull . . . and never fire until you are sure that you can kill. . . ."

And his tongue would crackle.

I should have thought. There was my father, whom I wanted to love.

There was Peregrine Storr, gambler, who had already demonstrated that he cared more for his vanity and his social aspirations than for his son.

My father was still there somewhere, a faint, ghostly blur in the double exposure.

But Perry Storr was his master.

Perry Storr, stalker.

Maria returned at a run. "We've got to get the horse out of here," she panted.

"Whoa, there." I eased her back into the office. "He's not going to shoot the horse. Not in the yard. He doesn't want to get himself arrested. If he'd been shooting at the yard, wherever he was, he'd have hit something. He's just trying to frighten us. I don't know why. It's just a childish ploy to torment us."

246

"I'm going to call the police."

"Maria." I put my hands on her shoulders. "Hold up, will you? What's the point? By the time they get up here, he'll be long gone. And what are we going to say? That there's a man up shooting on the moor? Big deal. He's got a license."

"But he could . . ." She spun from my grasp. She pushed back her hair. She did not even look at her hand as it reached for her cigarettes. "Listen. You know these things. Could a bullet go through the walls or the doors of one of these stalls and still do damage? Say he's, what? A quarter, a half mile away?"

"Maria —"

"Could it?"

I thought about those dog's-cock 130-grain bullets that could rip through clapboard wall as if through paper, thought about what would happen if one found its way into Ibn Saud's skull or his great artery, turning him over like a rack of skittles. Maria was watching my face. I did not need to answer.

"Right, that settles it," she said. "I'm sure you're right and he's just messing about, but I can't stand this. The old stone stalls at High Rigg — he'd be safe there. We could get the village motivated. They could scout around, keep that bastard at a healthy distance. I want to *know* that that horse is safe."

So now we fretted and awaited Rachel with the horse box. Maria rang the Rawcliffe Arms and the vicarage to drum up assistance at High Rigg. Corin and Jimmy returned to report that the gunman had gone. "Hear the shot, though?" Corin asked. "I think maybe he was a poacher not a tout all along. Maybe after deer, I don't know. Anyhow, he's buggered off."

"I'm sure that's right, Maria. He's gone," I said.

"Maybe," Maria snapped, "but he could come back. I want to be sure. I'm taking Ibn Saud home, Corin. He'll be safe there."

Corin winced. "What are you talking about, darling?"

The horse box came shuddering through the gate. Maria spoke as she walked across the yard. "That wasn't a stray poacher up there, Corin." She paused and announced over her shoulder, "That was Captain Peregrine Storr. Nick will explain to you, won't you, Nick? I'm going to load up our horse."

247

Corin said, "Oh, bloody hell," and reached blindly for a chair.

Maria had hurried me into the already shaking box with little stamps of the feet and flaps of the hands and pleas like a hunting horn — "Come on, come on, come oooon!" — and all the while I had been calm. I had smiled at Rachel. I had waved as I let out the hand brake. Now, only now, halfway to High Rigg, did the reality of our danger strike home, and I felt my hairline recede.

I had traveled this road a thousand times, yet only now, for the first time, did I see it. And seeing it, I shuddered, and something very large and heavy shifted from my diaphragm to my bowels. "Oh, sweet Jesus," I whispered, and my lungs fluttered. "God help us, he's given us his wind." I hit the steering wheel and sat forward. I made the engine shout.

"What?"

"Shut up! Get down!" I barked.

"Nick, you're going too fast."

"Not fast enough," I almost wailed. "For God's sake, get down on the floor, will you?"

Now I knew why my father had drawn attention to his presence above Corin's yard. I had seen him do the same with roe deer. It was no childish malice that had motivated him, but rather the desire to "bump" us into the open — out here, with that striding ridge encircling us like a lover's shoulder and the Kirkby Moorside Road climbing diagonally on the other side of the valley, not four hundred yards away.

We were climbing a gentle rise now, with nothing but open moor about us, uninterrupted save by granite boulders and the occasional shaggy sheep. I ran through the rest of the journey quickly in my mind. In half a mile a steepish decline would begin; then again through open country for three quarters of a mile; then the massive cliff of Spaunton Crags, hard by the road at our right, with the sheltering cover of the conifer plantations at the left . . . no. He would have to choose a spot near the road. He was unfit and had little time. It would be here, then, or on that forthcoming stretch downhill.

It was here, and now.

The old horse box hit a rock.

It felt like that, at least. There was a sudden hard jolt, then the slam of the gun, the rapid chorus of cawing echoes, a giant crow fleeing across the moors. The engine seemed to gulp, then screamed.

"Fuck it!" I shouted above the row. "He must be somewhere ahead."

"Stop, then!" Rachel's cheeks were spank pink. "Go back!"

"And give him twenty minutes to pepper the box while we lumber backward? No. If we can get down to the wood, we might be okay. More protection there. Get the horse out and into the trees. Into a drainage ditch if possible. Come on," I told the old engine. "Come on, please."

But there was little hope for Ibn Saud now. Even if the grinding, straining engine pulled us as far as the sheltering lea of Spaunton Crags, my father would merely have to drive his car half a mile up the road, walk a hundred yards or so to the edge of the cliff, and fire vertically down on the box. If we managed to get Ibn Saud into the woods, we might briefly be able to hide him, but that was the stalker's element, and it is not easy quietly to restrain a large, fit horse.

There were hours of daylight yet to come.

Time to kill.

I bounced on the seat to urge the box on as it strained to climb the hill. Already steam swirled on the juddering bonnet, but I could not afford to slow down.

"What's happening, Nick?" Rachel's voice quavered. "For God's sake, this can't be happening. Oh, God, oh, God . . ."

"Radiator!" I yelled. "He's hit the radiator. Engine's going to seize."

"He just can't . . . He can't be that crazy. Please, no."

"He is," I said grimly, through clenched teeth. "God save us, he is. The gambler. Has to win this hand, even at the risk of —" My voice shook so violently that I had to swallow hard, and then we were over. I shifted down. The engine barely noticed the easing of the strain. At our right, a kestrel, unaware of anything save hunger, flipped over a drystone wall.

"There!" Rachel sobbed. "There he is."

I looked where she pointed, up on the hillside to our right. There, halfway up the hook of scrub, the black car gleamed dully on the road that climbed parallel to ours. In a moment we would be broadside on, but the downward gradient meant that with every second we were sinking further away from him. He might take a potshot, but he must be four hundred, five hundred yards away, and there was room for three horses in the box. He would not know that he had achieved his end. He had to know. If we drew to a halt here, he would make quite sure. He would just have to crawl to within two hundred yards and systematically drill the box.

"Get into the back," I told Rachel. "Get Ibn Saud untied and turn him round. As soon as we stop, I'll get round to the back and let down the ramp, and as soon as I'm in the box, be ready to give me a leg up. I'll ride him out fast — he should come quite easily, but I hope to God he doesn't slip on the ramp — and I'll take him over the gate and into the woods. As soon as I'm gone, you climb back into the front of the box and slide out the driver's door, since that will give you more protection. Then run like hell for the woods — Dad won't be interested in you."

"I'd be a witness." Rachel's voice was suddenly steady.

"There's been nothing to witness. We haven't seen any-thing. . . . Go on, love."

She nodded. She sniffed. She got up from where she was crouched on the floor and clambered over the seats and into the box behind her through the connecting door. And as she went, the engine took a last asthmatic breath and died.

There was silence then, save for the rattle of the box, the thumping of the horse on straw, and the faint whisper of the wind.

"Oh, no," I heard Rachel whimper.

"I think we're all right," I called, and I pushed at the steering wheel. "Come on, damn you! Come on!"

We were traveling at perhaps twenty miles an hour. The slope was so gentle that we were losing speed with every rattling inch, but we were moving still, and the great wizened face of the cliff was drawing nearer. I could see the begging juniper on the bluffs, the wriggling black wrinkles in the rock. The horse box lumbered ever slower toward the bend beneath it.

My father saw it, too.

There was a thud behind me, a shriek from the horse, and again that hammer-crack with its ringing echoes. I ducked, and my stomach gulped. As the peals died and the horse thumped a dance of panic, I found my voice somewhere. "What's happened? Are you all right?" I called.

"Yes, yes." Rachel's voice was high-pitched and tremulous. "I don't believe this. It was over our heads. He's mad, Nick."

"I know."

"Are we there?"

"Nearly," I told her. "Nearly."

We were moving at a walking pace now, but we were on the bend, and I was riding the box out as though it were a flagging horse. When at last, with a groan, it drew to a halt, I was safe, protected from my father's fire by a wall of rock. I reckoned that he could still see the back of the box, but we were out of effective range.

How long would it take? He would climb back into the car and drive up to the top of the cliff that towered above us. I knew better than to believe yesterday's geriatric performance. He would stride — maybe run — to the edge. Say four minutes. Say he had set off immediately after firing that wild shot. Three minutes, then, to get Ibn Saud out, leap on his back, jump the gate, and get lost in the eight-foot-high dripping conifers at our left.

Go.

I scrambled out and scurried round to the back of the box. I looked up at where the car had been. It was gone; nor was it to be seen moving along the road. He was already above us, then, struggling through the heather, pitching into the becks, cursing.

"Ready?" I shouted.

"Nearly!" Rachel called from inside.

"Come on!"

"Hold on, damn it!"

I shot the bolt on the right. I crouched as I scurried across to the other side of the box. I reached up. The bolt was stiff. Twenty seconds were lost as I waggled it to work it free. Then

251

the weight of the door was on my hands. "Ready?" I called again, and my hands shook.

"Go on!" Rachel's voice was strong.

I let down the ramp.

It was at waist height when I fell, flung backward onto the wet gritty tarmac by what seemed to be an explosion from inside. I was vaguely aware of searing pain as the ramp was wrenched out of my hands, and of something hard and dark striking my temple before my head fell back to hit the road. There was the snort of a horse, the smell of a horse, the thudding and then the slithering clatter of hooves, and for a second the pressure of horse and ramp on my legs was increased. I rolled out from underneath it, my ears ringing like a cathedral.

What I saw from where I lay was familiar, as was the ringing of my ears, the blurring of my vision, the pain in my body as I saw it: a horse, a dark-brown horse, towering above me while booted feet kicked on.

"What the fuck are you . . . ," I managed to get out, and then everything — thought, words, sight — was wiped out by the tidal wave of sound.

When a high-velocity rifle is fired at you, time travels backward. First you hear the bullet strike flesh, then the crackling in the trees, then the huge crack of the gun, then the ringing echo.

Then time travels fast forward again, as though to catch up with the lost moment.

The horse took perhaps two paces forward and then went down like an abandoned puppet. Rachel was flung forward, somersaulting over his head and vanishing from my sight.

There was a long hiss from the dead horse as wind escaped from his great body. Then there was silence.

I climbed groggily and unsteadily to my feet. The world was spinning faster than it should. I dusted grit from my bloody hands. Somewhere a car started up and droned off like a disturbed bee.

I walked over to Rachel where she lay on the road. She was curled in a fetal comma. She was crying.

I knelt and laid a hand on her shoulder. "You bloody little fool," I panted. Breath was hard to come by. "You bloody little wonder. I was meant to . . ."

"Oh, God," she moaned like a foghorn. "Oh, *God.*"

"Come here." I drew her to me. There was a livid red mark on her forehead, and her right cheek had been grazed and burned by the asphalt. I kissed her forehead. I kissed her cheek. I kissed her eyes. "Oh, Christ, darling, are you all right?"

"I'm — I'm — I'm okay." Her breath shuddered out of her. She gulped in more air. My kissing her lips did not help.

"N-n-n-nick?"

"Oh, God, my love, I'm sorry."

She vacuumed up more air. "No, come on. S-s-s-no."

"Darling, darling idiot, please . . ."

"Please, Nick . . . no."

"I've been such a total . . . oh, God, such a total cunt. Please, my love . . ."

"Oh, yeah. Ha." She punched away her tears. She blinked fast. "Mean you've noticed I'm human? Oh, thanks a ton, Nick." And she sobbed for a minute against my chest.

I kissed her crown. "Oh, don't," I crooned. "Don't. Please, my love. I told you. I've been a complete ass."

"I mean" — she spoke against my mouth now — "I know I'm just the stable-girl, and —"

"Don't." I winced.

She hit my chest, and her eyes were wild. "But my father never tried to shoo-hoo-hoo . . ."

"Rachel, please."

I held her to me hard. Over her head I saw the dead horse, lying stiff-legged and somehow enlarged by death. Its lips were rolled back over a ghastly pink, black, and yellow grin.

I frowned.

It was a big dark bay. But it wasn't Ibn Saud.

"What . . . ?" I said stupidly, and the thudding and thumping from the box behind me at last penetrated my paralyzed skull. "What in Christ's name . . . ?"

Rachel turned to follow my gaze. Again a deep moan seeped from her.

The dead horse was Fleet.

Rachel flapped a hand dismissively. "Useless old thing, huh?" she sobbed, and her face crumpled like a burst balloon. "I — I brought him over to keep Ibn Saud com-company." Her voice was small. "I mean, he doesn't matter, does he . . . ?"

"Shut up," I wailed against her mouth. "Shut up, shut up, shut up . . ."

I had to make her.

I have an editor now for the telling of this story. I've never had one of those before. She says, "Come on. Bit embarrassing, this dialogue, isn't it?"

I say, "Yes."

"But we've scarcely seen Rachel before as a real human being."

I say, "No. That's the point."

She says, "But it's unrealistic."

I say, "Sure. Too bad. But it was real."

Beneath every coat and every suit in the snow-spattered paddock at Cheltenham, there was a naked body. Behind every polite smile, a passion hid. I had never been so aware of this, nor so grateful for ritual and disguise.

There was Lady Stratton, of whose naked body I had seen altogether too much. She smiled slyly at me as I rode past. There was Deirdre, carefully not looking at me or at Rashid as Len was flicked up on Slaney Star. There was Maria, chewing on her lower lip. She was instructing Dudley Knox, who had the ride on Pipistrelle. My mother appeared to be instructing him, too. And here, at my foot, leading Ibn Saud, was Rachel. My Rachel.

I knew her naked body, too. I loved every perfect inch of it.

For two nights those wide, wide eyes had watched me, as, to my bewilderment, she drained the marrow from my bones.

Snow peppered the hills and dribbled down onto the course. The sky was pewter, the air clean and sharp. It was a beautiful day for a battle.

And now we were all up and riding out about the thick gruel of the crowd, and Rachel quickly kissed my knee. She said, "Good luck, Nick. Love you."

I said, "Love you, too." Predictable, perhaps, but succinct.

And we were away.

Ibn Saud wanted to escape the people as much as I. I was happy now, with the power of a great horse beneath me and a cold wind wiping my brow. Would this, then, be the happy ending? Nick Storr wins the great race. His enemies are confounded. His reputation is restored. He is loved by a good woman. . . .

No. There are no endings.

If I won today, my father would be bankrupted and the deed of gift nullified. Waylands would have to be sold. If I won today, too, much of the credit must go to the man whom it would destroy. He, after all, had trained this magnificent animal until just eight months before.

But I was going to win today, because Ibn Saud said so, because he deserved his victory, and because I would do nothing to interfere with the course of nature and of history. I had seen too much of the consequences of such interference.

Dudley drew up alongside me in Maria's colors of green and red. He said, "Good little bugger, this."

"A darling," I agreed. "You look after him."

"Any tips?"

"Yeah. He doesn't like falling, he doesn't like the whip, he doesn't like Len Egan, and if he isn't going too well, make like a jackdaw."

"Straightforward." He grinned.

Len Egan trotted up on Slaney Star. "That's my fucking horse you're on," he snarled.

"Yeah, well, know how it feels now, don't you, Lenny?" Dudley said, and he smiled sweetly. "You had your chance last year."

Len said something like "Waargh."

I nodded after him as he walked up to the start. "Watch my back for me, would you?" I said to Dudley.

"And how'll I do that from ten lengths in front?" Dudley flicked at his breeches. "No. Don't worry. You get turned over, Lenny boy ends up six foot under."

"Thanks, mate. Same goes for you."

"Better'n last year, eh?"

"God." I thought back to my frantic, panic-stricken rushing about on this day a twelvemonth back. "Seems like an age."

"Hey, by the by, that girl does your feller . . ."

"Yeah?"

"She free?"

"Absolutely not."

"Oh. Like that, eh? Lucky bugger. Whoops. Here we go."
He pulled his goggles down.

The starter said, "Gentlemen . . ."

The flag rose. The wind threw up a quick flurry of snow-flakes. Ibn Saud pricked his ears. He had been here before. He knew what it was all about. I pulled down my goggles. We jogged forward at a bouncy trot. I was in no hurry to be up front; I needed to settle this boisterous fellow. He was too full of himself. I needed to get his back down, get him balanced and jumping studiously.

And we were off.

It seemed strange that back there, there were thousands of people watching us. It was very quiet, very private out here in the country. I tucked Ibn Saud in on the rails at the very back of the field. I told him that I knew how he felt, that I felt the same, but orders was orders. No course demands more guts and stamina than Cheltenham.

Ibn Saud snorted a little, but he accepted the restraint. He was a much more mature animal than he had been the year before. He knew his business.

From back here we could study the competition. Grimaldi, who had dismally failed in the King George VI but was said to be coming back to his best, led on the rails. He set a stiff-ish pace. Behind him J'Accuse, Stan Lloyd's black, and Prague Spring, last year's National winner, bowled along like a runaway carriage pair. Next came Pip, undaunted by the lofty company he was keeping (not that lofty: Len was on his outside), then old Appalachian, and finally us, a length far-ther back.

The rear is the comfiest place to be. You have as much light as you want, you can spot fallers in your way and avoid them, and you are spared the jostling in the pack.

I let Ibn Saud put himself right for the first. He jumped it big. At the second I got him to lengthen his stride so that he met it right and flew it. Initially, at least, we were just having a nice quiet school.

We were coming down to the water jump when the snow started in earnest. It came at first like rice at a wedding, flung across the track in quick spurts. By the time we reached the open ditch up the hill, though, it had thickened. It swirled about us like a strobe.

The field had opened up now. J'Accuse had made a break for it and was almost out of sight, nine, ten lengths ahead of Grimaldi. A good jump had put Len and Slaney Star into third. Pip was racing well within himself, and Prague Spring had come back to join me. Ibn Saud was going nicely on the bridle now, so I slipped him a bit of rein as the ditch emerged from the snow. I kicked on.

The approach was right. The takeoff was right. Just somehow he got it all wrong. He dwelt in the air and corkscrewed through the fence. At least he managed to get his forelegs out beneath him. Prague Spring, the good old reliable unerring jumper, was not so lucky. He erred. He hit the top of the fence with his forelegs, and they were still mixed up with the birch as the rest of him obeyed the dictates of gravity. He landed on his back with a thud that they must have felt in Gloucester.

I picked Ibn Saud up and told him to pay no attention to falling horses. He did not need telling. As we swung into the back straight, he pulled out, and suddenly Appalachian was at our near side. The snow was as thick now as feathers in a Saint Trinian's dorm, and were it not for the pink spots on Pat Kerslake's cap, the old gray might have disappeared altogether.

The course commentator had fallen strangely silent. We were racing in our own white world, out of sight of the eagerly watching millions. All sounds were intense amid the soft hushing of the falling snow.

"Like a bloody ticker-tape procession," Dudley called from up ahead.

"'Sright." Len was up there, too. "Can do what we bloody like, can't we? I think I'll do *you*, Mr. spoiled-brat Storr."

I saw the plain fence from just five yards away. I shook up Ibn Saud to make sure that he saw it, too.

"'Ware loose horse!" Dudley shouted.

"Where?" Len's voice was high-pitched. Then, "Fuck you!" he yelped. I saw his black and red colors spread for a second like a crucifix against the white. Then he was gone. Slaney Star arose to the fence alone.

Ibn Saud put in another of his big ones, and we landed a good length up on Appalachian. Dudley was now at my left. "What the hell happened there?" I panted.

"Oh, my foot just sort of got stuck under his," Dudley murmured. "These southern boys don't stick."

So fell the fortunes of the House of Storr.

J'Accuse lay sprawled beneath the last open ditch, which left just Grimaldi ahead of High Rigg's two as we came down the hill for the last time. "Let's make it a one-two," Dudley called. "Shake the snotty buggers up, eh?"

"Yeah."

We turned into the straight. Grimaldi was three lengths ahead of us. Dudley went for him first; I followed in his slipstream. We all three jumped the last upsides.

The crowd had seen us now. The stamping and shouting came at us like a storm. Now came the battle proper, the real heat in the muscles as we sat down and drove our mounts for the post. And there was gallant Pip on my near side, and Dudley pushing him out, shouting at him, "Come on, you old bugger! Come *on!*" and Grimaldi on my off, reeling from the whip but resolute as ever, and I in the center, straining every muscle as I worked at Ibn Saud.

And I pulled the whip through and gave him one quick down the near flank, and he found that fifth gear and edged ahead. Still Pip came back at him.

Again. It was like when you catch a great wave on a surfboard, the slow, mighty surge that Ibn Saud summoned from somewhere. And suddenly it was over, and I was soothing him, patting him, telling him that he was a wonder.

As if he needed telling.

I asked Rachel to stay in the car. I had, I suppose, an idea as to what I would find.

I walked up the steps and let myself into Waylands with my own key.

The hall was stripped. The tapestries, and the huge oil of the Battle of the Boyne that had hung above the fireplace, were gone. My footfalls made the bare marble sing. It was very cold.

"Dad!" I called. My voice came back to me in waves.

I glanced in the Chinese drawing room. Again, the better pieces were no longer there. The tables had been replaced with piecrust pieces from upstairs. The washed-silk rugs had been converted into Denny's Porsche — or my father's vengeful bets. The table was still in the dining room, but there was no silver on the sideboard, and my beloved Orpen was gone.

Dear God, the old man had gone for broke. The gambler had lost and could not face it. He had sought to recoup his losses with one last, crazed bet.

And he had lost again.

Joey had been among the first to congratulate me this afternoon. He had thrown his arms about me and hugged me close. "I taught you," he said. "Don't you ever forget. I taught you."

"Anyone asks, I'll tell 'em," I promised. "Wish this could have been with . . . the old way, you know."

"Sure. So do I. Still."

"Where's Dad?"

"Funked it. Said he'd stay home, watch it on TV. Poor old sod."

"Yup."

"All alone there, watching and envying."

"I know."

"Mrs. Storr's staying down here. At the Lygon. She's a hard one."

"I'll go see him. Tonight."

"He'd like that." Joey slowly shook his head. And I was whisked away by the man from the BBC.

I returned now to the hall. I ran up the curving staircase. It was dark on the landing. The prints of *The First Steeplechase on Record* still hung there, but the Thorburn of grouse in flight was gone.

259

I strode past my old room, the room of my childhood, and down to the double doors at the end of the corridor.

I opened them quietly.

There was a big cheval mirror.

I saw the resemblance to my father.

The curtains and the windows were open. It was freezing in here.

He lay on the big double bed, asleep. He looked very like me, now that those deep etched lines of pain were brushed from his face.

An almost empty decanter of port stood on the bedside table. A large red silk box of Leonidas truffles lay open beneath his right hand on the counterpane.

A diabetic's forbidden fruit.

I had heard that diabetic coma was sweet and euphoric.

And of course, there was a note by the port decanter. A gambler's last throw.

I held it under the dim bedside light. On Waylands writing paper, he had executed, in his familiar scrawl, his last, most brilliant exploitation: *Tell Nick well done. Please don't bring me back unless you love me. P.S.*

I replaced the note. I walked to the window. I gazed out at the snow-plump limes. I breathed deep. The air smelled of electricity. "Bastard," I murmured.

I turned back to the bed where he lay smiling in sleep. I bent over him and raised his left eyelid.

I wouldn't put it past him.

But no, the eye stared up at me, and the pupil was a pinhead. That much, at least, he had not faked.

I lowered the eyelid gently.

I bent and kissed him, because I loved him. And because I believed the words that he had written, I left the room.

"Not there?" said Rachel as I climbed back into the car.

"No." I sighed. "Nobody there. Come on, love. Quickly. Home."